TALES OF MYSTERY &

General Editor: David Stuart Davies

THE SHADOW ON THE BLIND
and other stories

with The Trainer's Ghost
and other ghost stories

THE SHADOW ON THE BLIND

and other stories

by Louisa Baldwin

with The Trainer's Ghost and other ghost stories

by Lettice Galbraith

WORDSWORTH EDITIONS

In loving memory of
MICHAEL TRAYLER
the founder of Wordsworth Editions

1

Readers who are interested in other titles from Wordsworth Editions are invited to visit our website at www.wordsworth-editions.com

For our latest list and a full mail-order service contact Bibliophile Books, 5 Thomas Road, London E14 7BN
Tel: +44 0207 515 9222 Fax: +44 0207 538 4115
e-mail: orders@bibliophilebooks.com

This edition published 2007 by
Wordsworth Editions Limited
8B East Street, Ware, Hertfordshire SG12 9HJ

ISBN 978 1 84022 612 6

Typeset in Great Britain by Chrissie Madden
Printed by Clays Ltd, St Ives plc

CONTENTS

THE SHADOW ON THE BLIND
and other stories

The Shadow on the Blind

Harbledon Hall had stood empty for seven years. For seven years no smoke had issued from its chimneys telling of the cheerful hearth within, no voice or laughter had been heard under its roof, no footstep coming or going across its threshold. A straggling growth of ivy and Virginia creeper, that covered the walls and veiled the windows, made the front of the house look forlorn and neglected, as the face of a sick man who has grown a ragged beard during a long illness. The window-sills were green with the drip of rain from the spouts choked with decaying leaves, and the brickwork was stained with dark patches of damp. The birds had built their nests undisturbed in every gable and projection of the roof, and in the wide chimneys, secure from danger of being smoked out of their comfortable quarters.

And within the house, though man had withdrawn his presence from it, other tenants were in possession. Rats and mice held revels in the empty rooms and passages, that resounded with the patter of their feet, the squeak of their voices, and the nibbling of their teeth. In the dead of night, bold as they had grown, they scared themselves by catching in wires that set bells ringing and echoing through the house, and an army of rats would rush helter-skelter down the great staircase, bounding over one another's backs in their panic, as we see them depicted in illustrations of the famous history of Dick Whittington and his cat.

If desolation reigned in Harbledon Hall, its gardens were returning to a state of savage nature, and the rank growth of weeds choked and overtopped the flowers and shrubs. No seeds had been sown, no lawns mown, no hedges clipped or tree or bush pruned, in seven long years, and the once orderly gardens had become a tangled thicket, where the fairy prince might seek the sleeping beauty. A bramble had sprung up by the sundial, and, clasping it in its thorny arms, threw its branches about it, effectually hiding it from the light of day. The stone basin of the disused fountain had become a nursery of young frogs, that hopped, swam, and croaked undisturbed, and nature was endeavouring to re-establish her sway where man had withdrawn his cultivating and restraining hand.

It was a radiant day in June. The hot sun poured down on the tangled overgrowth in the gardens of Harbledon Hall, the birds were in a perfect riot of song, and a south-west wind rocked them on the bough. Even the old house on such a day wore its least sombre aspect. One could imagine there had been happy household life within its walls, and it was possible to conceive that they might again resound to the laughter and voices of children at play.

Some such thought as this must have entered the mind of an elderly gentleman driving in an open carriage with his wife, a pale grey-haired lady, seated beside him. Mr Stackpoole was a cheerful, energetic man of sixty years of age, of strong likes and dislikes and sudden impulses. As he caught sight of the wide front of Harbledon Hall with its red gables glowing in the sun, its confused mass of creepers almost hiding the lower storeys from view, he told the coachman to draw up at the iron gates at the entrance.

'This is a very picturesque house, my dear; I should like to have a look at it,' he said to his wife; 'it may be the kind of place we are in search of,' and he alighted from the carriage as nimbly as a young man to read the notice painted on the weather-stained board fastened to the gates. 'For admission to view these premises, apply to Mr Judd, sexton, by the church.' Mr Stackpoole returned to the carriage and bade the coachman drive to the church, the tower of which they could see embowered among trees, apparently not more than a quarter of a mile distant. As they drove he continued, 'I like the look of the place very much. I am sure I could do something with it. I should just enjoy setting to work upon it to call order out of chaos, and in six months I would undertake to effect an entire transformation in the house and grounds, and make it one of the prettiest places in the neighbourhood. What do you think, my dear? Hey?'

The frail-looking elderly lady thus addressed made but a faint rejoinder, and her husband's sanguine enthusiasm by no means communicated itself to her. Harbledon Hall was the sixth old house Mr Stackpoole had taken a fancy to in the last ten years, and fallen out of love with as quickly, after exercising his ingenuity in putting it in perfect order and living in it for a short time. It was his diversion, now that he had retired from business and had nothing particular to do, to hunt up old country houses, put them in thorough modern repair and working order, live in them just long enough to induce his wife to hope that he had pitched his tent finally, when the demon of unrest would break out in him once more, and he was off again on the old quest.

This hunting of houses, catching them, and then letting them go, that he might pursue game of the same kind elsewhere, was naturally more entertaining to Mr Stackpoole than it could be to his wife and daughter. But the elder lady was patient and philosophic, and when her daughter said petulantly, 'Oh mamma, what a shame it is that we have to be dragged about the country like this! We have not been a year in this lovely house, and papa is tired of it already, and looking out again for some tumbledown old place to put that in good order, and leave it too, I suppose!' Mrs Stackpoole would reply, 'Never mind, Ella. Papa must do as he thinks best. The excitement and interest he finds in frequently changing house are necessary to him now that he has done with business; and remember, my dear, he has no home occupations to pass the time as you and I have.' But Ella Stackpoole was now married and settled in a home of her own, and the only other child, a son, was stationed with his regiment in Malta.

Therefore it was that when Mr Stackpoole became suddenly interested in the appearance of Harbledon Hall his wife was unable to feel any enthusiasm on the subject. Their last home had been in Cornwall, where, after six months spent in its most westerly corner, Mr Stackpoole discovered what everyone else had always known, that he was in a decidedly rainy part of England. He could scarcely have been more astonished at the quantity of rain that fell if it had been in Egypt, and he fled to London to make that his headquarters while he looked about for an old house to suit his fancy in the drier county of Surrey.

And on this bright June day he and his wife were driving through the fair country, house-hunting, and the more dilapidated a house looked, provided that his experienced eye saw capacities of improvement about it, the more attractive it appeared to Mr Stackpoole, as affording wider scope for his particular form of genius. His was a costly hobby, and strangers reaped the benefit of his lavish outlay on houses he perfected, tired of, and left so soon.

Mr Judd, the sexton, was found without difficulty, for indeed he was a conspicuous object, sitting in a large armchair by his cottage door reading the newspaper, and taking an occasional sip from a glass of cold brandy-and-water that stood beside him on the window-sill. He was a person of dignity in the village, accustomed to waste his own time and that of others, but Mr Stackpoole hurried him off to the carriage as soon as he had found the keys, and compelled him to unwonted activity. 'The garden be a wilderness, sir,' said the old man, opening one of the great iron gates, 'and it's four years since e'er an inquiry was made about the place.'

'It wouldn't be to everyone's taste, you see; it'll need a considerable outlay before it is fit for habitation,' said Mr Stackpoole complacently as he stooped to disentangle a briar from his wife's skirt. 'Who were the last tenants, and how long did they live here?' he said, turning to the old man and asking two questions at once.

'Sir Roland Shawe and his family had it last, sir. They took the place on a twenty-one years' lease, and they left uncommon sudden when it had five years and more to run. There was a deal o' talk about what made them leave i' that way,' and Judd opened wide the front door as he spoke, and they entered a large, lofty hall, smelling mouldy as though there were vaults below.

'Folks did say there was reasons more'n what they's own up to, for a large fam'ly to turn out all of a sudden, as if they was running away from the plague,' and the old sexton looked mysterious, and as though he longed to be questioned on the subject. Mr Stackpoole, however, was too much interested in pacing the length of the dining-room to notice any hints he might throw out.

'My dear,' he said to his wife, who was resting on the low window-seat, 'we will have the whole of this oak floor polished, and Turkish rugs laid down at intervals.'

'That was what we did in our house in Cumberland,' said Mrs Stackpoole gently, 'and if you remember you were not pleased with it when it was done;' then, turning to the old man: 'You were going to tell us why Sir Roland Shawe left so suddenly.'

'Forbid, ma'am, as I should say definite why he left, not knowing for certain,' said Mr Judd, swelling with importance as he spoke. 'I never believe more'n 'alf o' what I hear, and puts no faith in tales, whether master's or man's. But by what I can make out – and old Jemmy Judd can see through a stone wall as fer as most folks – I should say as ghosts was at the bottom of the whole kick-up.'

Mrs Stackpoole smiled at the old man's mode of expressing himself, and then looked anxiously towards her husband, who laughed heartily, and they left the dining-room for the upstairs regions, which he was impatient to explore.

'They fled before ghosts, did they?' said Mr Stackpoole, still laughing at the idea. 'If the house is supposed to be haunted I should like it all the better for its reputation,' and he swung open the door of a large, low room, with a deep projecting chimney-place and wide window letting in a flood of sunshine.

'This is certainly a very cheerful aspect,' said his wife, stepping to the window and looking out upon the wild garden enclosed by ragged yew hedges; 'there is nothing ghostly about this room, at all events!'

'Pooh! Ghosts indeed! Those who believe in them deserve to see them,' said Mr Stackpoole contemptuously. 'If we take the house this shall be your morning-room; you'll get plenty of sunshine, which is a great thing for you; and if I like the room under it I will have it done up for a business room for myself.' And they wandered from cellar to attic of the big house, Mr Stackpoole delighted with the possibilities of the place, and noting in his pocket-book the dimensions of the chief rooms and of the entrance hall.

'At all events I shall enquire on what terms the place is to be let,' he said, after spending two hours in energetically inspecting the premises, and as he slipped five shillings into Mr Judd's expectant palm, 'By the way, I have not asked who is the landlord?'

'The landlord, sir, be a many and not one,' and the old man named a well-known city Company to which the property belonged.

'I've rented from landlords, landladies, and trustees, but never yet from a Company: it's all one to me, and I'll see their agent in town tomorrow.' Then Mr Stackpoole took a farewell look at the room on the ground floor, immediately under the cheerful room at the head of the stairs that he had assigned to his wife's prospective use, and decided that it was exactly adapted to his requirements. After which they threaded their way back to the gates through the neglected maze of the garden.

'And how do you like the look of Harbledon Hall?' he asked his wife as they drove away; 'what do you think of the old place?'

'I confess that it does not impress me very favourably, though it is a handsome, well-built house, and might be made very comfortable, no doubt. But it struck me with a kind of chill.'

'So would any place, my dear, that had been shut up for seven years. I feel it in my back now; I wish it may not mean an attack of lumbago for me.' Mrs Stackpoole smiled at the literal interpretation of her words.

'I don't mean that kind of chill, but a sort of depressed foreboding feeling that I have never had before in any of the houses that you and I have been over together, and their name is legion.'

'Why, Anna, you don't mean to say that the old sexton has frightened you with his silly gossip! It was merely some nonsense or other he had made up to increase his importance. If I take the place I shall put in an army of workmen at once, and when next you see it, with good fires drying the rooms, windows bright and clean, and painters and paperers at work upon it, it will look very different, I can assure you. Any house that has been uninhabited as long as Harbledon Hall wears a forlorn look, but for all that I see the possibilities of it, and I could make it the prettiest place we have lived in yet.' And Mrs Stackpoole felt certain that her husband would take the old house.

The following day, when Mr Stackpoole saw the Company's agent, he was surprised at the very moderate rent asked for the house. Whether he wished to take it on lease or as a yearly tenant, the sum demanded was small enough to arouse suspicion in the most unwary.

'Why do you ask such a low rent for a fine old place like that?' he asked.

'It is so much out of repair from standing empty so long, I suppose the Company is willing to submit to a certain loss for the sake of having it inhabited again.'

'But with such a tempting low rent, how is it that it has not been taken long ago?'

'There have been any number of applications for it.'

'Indeed! The old fellow in charge of the keys who showed me over the house yesterday said that no-one had inquired about it for four years.'

A peculiar expression passed over the agent's face, but it was not one of surprise.

'He said so, did he? I've had plenty of enquiries.'

'He certainly said so. He was a talkative old man and anxious to impress us with the idea that Sir Roland Shawe left Harbledon Hall suddenly, some considerable time before his lease was up, in consequence of an absurd notion that the house was haunted. Now, personally, I care nothing about it, but my wife is sometimes nervous, and I thought I would ask you if you know anything of any unusual circumstances connected with his leaving so abruptly.'

'Judd is a chattering old fool! Did he tell you anything definite about it himself?' asked the agent.

'Nothing whatever, but he said some nonsense about ghosts driving them away from the place.'

'Of course there was an absurd story that got about at the time. It was some hocus-pocus about a magic lantern, I believe, got up by the young fellows to frighten the servants, with pictures of a skeleton on a sheet hung up somewhere or other. The whole thing was a stupid practical joke, only too successful, for the scare spread to the ladies of the house, and of course Sir Roland had to leave; they made the place too hot for him,' and the agent laughed uproariously. 'I remember all about it now that you ask me. The young Shawes got up the panic for their own purposes. They found the country too slow for them, they wanted to live in London, so with the simple apparatus of a magic lantern and a sheet they frightened the family back into town, and got what they wanted. Naturally Sir Roland used not to speak of it when he found it out, for no-one is proud of being made a fool of. And now, my dear sir,' he said, with an air of great candour, 'you know as much about this childish folly as I do myself. It has been magnified into something wonderful, till we've had that tempting property on our hands for all these years in consequence.'

Mr Stackpoole was pleased and amused with the agent's frank explanation of the basis of Mr Judd's mysterious allusions, and he and his wife laughed at it together over their dinner in the evening. Mrs Stackpoole was now willing that her husband should take Harbledon Hall, which he did as a yearly tenant, with the right of taking the property on a lease if at the end of three years he felt inclined to prolong his stay.

Then began the delightful bustle that Mr Stackpoole's soul loved – the drying, warming, painting, lighting, decorating and furnishing of the house, the taming and reclaiming of the garden; the stubbing up of old lawns and laying down of new turf; the clearing and re-gravelling of weed-grown paths. Such an army of workmen was engaged that Mr Stackpoole calculated that in less than five months the house would be ready to go into, and the gardens be looking clean and bare in their winter tidiness. 'It must be finished by the middle of December,' he said, 'that I may keep Christmas here with my family; and if every man has done his work well, and is out of the house by the twelfth of December, I will give each a bonus on his wages and a Christmas supper to you all.'

No wonder that the workmen caught something of Mr Stackpoole's enthusiasm, and that every time he brought his wife to see what was going on she was astonished with the progress made. All their friends were informed of the lucky find of the old house in Surrey, and invitations were issued long before for a series of entertainments, dances, and private theatricals they intended to give at

Harbledon Hall in the following January, when their daughter, Mrs Beaumont, and her husband would be staying with her parents.

Shortly before Mr and Mrs Stackpoole removed into Harbledon Hall they were dining out one evening, and after the ladies had left the room and the gentlemen had comfortably rearranged their chairs and were seated at their wine, Mr Stackpoole began on his favourite theme, the furnishing and repairing of the old house. As most of those present had frequently heard him on the same subject before, he was not much heeded, and prosed on without interruption till a tall, bald-headed gentleman opposite to him caught the words Harbledon Hall and at once became an attentive listener.

'Harbledon Hall did you say? Do you mean the old gabled, red brick house, three miles from Mendleton? I hope no friend of yours is thinking of taking it.'

Mr Stackpoole smiled. 'Not exactly a friend of mine, though probably I know him better than anyone else. I have taken Harbledon Hall myself, and intend moving into it in December.'

'The deuce you do!' said the bald gentleman, setting down his glass.

'I don't know why it should surprise you,' said Mr Stackpoole.

'Surprise me? Certainly not. Only I thought that the house was empty and likely to remain so.'

'Surely it has stood empty long enough – seven years. It requires an immense deal doing to it, of course, but I took a fancy to the place, and am putting it into thorough repair, introducing the electric light among other modern improvements; in fact I am sparing no expense. Do you know anything about Harbledon Hall?'

'I used to do. Sir Roland Shawe, the last tenant, is my brother,' and the bald-headed gentleman spoke in a dry and uncommunicative manner. But a hint was not enough for Mr Stackpoole.

'Then you are the very person to tell me about an absurd story I have heard – it had something to do with a magic lantern, I believe, some kind of scare the young people got up to pretend there were bogies in the house, and frighten their parents back to town, where they preferred to live. You see, I've heard all about it, and I only want it corroborated by a member of the family,' and he laughed heartily, as though it were the best joke in the world. But the gentleman opposite him grew grave to severity and said, 'I am unable to understand your allusion to a magic lantern performance which is supposed to have tried my brother's nerves, and absurd is the last word applicable to the circumstances under which Sir Roland was compelled to leave Harbledon Hall.'

'Then I must have been misinformed,' replied the undaunted Mr Stackpoole, whose curiosity was now thoroughly aroused. 'As I am about to live in the house, will you not tell me the real circumstances, that I may be able to contradict the foolish stories that one hears?'

'Why should it be necessary for you to contradict gossip on the subject? Sir Roland never mentions it. It is possible that some time you may learn for yourself why my brother left the house; then I think you will be satisfied that he acted wisely, and if not, I should be sorry to prejudice you against Harbledon Hall.' And the gentlemen rose to join the ladies, and Mr Stackpoole remained in a state of mystification. Evidently something had happened to drive Sir Roland Shawe and his family from Harbledon Hall, with which neither old Judd nor the agent were acquainted. What could it be? For himself, so long as it was neither rats nor drains, he did not care, but with his wife it was different. If she had an inkling that there was anything uncanny about the house, she would refuse to go into it at the eleventh hour, or, if she went, would make a point of seeing a ghost the very first dark night.

But she must hear no silly talk about it. Any ghosts that former inhabitants of the Hall had imagined they saw was when they went about the house starting at their own shadows by the dim light of oil lamps. The electric light would put all that to rights. It was the best cure for such preposterous folly, and in its illumination Mr Stackpoole felt that he should be more than a match for all the powers of darkness.

But shortly after meeting Sir Roland Shawe's brother an odd coincidence happened that drew his attention again to the subject of their conversation. Mrs Stackpoole had written to her son at Malta telling him that his father had taken an old house in Surrey with which he had fallen in love, how beautifully he was fitting it up, that they expected to keep Christmas in it, and that it was at Harbledon Hall they hoped to welcome him on his return to England. In reply Jack wrote, 'So my father is again on the wing. Well, this time I am glad he is taking you to a thoroughly accessible place, and not to Cornwall or Cumberland. But is the old house he has taken a fancy to not far from Mèndleton? I suppose there can't be two Harbledon Halls in the same county, but it is odd if it is the house of that name that I have lately heard something about. There was a young civilian out here for his health – he has gone to Egypt now – and he told me that his uncle, Sir Roland Smith, or some such name, had been fairly driven out of an old house in Surrey by ghosts. I'm sure he called it Harbledon Hall, and he said that his uncle was not in the least a nervous man, but it was more than he could stand, and he had to leave. I wish now that I had asked him all about it, but he was such a dull chap, nothing he said interested me, so I lost the chance of learning particulars. Don't be timid, dear mother. Let me tackle the bogies when I come home; I should enjoy nothing better.'

Mrs Stackpoole did not like this at all. It produced an eerie and creepy sensation, and her husband took care not to increase her discomfort by telling her of his conversation with Mr Shawe.

'It is odd, my dear, very odd,' he said, in his most cheerful tones; 'and we are obliged to admit that, somehow or other, someone or other received some sort of a fright at Harbledon Hall. Nothing can be more vague, yet that is all that is known about it. A pity the whole silly business was not inquired into on the spot, for of course it would admit of a perfectly simple solution. Very likely one of the maids had supped rather more heavily than usual on cold pork, and in a paroxysm of indigestion walked in her sleep; someone saw her in her white nightgown, took her for a ghost, and got up a scare – for it is always easier to cry out than to investigate. And there you have the history of a ghost story in a nutshell, my dear – in a nutshell.'

The workmen were punctually out of Harbledon Hall on the day agreed upon, and as punctually received their pay and Christmas supper, and the house was ready for the reception of the new tenant, with the good wishes of all who had helped to prepare it for him. Mr Stackpoole arranged that his family should arrive after dark, that he might surprise his wife with the electric light in every room and passage, and introduce her to her new home under its most cheerful and attractive aspect.

As they approached the house both Mrs Stackpoole and her daughter exclaimed with delight, and Ella said it was too pretty to be real, it was like something on the stage. From every window, from the basement to the garrets, streamed the pure radiance of the electric light, undimmed by curtain or blind, sending shafts of light far into the surrounding darkness. From the porch the white light illumined the drive like a cold sunshine, and showed every pebble on the ground and every twig on the bare boughs.

'There, my dears,' said Mr Stackpoole triumphantly, as he led his wife and daughter into the brilliant hall; 'this is how modern science drives away foolish fears of darkness by turning night into day. No-one could be nervous or afraid of ghosts in a house like this.'

'No, indeed, the thing would be impossible,' replied Mrs Stackpoole, her daughter, and son-in-law in confident chorus.

Christmas was kept with much festivity at Harbledon Hall, and it was impossible to say who was most delighted with the house – the host or hostess, or the guests under its hospitable roof. Each was charmed with his own room, but Mrs Stackpoole's morning-room was the general favourite, and afternoon tea was frequently taken there in preference to the more stately drawing-room. The grandchildren played in the empty rooms upstairs on rainy days, and every evening watched the miracle of lighting the house with the electric light with breathless interest. They regarded grandpapa as a light-producing wizard, so that something of awe was mingled with their wildest frolics, and they did not dare to open the door of his own particular room, which was respectfully called the study, though its principal use was to smoke in, or to take a quiet nap in before dinner.

It was the end of January, and the Stackpooles were daily congratulating themselves on their good fortune in meeting with a house so perfectly suited to their requirements, when they wound up their festivities with a fancy ball. Several young people were staying in the house for the occasion, who were to depart the day after the ball, leaving their host and hostess for the first time alone in their new home. Numbers of guests were coming from a distance, many of whom had accepted the invitation out of curiosity, as a dance afforded a good opportunity of spending a night under cheerful auspices in a house with the reputation of being haunted.

All their entertainments had so far been successful, but the last was to be the best, and Mr and Mrs Stackpoole threw their whole souls into the preparations to ensure its complete success. The room was charming, the floor perfect, the band that came from town the most renowned of the season. The costumes to be worn were of no special period or country, and the Stackpooles themselves set an example of reckless catholicity in the matter, the hostess being dressed as Queen Elizabeth, and her husband as an Admiral of the Fleet of today, while Mr and Mrs Beaumont figured respectively as a Japanese lady and Spanish matador! By the time that the guests had arrived, clad in the garb of all ages and countries, the ballroom appeared to contain such a motley throng as only the Day of Judgement could bring together. Here an ancient Greek danced with a Swedish peasant, and the Black

Prince with a female captain of the Salvation Army, and there a clown and a nun waltzed gaily past Mahomet and a ballet-girl.

The electric light was a greater novelty then than it is now, and the guests were loud in their admiration of the fairy-palace appearance of the house as they approached, and of its brilliance within. Mr Stackpoole was as delighted as a child with a new toy, and led his friends about showing them how, by merely turning a button on the wall, he could plunge a room in darkness, or flood it with radiant light.

Dancing was kept up with great spirit till the small hours, and as the clock in the hall chimed a quarter-past three, the old house resounded to the half sad and wholly romantic strains of a waltz by Waldteufel. The guests who came from a distance had begun to depart, and Mr Beaumont stood in the porch laughingly seeing Lady Jane Grey and Flora Macdonald into their carriage. Just then a maid gave a message to one of the footmen for Mrs Beaumont, who sat fanning herself near the door of the ballroom. 'If you please, nurse says Master Harry won't go to sleep till he sees you, ma'am.'

'Tell nurse I will come directly,' and, excusing herself to the lady who sat next to her, she slipped out of the room. In the hall she met her father as he was entering his study.

'I'm going to put this miserable encumbrance by,' he said, smiling and flourishing the Admiral's cocked hat, which he had gallantly carried the whole evening to his great inconvenience.

'And I am on my way to the nursery to see little Harry,' and Mrs Beaumont ran upstairs, singing softly to the sweet music that came floating from the ballroom below. Mr Stackpoole laid his hat on the table, and looked at the clock on the mantel-piece. 'A quarter-past three! I'm tired, and the young people ought to be. Heigh-ho! I'd rather give ten dinners than one dance,' and he sank into a low chair by the fire, yawned profoundly, stretched his legs out before him, and closed his eyes. Sleep fell upon him instantly, and for a few minutes he was lost in its depths, light and sound had ceased to exist for him, his brain was steeped in silent darkness.

Mr Beaumont still stood in the porch, the servants had returned to the house, and he was alone. It was a mild winter's night. He flung a cloak over his shoulders, and stepped into the open air. 'I shan't be missed for five minutes,' he said to himself, 'while I smoke a cigarette,' and he walked briskly along a broad path some thirty yards from the house, from which he had a perfect view of Harbledon Hall. And very pretty its cheerful brightness looked against the dark background of star-set sky. Brilliant rays of light shot from the undraped windows, and those that had the blinds drawn down showed the outline of objects in the room thrown upon them in shadow, as clearly as from a magic lantern.

Involuntarily, he raised his eyes to the window of Mrs Stackpoole's sitting-room, and stood rooted to the spot. Two figures as clearly defined as silhouettes were visible on the pure square of the blind – the shadows of an old man and a young man struggling together. From the shape of the heads, George Beaumont saw that they wore wigs, and there was the clearly-cut shadow of the ruffles at the wrists, and the younger and taller man wore a large Steinkirk with laced ends round his neck. At first he thought that they were guests dressed in the costume of the early Georgian period, though how they had gone upstairs into that room, or why there was a deadly struggle between them, he did not know. But wonder and speculation were swallowed up in terrified interest as he watched the course of the brief conflict. The elder and shorter man, who stooped considerably, appeared to be unarmed, and seized the younger man by the throat, when he shook himself free, stepped quickly back, drew his sword, and, plunging forward on his right foot, ran his opponent through the body. He staggered backward and fell out of sight below the level of the window, and there remained only the shadow of the younger man in clear profile on the blind. He stood for a minute looking down, and George Beaumont had time to observe the finely cut features of a total stranger. Then he wiped the blade of his sword, turned, and walked away, and his shadow passed out of sight, leaving the window blind a blank, luminous square.

Indoors at the same time Mr Stackpoole had been waked from his short sleep by a sound in his wife's sitting-room overhead, and he sprang to his feet with every faculty concentrated in listening. A noise as of chairs pushed back and upset on the polished floor, and a scuffling of feet as though two men were struggling together. Then a moment of silence, a loud stamp, and a heavy fall that seemed to shake the ceiling, followed by deep groans. 'Good God! What can be the matter!' cried Mr Stackpoole, and he rushed out of the room into the hall. The front door stood open, though the inner glass doors were closed, and neither his son-in-law nor any of the servants were there. He stopped to call nobody, but ran upstairs to his wife's room as his daughter came downstairs from the storey above with a white and terrified face. 'Oh, Papa, someone has just frightened me so, but whoever he is he is in there! I saw him go into Mamma's room a few minutes ago, and I'm so glad you've come, for I dare not follow him,' and without asking her of whom she was speaking, Mr Stackpoole flung the door wide open and rushed into the room. No-one was there. Not a chair or table displaced, and the electric light illuminating every corner of the room forbade the possibility of anyone being in hiding.

'It is the most extraordinary thing!' he exclaimed, wiping the moisture of terror from his brow as he spoke. 'I would not have your mother know of it for the world!'

'Have you seen him too?' said his daughter faintly.

'Seen whom, child? Seen what? No, I've seen nothing, but I've heard enough to last me my lifetime. God forbid that I should hear it again!' and he looked about the room and under the table, fairly stupefied with amazement.

'He passed me on the stairs just as I came out of the night nursery,' said Mrs Beaumont, anxious to tell her experience without waiting to hear her father's. 'A tall young man ran quickly by me dressed in a blue coat, with ruffles at the wrists and a great laced cravat and a wig tied with ribbon at the back. He carried a long thin sword in his hand. At first I thought it was Arthur Newton, who wore a powdered wig like his this evening, but I remembered his coat was black, and that he left early. When I saw his face it was a stranger's, and he looked cruel and passionate. I followed him till I saw him go into this room and shut the door after him.'

'Then where the devil is he now?' said Mr Stackpoole. 'This is some miserable practical joke, but I'll get to the bottom of it and be even with them yet – I'll get to the bottom of it!' and as he spoke the door that he had taken the precaution to close burst open, and his son-in-law entered in his matador's dress, pale and breathless, as if the bull had turned and given him chase.

'Oh, George, have you seen him too?' said his wife.

'Did you hear anything?' asked Mr Stackpoole. 'Sit down, man; you are trembling like a leaf.'

'There were two of them, an old man and a young man, in this room a minute ago! In God's name, who were they, and why did you not stop them before murder was done?' he said excitedly.

Mr Stackpoole grew quiet and self-collected at the sight of his son-in-law's agitation. 'Pull yourself together, George, and tell me what you mean. There is something up tonight that needs explaining.'

'But where are they? They were in this room, and if you were with them you must have witnessed what happened, or if you only came upstairs this minute, you must have met the young man leaving the room. The old man will never stir again,' and he lifted the tablecloth and looked under the table.

'How come you to speak confidently of who was in this room a few minutes ago, when you were downstairs all the while?' asked Mr Stackpoole.

'I was smoking a cigarette in the garden after seeing the Westons off, walking in the broad path, when I looked up at mamma's sitting-room window and saw the shadow of two men on the blind, shown up by the electric light as clear and sharp as in a magic lantern. I saw their profiles perfectly, but I did not know their faces. They wore wigs tied behind, and ruffles at their wrists, and the younger, taller man, as I saw by the shadow, had a laced Steinkirk round his neck. They struggled together, and the old man grasped the young man by the throat. But he tore himself free, drew his sword, and ran him through the body, then moved away, and left the blind a blank sheet of white.'

'Good God! And I heard it all in my room below, the struggle and the fall, and deep groans!' said Mr Stackpoole.

'And I met the young man – if it was anything human – he passed me on the stairs!' said his daughter, seizing her father by the arm. 'Oh, papa, Harbledon Hall *is* haunted; people were right about it! Do let us leave this dreadful place tomorrow!' And the concluding notes of the Waldteufel waltz sighed through the house as she spoke.

Mr Stackpoole shook his head. 'I don't know how that is to be done, for your mother must not be frightened. For heaven's sake try to look as if nothing had happened. We shall be missed downstairs; I'll go, and you two must manage to bid our guests goodnight decently, and not to alarm those who remain till tomorrow. We must rouse no suspicions. George, fetch Ella a glass of champagne, it will do her good.'

'Oh, don't leave me alone!' cried Mrs Beaumont like a frightened child. 'Then I'll send wine up for you both,' said her father, 'and mind, you must follow me directly.'

Mr Stackpoole rejoined his guests, who had not missed him, and had begun the last dance with as much freshness and enjoyment as though it were the first in the evening. At length all the guests had departed except those composing the house party, and the ladies retired, leaving the gentlemen to have a smoke in the billiard-room.

'You don't look very well, Beaumont,' said a young man dressed as a Tyrolean peasant, as he lit a cigar and looked up at his friend's pale face.

'It's nothing, only waltzing makes me giddy,' and he mixed himself some brandy and soda.

One by one the guests bade goodnight and left the room, till there remained only Mr Stackpoole, his son-in-law, and Mr Liston, a gentleman with very long legs, wearing tights that displayed them to advantage.

'Did your father-in-law know when he took Harbledon Hall that it was supposed to be haunted?' he said in a low voice to Mr Beaumont. Mr Stackpoole happened to hear the question and replied to it himself.

'We heard some foolish gossip on the subject, for of course no place stands empty so long without legends being invented to account for the fact. But I am not the man to listen to vulgar chatter. I took the house, and have been highly delighted with it.' And Mr Beaumont could only admire his father-in-law's admirable self-possession.

'Just so, and the electric light is the true cure for the supposed supernatural. Of course you know how suddenly Sir Roland Shawe left the place?'

'Oh yes, we've heard all about that,' said Mr Stackpoole, forcing a laugh.

'Do you know, I doubt whether you have heard *all* about it; at least if you have, you must be a cheerful sort of person if you can laugh at it,' said Mr Liston.

'Why, of course the whole thing was a foolish practical joke, something connected with a magic lantern, if I remember rightly.'

'Magic lantern! I never even heard the word mentioned. No; if you care to hear the truth about it, I think I can tell it you. I've lived in the county all my life, and I know the story of Harbledon Hall by heart. I only wonder you don't. I should not tell it you now if I thought it would make you nervous; but since you've put in the electric light, and done up the house in such cheerful modern style, the whole place is changed, and anyone might enjoy living here.'

'Let us hear the story,' said Mr Stackpoole abruptly.

'I see I've roused your curiosity. The story goes that some hundred and fifty years ago there lived in this house a certain father and son who hated one another like the devil, and it is needless to say there was a woman in the case and a fortune at stake. The old man must have been an uncommonly bad lot, and he is said to have grossly insulted the young lady his son was about to marry, having in the first instance proposed to her himself and been refused. The two men had a deadly quarrel about it in this very house, and the upshot was that the son, mad with passion, ran his father through the body, and killed him on the spot. There, I shan't say anything more about it, if it is too much for you,' said Mr Liston, struck by the blanched faces before him.

'Go on, go on,' said Mr Stackpoole.

'Well, one winter's night, now eight years ago, as Sir Roland Shawe was coming home late, walking across the garden, he looked up at a window on the first floor where a light was burning, and he saw on the blind, in clear outline, the shadows of the old man and his son struggling together, and he saw the young man run his father through the body with his rapier.'

'I cannot bear it! I cannot bear it!' said George Beaumont, pale as death, and looking ready to faint.

'You could but say that if you had seen the grim shadows yourself. It certainly is a horrid story, and though I can't say that I believe in ghosts myself, I can offer no explication of the details I have given you. Sir Roland believed it, and he was a clear-headed, matter-of-fact sort of person. Other members of his family, too, saw and heard unaccountable sights and sounds that night. One of his sons who was sitting up late for his father, met the shadow of an evil-looking fellow dressed in a blue coat and wearing a powdered tie-wig, hurrying along an upper passage, carrying a naked rapier in his hand. And Lady Shawe was waked by a sound in the room next to hers, which was the room where the shadows were seen on the blind – a sound of struggling and upsetting of chairs, followed by a heavy fall and deep groans. Now, if only one person had thought he had heard or seen unaccountable things, Sir Roland would have made the best of it and stayed on at Harbledon Hall; but, by Jove! when three rational beings are each an eye- or ear-witness it becomes intolerable. Whether you believe in ghosts or not, you can't put up with a thing like that!'

'By Heaven, you can't, that's true!' said Mr Stackpoole, wiping his moist brow. 'And now, Liston, that you have told me this, I'll tell you something in return. I and my family leave Harbledon Hall tomorrow for the precise reasons that drove Sir Roland Shawe out of it eight years ago.'

'Never!'

'As sure as I'm alive we leave here tomorrow! I must find some reason for our sudden flight, but go we must, and I cannot have my wife alarmed.'

'I would not spend another night in the house for the world!' said Mr Beaumont.

'But, my dear Mr Stackpoole, I hope that nothing that I have said leads you to make this extraordinary resolution. Your imagination is excited by what you have heard; there cannot be any cause why you should leave this charming place that you have just fitted up to your own taste,' said Mr Liston soothingly.

'The story you have told us has only helped to explain what we already know. I'll tell you that this very night, not a couple of hours ago, in the blaze of the electric light and with the house full of company, Beaumont, my daughter, and myself have seen and heard the sights and sounds that drove Sir Roland Shawe out of Harbledon Hall; and we leave tomorrow – or rather today, for it is nearly six o'clock now – never to spend another night under this accursed roof!' and Mr Stackpoole's voice shook as he spoke. 'I have only to request,' he added, 'that you will treat this communication as confidential, for neither Beaumont nor I shall care to speak or to be spoken to about what has occurred tonight.'

Where was Mr Stackpoole's intelligent curiosity on the subject of ghosts, and what had become of his courage? The one had been satisfied and the other daunted, and he had not the slightest desire to remain and investigate the mystery.

At late breakfast Mrs Stackpoole was shocked by the appearance of her family. It would have been difficult to say which was most pale and haggard, her husband, her daughter, or her son-in-law. They made the poor excuse that late hours did not suit them and that dancing knocked them up, and she told them that they looked like young children who had been to their first pantomime the night before. When the last guest was gone Mrs Stackpoole saw that there was something seriously amiss with her husband, and was at a loss to account for his changed humour.

'My dear, we will go up to town with George and Ella,' he said, with quick decision.

'Impossible,' replied his wife calmly. 'You, of course, will go if you like to do so, but I really cannot.'

'Oh, do come with us, mamma? You know how much papa wishes it,' said her daughter.

'Yes, do come with us,' urged her son-in-law with unwonted ardour, 'it is so long since we met,' forgetting that they had spent the last month together.

Mrs Stackpoole laughed. 'There is evidently some deep-laid plot among you to hurry me off. Well, if you will be any the happier for my coming with you, I will do so, though it is most inconvenient to leave home in this sudden way,' said the good-tempered lady.

And they travelled up to London that day, never to return to Harbledon Hall. Mr Stackpoole so managed it that his wife did not know the reason for so soon quitting the most delightful house they had ever lived in. He preferred that she should attribute it to his restlessness and caprice, anything rather than that her nerves should be shaken by hearing the truth.

He consulted a fashionable physician, first giving him a hint that he wished to be ordered to the South of France immediately, and the hint being taken he told his long-suffering wife that Dr Blank had recommended him to go at once, and in two days they were *en route* for Marseilles.

Mrs Stackpoole was used to her husband's impulsive, angular movements, so that it did not greatly disturb her; but when a week later he said that he had decided to give up Harbledon Hall and to look for a place somewhere in the eastern counties which were as yet untrodden ground, she shed tears of present disappointment and prospective fatigue. When the much enduring lady had dried her eyes and her husband had enumerated to her in detail every reason but the real one for which he was leaving their beautiful home, she said, 'My dear, if I did not know better, I should be forced to believe that you too had seen the ghost that frightened Sir Roland Shawe out of Harbledon Hall eight years ago!'

The Weird of the Walfords

On a Summer's Day in the year 1860, I, Humphrey Walford, did a deed for which I should have been disinherited by my father and disowned by my ancestors. I laid sacrilegious hands on the old carved oak four-post family bedstead and destroyed it.

Alone I could not have accomplished the work of destruction. The massive posts, canopy, and panels would have resisted my single efforts; but I compelled two reluctant men to lend me their aid, and by the help of saws and hatchets we reduced the whole structure to billets of wood such as one might kindle a cheerful flame with in the parlour grate on a damp summer evening.

It was a bed with a history to me so unspeakably melancholy that I had resolved when I was my own master I would destroy the gloomy structure, and rid me of the nightmare-like feeling with which the sight of it never failed to inspire me.

The bed itself was upwards of three hundred years old, carved in oak grown on our land, while the heavy dark-green hangings, faded and musty-smelling, dated only from the time of my great-grandfather Walford. I have the dimensions of the huge hearse-like thing by heart. It was ten feet long by eight feet wide, and ten feet high; and when as a small child I was brought to see my young mother die in the recesses of the vast bed, I looked up at its tall posts with something of the awe with which I should now regard the loftiest tree.

For three centuries this bed had been the cradle and grave of our family. Its heavy drapery had deadened the sound of the first cry and the last groan of the generations of Walfords who had been born or died in Walford Grange. In its solemn depths the newly-wedded brides of the family lay the first few nights in their new home, till the wedding festivities were ended, and the squire and his wife began their everyday married life by occupying a less stately but more comfortable bed. I knew the history of the gloomy old piece of furniture as family tradition had preserved it for three centuries. Ten Squire Walfords had either died in that bed or had lain on it after death awaiting their burial. I was the eleventh squire dating from the epoch of the bed, and I would neither die in it nor be laid upon it after my death. And to make sure of this there was no way but now, in my youth and strength, to fall upon it with hatchet and saw and utterly destroy it.

I did not fear death more than my forefathers, but I resented being bidden by family tradition and custom to die in a given spot. I rebelled at having a definite place assigned to me to lie down in and die – a place so fraught with dismal associations as the ancient, hearse-like bed. I could not endure to think that, wander wide as I would, I must return to this bed of death at last, and here, among stifling pillows and heavy curtains, end my life precisely where it began.

Must this ghastly horror of my childhood be the goal towards which I tend? When I am sailing on mid-ocean, the ship ploughing her way through the furrows of the sea, shall I only be speeding, sooner or later, towards this dismal bed? When I climb mountains and breathe the keen air of the heights, is it but to end in the exclusion of light and air? Must every step I take, every journey I make, be but a stage on the road that ends in the stifling pillows of this bed of death? No, a thousand times no, and I brought my axe down on the footboard with a crash.

How vividly both the dead and living who had occupied this ancient bed rose before my mind's eye! Here had lain Ralph Walford, killed in the Civil Wars, fighting for the king, and his wounded body was brought home and stretched on what had been his bridal bed to await his burial. And here died Squire Ralph's young widow, who, a short time after her husband's sad homecoming, gave birth to his posthumous child, and never again left this ill-omened bed till they carried her out feet foremost. Ralph Walford's brother Heneage, the next Squire, thought to make the old bed festive with gold and crimson hangings, to forget that his brother's corpse had lain on it, his orphan child been born in it, and his widow died in it, and by the upholsterer's wit to convert a hearse into a bridal bower.

Brighter times came to our family with the Restoration. We had spent our blood and treasure in the king's cause, for which he did not suffer us to go unhonoured; for shortly after his joyful restoration his gracious majesty was travelling within ten miles of Walford Grange, and, the weather proving stormy, and there being no other Royalist house of consideration near, he made shift to pass a night under the roof of his faithful servant Heneage Walford.

My father often told me the history of that memorable visit, as it had been handed down from generation to generation. How gracious and witty was the king's majesty, how merry and light-hearted, as little troubled by the murder of his royal father and the heavy misfortunes of his house as by the brave lives lost and families impoverished in his cause!

Squire Heneage was as loyal a man as ever drew sword for the king, yet he was heard to say that it was a cursed day for him when his gracious majesty honoured him by being his guest, for it turned his wife Mistress Johanna's head, and she was never again the woman she had been. She grumbled and bemoaned herself that the king had not knighted her husband, so that she might have ruffled it a step above the squirearchy. But one abiding comfort remained with her from the royal visit. And this was that both at coming and going the king had saluted her, and she ever after prettily described the royal manner of kissing, which she affirmed to differ from that practised by ordinary men. Mistress Johanna's serving woman, Anne Grimshaw, said that the king had saluted her too; but this her mistress would not hear of, and when she appealed to Squire Heneage he set the vexed question at rest by giving his opinion that, judging it as a matter of probability, it was more likely that a vain woman should lie, than that his sacred majesty should kiss Anne Grimshaw, who had a foul face of her own.

If I have somewhat enlarged on the fact of the king's visit to Walford Grange, it is not so much on account of any tokens of his royal favour that he was pleased to bestow on my ancestors, as because he lay in the best chamber, in the great oak bed with its brave new hangings. But the king was tormented by terrible dreams, and woke in the morning haggard and weary, as though he had been ridden by witches. And that I attributed to a malign influence in the hearse-like bed itself, and with that I crashed into it afresh.

I had long promised myself this fierce destructive joy, when I in my turn should be master of Walford Grange. My father had died in this bed three years ago, and I had been travelling in the south of Europe ever since, urged partly by the restless curiosity of youth, and partly by the belief that no Squire Walford had ever crossed the seas before. Some younger sons and thriftless members of our family, in pursuit of the fortune denied them at home, had ventured into foreign lands, but the head of the house never. My father met any wishes or arguments I advanced on the subject of travel by a statement that seemed to him conclusive – that a man sees enough in his own country that he can't understand, without going abroad to complete his confusion. But now on my return home I hastened to carry out my design on the hated ancestral bed.

What consternation prevailed in the house when it was understood what I was about, and when I and Gillam the carpenter and his man, having stripped the great bed of its drapery, proceeded to take to pieces the panels of the carved oak canopy! Mrs Barrett, the old housekeeper, stood wiping her honest eyes and bewailing my impiety.

'Don't 'ee do it, squire, don't 'ee do it! You may come to know the want of a good feather bed to die in yet! Such a bed as it's been for lyings in and layings out, and I'd hoped to ha' seen you laid in it, like your poor father before you.'

What Mrs Barrett's expectation of life may have been I know not, but she was sixty-five, and I twenty-four years of age.

'My good Barrett, I have determined that this bed shall utterly perish. We will not contribute one more corpse to its greedy maw. But if it be its feathers that you bewail, you are welcome to its pillows to line your nest with, but the bed itself must perish.'

'What, squire, the bed that your great uncle Geoffrey was found dead in, when he'd gone upstairs overnight as well and as hearty as ever man was, and making his ungodly jokes, the Lord forgive him! The very bed as your grandfather lay in two whole years before he died, and all the house heard his groans; and where your Aunt Hester was laid with the water drip, drip from every limb, just as they brought her in drowned from the brook!'

'Yes, my good Barrett, because of these very things the bed must perish.'

Then Gillam began, as he took off his paper cap and wiped his brow: 'If it's as the bed don't seem nateral like to sleep in after so many o' your kin has laid stiff and stark in it, won't you sell it, squire, to them as knows nothing of its ways? That there panel with the berried ivy on it is a deal too pretty a bit of carving to make firewood on.'

'No, Gillam, I shall not sell it. The man who would take money for the bed his ancestors died in, would sell their bones to make knife-handles of. Besides, the bed has existed long enough; it has served my family to die in for ten generations. It's my own property, Gillam; mayn't I do what I will with my own?'

'Ay, surely, squire; there's no law to hinder a man making any fool of hisself as he pleases wi' what's his own. But I sides with the chap as made the bedstead, and I shouldn't like to think as in a matter o' two or three hundred years a bit o' my work 'ud be chopped up for firing.'

'Be under no uneasiness, Gillam; you and I do not live in an age that produces lasting work. Our glue-and-tintack carpentry is not done with a view to posterity.'

'Well, squire,' continued Gillam, returning to his first idea, 'if you won't sell the bedstead whole nor piecemeal, you might give me them panels with the carved ivy on 'em. I could find you some bits o' wood as 'ud burn brighter and better.'

'I don't mind giving you the old ivy carving, Gillam,' I said, 'but only on condition that I shall never see anything more of it, in any shape or form.'

'That's easy promised, sir, and thank you kindly. I'll make it up into something as'll surprise itself.'

Having weakly consented to his request, I saw him lay aside two or three beautiful panels, richly carved with branches of berried ivy, as salvage from the general wreck. If the gloomy horrors of the old bed had not eaten into my very heart, I could never have lent a hand at such a work of destruction. I should at least have saved the footboard with its carving in high relief of Adam and Eve under the tree, a man-headed serpent twining round the trunk, and the branches bending beneath their load of fruit. But I could not look at it without thinking of the dying eyes that had fixed their fading gaze on it, so my axe and saw made havoc of a work of art. When the floor was littered over with billets of wood, and the men were wiping their hot faces, I felt a strange lightness of heart, a comfortable sense of work postponed at length happily accomplished.

'Gillam,' I said, 'there was timber enough in that huge thing to build a man-of-war, drapery to make her sails, and rope enough for all her rigging.'

'Ay, there was a'most;' and, hastily throwing his tools into his basket, he added, sarcastically I thought, 'There'll be nothing else I can help you to pull down or to smash up, squire?'

I soon found that my destructive toil had benefited me in more ways than one. Not only had it freed me from an intolerable oppression of spirit, but it had established for me in the neighbourhood a reputation for eccentricity, which I maintained afterwards at the smallest cost, and found of great service. The carrying out of my long-cherished purpose was regarded as evidence of a wild and lawless disposition, bordering on mental derangement. Night after night at the alehouse Gillam recounted to a breathless audience the story of the scene of destruction at which he had assisted professionally. And it grew in the telling till, without the slightest intention of lying, he added that the squire's rage against the old place was such, that he had been obliged to menace him with the screwdriver to keep him from tearing down the mantelshelf and wainscot.

I was evidently a man whom it was not wise to thwart or contradict. My servants flew at my least word with an alacrity I had not before observed. My bidding was promptly done, my orders were not disputed, and whatever I said was agreed to with servility. While enjoying the sweets of mental health, as my neighbours voted me on such insufficient grounds on the borderland of insanity, I availed myself of the liberty it gave me to speak and act as I chose. Their hasty judgement had made me free of the wide domain of conduct. There was nothing I could do, however extravagant, but was clearly shadowed forth in the destruction of the ancestral oak bed.

I began to grow lonely in Walford Grange. My good Barrett died suddenly, and in my solitude I wanted someone to sit and talk with me in the long evenings, for even the bright wood fire flickering on the hearth could not satisfy all my desires for cheerful companionship. I should not have wished to marry if I had had a brother to live with me, to share my thoughts and occupations, and who would himself marry and preserve the name. But I was the last of the family, and I did not mean to let an ancient race die out.

I began seriously to think of marrying, though whom, I had not an idea, for so far I had not seen the woman I should care to marry, nor could I suppose that anyone looked with an eye of favour upon me. But when a man makes up his mind to marry, and sets out on his travels by land and sea, resolved never to return to his home till he brings a wife with him, it would be hard if he could not effect his purpose.

It happened that I met with my wife unexpectedly, and where I should have thought I was least likely to meet her – in a log house in the far west of America. Her name was Grace Calvert, and she was only eighteen years old, fair and fresh as an unfolding flower, and full of the high spirits and delight of life suited to her age and her free and simple bringing up. I fell in love with her at first sight, and we were married after a short courtship, for I had obtained the object of my travel, and my little wife was wild with curiosity and impatience to see England. She had a most romantic conception of the land of her forefathers, and delighted me by her belief that every village in England contained a church, vast and venerable as Westminster Abbey, and was engirt with hills crowned by frowning fortresses.

Grace had never seen houses built either of brick or stone, and had I not been able to show her a photograph of Walford Grange, it would have been impossible to give her any idea of an object so strange that there was nothing within the narrow limits of her experience with which to compare it. Her imagination was greatly stirred by the picture of the old house. Not a detail escaped her, from the fluted chimneys to the stone seats in the wide porch. The oriel windows, with their diamond panes, pleased my young wife more than anything, and especially she admired the broad windows of the best bed-chamber, in which some two years before I had wrought my destructive will on the ancestral bed. The room was now bare and stripped of furniture, and since Mrs Barrett's death I had kept it constantly locked.

Grace was fascinated with the position of the room, with its large window over the porch, looking down the avenue of limes by which the house was approached, to the open country, and the line of low hills that bounded the horizon.

'That room must be lighter than those on the ground floor,' she said, 'see how the upper storey projects and throws a shadow over the lower rooms. We will make it our sitting-room, will we not?'

The request gave me a strange sinking of heart, and I felt that not even the society of my young wife could induce me to live in the room that had so long contained the hearse-like bed. I temporised with her in a vague manner, neither granting nor denying her request. I begged her to wait till she could see for herself how much better adapted to the comfort of daily life were the rooms on the ground floor than those on the upper storey.

In all her short life, Grace had not been further than twenty miles from the spot where she was born, and I feared lest taking her away from all she loved, and from everything with which she was familiar, might prove too keen a pain.

There was a brief tempest of tears at parting with the dear ones she was never to meet again, but it was an April shower succeeded by smiles. Each outburst of weeping was of shorter duration, and the sunny intervals between them were longer, till in a few days Grace was her bright self again. The excitement of the journey was so overwhelming as to swallow up every other feeling.

We reached our home one November afternoon, as the setting sun looked out through a rift in the clouds, and his level beams lighted up every casement with a red glow. As we drove up the leafless avenue, heavy drops fell from the bare boughs overhead, and Grace, clinging to my arm, said in a frightened whisper: 'Oh Humphrey, that light in the window is not like sunshine! It looks as if your old house was on fire!' and raising my eyes I caught for one moment the full effect of the illusion. But, the sun sinking into his bed of cloud, the red glow faded from the windows and left them dark and dim. 'Welcome, my darling, to your English home!' I said, and I took my little wife by the hand and led her up the wide oak staircase; and before we sat down to our evening meal I had taken her over the house from garret to basement, preceding her, candle in hand, through the darkening rooms.

She expressed unbounded admiration for the house and its furniture, but the old family portraits and pictures excited her utmost enthusiasm, for Grace had never seen anything more venerable or older than her grandparents and the log house in which she was born. When her raptures had toned down sufficiently to allow her to eat a little, and we were seated at supper in the oak parlour, my little wife suddenly said: 'Humphrey, there ought to be a ghost in a house like this.'

'Why should there be?' I asked, while I smiled at her extreme gravity.

'Because so many generations of men and women cannot have been born and died in this house without leaving some trace of themselves for us who come after,' and I saw that works of fiction had penetrated into the far west, for Grace had certainly been reading romances.

'I object to talking about ghosts at supper,' I said; 'breakfast is the best time for such conversation, and not a word should be uttered on the subject later than twelve o'clock at noon;' and I rose, and taking one of the candles with me, and holding it so as to throw the light on a dark painting over the mantelshelf, I asked: 'Do you know who that is?'

My little wife looked earnestly at the portrait, with her head inclined dubiously, and with a puzzled expression of face.

'I am not surprised that you do not know who that dark sinister-looking man is, for the backwoods of America are not hung with portraits of Charles the Second. Yes, that is King Charles; and the melancholy cast of his features must be merely an inherited expression – certainly nothing in his nature answered to it – for he passed through grief and tragedy with a light heart. He once spent a night in this very house; we have the tradition of his visit, with many quaint details, preserved to this day.'

'Oh how wonderful to think of it!' said Grace eagerly; 'and would the king sup in this very room where you and I are now?'

'Yes, in this very room, and would you like to know what he had for supper?'

'No, that is not the kind of thing that makes me curious. I want to know how the king looked, how he was dressed, and in which of those solemn-looking old bedrooms upstairs he slept. No doubt you still have the bed the king slept in?'

'No,' I replied with decision, 'that I am sure we have not.'

'Then tomorrow, Humphrey, you will shew me the room the king slept in, and the bed I can imagine for myself.'

The bed she could imagine for herself! My little wife did not know what she was talking about. The next day the event occurred which might have been expected. I was walking in the garden, when Grace came to me, and slipping her hand through my arm, drew me towards the porch.

'You see that large window,' she said, pointing towards it as she spoke; 'that is the one I admired so much in the picture of the house. I have looked out of every window but that, and I fancy the room must be locked, for I cannot open it, so I have fetched you to unlock it for me.'

I walked in silence by her side while she led me into the house and upstairs to the door of the hated room, talking with so much animation herself that she did not notice that I had not spoken a word.

'This is the room,' she said gaily, and she turned the latch of the door to and fro, saying as she did so, 'You see it is locked.'

'I know it is,' I said sullenly.

'Then fetch the key and open it,' and Grace gave the door handle a little impetuous shake.

'My dearest, don't ask me again to open that door, for I shall not do it.'

'Not do what I ask you to do? How cruel of you!' and her eyes filled with tears.

I knew that my young wife thought me brutal, but I could only say 'Anything else in my power I will do for you, only this one thing, this one little thing, I beg you will not ask me to do.'

'If you admit that it is such a very small thing, there can be no reason why you should refuse to grant me such a trivial request,' persisted Grace; 'when I ask you simply to unlock a door in your own house, and you refuse to do it, I can only think that you do not love me, or else that there is some horrid mystery about the room that you wish to keep hidden from me;' and she wiped away a hasty tear, that proceeded rather from indignation than from grief.

'My dear Grace, do not let us be tragic about nothing. There is no secret connected with this room that I have ever heard of, and I love you so much that I cannot bear to see you troubling yourself with absurd imaginations. The fact is this. I have a feeling – call it superstition, what you will – but I have a feeling that would make it very painful to me to open this door and take you into the room. And what pleasure could there be in seeing a bare, unfurnished room, precisely like any other empty room?'

'But I should set about furnishing it at once.'

'Let us come away,' I said, gently removing her dear obstinate hand from the lock. 'I repeat, I have a feeling about that room that would prevent my ever being happy in it,' and, I added lightly, 'Don't let my Eve spoil our paradise by longing after the forbidden fruit.'

But Grace said quickly, 'It was not Adam who forbade Eve to eat of the fruit. If it had been, I can't see that there would have been any great harm in disobeying him.' And we said no more about the locked door, but a cloud had come between us, and the unalloyed sweetness of our first happiness was lost.

One day, a few weeks after this folly, when I was beginning to hope that my little wife had forgotten her curiosity, I saw from her constrained and uneasy manner that something had happened to disturb her.

'My dear Grace, you certainly are not happy this morning – will you not tell me what ails you?' I asked.

Her voice trembled and her face flushed as she replied. 'Humphrey, I did not think you could tell me an untruth.'

'My child, what do you mean? We are playing at cross purposes. Be so good as to explain your meaning, that we may not misunderstand each other for a moment.'

'You told me that the big bedroom you keep locked was empty.'

'So it is,' I said, growing impatient at this childish scene, 'but what is the untruth I have told you?'

'Why, the room is not empty. I can prove what I say.'

'The room not empty! Nonsense! I keep the key, and none but myself has entered it these two years.'

'How can you persist in such an untruth, Humphrey? I am not ashamed to confess that I looked through the keyhole – I wonder I did not do it before – and I saw in the middle of the room, between the door and the window, an enormous old bed. I could only see the two foot-posts, but they went up to the ceiling, and the footboard was high and richly carved, and the curtains a gloomy, dark green. So you have deceived me about the room, and I am afraid there is some secret connected with it that you dare not tell me. What ails you, Humphrey?' and my wife rose with a terrified exclamation, for I thought I was fainting, and all the life seemed to have gone out of the air.

'Grace,' I said, when I had shaken off the sense of oppression, 'let us go at once to that unlucky room, and settle this preposterous dispute. You say that the room has furniture in it – I say that it is empty. We will see which of us is right, and then we will never mention the subject again;' and I asked my wife to come with me and assure herself that the room was, as I said, absolutely bare and unfurnished. My hand shook as I turned the key, and, flinging the door open till it strained on its hinges, we entered the room together.

Grace shrank back with a low cry, and covered her face with her hands.

'Where is it gone to, the great bed that I saw standing on this very spot? I cannot have been deceived. Oh Humphrey! why do you play me such cruel tricks? You terrify me.'

'My little wife,' I said, assuming an air of cheerfulness I was far from feeling, 'this comes of what I must call your overweening curiosity. If my dear girl had been content to let me keep this door locked, she would not have grown so curious that her little brain is almost turned, and she has taken to seeing housewifely spectral illusions of domestic furniture. Depend upon it, what you think you saw was nothing but the creature of your own imagination, that has dwelt so long on the idea of furnishing the room that you have only to peep through the keyhole, and, hey, presto! the thing is done, and beds and tables start forward at your bidding. But henceforward you can enter the room as often as you like, only we will not live in it, and I will not have it furnished.'

This appeared to satisfy Grace, and though I could not fully persuade her that the great bed she had seen when she peeped through the keyhole was an illusion begotten of curiosity and a lively imagination, yet with the door of the room unlocked, she felt that she had some control over any tricks I might play her in the future.

I was deeply disturbed by what she had told me. I had not breathed a word to my wife about the destruction of the ancestral bed. Mrs Barrett was dead before we were married, and I had changed my servants since her death, and, as we saw nothing of our neighbours,

Grace could not have heard from anyone of the ghastly old bed, which nevertheless she had accurately described to me.

I could never tell her the truth now. It would shake her nerves, and impress her with the idea that there was something weird about the house. I wished I had not destroyed the old bed. Better far that she should have known the gloomy reality than behold a presentment of it that was neither an embodiment of memory nor a vivid picturing of it from imagination. I tried if I could summon up a like hallucination, but in vain. Though my memory of the ancient bed was perfect, and every detail stamped on my mind, never could I call it up before my external vision, however earnestly I tried to do so.

Grace completely regained her accustomed cheerfulness, and in the spring was busy making a thousand little preparations for the expected arrival of an infant, which was to surpass any yet born into this world. I could hardly believe the gentle obstinacy of my wife, when, after all I had said about the empty room, she asked one day if she might not make it into a nursery.

'Do you not remember, dear, that I said we would not furnish that room?' I said.

'Oh, of course, not furnish it; a nursery needs no furniture; but it is much the most cheerful and sunny room in the house.'

And again I had to appear inhuman and refuse my little wife a trivial request.

One morning as I sat in my room busy with my accounts, Grace came to tell me that she was going to drive to the county town, some eight miles distant, for a round of shopping, such as her soul loved. I said that if she would wait till the next day I should be able to take her myself, but she tapped the barometer on the wall, that had stood for some time at 'set fair', and assured me it would rain tomorrow, and that she must avail herself of the fine weather today. So away drove my self-willed darling, nodding a gay farewell as the carriage drove away from the house.

Grace returned late in the afternoon in the best of spirits, bringing with her an enormous package such as none but a country woman, or one, like my little wife, from the far west, would dream of bringing with her in an open carriage. It must have broken the coachman's heart to drive with it through the streets of the county town.

'What in the name of wonder have you brought home with you?' I asked.

'Ah!' she said, laughing, 'it is a trial for your curiosity now! Anything else you may ask me I will tell you, only I cannot let you know anything about this mysterious package.'

'Then have it put out of sight,' I said, 'or depend upon it I shall find some hole in the wrapper to peep through. You ought to know what a devouring passion curiosity is.'

As the unwieldy bundle was carried upstairs, its cover slipped aside and revealed a pair of black oak rockers. But I said nothing; Grace should tell me her little secret in her own way, and at her own time.

We thought ourselves the happiest creatures in the world when our little son Heneage was born. The gloom that brooded over the house from the death of many generations was lessened by the joy of birth, and my young son's life was like the sprouting acorn that sends up its vigorous shoot through the earth, fed by the fallen leaves of a hundred autumns. On the third day of our happiness my wife sent for me, and told me she had a very pretty surprise for me.

'I can tell you all about the big mysterious package now. It was a beautiful old-fashioned cradle that I bought in Carlyon from a man called Gillam, who keeps an old furniture shop here. I fell in love with it at once, for I knew how well it would suit this house with its old oak. Gillam said he could swear it was old work; in fact, he said it was originally part of a fine old bedstead a poor mad gentleman in the neighbourhood actually destroyed in a fit of frenzy, but he was lucky enough to secure a portion of the wreck, and made it up into that cradle, and baby looks lovely in it. I'm afraid I gave a great deal of money for it, but one does not meet with such a beautiful thing every day:' and the nurse removed a screen from before the cradle, that its beauties might burst upon me suddenly and with the more effect.

Cold drops stood on my brow as I recognised, in the high sides and head of the cradle, the carving of ivy branches and berries I had so madly given Gillam when I destroyed the old bed.

'I thought you would have been so pleased,' said Grace, disappointed by my silence as I stood spellbound, my eyes following every line of the hatred carving. 'I thought you would have been so pleased to see baby in a cradle really worthy of him.'

But I could not speak; I was oppressed by a sense of coming doom.

'It is very unkind of you,' said Grace. 'I had prepared a pretty surprise for you, and instead of being pleased, you stand and sigh and look as if you saw a ghost. Nurse, take baby out of his lovely cradle; we must get him a common wicker thing to lie in instead!' And the nurse did as her mistress bade her, and lifted little Heneage from his cradle of death, for while we talked the child had slept his feeble life away.

I have no memory of what happened day by day during the few weeks following. It was my one consuming fear that my wife too should die. Six weeks after our child's death I carried her downstairs, and this was the only progress made towards recovery. She remained at the same stage of convalescence, made wayward by grief, with shattered nerves, and so weak in mind and body that I dared not thwart her in anything. As the dim, sunless days of autumn drew on, my little wife said to me as though we had never spoken on the subject before: 'I want the big empty room furnished for my sitting-room, Humphrey. I shall have a little sunshine there sometimes to cheer me in your dismal English winter, and it will amuse me to furnish it.'

As I looked at her white wishful face, I felt that nothing mattered to me now, and I said, 'Do exactly as you like, dear, in everything,' and she was too listless to thank me.

But the work of transforming the sombre room into a bright boudoir proceeded rapidly, for Grace said with a shudder, 'I will have no more old oak furniture.'

My little wife always went to extremes, and now, in her antipathy to old oak, she filled the room with tawdry chips of furniture, chairs made of gilded match-sticks tied together with ribbons, that must sink into feeble ruins if a cat so much as jumped on them.

I entered into all her little fancies, and feigned excessive admiration of each fresh idea she had on the subject of decoration. I did her bidding, even to placing her couch on the very spot where the hated bed had stood. Thus was my resistance broken down, and I, who three years ago had tried by sheer physical force to thwart destiny, was now unconsciously working to bring about its fulfilment. It did not tarry long.

One gloomy November afternoon, Grace lay on her couch covered with soft shawls, and the window curtains were drawn back to give as much light as possible. The glow of the setting sun illuminated the room, and lent a more living hue to the grey pallor of her face.

'How like the day when I first came to Walford Grange!' she said; 'the sun is setting with the same fiery light. Do go into the garden, Humphrey, and see if the windows are aglow with red light as they were then.' And I left her to do as she asked me.

Seen from the garden, the house looked precisely as it had done on the day of our homecoming. From garret to basement every window glowed red in the light of the setting sun, as though from fire within. Everything that my eyes rested on was as it had been a year ago. Grace and I only were changed – changed in ourselves and changed to each other. I felt impatient of the changeless aspect of nature and of inanimate things around me, and I entered the house, now dark in contrast with the twilight without, and returned to my wife's room with a heavy heart.

'The house looks as it did when you first saw it,' I said. 'Till the sun sank behind the hill, the windows were lighted up with the same strange effect of fire that you noticed a year ago,' and I threw a fresh log on the embers as I spoke, sending a bright train of sparks up the wide chimney. 'Shall I light the candles?' I asked, turning towards my wife's couch; 'the room is growing dark.' But there was no reply. I was speaking to the dead.

In vain I had baulked the old bed of its prey, for there on the very spot where it had stood for three centuries and generations of my ancestors had died, the wife of the last of the Walfords lay dead.

I buried my sweet Grace by our little son, and on the night of the funeral, alone in my desolate home, I conceived the idea of freeing myself for ever from the horror of darkness that had fallen on Walford Grange. I sent every servant away. I would have the house and my sorrow to myself.

When I was assured that I was alone in the house, I went rapidly from room to room in a strange exultation, speaking aloud and flinging open doors and windows till the cold night air rushed through chambers and passages, and curtains and hangings flapped in the wind.

'When I destroyed the old bed of death,' I said, 'I thought to restore joy and brightness to Walford Grange. But I should have destroyed not it alone, but the room in which it stood, and the very house of which it formed a part. Never more shall man dwell in this house glutted with death. Never more shall the voice of the bride and bridegroom be heard in its chambers, or footsteps of children be heard on its stairs. Never more shall fire subdued to harmless household use be kindled on its hearth, but fire untamed in its ferocity shall devour the accursed pile.' And I seized the burning log from the hearth and threw it on the couch where Grace had died.

Carrying a lighted brand, I sped from room to room of the doomed house, leaving in each a fiery token of my presence, and then, descending the wide staircase, where flickering shadows were cast from every open door, and the silence was broken by the crackling sound of flames, I let myself out into the darkness, closing the heavy door behind me with a crash.

On through the cold damp air I ran, the moon through a rift in the clouds guiding me by her fitful light, till, drawing her shroud around her, she left me again in darkness. Not once did I turn to right or left or look behind me till I had gained the summit of the hills that bounded the valley. Then I stood and turned to take a last look at the home of my fathers. Just then the moon, issuing forth in cold splendour from her bed of cloud, shed a solemn lustre far and wide. And I saw for the last time the house of my birth, the cradle and grave of my race, and every window from basement to garret glowed with fire, no mere reflected glare, but red from the raging fire within, and keen flames darted from the casement of the room above the porch.

I stood long to watch the fire of my own kindling, till when a sudden burst of light and leaping splendour of flame showed me that the gabled roof had fallen in, I shouted, took off my hat, and waved a last farewell to Walford Grange.

The Uncanny Bairn

A Story of the Second Sight

David Galbraith owned a compact estate in East Lothian which he farmed at a considerable profit. The land had passed from father to son for a couple of hundred years. It had always yielded a good livelihood to the owner, but never had it been so highly cultivated or produced such abundant crops as under David Galbraith's liberal and skilful management. The oats and potatoes grown on his farm commanded the highest prices in the market, and his root crops were superior to any in the district. The large, solidly built stone house in which generations of Galbraiths had lived and died stood in the midst of the property, sheltered by a belt of trees on rising ground from the sweeping east wind. And the labourers' cottages, equally well constructed to resist the gales that blew across the Firth of Forth, were models of decent comfort. The livestock on the farm was well fed and cared for. The whole property bore evidence to the wealth, thrift, and intelligence of its owner.

And David Galbraith's wife was well-to-do and thrifty like himself. She too was the child of a Lowland landowner and farmer, and brought her husband no inconsiderable tocher, while her industry and housewifely accomplishments might in themselves have served as a marriage portion. She too, like her husband, came of a douce Presbyterian stock, worthy, upright folk, holding by the faith and practice of their forbears; orthodox and thrifty, worshipping as their fathers had done, and hauding the gear as tightly, nothing doubting but that to them was especially assigned not only the good things of this world, but also of that which is to come.

Galbraith did not marry till he was a middle-aged man. But he had long had the cares of a family on his shoulders without its pleasures to lighten the burden. He was the eldest of six orphan sisters and brothers, to whom he had acted the part of a father. And it was not till Colin, the last and youngest, had left Scotland for a sheep run in Australia, with money lent him by his brother, that he felt himself at liberty to marry. But now that his pious duty towards his family was fulfilled, David Galbraith did not hesitate to take to himself a wife in the person of Miss Alison McGilivray, a lady of some five-and-thirty years of age, with large hands and feet, small grey eyes, high cheek-bones, and a complexion betokening exposure to a harsh climate. She was well educated and intelligent, and in talking with her servants and poor neighbours, commonly fell into the comfortable Lowland Scotch that her father and mother had taken a pride in speaking.

Only one child was born to David and his wife in the ample home where there was space, maintenance, and welcome for a dozen. Yet this one was a son, and the Galbraiths were not doomed to die out. The boy was christened Alexander, after his two grandfathers, both of whom were Alexanders, so that there was no chance of dispute as to which side of the house should have the naming of the child.

And a poor, wee, frail child he was, apparently inheriting nothing of the strength and vigour of the Galbraiths and McGilivrays, nor did he resemble father or mother in feature. He seemed a little foreigner that had come to stay with them for a while, and often in his feeble infancy he bade fair to depart and leave his parents child-less. The shrewd bracing winds, that were life and health to them, nipped and shrivelled him. He took every ailment that was to be had, and when there was nothing catching in the neighbourhood, he would originate some illness of his own, severe enough to have shaken the constitution of any but a seasoned weakling like himself. The Lowland farmer would hang over the cradle of his waxen-faced baby, holding his breath for very fear as he looked at the puny thing, and would say, dropping into broad Scotch, as his wont was when strongly moved, 'Wha wad ken this for a bairn o' mine, sae strang and bonny and weel set up as the Galbraiths have aye been?'

But the babe won through the troubles and perils of his sickly infancy, and at six years of age had grown into a delicate slip of a child, with an interesting pair of grey eyes in his pale face, and a bright spark of intellect in his big head. The family doctor, to whose unceasing care Sandie owed his life almost as much as to his mother's devoted nursing, forbade his parents to attempt anything in the way of systematic education till the boy was eight or nine years of age.

'Canna ye be content to let weel alane,' he would say, 'and bide till the bairn's strang and healthy before ye trouble him to read and write? Gin ye set his brains ableeze wi' letters and figures, ye'll just be burnin' down the house that's meant to be the habitation of a fine soul; gin ye wad haud your hands aff it, and leave it alane!'

And little Sandie did very well, though unable to read or write till long after the age at which the children of his father's labourers could spell out a psalm, and sign their names in a big round hand. But the child had a memory such as must have been commoner in the world before there were books to refer to at every turn than it is now, and his mind was stored with fairytales and old border ballads that his mother and his nurse told or sung to him in the winter evenings. But Mrs Galbraith and Effie were careful never to tell him stories of a weird or ghostly nature, for the doctor had impressed upon them before all things that Sandie must never be frightened. 'For gin the bairn be frighted he will na sleep,' said the astute mistress to the maid, 'and ye'll just hae to sit the lang mirk evenings by his bed, while ye hear the maids daffin' by candlelicht below, or walking wi' their laddies; but gin ye never let him hear o' ghaists and wraiths, he'll just sleep like a bird wi' its head under its wing; and whiles ye'll be able to leave him and hae a crack wi' your neebors like ony ither body!'

Though mother and nurse, actuated by different but equally strong motives, kept all knowledge of the supernatural from the child, there came a day when his father accused them both of poisoning his mind with stories of witches, warlocks, and ghosts, and making an uncanny bairn of the boy.

When Sandie was seven years of age, a lean and overgrown child without his front teeth, and any comeliness he might possess existed only in his mother's eyes, a strange circumstance happened that greatly perplexed and distressed his parents. One cold afternoon late in October Mrs Galbraith told Effie to take a pudding and a can of broth to an old and very poor woman, called Elspeth McFie, who lived in a lone cottage a mile from the farm, and Sandie was to go with her for the sake of the walk. The trees were already stripped by the autumn gales, to which a dead calm succeeded, and a cold fog had crept up from the sea and brooded over the bare fields, settling on the naked boughs in chilly drops of moisture. The careful mother wrapped a plaid round the boy, and bade him run as he went, to keep himself warm. Away sped Sandie along the high road, driving a ball before him, running after it to send it flying again with a dextrous blow of his stick, till his pale cheeks glowed with exercise, and he overshot his mark, ran past old Elspeth's cottage, and had to be recalled by Effie.

'Ye maun pit the basket in her hand your ain sel',' she said, as she led the reluctant child into the dark close room where the old woman sat shivering by the fire, spreading her skinny hands over the dying embers. But Sandie held back, and neither threatening nor coaxing would induce him to move a step nearer to Elspeth, so that, stigmatising him as 'a dour limb', Effie was obliged to set the basket on the table herself.

'It's just a pudding and a few broth that Mistress Galbraith has sent ye, for she's aye mindfu'o' the puir,' she said, as she set out the can and bowl before the old woman. Elspeth looked with a bitter smile at the good things spread before her.

'It's a' verra gude sae far as it gaes, but gin I'd been the rich body, and Mistress Galbraith the puir carline, I wad hae sent her a mutchkin' o' something stronger than mutton broth. Does she no warm her ain thrapple wi' a drap whusky hersel'?'

'For shame, Elspeth! Ye maun just tak' what's sent ye and be thankfu'!' said Effie sharply; and turning to Sandie, who stood gazing intently at the old woman, 'What ails the bairn that he canna tak' his eyes aff your face? It's no your beauty, I'm thinking, Elspeth, that draws him sae!'

The ill-favoured old woman cackled to herself, displaying a few yellow tusks, the last survivors of a set of teeth that had once been as white and strong as Effie's.

'It's lang since man or bairn looked at auld Elspeth wi' sic a gaze. What does the bairn see in an auld wife's face? Ye suld look at the lasses, Sandie, lad,' and Elspeth stretched out her lean arm, caught the boy by the wrist, and drew him towards her. She was a hideous old woman, and in the gathering twilight, when the red glare of the embers shed a glow on her harsh features, she appeared positively witch-like. Sandie suffered himself to be drawn close to her as one who walks in his sleep, with wide-open eyes void of expression, and then stood opposite her for a moment pale and silent. Before either of the women could speak, the child's voice was heard.

'What for ha'e ye bawbees on your een, Elspeth McFie, and a white claith lappit under your chin?'

Old Elspeth dropped Sandie's hand and sank back with a groan.

'Effie, Effie, hark till him! The bairn has the second sight, and he sees me stricket for the grave, aye, and ye'll all see it sune! I feel the mouls upon me a'ready! Tak' him awa', tak him awa', he's an awesome bairn!' and Sandie quietly put on his cap and went out into the could mist. Effie followed him, and relieved her fright and agitation by speaking sharply to the child.

'For shame of yoursel', Sandie, to fright an old woman wi' gruesome words that ye never heard from your mither nor me!'

'But what for suld Elspeth be frighted? There were bawbees on her 'een, and a white claith round her heid, and I just tauld her aboot it; and gin I see the like of it on your face, Effie, I will tell ye!'

'My certie! but ye'll be brent for a warlock gin ye read folks' deaths on their faces, and ye'd best haud your clavers!' and Effie said no more, but thought much on her way back to the farm. She was sure that Sandie did not know the meaning of his own words. He had never seen a dead body, and he did not know how a corpse is prepared for the grave, and he certainly had no information on the subject from books, for he could not read. And the appearance he described on old Elspeth's face did not seem to frighten him. He had gazed at her from the moment in which they entered the cottage till they left it, but with wonder and interest rather than fear. The fright was for Elspeth McFie and herself, and as she watched the child, unconscious of the death wound he had given, bounding along the road still playing with his ball and stick, Effie shuddered with vague and nameless fears.

That night at supper Effie told her fellow servants of Sandie's weird words, and they took counsel together whether his mother should be told about it or not, and they decided only to speak to her if anything untoward happened to old Elspeth. It was on Thursday that Effie had been sent to Elspeth McFie's cottage, and she resolved to go there again on her own account on the following Sunday afternoon. Her native superstitions were strong upon her, though she had never imparted them to her young charge, and she drew near to Elspeth's cottage with a boding heart. It scarcely surprised her when she entered to find old Elspeth lying dead on the bed, with coins on her eyes and a white cloth bound round her head, precisely as Sandy had seen her on Thursday.

Two women were in the room with the dead, eager to tell how Elspeth had taken to her bed on Thursday evening, refused bit or sup, and had died early that morning. Effie trembled, but merely asked of what old Elspeth had died, for three days before she seemed in no likelihood of death. But the only account the women could give of her sudden death was that she appeared to have had no illness at all, and that she had said, 'I'm no a sick woman, but a dying, and I maun gae!'

Effie hastened home to tell her mistress everything, repeating faithfully every word that old Elspeth and Sandie had said on the previous Thursday. And Mrs Galbraith listened with a white and awe-struck face.

'Ye'll just say naething about it, Effie; it'll be a sair prejudice against the poor bairn, and stand in his way, gin folks think Sandie has the second sight.' And Effie did not think it necessary to mention that every servant in the house was acquainted with the result of her visit to old Elspeth's cottage. But she hinted that if she continued to wait on such an awesome bairn, that might see the death tokens on her face any day, and fright her into an early grave, her wages should be raised in proportion to the danger of her service.

When Mrs Galbraith told her husband of Sandie's ghastly remark, its tragic result, and the child's unconsciousness in the matter, he disguised the fears that possessed him beneath a bluster of wrath, and rated her and Effie soundly. 'It stands to reason that the bairn canna speak o' what he does na ken, and you and Effie, but mair likely Effie than you – for I was used to think you a woman of sense – hae been telling Sandie auld wives' tales about the second sight, till he thinks it a fine thing to practise what ye've taught him, and the auld doitered fule Elspeth dies out o' sheer fright in consequence, and ye maun see for your ain sel' what your ain folly has brought about!'

But Mrs Galbraith protested that neither she nor Effie had ever uttered a word about the second sight in the boy's hearing. And David, who in his heart believed his wife, though he did not deem it consistent with his dignity to own as much, abruptly ended the unpleasant affair by saying peremptorily, 'I'll no permit the bairn to be tauld any mair ungodly superstitions and auld wives' tales. Effie may gang to the deil and Sandie sall be wi' me in his walks and rides and I'se warrant ye'll hear naething from him but what he learns fra' me, guid sense and sound doctrine.'

And Effie was dismissed to her own great relief, and from that day forth Sandie became his father's outdoor companion, to the visible benefit of his health and spirits.

But no-one was so really alarmed at Sandie's uncanny remark and its consequences as David Galbraith himself. His grandmother, a Highland woman, had had the second sight, and his father had told him how she lived to become the terror of her family. Her premonitions of death and calamity were unfailingly true, and the spirit within her never enlightened her as to how the impending evil might be averted. She was simply the medium of announcing approaching doom. What if her ghostly gift had descended to her grandson, a barren heritage that would make him shunned by his kind!

Poor Alison Galbraith, finding her husband irritable and unreasonable on the subject of Sandie's weird speech, sought comfort in pouring out her fears to their minister, The Revd Ewan Macfarlane, who gave ear to her with as much patience as could be expected from a man whose chief business it was in life to speak and not to listen.

He drew the very worst inference from what he heard. 'It's a clear case o' the second sight, and I canna but fear that there may be waur to come. When the uncanny spirit lights on a body there's nae predicting what its manifestations may be, and for aught that we ken it may be you or me that Sandie'll see the death tokens on neist. And if ye continue to bring him to the kirk, I wad request that ye'll no let him sit glowering at me, for though sudden death wad doubtless be sudden glory to me, it wad no be consistent wi' the dignity of a Minister o' the Free Kirk that he suld be harried untimely into his grave by an uncanny bairn, that wad hae been burnt for a warlock in times gane by. And if I was spared such a sair visitation, the bairn might yet be permitted to wark a certain perturbation of spirit in me, that wad cause me to curtail the word of God, and bring my discourse to a premature end, to the grievous loss of them that hear. And, Mistress Galbraith, let me tell ye, ye'll fa' into disrepute wi' your neighbours gin Sandie sees bawbees on your minister's honoured een, and aught came of it to his prejudice!'

In the following spring David Galbraith's youngest brother Colin returned, after an absence of ten years, to spend a few months with his relations in Scotland. His industry had been prospered in Australia, and he was in a better position than he could have attained by any exertions of his own in the old country. He and his nephew struck up a warm friendship together, and it was a pretty sight to see them golfing on the links at North Berwick, the strong man accommodating his play to that of the puny boy by his side, and restraining his speech so that not a word fell from his lips but what was fit for a child to hear.

One day when they had played till Sandie was tired they sauntered down to the beach, Uncle Colin to sit on the rocks smoking his morning pipe, his nephew to perch beside him and amuse himself with the shells and seaweed that abound there. Presently Sandie grew weary of sitting still, threw away the handful of shells he had picked up, and proposed that they should go further along the sands to where the children were bathing. 'And gi'e me your hand, Uncle Colin, and I'll tell ye something while we walk that I canna just understand mysel'. I've seen an unco' strange thing; I've seen your house in Australia!'

'Hoot, mon! what havers are ye talking? Ye've been dreaming!' said Uncle Colin cheerily.

'Na, I saw it. It was no dream; I ken weel the difference between dreaming and seeing. Your house has na slates on the roof, like our house; it was theckit like a hay-rick, and it had a wide place round it covered with another little theckit roof, and windows like big glass doors opened on it. And there was fire all about, and tall grass all ableeze, and sheep rinning hither and thither frighted, and a man with a black beard and a gun in his hand ran out o' the house and shouted: "O'Grady, save the mare and foal! If they're lost, the master will never forgi'e ye!" What ails ye, Uncle Colin, that ye look sae gash?' and the boy looked up in his uncle's face with wonder.

'It's no canny to see such a sight, Sandie! What do ye ken o' bush fires? And ye've never seen a picture of my house; and who tauld ye that my groom is an Irishman named O'Grady? I've tauld naebody here, and the man with the black beard is my Scotch shepherd.'

'There was no need to tell me onything about it, Uncle Colin, for I saw it a'; but if the man at the door had na shouted O'Grady, then I suld na hae kenned his name.'

Colin made a poor attempt at laughter, that he might hide from the child how shocked and startled he was. But as soon as they reached home he told his brother about his son's vision, and heard from him in return the story of Sandie and old Elspeth. A few days later Colin Galbraith received a telegram from his head shepherd informing him of the heavy loss he had just sustained from a very serious bush fire, and both he and David were convinced that Sandie was an uncanny bairn.

Colin returned to Australia immediately afterwards, and as he parted from his brother and sister-in-law he said with a melancholy smile, 'If ony mischance befa's me, ye'll ken as sune as I do mysel'. Your awesome bairn will see it a', and ye may tak for gospel aught tauld ye by ane that has the second sight.'

One fine afternoon, some three weeks after Colin had sailed, David having just then no particular work to keep him on the farm all day, proposed for a great treat to row Sandie to the Bass Rock. Oat-cutting would shortly begin, and then he would not have a spare hour from morning to night. But today he and his son would enjoy a holiday together, and Sandie was to take with him the small gun that his father gave him on his last birthday, for he was now nine years of age, and high time that he set about learning to kill something or other. All the latent boy seemed developed in the delicate child by the possession of the small fowling-piece, and he blazed away at the rats under the hay-ricks and at the sparrows on the roof, to the peril alike of the poultry and of the bedroom windows. 'Mother, mother, I'll shoot ye a gannet and mak' ye a cushion o' the down!' he shouted in wild excitement as he set forth on the expedition.

Mrs Galbraith stood on the doorstep watching her husband and son leave the house together, David a stout, tall man in the prime of late middle life, red-faced and grey-haired, and Sandie a lanky lad with pale freckled face, but with more vigour in his step than the fond mother had ever expected to see. He carried his gun over his shoulder and strode along by his father's side, glancing up at him frequently to try to imitate his every look and gesture. David Galbraith was fond of rowing, and as it was a very calm day he dismissed the man in charge of the boat, and taking the oars himself said it would do him good to row as far as the Bass Rock and back again. The sea was like a mill-pond, a glassy stretch of water with here and there a wind flaw wrinkling its smooth surface. There was not a wave that could have displaced a pebble on the beach, and masses of olive-green seaweed floated motionless in its clear depths. To the left, high above them, stood the ruins of Tantallon Castle, bathed in August sunshine, its grey walls taking warmth and colour from the glow of light that softened and beautified its rugged outline. Before them the sullen mass of the Bass Rock towered above the blue water, circled by countless thousands of sea birds, the glitter of whose white wings was seen as silvery flashes of light, from a distance too great to distinguish the birds themselves.

They were near enough to the shore to hear voices and laughter borne over the water from the grassy enclosure before Tantallon Castle, and lowing of kine in the pastures, and as they neared the Bass Rock these sounds were exchanged for the squealing of wild fowl and the clang of their wings. To Sandie's delight he was allowed to shoot from the boat, which he did with as little danger to the birds as to the fishes, and the only condition his father imposed was that he should fire with his back towards him, 'till your aim is mair preceese, mon'. Though it soon became evident even to the sanguine Sandie that he would bring home neither gannet nor kittiwake, it was a rapturous delight to be rowed about the island by his father, who told him the name of every bird he saw, and pointed out their nests on the precipitous face of the rock. Then David rested on his oars, and the boat scarcely moved on the still water while Sandie ate the oatcake and drank the milk provided for him by his mother, and his father took a deep draught from his flask till his face grew crimson.

'Father, gi'e me a drink, too,' said Sandie, stretching out his hand.

'Na, na; ye'll stick to your milk-drinking till ye ha'e built up a strong frame, and then ye may tak' as much whusky as ye wull to keep it in guid repair.'

And now the boat was turned landward once more, and they soon lost sound of the clang of the sea birds' wings, and the lowing of kine was again heard, and David rowed slowly past the rock of Tantallon. Sandie had fallen silent, and sat leaning his arm on the gunwale of the boat looking into the limpid water, dipping his hand into a soft swelling wave, and scattering a shower of glittering drops from his fingers. Suddenly he ceased his play, and kneeling in the bottom of the boat, clung firmly to the side with both hands, leaned over, and gazed intently in the water. His father, who was always on the alert where his son was concerned, at once noticed the change that had come over him, rowed quicker, and said cheerily, 'What are ye glowering at, mon? Did ye never see a herring in the sea before?'

Sandie neither spoke nor stirred, and David took comfort in thinking that after all the lad could see nothing uncanny in the water; it was just some daft folly or other he was after, best unnoticed. But when Sandie did speak it was to utter words for which he was unprepared.

'Father, I see Uncle Colin in the water wi' his face turned up to me, and his een wide open, but he canna see wi' them.' And the boy did not raise his head, but continued to gaze into the water. Drops of sweat broke out on Galbraith's brow, and he lifted the dripping oars high in the rowlocks and leaned towards Sandie, his red face now as white as the boy's.

'Whether it's God or the de'il speaks in ye, I dinna ken, but ye'll drive me mad wi' your gruesome clavers! Haud up, man! And fling yoursel' back in the boat, where ye'll see naething waur than yoursel'.'

But Sandie did not stir. 'It's Uncle Colin that I see floating in the water, lappit in seaweed, and he's nae sleeping, for his een stare sae wide,' and Galbraith, who would not have looked over the gunwale of the boat for his life, with an oath plunged the oars deep into the water and rowed with furious strokes.

'Ye've struck the oar on his white face!' shrieked the boy, and fell back crying in the boat.

A heavy gloom settled on the Galbraiths, and this last hideous vision of Sandie's they kept strictly to themselves. They did not seek counsel of their minister or of anyone. They were certain that Colin was drowned. It was a mere question of time when they could hear how it had happened, but hear it they assuredly would. And Sandie, too, was gloomy and depressed. 'The bairn has frighted himself this time as weel as others,' said his father, 'and sma' blame to him. But I would rather follow him to the kirkyard than that he suld grow up wi' the second sight! It may ha'e been a' varra weel in a breekless, starving Hielander a hundred years ago, but it's no consistent for a well-fed Lowlander in these days o' trousers and high farming. How is Sandie to do justice to the land and mind the rotation of crops if he goes daft wi' the second sight?'

The oat harvest was plentiful and got together in fine condition, but neither David nor his wife had any heart to enjoy it. They simply lived through each day waiting for the tidings that must come. Nor had they long to wait. A month after Sandie's vision David read in the newspaper of the safe arrival of his brother's ship at its destination. It reported a prosperous voyage with but one casualty during its course. On the twenty-fourth day after sailing, a passenger booked for Sydney had mysteriously fallen overboard in perfectly calm weather and was drowned. The gentleman's name was Mr Colin Galbraith, and his sudden untimely end had cast a gloom over the ship's company. So far the newspaper report, which, brief as it was, was all that David and Alison could ever learn of their poor brother's fate. They carefully compared the dates, and found that Colin had been drowned three days after Sandie had seen the vision of the body in the sea.

'I winna tell the bairn that puir Colin is dead,' said David gloomily.

'Ye'll just tell the bairn he's dead, but you'll say naething of drowning.'

'Ye maun do as ye think best, but I canna mention puir Colin's name to him.' And it was from his mother that Sandie heard of his Uncle Colin's death. He listened gravely and thoughtfully to the tidings. 'Aye, it was him that I saw in the water.' And that was all that he had to say about the death of his favourite uncle. He asked no question and made no further remark.

From this time forward a great change came over David Galbraith. From being wholly matter of fact and little inclined to believe more than his senses could attest, he became credulous and superstitious. He trembled at omens, and was unnerved for his day's work if his dreams overnight were unpropitious. He disliked being out on dark nights, and cast uneasy glances over his shoulder as though he heard steps behind him. At times when he was riding he thought that he heard someone following hard on his heels, and he would gallop for miles and reach home, horse and rider both in a sweat of fear. And Sandie, the unconscious cause of the evil change in his father, mutely wondered what had come over him. David scarcely let the boy out of his sight, though his society was a torment to him, and he was always wondering what would be the next shock he would receive. Unhappily he tried to restore tone to his shaken nerves by drinking, and the habit grew quickly on him to his good wife's great distress. And times were now so changed that Sandie was often more frightened of his father than his father was of him. Mrs Galbraith proposed sending Sandie to stay with some relations of her own at Linlithgow, thinking that it would do her husband good to have the strain of the boy's constant society removed for a while. But he would not hear of it, and merely said, 'The bairn sall bide at hame. It's my ain weird, and I maun dree it.'

Some two years passed by in which Sandie had no visions, and grew steadily healthier and stronger and more like other boys of his age, so that his mother began to think they should make a man of him yet. But though his father noticed the physical improvement in his son with pride, nothing could persuade him that the dreaded gift had departed from him. In vain his wife tried to convince him that there was no further cause for anxiety. He shook his head and said, 'Ye'll no get rid of an ill gift sae lightly. It's a fire that burns low, but it'll burst out into flame for a' that.'

In the third summer after Colin Galbraith was lost at sea, on a lovely summer evening Mrs Galbraith sat at the open window, knitting and smiling placidly, as she watched her son at work in his little plot of garden watering the tufts of pinks and pansies. She laid her work in her lap, and her eyes followed his every movement with quiet pleasure. Sandie would make a good gardener. There was not a weed nor a straggling growth in his plot, all was neat and trim. And the flower beds were prettily bordered with shells he had collected on the beach at North Berwick.

He was gathering a posy with fastidious care, and his mother knew that it was for her, and thought to herself that if he had been uncanny in time past, he was a good boy, his heart was in the right place. But something disturbed him in his work. He rose from stooping over the bed, dropped his flowers to the ground, and Alison thought he was listening to some far-away sound, till a change that passed over his face showed her that she was mistaken. Sandie was not listening, he was seeing. His face grew pale and his features pinched, his grey eyes were fixed while the colour faded out of them till they were almost white, and he shuddered as though a cold wind blew over him.

Mrs Galbraith rose silently, and assured by the deep breathing of her husband, who was sitting in an armchair by the hearth, that he was asleep, opened the door softly, left the room, and hurried into the garden. There in the sunshine, surrounded by summer sights and summer scents, stood Sandie, a very image of midnight terror. His mother laid her large warm hands on his shoulders, and gently shook him.

'Sandie, Sandie, if you're seeing again, for God's sake say nothing to your father! He canna bear it; ye'll tell me,' she said in a frightened whisper.

The boy gave a sigh, passed his hands over his eyes, and staggered as though he were dizzy. Alison grasped her son firmly by the arm. 'Come awa'! If your father wakes and goes to the window he'll see us; come awa'!' And she hurried the boy through the warm evening sunshine that had suddenly grown cold and dim to her, and led him to a retired part of the garden.

'And now what was it that ye saw?' And looking at her with a strange expression of fear and compassion, Sandie said, 'I saw my father lying on the road at the foot of the steep brae by Sir Ewen Campbell's gates, and his een were shut, but for a' that he was the same as Uncle Colin!'

The self-controlled, unemotional Alison Galbraith gave a smothered scream as she listened to her son, and seizing his arm in a passion of fear, with a grip like a vice, said 'Elspeth McFie was right when she called you an awesome bairn! What for has God in His wrath given me such a child?' and she shook him off, and left him alone in his confused misery.

If David Galbraith had not been overcome with drink that night, he would have seen that something terrible had occurred to agitate his wife. But when the drunken fit was spent he noticed that she looked white and ill.

'Alison, woman, you keep too close in the house,' he said; 'ye should walk to the sea and breathe the caller air, to bring the colour back to your cheeks.'

The following Friday was the corn market at Haddington, and David Galbraith, sober, shrewd, and business-like, set out to attend it, bent on driving a hard bargain. Alison stood at the gate as he mounted his horse to wish him good luck, and to add a word of wifely admonition as to the advisability of not drinking too much whisky before the return journey, and 'Ye'll no be late coming home the night, Davie?'

'There is no night at this time o' year, Alison.'

'And ye'll mind to come by the level road. There's the steep brae beyond the Campbell's gates, and I'd rather ye gave it a wide berth, and came by the long road.'

'Not I, woman! Do ye expect me to mak' a midnight ride a mile longer just to avoid a brae that I ken as weel as my ain doorstep? Kelpie'll be sober, douce beast, if his master's not, and he kens every stane on the brae. Ye'll go to bed and leave the house door unlocked for me,' and David gave his horse a touch with the whip and away he trotted.

Alison stood till the sound of hoofs had died away and then went back into the house with a boding heart. Sandie returned from school at noon in high spirits, and asked his mother's leave to bring home a schoolfellow to play with him in the afternoon. It was wonderful how his spirits had rallied since his vision of a few days before. It seemed as though his body had now grown strong enough to shake off the ghastly influence entirely. But his mother was shattered both by memory and apprehension.

A dreadful restlessness possessed her as night drew on, and after the shouts of the boys at play were over, and silence fell on house and garden, she slipped out unnoticed and walked in the twilight to the beach. It was high midsummer, when in those latitudes the sunset lingers on the western horizon till in the east the vigorous dawn breaks to quench its lesser light. The crescent moon hung low in the sky over the gently murmuring sea that glimmered mysteriously in the diffused twilight, and the brown rocks loomed dark above the water. A time and a place to suggest eerie feelings to the most unimpressionable. But Alison's whole mind was so filled with apprehensions of approaching doom that the scene had no effect upon her – she scarcely noticed where she was. The fear that possessed her was an inward fear, neither suggested nor increased by the aspect of familiar things. She did not meet a soul in her restless wanderings. As she opened the house door on her return the clock struck twelve. Oh, when would David be home? He was seldom later than midnight. Alison needed no light, and creeping softly upstairs she entered Sandie's room, and drawing aside the curtain, by the solemn twilight of the northern night she saw his sleeping face calm and peaceful as an infant's. Did she grudge him his untroubled slumber, that she would rather have found him awake and oppressed with terror as herself?

While she stood listening to the beating of her own heart, that sounded louder than the breathing of her child, she heard the first distant sound of approaching hoofs, and as they rapidly drew nearer she recognised Kelpie's familiar steps.

'Thank God, he is safe home!' she said, and lest her husband should be displeased to find her sitting up for him she hastened to her room and lighted a candle. The horse had stopped opposite the house, and David had had time to dismount, but he had not opened the gate. Someone might be detaining him there. Yet there was no sound of voices to be heard, only Kelpie impatiently striking the ground with one of his fore feet. Alison looked out of the window, but could see nothing for the high wall. As several minutes passed and still her husband did not come, and the horse stamped with increasing impatience, she slipped downstairs out of doors and across the garden to the gate. So deadly a fear lay upon her spirit that when she flung the gate open and saw Kelpie standing riderless on the dusky highway she felt no surprise, only an assurance that Sandie's vision was about to come true.

'Oh, Kelpie lad, your master's no far to seek!' she said as she led the trembling, sweating beast towards the stable yard. Then, without calling up any of the men, just as she was with uncovered head, Alison Galbraith sped through the dusk and silence of the summer night.

'The steep brae by Sir Ewen Campbell's gates! The steep brae by Sir Ewen Campbell's gates!' she said to herself as she ran, and when the dark firs and high wall bounding the park came in sight her limbs almost gave way beneath her. Then she reached the great iron gates between granite pillars, and in the twilight she caught sight through their bars of the black avenue within, and heard the wind sigh in the boughs. Alison pressed her hand to her heart and urged herself on. Now a bat cut its zig-zag flight through the air and startled her. The white scut of a frightened rabbit shone out in the dusk as it flashed across her path in search of a friendly burrow, and her echoing steps woke many a sleeping bird and set it fluttering with fear.

The next turn in the road would bring her to the foot of the brae, and to something that she dared not name that she knew was waiting for her there. She closed her eyes for an instant as she rounded the curve of the road and clenched her hands. Then the soft silence of the summer night was broken by a wailing cry, and Alison Galbraith fell senseless on the dead body of her husband.

David was sober that night, but as he rode through the mirk lanes the old horror had overtaken him. He thought that he heard a horseman following hard upon him, and clapped spurs to his beast and galloped down the hill, at the foot of which Kelpie slipped on a rolling stone, threw his rider heavily to the ground, and he neither spoke nor moved again.

Alison Galbraith did not long survive her husband, and her death took place without Sandie having any intimation of its approach. He never had vision or prophetic foresight again after his father died. The weird gift departed from him with his weakly childhood, and he grew up robust and stout, thriving and commonplace as his forebears. Sandie is even a better farmer than his father before him, and is in a fair way to solve the problem of how to make two blades of wheat grow where only one had grown before. He has married a wife, practical and matter of fact as himself, and their sons and daughters are as guiltless of imagination as they are of any touch of the uncanny. The burly Lowland farmer can never be induced to speak of the second sight, even to his most intimate friends. In the early days of their married life his young wife ventured to ask him about the visions of his childhood, of which she had heard. But he silenced her with such severity that she did not again dare to approach the subject, and she will never know whether the stories of her husband's uncanny childhood are wild legends or plain truth.

Many Waters Cannot Quench Love

Did I not know my old friend John Horton to be as truthful as he is devoid of imagination, I should have believed that he was romancing or dreaming when he told me of a circumstance that happened to him some thirty years ago. He was at that time a bachelor, living in London and practising as a solicitor in Bedford Row. He was not a strong man, though neither nervous nor excitable, and as I said before singularly unimaginative.

If Horton told you a fact, you might be certain that it had occurred in the precise manner he stated. If he told it you a hundred times, he would not vary it in the repetition. This literal and conscientious habit of mind made his testimony of value, and when he told me a fact that I should have disbelieved from any other man, from my friend I was obliged to accept it as truth.

It was during the long vacation in the autumn of 1857, that Horton determined to take a few weeks holiday in the country. He was such an inveterate Londoner he had not been able to tear himself away from town for more than a few days at a time for many years past. But at length he felt the necessity for quiet and pure air, only he would not go far to seek them. It was easier then than it is now to find a lodging that would meet his requirements, a place in the country yet close to the town, and it was near Wandsworth that Horton found what he sought, rooms for a single gentleman in an old farmhouse. He read the advertisement of the lodgings in the paper at luncheon, and went that very afternoon to see if they answered to the tempting description given. He had some little difficulty in finding Maitland's Farm. It was not easy to find his way through country lanes that to his town eyes looked precisely alike, and with nothing to indicate whether he had taken a right or wrong turning. The railway now runs shrieking over what were then green fields, lanes have been transformed into gas-lighted streets, and Maitland's Farm, the old red-brick house standing in its high-walled garden, has been pulled down long ago. The last time Horton went to look at the old place it was changed beyond recognition, and the orchard in which he had gathered pears and apples during his stay at the farm, was now the site of a public house and a dissenting chapel.

It was on a hot afternoon early in September when Horton opened the big iron gates and walked up the path bordered with dahlias and hollyhocks leading to the front door, and rang for admittance at Maitland's Farm. The bell echoed in a distant part of the empty house and died away into silence, but no-one came to answer its summons. As Horton stood waiting he took the opportunity of thoroughly examining the outside of the house. Though it was called a farm it had not been built for one originally. It was a substantial, four-storey brick house of Queen Anne's period, with five tall sash windows on each floor, and dormer windows in the tiled roof. The front door was approached by a shallow flight of stone steps, and above the fan-light projected a penthouse of solidly carved woodwork. On either side were brackets of wrought iron, supporting extinguishers that had quenched the torch of many a late returning reveller a century ago. Only the windows to right and left of the door had blinds or curtains, or betrayed any sign of habitation. 'Those are the rooms to be let, I wonder which is the bedroom,' thought my friend as he rang the bell for the second time. Presently he heard within the sound of approaching footsteps, there was a great drawing of bolts, and after a final struggle with the rusty lock, the door was opened by an old woman of severe and cheerless aspect. Horton was the first to speak.

'I have called to see the rooms advertised to be let in this house.'

The old woman eyed him from head to foot without making any reply, then opening the door wider, nodded to him to enter. He did so and found himself in a large paved hall lighted from the fan-light over the door, and by a high narrow window facing him at the top of a short flight of oak stairs. The air was musty and damp as that of an old church.

'A hall this size should have a fire in it,' said Horton, glancing at the empty rusty grate.

'Farmers and folks that work out of doors keep themselves warm without fires,' said the old woman sharply.

'This house was never built for a farm, why is it called one?' enquired Horton of his taciturn guide as she opened the door of the sitting-room.

'Because it was one,' was the blunt reply. 'When I was a girl it was the Manor House, and may be called that again for all I know, but thirty years since, a man named Maitland took it on a lease and farmed the land, and folks forgot the old name, and called it Maitland's Farm.'

'When did Maitland leave?'

'About two months ago.'

'Why did he go away from a nice place like this?'

'You are fond of asking questions,' remarked the old woman drily. 'He went for two good reasons: his lease was up, and his family was a big one. Nine children he had, from a girl of two-and-twenty down to a little lad of four years old. His wife and him thought it best to take 'em out to Australia, where there's room for all. They were glad to go, all but the eldest, Esther, and she nearly broke her heart over it. But then she had to leave her sweetheart behind her. He's a young man on a dairy farm near here, and though he's to follow her out and marry her in twelve months, she did nothing but mourn, same as if she was leaving him altogether.'

'Ah, indeed!' said Horton, who could not readily enter into details about people whom he did not know. 'So this is the sitting-room; it's large and airy, and has as much furniture in it as a man needs by himself. Now show me the bedroom, if you please.'

'Follow me upstairs, sir,' and the old woman preceded him slowly up the oak staircase, and opened the door of the back room on the first floor.

'Then the bedroom that you let is not over the sitting-room?'

'No, the front room is mine, and the room next to it is my son's. He's out all day at his work, but he sleeps here, and mostly keeps me company of an evening. I'm alone here all day looking after the place, and if you take the rooms I shall cook for you and wait on you myself.'

Horton liked the look of the bedroom. It was large and airy, with little furniture in it beyond a bed and a chest of drawers. But it was delicately clean, and silent as the grave. How a tired man might sleep here! The walls were decorated with old prints in black frames of the 'Rake's Progress' and 'Marriage à la Mode', and above the high carved mantelpiece hung an engraving of the famous portrait of Charles the First, on a prancing brown horse.

'Those things were on the walls when the Maitlands took the place, and they had to leave 'em where they found 'em,' said the old woman. 'And they found that sword too,' she added, pointing to a rusty cutlass that hung from a nail by the head of the bed; 'but I think they'd have done no great harm if they'd sold it for old iron.'

Horton took down the weapon and examined it. It was an ordinary cutlass, such as was worn by the marines in George the Third's reign, not old enough to be of antiquarian interest, nor of sufficient beauty of workmanship to make it of artistic value. He replaced it, and stepped to the windows and looked into the garden below. It was bounded by a high wall enclosing a row of poplars, and beyond lay the open country, visible for miles in the clear air, a sight to rest and fascinate the eye of a Londoner.

Horton made his bargain with the old woman whom the landlord had put into the house as caretaker, pending his decision about the disposition of the property. She was allowed to take a lodger for her own profit, and as soon as Mrs Belt found that the stranger agreed to her terms, she assured him that everything should be comfortably arranged for his reception by the following Wednesday.

* * *

Horton arrived at Maitland's Farm on the evening of the appointed day. A stormy autumnal sunset was casting an angry glow on the windows of the house, the rising wind filled the air with mournful sounds, and the poplars swayed against a background of lurid sky.

Mrs Belt was expecting her lodger, and promptly opened the door, candle in hand, when she heard wheels stopping at the gate. The driver of the fly carried Horton's portmanteau into the hall, was paid his fare, and drove away thinking the darkening lanes more cheerful than the glimpse he had had of the inside of Maitland's Farm.

Horton was thoroughly pleased with his country quarters. The intense quiet of the almost empty house, that might have made another man melancholy, soothed and rested him. In the daytime he wandered about the country, or amused himself in the garden and orchard, and he spent the long evenings alone, reading and smoking in his sitting-room. Mrs Belt brought in supper at nine o'clock, and usually stayed to have a chat with her lodger, and many a long story she related of her neighbours, and the Maitland family, while she waited upon him at his evening meal.

On several occasions she told him that Esther Maitland's sweetheart, Michael Winn, had come to talk with her about the Maitlands, or to bring her a newspaper containing tidings that their ship had reached some point on its long voyage in safety.

'You see the *Petrel* is a sailing vessel, sir, and there's no saying how long she'll take getting to Australia. The last news Michael had, she'd got as far as some islands with an outlandish name, and he's had a letter from Esther posted at a place called Madeira. And now he gives himself no peace till he can hear that the ship's safe as far as – somewhere, I think he said, in Africa.'

'It would be the Cape, Mrs Belt.'

'That's the name, sir, the Cape, and he werrits all the time for fear of storms and shipwrecks. But I tell him the world's a wide place, and the sea wider than all, and very likely when the chimney pots is flying about our heads in a gale here, the *Petrel*'s lying becalmed somewhere. And then he takes up my thought and turns it against me. "Yes," he says, "and when it's a dead calm here on shore, the ship may be sinking in a storm, and my Esther being drowned." '

'Michael Winn must be a very nervous young man.'

'That's where it is, sir, and I tell him when he follows the Maitlands it's a good job that he leaves no-one behind him that'll werrit after him, same as he's werrited after Esther.'

It was the middle of October, and Horton had been a month at the farm. The weather was now cold and wet, and he began to think it was time he returned to his snug London home, for the autumn rain made everything at Maitland's Farm damp and mouldy. It had blown half a gale all day, and the rain had fallen in torrents, keeping him a prisoner indoors. But he occupied himself in writing letters, and reading some legal documents his clerk had bought out to him, and the time passed rapidly. Indeed the evening flew by so quickly he had no idea it was nine o'clock, when Mrs Belt entered the room to lay the cloth for supper.

'It's stopped raining now, sir,' she said, as she poked the fire into a cheerful blaze, 'and a good job too, for Michael Winn brings me word the Wandle's risen fearful since morning, and it's out in places more than it's been for years. But there's a full moon tonight, so no-one need walk into the water unless they've a mind to.'

Horton's head was too full of a knotty legal point to pay much heed to Mrs Belt, and the old woman, seeing that he was not in a mood for conversation, said nothing further. At half-past ten she brought her lodger some spirits and hot water, and his bedroom candle, and wished him good-night. Horton sat reading for some time, and then made an entry in his diary concerning a day of which there was absolutely nothing to record, lighted his candle, and went upstairs. I am familiar with the precise order of each trifling circumstance. My friend has so often told me the events of that night, and never with the slightest addition or omission in the telling. It was his habit, the last thing at night, to draw up the blinds. He looked out of the window, and though the moon was at the full, the clouds had not yet dispersed, and her light was fitful and obscure. It was twenty minutes to twelve as he extinguished the candle by his bedside. Everything was propitious for rest. He was weary, and the house profoundly silent. The rain had stopped, the wind fallen to a sigh, and it seemed to him that as soon as his head pressed the pillow he sank into a dreamless slumber.

Shortly after two o'clock Horton awoke suddenly, passing instantaneously from deep sleep to the possession of every faculty in a heightened degree, and with an insupportable sense of fear weighing upon him like a thousand nightmares. He started up and looked around him. The perspiration poured from his brow, and his heart beat to suffocation. He was convinced that he had been waked by some strange and terrible noise, that had thrilled through the depths of sleep, and he dreaded the repetition of it inexpressibly. The room was flooded with moonlight streaming through the narrow windows, lying like sheets of molten silver on the floor, and the poplars in the garden cast tremulous shadows on the ceiling.

Then Horton heard through the silence of the house a sound that was not the moan of the wind, nor the rustling of trees, nor any sound he had heard before. Clear and distinct, as though it were in the room with him, he heard a voice of weeping and lamentation, with more than human sorrow in the cry, so that it seemed to him as though he listened to the mourning of a lost soul. He leaped up, struck a match, and lighted the candle, and seizing the cutlass that hung by the bed, unlocked the door, and opened it to listen.

So far as all ordinary sounds were concerned, the house was silent as death, and the moonlight streamed through the staircase window in a flood of pale light. But the unearthly sound of weeping, thrilling through heart and soul, came from the hall below, and Horton walked downstairs to the landing at the top of the first flight. There, on the lowest step, a woman was seated with bowed head, her face hidden in her hands, rocking to and fro in extremity of grief. The moonlight fell full on her, and he saw that she was only partly clothed, and her dark hair lay in confusion on her bare shoulders.

'Who are you, and what is the matter with you?' said Horton, and his trembling voice echoed in the silent house. But she neither stirred nor spoke, nor abated her weeping. Slowly he descended the moonlit staircase till there were but four steps between him and the woman. A mortal fear was growing upon him.

'Speak! if you are a living being!' he cried. The figure rose to its full height, turned and faced him for a moment that seemed an eternity, and rushed full on the point of the cutlass Horton involuntarily presented. As the impalpable form glided up the blade of the weapon, a cold wave seemed to break over him, and he fell in a dead faint on the stairs.

How long he remained insensible he could not tell. When he came to himself and opened his eyes, the moon had set, and he groped his way in darkness to his room, where the candle had burnt itself out.

When Horton came down to breakfast, he looked as though he had been ill for a month, and his hands trembled like a drunkard's. At any other time Mrs Belt would have been struck by his appearance, but this morning she was too much excited by some bad news she had heard, to notice whether her lodger was looking well or ill. Horton asked her how she had slept, for if she had not heard the terrible sounds that waked him, it still seemed impossible she should not have heard his heavy fall on the stairs. Mrs Belt replied, with some astonishment at her lodger's concern for her welfare, that she had never had a better night, it was so quiet after the wind fell.

'But did your son think the house was quiet, did he sleep too?' asked Horton with feverish eagerness.

Mrs Belt was yearning to impart her bad news to her lodger, and remarking that she had something else to do than ask folks how they slept o' nights, she said a neighbour had just told her that Michael Winn had fallen into the Wandle during the night – no-one knew how – and was drowned, and they were carrying his body home then.

'What a terrible blow for his sweetheart,' said Horton, greatly shocked.

'Aye! there's a pretty piece of news to send her, when she's expecting to see poor Michael himself soon.'

'Mrs Belt, have you any portrait of Esther Maitland you could show me? I've heard the girl's name so often I'm curious to know what she is like.' And the old woman retired to hunt among her treasures for a small photograph on glass, that Esther had given her before she went away. Presently Mrs Belt returned, polishing the picture with her apron.

'It's but a poor affair, sir, taken in a caravan on the Common, yet it's like the girl, it's very like.'

It was a miserable production, a cheap and early effort in photography, and Horton rose from the table with the picture in his hand to examine it at the window. And there, surrounded by the thin brass frame, he recognised the face of all faces that had dismayed him, the face he beheld in the vision of the preceding night. He suppressed a groan, and turned from the window with a face so white, that, as he handed the picture back to Mrs Belt, she said, 'You're not feeling well this morning, sir.'

'No, I'm feeling very ill. I must get back to town today to be near to my own doctor. You shall be no loser by my leaving you so suddenly, but if I am going to be ill, I am best in my own home.' For Horton could not have stayed another night at Maitland's Farm to save his life.

He was at his office in Bedford Row by noon, and his clerks thought that he looked ten years older for his visit to the country.

A little more than three weeks after Horton returned to town, when his nerves were beginning to recover their accustomed tone, his attention was unexpectedly recalled to the abhorrent subject of the apparition he had seen. He read in his daily paper that the mail from the Cape had brought news of the wreck of the sailing vessel *Petrel* bound for Australia, with loss of all on board, in a violent storm off the coast, shortly before the steamer left for England. By a careful comparison of dates, allowing for the variation of time, the conviction was forced upon John Horton that the ill-fated ship foundered at the very hour in which he beheld the wraith of Esther Maitland. She and her lover, divided by thousands of miles, both perished by drowning at the same time – Michael Winn in the little river at home, and Esther Maitland in the depths of a distant ocean.

How He Left the Hotel

I used to work the passenger lift in the Empire Hotel, that big block of building in lines of red and white brick like streaky bacon, that stands at the corner of Bath Street. I'd served my time in the army and got my discharge with good conduct stripes, and how I got the job was in this way. The hotel was a big company affair, with a managing committee of retired officers and suchlike, gentlemen with a bit o' money in the concern and nothing to do but fidget about it, and my late Colonel was one of 'em. He was as good-tempered a man as ever stepped when his will wasn't crossed, and when I asked him for a job, 'Mole,' says he, 'you're the very man to work the lift at our big hotel. Soldiers are civil and businesslike, and the public like 'em only second-best to sailors. We've had to give our last man the sack, and you can take his place.'

I liked my work well enough and my pay, and kept my place a year, and I should have been there still if it hadn't been for a circumstance – but more about that just now. Ours was a hydraulic lift. None o' them rickety things swung up like a poll parrot's cage in a well staircase, that I shouldn't care to trust my neck to. It ran as smooth as oil, a child might have worked it, and safe as standing on the ground. Instead of being stuck full of advertisements like a' omnibus, we'd mirrors in it, and the ladies would look at themselves, and pat their hair, and set their mouths when I was taking 'em downstairs drest of an evening. It was a little sitting-room with red velvet cushions to sit down on, and you'd nothing to do but get into it, and it 'ud float you up, or float you down, as light as a bird.

All the visitors used the lift one time or another, going up or coming down. Some of them was French, and they called the lift the 'assenser', and good enough for them in their language no doubt, but why the Americans, that can speak English when they choose, and are always finding out ways o' doing things quicker than other folks, should waste time and breath calling a lift an 'elevator', I can't make out.

I was in charge of the lift from noon till midnight. By that time the theatre and dining-out folks had come in, and anyone returning later walked upstairs, for my day's work was done. One of the porters worked the lift till I came on duty in the morning, but before twelve there was nothing particular going on, and not much till after two o'clock. Then it was pretty hot work with visitors going up and down constant, and the electric bell ringing you from one floor to another like a house on fire. Then came a quiet spell while dinner was on, and I'd sit down comfortable in the lift and read my paper, only I mightn't smoke. But nobody else might neither, and I had to ask furren gentlemen to please not to smoke in it, it was against the rule. I hadn't so often to tell English gentlemen. They're not like furreners, that seem as if their cigars was glued to their lips.

I always noticed faces as folks got into the lift, for I've sharp sight and a good memory, and none of the visitors needed to tell me twice where to take them. I knew them, and I knew their floor as well as they did themselves.

It was in November that Colonel Saxby came to the Empire Hotel. I noticed him particularly because you could see at once that he was a soldier. He was a tall, thin man about fifty, with a hawk nose, keen eyes, and a grey moustache, and walked stiff from a gunshot wound in the knee. But what I noticed most was the scar of a sabre cut across the right side of the face. As he got in the lift to go to his room on the fourth floor, I thought what a difference there is among officers. Colonel Saxby put me in mind of a telegraph post for height and thinness, and my old Colonel was like a barrel in uniform, but a brave soldier and a gentleman all the same. Colonel Saxby's room was number 210, just opposite the glass door leading to the lift, and every time I stopt on the fourth floor Number 210 stared me in the face.

The Colonel used to go up in the lift every day regular, though he never came down in it, till – but I'm coming to that presently. Sometimes, when we was alone in the lift, he'd speak to me. He asked me in what regiment I'd served, and said he knew the officers in it. But I can't say he was comfortable to talk to. There was something stand-off about him, and he always seemed deep in his own thoughts. He never sat down in the lift. Whether it was empty or full he stood bolt upright, under the lamp, where the light fell on his pale face and scarred cheek.

One day in February I didn't take the Colonel up in the lift, and as he was regular as clockwork, I noticed it, but I supposed he'd gone away for a few days, and I thought no more about it. Whenever I stopt on the fourth floor the door of Number 210 was shut, and as he often left it open, I made sure the Colonel was away. At the end of a week I heard a chambermaid say that Colonel Saxby was ill, so thinks I that's why he hadn't been in the lift lately.

It was a Tuesday night, and I'd had an uncommonly busy time of it. It was one stream of traffic up and down, and so it went on the whole evening. It was on the stroke of midnight, and I was about to put out the light in the lift, lock the door, and leave the key in the office for the man in the morning, when the electric bell rang out sharp. I looked at the dial, and saw I was wanted on the fourth floor. It struck twelve as I stept into the lift. As I passed the second and third floors I wondered who it was that had rung so late, and thought it must be a stranger that didn't know the rule of the house. But when I stopt at the fourth floor and flung open the door of the lift, Colonel Saxby was standing there wrapt in his military cloak. His room door was shut behind him, for I read the number on it. I thought he was ill in his bed, and ill enough he looked, but he had his hat on, and what could a man that had been in bed ten days want with going out on a winter midnight? I don't think he saw me, but when I'd set the lift in motion, I looked at him standing under the lamp, with the shadow of his hat hiding his eyes, and the light full on the lower part of his face that was deadly pale, the scar on his cheek showing still paler.

'Glad to see you're better, sir,' but he said nothing, and I didn't like to look at him again. He stood like a statue with his cloak about him, and I was downright glad when I opened the door for him to step out in the hall. I saluted as he got out, and he went past me towards the door.

'The Colonel wants to go out,' I said to the porter, who stood staring. He opened the front door and Colonel Saxby walked out into the snow.

'That's a queer go,' said the porter.

'It is,' said I. 'I don't like the Colonel's looks; he doesn't seem himself at all. He's ill enough to be in his bed, and there he is, gone out on a night like this.'

'Anyhow he's got a famous cloak to keep him warm. I say, supposing he's gone to a fancy ball and got that cloak on to hide his dress,' said the porter, laughing uneasily. For we both felt queerer than we cared to say, and as we spoke there came a loud ring at the door bell.

'No more passengers for me,' I said, and I was really putting the light out this time, when Joe opened the door and two gentlemen entered that I knew at a glance were doctors. One was tall and the other short and stout, and they both came to the lift.

'Sorry, gentlemen, but it's against the rule for the lift to go up after midnight.'

'Nonsense!' said the stout gentleman, 'it's only just past twelve, and it's a matter of life and death. Take us up at once to the fourth floor,' and they were in the lift like a shot.

When I opened the door, they went straight to Number 210. A nurse came out to meet them, and the stout doctor said, 'No change for the worse, I hope.' And I heard her reply, 'The patient died five minutes ago, sir.'

Though I'd no business to speak, that was more than I could stand. I followed the doctors to the door and said, 'There's some mistake here, gentlemen; I took the Colonel down in the lift since the clock struck twelve, and he went out.'

The stout doctor said sharply, 'A case of mistaken identity. It was someone else you took for the Colonel.'

'Begging your pardon, gentlemen, it was the Colonel himself, and the night porter that opened the door for him knew him as well as me. He was dressed for a night like this, with his military cloak wrapt round him.'

'Step in and see for yourself,' said the nurse. I followed the doctors into the room, and there lay Colonel Saxby looking just as I'd seen him a few minutes before. There he lay, dead as his forefathers, and the great cloak spread over the bed to keep him warm that would feel heat and cold no more.

I never slept that night. I sat up with Joe, expecting every minute to hear the Colonel ring the front door bell. Next day every time the bell for the lift rang sharp and sudden, the sweat broke out on me and I shook again. I felt as bad as I did the first time I was in action. Me and Joe told the manager all about it, and he said we'd been dreaming, but, said he, 'Mind you, don't you talk about it, or the house'll be empty in a week.'

The Colonel's coffin was smuggled into the house the next night. Me and the manager, and the undertaker's men, took it up in the lift, and it lay right across it, and not an inch to spare. They carried it into Number 210, and while I waited for them to come out again, a queer feeling came over me. Then the door opened softly, and six men carried out the long coffin straight across the passage, and set it down with its foot towards the door of the lift, and the manager looked round for me.

'I can't do it, sir,' I said. 'I can't take the Colonel down *again*, I took him down at midnight yesterday, and that was enough for me.'

'Push it in!' said the manager, speaking short and sharp, and they ran the coffin into the lift without a sound. The manager got in last, and before he closed the door he said, 'Mole, you've worked this lift for the last time, it strikes me.' And I had, for I wouldn't have stayed on at the Empire Hotel after what had happened, not if they'd doubled my wages, and me and the night porter left together.

The Real and the Counterfeit

Will Musgrave determined that he would neither keep Christmas alone, nor spend it again with his parents and sisters in the south of France. The Musgrave family annually migrated southward from their home in Northumberland, and Will as regularly followed them to spend a month with them in the Riviera, till he had almost forgotten what Christmas was like in England. He rebelled at having to leave the country at a time when, if the weather was mild, he should be hunting, or if it was severe, skating, and he had no real or imaginary need to winter in the south. His chest was of iron and his lungs of brass. A raking east wind that drove his parents into their thickest furs, and taught them the number of their teeth by enabling them to count a separate and well defined ache for each, only brought a deeper colour into the cheek, and a brighter light into the eye of the weather-proof youth. Decidedly he would not go to Cannes, though it was no use annoying his father and mother, and disappointing his sisters, by telling them beforehand of his determination.

Will knew very well how to write a letter to his mother in which his defection should appear as an event brought about by the over-mastering power of circumstances, to which the sons of Adam must submit. No doubt that a prospect of hunting or skating, as the fates might decree, influenced his decision. But he had also long promised himself the pleasure of a visit from two of his college friends, Hugh Armitage and Horace Lawley, and he asked that they might spend a fortnight with him at Stonecroft, as a little relaxation had been positively ordered for him by his tutor.

'Bless him,' said his mother fondly, when she had read his letter, 'I will write to the dear boy and tell him how pleased I am with his firmness and determination.' But Mr Musgrave muttered inarticulate sounds as he listened to his wife, expressive of incredulity rather than of acquiescence, and when he spoke it was to say, 'Devil of a row three young fellows will kick up alone at Stonecroft!

We shall find the stables full of broken-kneed horses when we go home again.'

Will Musgrave spent Christmas day with the Armitages at their place near Ripon. And the following night they gave a dance at which he enjoyed himself as only a very young man can do, who has not yet had his fill of dancing, and who would like nothing better than to waltz through life with his arm round his pretty partner's waist. The following day, Musgrave and Armitage left for Stonecroft, picking up Lawley on the way, and arriving at their destination late in the evening, in the highest spirits and with the keenest appetites. Stonecroft was a delightful haven of refuge at the end of a long journey across country in bitter weather, when the east wind was driving the light dry snow into every nook and cranny. The wide, hospitable front door opened into an oak-panelled hall with a great open fire burning cheerily, and lighted by lamps from overhead that effectually dispelled all gloomy shadows. As soon as Musgrave had entered the house he seized his friends, and before they had time to shake the snow from their coats, kissed them both under the mistletoe bough and set the servants tittering in the background.

'You're miserable substitutes for your betters,' he said, laughing and pushing them from him, 'but it's awfully unlucky not to use the mistletoe. Barker, I hope supper's ready, and that it is something very hot and plenty of it, for we've travelled on empty stomachs and brought them with us,' and he led his guests upstairs to their rooms.

'What a jolly gallery!' said Lawley enthusiastically as they entered a long wide corridor, with many doors and several windows in it, and hung with pictures and trophies of arms.

'Yes, it's our one distinguishing feature at Stonecroft,' said Musgrave. 'It runs the whole length of the house, from the modern end of it to the back, which is very old, and built on the foundations of a Cistercian monastery which once stood on this spot. The gallery's wide enough to drive a carriage and pair down it, and it's the main thoroughfare of the house. My mother takes a constitutional here in bad weather, as though it were the open air, and does it with her bonnet on to aid the delusion.'

Armitage's attention was attracted by the pictures on the walls, and especially by the life-size portrait of a young man in a blue coat, with powdered hair, sitting under a tree with a staghound lying at his feet.

'An ancestor of yours?' he said, pointing at the picture.

'Oh, they're all one's ancestors, and a motley crew they are, I must say for them. It may amuse you and Lawley to find from which of them I derive my good looks. That pretty youth whom you seem to admire is my great-great-grandfather. He died at twenty-two, a preposterous age for an ancestor. But come along Armitage, you'll have plenty of time to do justice to the pictures by daylight, and I want to show you your rooms. I see everything is arranged comfortably, we are close together. Our pleasantest rooms are on the gallery, and here we are nearly at the end of it. Your rooms are opposite to mine, and open into Lawley's in case you should be nervous in the night and feel lonely so far from home, my dear children.'

And Musgrave bade his friends make haste, and hurried away whistling cheerfully to his own room.

The following morning the friends rose to a white world. Six inches of fine snow, dry as salt, lay everywhere, the sky overhead a leaden lid, and all the signs of a deep fall yet to come.

'Cheerful this, very,' said Lawley, as he stood with his hands in his pockets, looking out of the window after breakfast. 'The snow will have spoilt the ice for skating.'

'But it won't prevent wild duck shooting,' said Armitage, 'and I say, Musgrave, we'll rig up a toboggan out there. I see a slope that might have been made on purpose for it. If we get some tobogganing, it may snow day and night for all I care, we shall be masters of the situation any way.'

'Well thought of, Armitage,' said Musgrave, jumping at the idea.

'Yes, but you need two slopes and a little valley between for real good tobogganing,' objected Lawley, 'otherwise you only rush down the hillock like you do from the Mount Church to Funchal, and then have to retrace your steps as you do there, carrying your car on your back. Which lessens the fun considerably.'

'Well, we can only work with the material at hand,' said Armitage; 'let's go and see if we can't find a better place for our toboggan, and something that will do for a car to slide in.'

'That's easily found – empty wine cases are the thing, and stout sticks to steer with,' and away rushed the young men into the open air, followed by half a dozen dogs barking joyfully.

'By Jove! if the snow keeps firm, we'll put runners on strong chairs and walk over to see the Harradines at Garthside, and ask the girls to come out sledging, and we'll push them,' shouted Musgrave to Lawley and Armitage, who had outrun him in the vain attempt to keep up with a deer-hound that headed the party. After a long and careful search they found a piece of land exactly suited to their purpose, and it would have amused their friends to see how hard the young men worked under the beguiling name of pleasure. For four hours they worked like navvies making a toboggan slide. They shovelled away the snow, then with pickaxe and spade, levelled the ground, so that when a carpet of fresh snow was spread over it, their improvised car would run down a steep incline and be carried by the impetus up another, till it came to a standstill in a snow drift.

'If we can only get this bit of engineering done today,' said Lawley, chucking a spadeful of earth aside as he spoke, 'the slide will be in perfect order for tomorrow.'

'Yes, and when once it's done, it's done for ever,' said Armitage, working away cheerfully with his pick where the ground was frozen hard and full of stones, and cleverly keeping his balance on the slope as he did so. 'Good work lasts no end of a time, and posterity will bless us for leaving them this magnificent slide.'

'Posterity may, my dear fellow, but hardly our progenitors if my father should happen to slip down it,' said Musgrave.

When their task was finished, and the friends were transformed in appearance from navvies into gentlemen, they set out through thick falling snow to walk to Garthside to call on their neighbours the Harradines. They had earned their pleasant tea and lively talk, their blood was still aglow from their exhilarating work, and their spirits at the highest point. They did not return to Stonecroft till they had compelled the girls to name a time when they would come with their brothers and be launched down the scientifically prepared slide, in wine cases well padded with cushions for the occasion.

Late that night the young men sat smoking and chatting together in the library. They had played billiards till they were tired, and Lawley had sung sentimental songs, accompanying himself on the banjo, till even he was weary, to say nothing of what his listeners might be. Armitage sat leaning his light curly head back in the chair, gently puffing out a cloud of tobacco smoke. And he was the first to break the silence that had fallen on the little company.

'Musgrave,' he said suddenly, 'an old house is not complete unless it is haunted. You ought to have a ghost of your own at Stonecroft.'

Musgrave threw down the yellow-backed novel he had just picked up, and became all attention.

'So we have, my dear fellow. Only it has not been seen by any of us since my grandfather's time. It is the desire of my life to become personally acquainted with our family ghost.'

Armitage laughed. But Lawley said, 'You would not say that if you really believed in ghosts.'

'I believe in them most devoutly, but I naturally wish to have my faith confirmed by sight. You believe in them too, I can see.'

'Then you see what does not exist, and so far you are in a fair way to see ghosts. No, my state of mind is this,' continued Lawley, 'I neither believe, nor entirely disbelieve in ghosts. I am open to conviction on the subject. Many men of sound judgement believe in them, and others of equally good mental capacity don't believe in them. I merely regard the case of the bogies as not proven. They may or may not exist, but till their existence is plainly demonstrated, I decline to add such an uncomfortable article to my creed as a belief in bogies.'

Musgrave did not reply, but Armitage laughed a strident laugh.

'I'm one against two, I'm in an overwhelming minority,' he said. 'Musgrave frankly confesses his belief in ghosts, and you are neutral, neither believing nor disbelieving, but open to conviction. Now I'm a complete unbeliever in the supernatural, root and branch. People's nerves no doubt play them queer tricks, and will continue to do so to the end of the chapter, and if I were so fortunate as to see Musgrave's family ghost tonight, I should no more believe in it than I do now. By the way, Musgrave, is the ghost a lady or a gentleman?' he asked flippantly.

'I don't think you deserve to be told.'

'Don't you know that a ghost is neither he nor she?' said Lawley. 'Like a corpse, it is always *it*.'

'That is a piece of very definite information from a man who neither believes nor disbelieves in ghosts. How do you come by it, Lawley?' asked Armitage.

'Mayn't a man be well informed on a subject although he suspends his judgement about it? I think I have the only logical mind among us. Musgrave believes in ghosts though he has never seen one, you don't believe in them, and say that you would not be convinced if you saw one, which is not wise, it seems to me.'

'It is not necessary to my peace of mind to have a definite opinion on the subject. After all, it is only a matter of patience, for if ghosts really exist we shall each be one in the course of time, and then, if we've nothing better to do, and are allowed to play such unworthy pranks, we may appear again on the scene, and impartially scare our credulous and incredulous surviving friends.'

'Then I shall try to be beforehand with you, Lawley, and turn bogie first; it would suit me better to scare than to be scared. But, Musgrave, do tell me about your family ghost; I'm really interested in it, and I'm quite respectful now.'

'Well, mind you are, and I shall have no objection to tell you what I know about it, which is briefly this: Stonecroft, as I told you, is built on the site of an old Cistercian Monastery destroyed at the time of the Reformation. The back part of the house rests on the old foundations, and its walls are built with the stones that were once part and parcel of the monastery. The ghost that has been seen by members of the Musgrave family for three centuries past, is that of a Cistercian monk, dressed in the white habit of his order. Who he was, or why he has haunted the scenes of his earthly life so long, there is no tradition to enlighten us. The ghost has usually been seen once or twice in each generation. But as I said, it has not visited us since my grandfather's time, so, like a comet, it should be due again presently.'

'How you must regret that was before your time,' said Armitage.

'Of course I do, but I don't despair of seeing it yet. At least I know where to look for it. It has always made its appearance in the gallery, and I have my bedroom close to the spot where it was last seen, in the hope that if I open my door suddenly some moonlight night I may find the monk standing there.'

'Standing where?' asked the incredulous Armitage.

'In the gallery, to be sure, midway between your two doors and mine. That is where my grandfather last saw it. He was waked in the dead of night by the sound of a heavy door shutting. He ran into the gallery where the noise came from, and, standing opposite the door of the room I occupy, was the white figure of the Cistercian monk. As he looked, it glided the length of the gallery and melted like mist into the wall. The spot where he disappeared is on the old foundations of the monastery, so that he was evidently returning to his own quarters.'

'And your grandfather believed that he saw a ghost?' asked Armitage disdainfully.

'Could he doubt the evidence of his senses? He saw the thing as clearly as we see each other now, and it disappeared like a thin vapour against the wall.'

'My dear fellow, don't you think that it sounds more like an anecdote of your grandmother than of your grandfather?' remarked Armitage. He did not intend to be rude, though he succeeded in being so, as he was instantly aware by the expression of cold reserve that came over Musgrave's frank face.

'Forgive me, but I never can take a ghost story seriously,' he said. 'But this much I will concede – they may have existed long ago in what were literally the dark ages, when rushlights and sputtering dip candles could not keep the shadows at bay. But in this latter part of the nineteenth century, when gas and the electric light have turned night into day, you have destroyed the very conditions that produced the ghost – or rather the belief in it, which is the same thing. Darkness has always been bad for human nerves. I can't explain why, but so it is. My mother was in advance of the age on the subject, and always insisted on having a good light burning in the night nursery, so that when as a child I woke from a bad dream I was never frightened by the darkness. And in consequence I have grown up a complete unbeliever in ghosts, spectres, wraiths, apparitions, *doppelgänger*, and the whole bogie crew of them,' and Armitage looked round calmly and complacently.

'Perhaps I might have felt as you do if I had not begun life with the knowledge that our house was haunted,' replied Musgrave with visible pride in the ancestral ghost. 'I only wish that I could convince you of the existence of the supernatural from my own personal experience. I always feel it to be the weak point in a ghost story, that it is never told in the first person. It is a friend, or a friend of one's friend, who was the lucky man, and actually saw the ghosts.' And Armitage registered a vow to himself, that within a week from that time Musgrave should see his family ghost with his own eyes, and ever after be able to speak with his enemy in the gate.

Several ingenious schemes occurred to his inventive mind for producing the desired apparition. But he had to keep them burning in his breast. Lawley was the last man to aid and abet him in playing a practical joke on their host, and he feared he should have to work without an ally. And though he would have enjoyed his help and sympathy, it struck him that it would be a double triumph achieved, if both his friends should see the Cistercian monk. Musgrave already believed in ghosts, and was prepared to meet one more than half-way, and Lawley, though he pretended to a judicial and impartial mind concerning them, was not unwilling to be convinced of their existence, if it could be visibly demonstrated to him.

Armitage became more cheerful than usual as circumstances favoured his impious plot. The weather was propitious for the attempt he meditated, as the moon rose late and was approaching the full. On consulting the almanac he saw with delight that three nights hence she would rise at 2 a.m., and an hour later the end of the gallery nearest Musgrave's room would be flooded with her light.

Though Armitage could not have an accomplice under the roof, he needed one within reach, who could use needle and thread, to run up a specious imitation of the white robe and hood of a Cistercian monk. And the next day, when they went to the Harradines to take the girls out in their improvised sledges, it fell to his lot to take charge of the youngest Miss Harradine. As he pushed the low chair on runners over the hard snow, nothing was easier than to bend forward and whisper to Kate, 'I am going to take you as fast as I can, so that no-one can hear what we are saying. I want you to be very kind, and help me to play a perfectly harmless practical joke on Musgrave. Will you promise to keep my secret for a couple of days, when we shall all enjoy a laugh over it together?'

'Oh yes, I'll help you with pleasure, but make haste and tell me what your practical joke is to be.'

'I want to play ancestral ghost to Musgrave, and make him believe that he has seen the Cistercian monk in his white robe and cowl, that was last seen by his respected credulous grandpapa.'

'What a good idea! I know he is always longing to see the ghost, and takes it as a personal affront that it has never appeared to him. But might it not startle him more than you intend?' and Kate turned her glowing face towards him, and Armitage involuntarily stopped the little sledge, 'for it is one thing to wish to see a ghost, you know, and quite another to think that you see it.'

'Oh, you need not fear for Musgrave! We shall be conferring a positive favour on him, in helping him to see what he's so wishful to see. I'm arranging it so that Lawley shall have the benefit of the show as well, and see the ghost at the same time with him. And if two strong men are not a match for one bogie, leave alone a home-made counterfeit one, it's a pity.'

'Well, if you think it's a safe trick to play, no doubt you are right. But how can I help you? With the monk's habit, I suppose?'

'Exactly. I shall be so grateful to you if you will run up some sort of garment, that will look passably like a white Cistercian habit to a couple of men, who I don't think will be in a critical frame of mind during the short time they are allowed to see it. I really wouldn't trouble you if I were anything of a sempster (is that the masculine of sempstress?) myself, but I'm not. A thimble bothers me very much, and at college, when I have to sew on a button, I push the needle through on one side with a threepenny bit, and pull it out on the other with my teeth, and it's a laborious process.'

Kate laughed merrily. 'Oh, I can easily make something or other out of a white dressing-gown, fit for a ghost to wear, and fasten a hood to it.'

Armitage then told her the details of his deeply-laid scheme, how he would go to his room when Musgrave and Lawley went to theirs on the eventful night, and sit up till he was sure that they were fast asleep. Then when the moon had risen, and if her light was obscured by clouds he would be obliged to postpone the entertainment till he could be sure of her aid, he would dress himself as the ghostly monk, put out the candles, softly open the door, and look into the gallery to see that all was ready. 'Then I shall slam the door with an awful bang, for that was the noise that heralded the ghost's last appearance, and it will wake Musgrave and Lawley, and bring them both out of their rooms like a shot. Lawley's door is next to mine, and Musgrave's opposite, so that each will command a magnificent view of the monk at the same instant, and they can compare notes afterwards at their leisure.'

'But what shall you do if they find you out at once?'

'Oh, they won't do that! The cowl will be drawn over my face, and I shall stand with my back to the moonlight. My private belief is, that in spite of Musgrave's yearnings after a ghost, he won't like it when he thinks he sees it. Nor will Lawley, and I expect they'll dart back into their rooms and lock themselves in as soon as they catch sight of the monk. That would give me time to whip back into my room, turn the key, strip off my finery, hide it, and be roused with difficulty from a deep sleep when they come knocking at my door to tell me what a horrible thing has happened. And one more ghost story will be added to those already in circulation,' and Armitage laughed aloud in anticipation of the fun.

'It is to be hoped that everything will happen just as you have planned it, and then we shall all be pleased. And now will you turn the sledge round and let us join the others, we have done conspiring for the present. If we are seen talking so exclusively to each other, they will suspect that we are brewing some mischief together. Oh, how cold the wind is! I like to hear it whistle in my hair!' said Kate as Armitage deftly swung the little sledge round and drove it quickly before him, facing the keen north wind, as she buried her chin in her warm furs.

Armitage found an opportunity to arrange with Kate, that he would meet her half-way between Stonecroft and her home, on the afternoon of the next day but one, when she would give him a parcel containing the monk's habit. The Harradines and their house party were coming on Thursday afternoon to try the toboggan slide at Stonecroft. But Kate and Armitage were willing to sacrifice their pleasure to the business they had in hand.

There was no other way but for the conspirators to give their friends the slip for a couple of hours, when the important parcel would be safely given to Armitage, secretly conveyed by him to his own room, and locked up till he should want it in the small hours of the morning.

When the young people arrived at Stonecroft Miss Harradine apologised for her younger sister's absence – occasioned, she said, by a severe headache. Armitage's heart beat rapidly when he heard the excuse, and he thought how convenient it was for the inscrutable sex to be able to turn on a headache at will, as one turns on hot or cold water from a tap.

After luncheon, as there were more gentlemen than ladies, and Armitage's services were not necessary at the toboggan slide, he elected to take the dogs for a walk, and set off in the gayest spirits to keep his appointment with Kate. Much as he enjoyed maturing his ghost plot, he enjoyed still more the confidential talks with Kate that had sprung out of it, and he was sorry that this was to be the last of them. But the moon in heaven could not be stayed for the performance of his little comedy, and her light was necessary to its due performance. The ghost must be seen at three o'clock next morning, at the time and place arranged, when the proper illumination for its display would be forthcoming.

As Armitage walked swiftly over the hard snow, he caught sight of Kate at a distance. She waved her hand gaily and pointed smiling to the rather large parcel she was carrying. The red glow of the winter sun shone full upon her, bringing out the warm tints in her chestnut hair, and filling her brown eyes with soft lustre, and Armitage looked at her with undisguised admiration.

'It's awfully good of you to help me so kindly,' he said as he took the parcel from her, 'and I shall come round tomorrow to tell you the result of our practical joke. But how is the headache?' he asked smiling, 'you look so unlike aches or pains of any kind, I was forgetting to enquire about it.'

'Thank you, it is better. It was not altogether a made-up headache, though it happened opportunely. I was awake in the night, not in the least repenting that I was helping you, of course, but wishing it was all well over. One has heard of this kind of trick sometimes proving too successful, of people being frightened out of their wits by a make-believe ghost, and I should never forgive myself if Mr Musgrave or Mr Lawley were seriously alarmed.'

'Really, Miss Harradine, I don't think that you need give yourself a moment's anxiety about the nerves of a couple of burly young men. If you are afraid for anyone, let it be for me. If they find me out, they will fall upon me and rend me limb from limb on the spot. I can assure you I am the only one for whom there is anything to fear,' and the transient gravity passed like a cloud from Kate's bright face. And she admitted that it was rather absurd to be uneasy about two stalwart young men compounded more of muscle than of nerves. And they parted, Kate hastening home as the early twilight fell, and Armitage, after watching her out of sight, retracing his steps with the precious parcel under his arm.

He entered the house unobserved, and reaching the gallery by a back staircase, felt his way in the dark to his room. He deposited his treasure in the wardrobe, locked it up, and attracted by the sound of laughter, ran downstairs to the drawing-room. Will Musgrave and his friends, after a couple of hours of glowing exercise, had been driven indoors by the darkness, nothing loath to partake of tea and hot cakes, while they talked and laughed over the adventures of the afternoon.

'Wherever have you been, old fellow?' said Musgrave as Armitage entered the room. 'I believe you've a private toboggan of your own somewhere that you keep quiet. If only the moon rose at a decent time, instead of at some unearthly hour in the night, when it's not of the slightest use to anyone, we would have gone out looking for you.'

'You wouldn't have had far to seek, you'd have met me on the turnpike road.'

'But why this subdued and chastened taste? Imagine preferring a constitutional on the high road when you might have been tobogganing with us! My poor friend, I'm afraid you are not feeling well!' said Musgrave with an affectation of sympathy that ended in boyish laughter and a wrestling match between the two young men, in the course of which Lawley more than once saved the tea table from being violently overthrown.

Presently, when the cakes and toast had disappeared before the youthful appetites, lanterns were lighted, and Musgrave and his friends, and the Harradine brothers, set out as a bodyguard to take the young ladies home. Armitage was in riotous spirits, and finding that Musgrave and Lawley had appropriated the two prettiest girls in the company, waltzed untrammelled along the road before them lantern in hand, like a very will-o'-the-wisp.

The young people did not part till they had planned fresh pleasures for the morrow, and Musgrave, Lawley, and Armitage returned to Stonecroft to dinner, making the thin air ring to the jovial songs with which they beguiled the homeward journey.

Late in the evening, when the young men were sitting in the library, Musgrave suddenly exclaimed, as he reached down a book from an upper shelf, 'Hallo! I've come on my grandfather's diary! Here's his own account of how he saw the white monk in the gallery. Lawley, you may read it if you like, but it shan't be wasted on an unbeliever like Armitage. By Jove! what an odd coincidence! It's forty years this very night, the thirtieth of December, since he saw the ghost,' and he handed the book to Lawley, who read Mr Musgrave's narrative with close attention.

'Is it a case of "almost thou persuadest me"?' asked Armitage, looking at his intent and knitted brow.

'I hardly know what I think. Nothing positive either way at any rate.' And he dropped the subject, for he saw Musgrave did not wish to discuss the family ghost in Armitage's unsympathetic presence.

They retired late, and the hour that Armitage had so gleefully anticipated drew near. 'Good night both of you,' said Musgrave as he entered his room, 'I shall be asleep in five minutes. All this excercise in the open air makes a man absurdly sleepy at night,' and the young men closed their doors, and silence settled down upon Stonecroft Hall. Armitage and Lawley's rooms were next to each other, and in less than a quarter of an hour Lawley shouted a cheery goodnight, which was loudly returned by his friend. Then Armitage felt somewhat mean and stealthy. Musgrave and Lawley were both confidingly asleep, while he sat up alert and vigilant maturing a mischievous plot that had for its object the awakening and scaring of both the innocent sleepers. He dared not smoke to pass the tedious time, lest the tell-tale fumes should penetrate into the next room through the keyhole, and inform Lawley if he woke for an instant that his friend was awake too, and behaving as though it were high noon.

Armitage spread the monk's white habit on the bed, and smiled as he touched it to think that Kate's pretty fingers had been so recently at work upon it. He need not put it on for a couple of hours yet, and to occupy the time he sat down to write. He would have liked to take a nap. But he knew that if he once yielded to sleep, nothing would wake him till he was called at eight o'clock in the morning. As he bent over his desk the big clock in the hall struck one, so suddenly and sharply it was like a blow on the head, and he started violently. 'What a swinish sleep Lawley must be in that he can't hear a noise like that!' he thought, as snoring became audible from the next room. Then he drew the candles nearer to him, and settled once more to his writing, and a pile of letters testified to his industry, when again the clock struck. But this time he expected it, and it did not startle him, only the cold made him shiver. 'If I hadn't made up my mind to go through with this confounded piece of folly, I'd go to bed now,' he thought, 'but I can't break faith with Kate. She's made the robe and I've got to wear it, worse luck,' and with a great yawn he threw down his pen, and rose to look out of the window. It was a clear frosty night. At the edge of the dark sky, sprinkled with stars, a faint band of cold light heralded the rising moon. How different from the grey light of dawn, that ushers in the cheerful day, is the solemn rising of the moon in the depth of a winter night. Her light is not to rouse a sleeping world and lead men forth to their labour, it falls on the closed eyes of the weary, and silvers the graves of those whose rest shall be broken no more. Armitage was not easily impressed by the sombre aspect of nature, though he was quick to feel her gay and cheerful influence, but he would be glad when the farce was over, and he no longer obliged to watch the rise and spread of the pale light, solemn as the dawn of the last day.

He turned from the window, and proceeded to make himself into the best imitation of a Cistercian monk that he could contrive. He slipt the white habit over all his clothing, that he might seem of portly size, and marked dark circles round his eyes, and thickly powdered his face a ghastly white.

Armitage silently laughed at his reflection in the glass, and wished that Kate could see him now. Then he softly opened the door and looked into the gallery. The moonlight was shimmering duskily on the end window to the right of his door and Lawley's. It would soon be where he wanted it, and neither too light nor too dark for the success of his plan. He stepped silently back again to wait, and a feeling as much akin to nervousness as he had ever known came over him. His heart beat rapidly, he started like a timid girl when the silence was suddenly broken by the hooting of an owl. He no longer cared to look at himself in the glass. He had taken fright at the mortal pallor of his powdered face. 'Hang it all! I wish Lawley hadn't left off snoring. It was quite companionable to hear him.' And again he looked into the gallery, and now the moon shed her cold beams where he intended to stand. He put out the light and opened the door wide, and stepping into the gallery threw it to with an echoing slam that only caused Musgrave and Lawley to start and turn on their pillows. Armitage stood dressed as the ghostly monk of Stonecroft, in the pale moonlight in the middle of the gallery, waiting for the door on either side to fly open and reveal the terrified faces of his friends.

He had time to curse the ill-luck that made them sleep so heavily that night of all nights, and to fear lest the servants had heard the noise their master had been deaf to, and would come hurrying to the spot and spoil the sport. But no-one came, and as Armitage stood, the objects in the long gallery became clearer every moment, as his sight accommodated itself to the dim light. 'I never noticed before that there was a mirror at the end of the gallery! I should not have believed the moonlight was bright enough for me to see my own reflection so far off, only white stands out so in the dark. But is it my own reflection? Confound it all, the thing's moving and I'm standing still! I know what it is! It's Musgrave dressed up to try to give me a fright, and Lawley's helping him. They've forestalled me, that's why they didn't come out of their rooms when I made a noise fit to wake the dead. Odd we're both playing the same practical joke at the same moment! Come on, my counterfeit bogie, and we'll see which of us turns white-livered first!'

But to Armitage's surprise, that rapidly became terror, the white figure that he believed to be Musgrave disguised, and like himself playing ghost, advanced towards him, slowly gliding over the floor which its feet did not touch. Armitage's courage was high, and he determined to hold his ground against the something ingeniously contrived by Musgrave and Lawley to terrify him into belief in the supernatural. But a feeling was creeping over the strong young man that he had never known before. He opened his dry mouth as the thing floated towards him, and there issued a hoarse inarticulate cry, that woke Musgrave and Lawley and brought them to their doors in a moment, not knowing by what strange fright they had been startled out of their sleep. Do not think them cowards that they shrank back appalled from the ghostly forms the moonlight revealed to them in the gallery. But as Armitage vehemently repelled the horror that drifted nearer and nearer to him, the cowl slipped from his head, and his friends recognised his white face, distorted by fear, and, springing towards him as he staggered, supported him in their arms. The Cistercian monk passed them like a white mist that sank into the wall, and Musgrave and Lawley were alone with the dead body of their friend, whose masquerading dress had become his shroud.

My Next Door Neighbour

Some years ago it was my doleful hap to spend five months as a patient in one of our London hospitals. They were the dreariest months in the whole year, from November to February, when the great city is shorn of its summer attractions, and rain, fog and frost alternately strive for the supremacy, so that I did not lose many outdoor pleasures owing to my illness. My life had been an up-and-down-hill journey, full of varied experiences. I had travelled much and seen many peoples and countries, I had had wealth and squandered it, and now at length poverty and I were fairly face to face. I had only myself to thank for my reverse of fortune, and I could not complain of the result of my own actions. The boon companions who helped me to spend my money forsook me at the approach of adversity, as midges that dance in the sunshine disappear when the sky is overcast.

I could not but admire the symmetry and completeness of my misfortunes. Penniless, friendless, and for the first time in my life, at thirty-five years of age, fallen seriously ill. Health, without which I could do nothing and be nothing, was withdrawn precisely at the time when it was the one thing needful to enable me to retrieve my position. I had wealthy relations, but as I had not cared to know them in my prosperity I had no claim on them in my adversity, nor any desire to imitate the return of the Prodigal Son on the baseless presumption that a fatted calf would be killed for me. I remember it struck me as odd, when the doctor who visited me in my cheap lodgings gave me an in-patient's ticket for the hospital, whose pleasant lot it had been hitherto to bestow, instead of receive favours. But there was no flavour of private charity in the proffered aid. I accepted it as coming from that great impersonal body, the public, towards whom no-one ever felt a burdensome sense of obligation.

The principle on which I had always chosen my friends probably made it easier than it would have been to most men of my education, to pass twenty weeks on amicable terms with the very mixed specimens of humanity that passed through the hospital ward as my fellow patients. If a man pleased and interested me, that was his letter of recommendation. I enjoyed his society regardless of social distinctions. I thought no more of him if he happened to be a duke, or less if he chanced to be a cabman.

Many were the changes I saw during my long stay in the hospital. Some of my fellow patients died, but most recovered and went away, while I remained till the population of the beds had changed repeatedly, and I grew to be the oldest inhabitant and father of the house. Our ward was a long narrow room with folding doors at each end, a large fireplace in the middle, with four high windows at either side, six beds under each row of windows, and twelve beds along the opposite side of the room, making twenty-four in all. The walls were stained a cheerful blue, and hung with engravings of more or less merit, and garnished here and there with texts and mottoes inciting us to be very joyful, or, where that was not possible, to try resignation as a useful work-a-day substitute. The floor was of polished wood, unrelieved by carpet or rug. The windows opened easily by an arrangement of ropes and pulleys, and ventilators close under the ceiling at the opposite side of the ward ensured a thorough current of air when it was necessary to change the atmosphere. But nothing can prevent the peculiar flatness of hospital air. I never lost the consciousness of it, while the smell of carbolic filled with me loathing. It is supposed to overpower other and so-called worse odours than itself; but to me it seemed merely a substituting of one evil for another.

The illness that kept me so long in the hospital was a surgical case of great interest to the doctors and considerable suffering to myself, but gratifying to my invalid's egotism, because it was the only case of the kind in the ward, where nine diseases were apportioned among twenty-four patients. To have one all to oneself out of that limited number conferred a certain distinction upon one.

An Anglican sisterhood was in charge of the nursing at the hospital, and splendidly they performed their duties. I think of them still with respect and gratitude. The nurses were strong, capable women, for the most part wonderfully forbearing with ill-tempered and thankless patients. During the time I spent under their care I gained some insight into the trials and difficulties of a hospital nurse's life. I came to the conclusion that, if I were a woman, I would do or be anything that was honest, except stewardess on board ship, rather than nurse sick people for a livelihood.

It is a marvel to me how anyone used to quiet and privacy in his own home when he is ill ever recovers in a hospital, where he has neither one nor the other. But I had such a splendid nervous system that it was only on days of prostration following an operation that I really suffered from living in public, and then I did so acutely. In spite of the screen put round my bed to form a make-believe room to myself, in imagination I still saw the seven faces on the pillows to my right hand and four to my left in the long row of beds. I heard every groan, every impatient exclamation of the weary sufferers, and at night I listened with a frightfully exalted sense of hearing to the long-drawn snores of such of them as were happy enough to be able to sleep. The crowd of medical students, who accompanied and thronged about the doctors when they made the round of the wards, was in itself enough to kill a sensitive and nervous patient. They clustered like bees round any especially interesting case, and the more hideous the sights they saw, or the details they listened to, the happier they were and the more notes they took. I looked at the dignified bearing and the fine face of the celebrated operating surgeon to whom they were listening by a patient's bedside, and wondered could he ever have been an uncouth lad like so many of his pupils. Could those penetrating eyes, full of the fire of genius, ever have winked at a fellow student behind the back of the great doctor of the day some forty years ago?

I soon became interested in the routine of hospital life, and on those days when I was fairly well and free from pain I should never wish to be better entertained than I was in studying my fellow-patients.

We were a motley crew, surely the oddest four-and-twenty men that circumstances could have thrown together. The changes in our population were so rapid that a bed had scarcely time to grow cold before it was in possession of a fresh occupant. We were of all ages, shapes, and sizes, and of a variety of nationalities; being, I think, at our most representative when our company consisted of Englishmen, Irishmen, and Scotchmen, with a choleric little Welshman, Germans, a Yankee, a Frenchman, a Swede, a Lascar seaman, a Jew, and a Negro. By chance the Yankee on the day of his arrival was put in the next bed to the Negro; but after much nasal vituperation, the arrangement was altered for peace and quiet's sake. We also represented many trades, and had amongst us tailors, policemen, costermongers, postmen, a butler, cabmen, a grave-digger, a sugar refiner, shoemakers, and an omnibus conductor.

We also had some of those mysterious gentlemen of no particular calling or visible means of sustenance, who live at the back of everywhere, that a crowd or an accident brings into the street in swarms, as heavy rain brings worms to the surface of the soil. They are always open to an odd job, when it is highly paid for and not of an arduous nature. They spend their Sunday afternoons demonstrating in the park, clothed in long topcoats and woollen comforters, and never without a short pipe and tobacco, which presumably cost money. Where they sleep at night when they are not in hospital I have no idea. One of our company, who afforded me much amusement, was a genteel and sensitive young clerk, who had it on his mind to explain to me how he came to be in such a vulgar institution as a public hospital. He was consumed by a haunting dread lest, when he had recovered and returned to his place in the office of Messrs Scrawley and McNib in Lincoln's Inn, he might be recognised in the street and spoken to by one of his fellow patients, a chimney-sweep of too friendly a disposition. 'His face, sir, would be black in the pursuit of his avocation and I shouldn't know him, but he'd see me a mile off and run after me; and if a man in my position is seen talking to a sweep I shall be ruined,' said my sensitive little clerk.

I made a great variety of friends among my fellow patients who stayed long enough to feel some interest in others, as the terrible egotism of their own sufferings abated. I parted on excellent terms with a butler, who taught me the kind of whistle I must give at the area gate when I called to see him after nightfall. A hansom-driver, bidding me goodbye, in the fullness of his heart, offered to take me in his cab down Piccadilly for my first airing after I left the hospital. A thoughtful little German baker with whom I talked metaphysics in accordance with the definition, that, 'when a man talks to you in a way that you don't understand, about a thing which he doesn't understand, them's metaphysics,' as a parting gift presented me with a list of shops whose bread one would do well to avoid, from the baker's custom of working the sponge with unwashen hands, and I thanked him. A costermonger acquaintance taught me how, when buying fruit off a barrow in the street, to detect the tricks of the trade. In short, I picked up a great deal of information that, if it was not useful, amused me and afforded me a glimpse into the lives of other men.

I had been three months in bed, and was recovering from the effects of an operation, when I became acquainted with a man who interested me more than any other of my fellow patients.

I remember the day that he came into the hospital. It was in the first week of the new year, and a nurse had congratulated me on the good luck of having had the bed to the right of mine standing empty for two whole days. Its last occupant had been a dull, heavy fellow, absorbed in the contemplation of his own symptoms and doggedly convinced that he was the head martyr in the universe, unable perhaps, and certainly unwilling, to take part in the courtesies and amenities of invalid life. We did not miss him when he left, and the blank pillow was a pleasanter object to look at than the furrowed, irritable face and bald head that had lain upon it. It occurred to me, how fortunate I should be if the fates should send me an intelligent, sympathetic fellow sufferer in the bed that I had seen so diversely occupied during the past twelve weeks.

The previous night my rest had been troubled, and in the forenoon, between the disturbance of the doctor's visit and dinner being brought to us, I fell asleep. When I awoke I was astonished to find the bed that an hour and a half before had been empty occupied by a fresh patient, looking as comfortable and established as though he had been there a week.

The newcomer was a tall, swarthy-complexioned man of about thirty years of age. He lay on his back with his eyes closed and his head inclined towards me, so that I had a good view of his very remarkable face. That he was not an Englishman I felt sure, though to what country he belonged I could not tell. He was clean-shaven as I thought, but I afterwards found that no hair grew on his face, and a month without a razor did not darken his lip or chin. His skin was of a yellowish-brown, and his straight black hair that covered his ears and lay on his cheek was cut square across the forehead. The nose was large and prominent, the mouth large, thin-lipped, and well-shaped, and the jaw formed a powerful angle from the ear. The length of the face from the eyes to the mouth was greater than is usual, and the finely-modelled long hollow of the cheek gave a melancholy and dignified outline to his countenance. I wondered what he would be like when he awoke, and as I watched he opened his dark eyes, large and set wide apart, with a clear and penetrating expression.

As I looked in his face, that in spite of its smoothness was essentially masculine, and in expression a quaint mixture of shrewdness and childlike simplicity, I said to myself, 'My friend, I cannot offhand assign you to any particular country, but I can date your type of face for you. You have no business at all wandering about in the nineteenth century. You ought never to have stirred from the fourteenth, nor emerged from the pages of Froissart, to which you really belong.'

There was a quiet dignity about the man that forbade me to ask the usual questions that inaugurate a hospital acquaintance, such as, 'What's your name? Where do you come from? And what's the matter with you?' and I waited my time for a favourable opportunity of speaking to him.

When the nurse gave me my dinner I asked her, 'Who is the man in the next bed?'

'A Frenchman; he was brought here while you were asleep.'

'Good,' thought I; 'then I shall amuse myself by rubbing up my rusty French with him. Can you tell me his name?'

'No, I can't remember French names, and besides, he has a string of them, those foreigners always have.'

I reached paper and pencil from the locker by my side and gave them to the nurse. 'Just oblige me by copying his name from the card over his bed and bring it to me, will you?' She did as she was requested, and returning handed me the paper, on which she had written the names Jean-Marie Thégonnec Pipraic. 'Why, the man must be a Breton,' said I, repeating the two last names to myself.

'A Briton! A Frenchman never yet was a Briton, and couldn't be if he tried,' said the nurse promptly, her national susceptibilities rubbed the wrong way in an instant through her misapprehension.

'A Breton, my good woman, a Breton, not a Briton,' said I; 'and a Breton is no more a Frenchman, though he may happen to speak French, than a Welshman is an Englishman, even if he talks English. When did that solemn, dignified, fourteenth-century face ever belong to a Frenchman I should like to know?' and I wished to argue with my nurse concerning racial differences. But she cut the matter short by turning to the new patient and asking him plainly whether he was a Frenchman or what, for an Englishman in the next bed would not take her word for it. Our stranger, who was sitting up with his table across his knees, waiting for dinner, bowed gravely, first to the nurse and then to me.

'I am a Breton, madame, and I come from Roscoff, in the *département* of Finistère,' he said in a low, melancholy voice, speaking with a strong foreign accent; and he added with dignified simplicity: 'My name is Jean-Marie Thégonnec Pipraic, but I am everywhere called Jean-Marie.'

'I thought you a Breton from your name,' I said. 'I know your part of Brittany very well. I used to know Finistère and Morbihan from end to end. I once spent a summer there.'

'Does monsieur know Bretagne?' said my new acquaintance, with flashing eyes. 'Has he been to Morlaix, Landenau, Quimper, St Pol de Léon, Carnac, Plougastel?' and then followed a torrent of names of places, some on the coast and some inland, just as they rushed into his mind.

'I know them all, my friend,' I said, smiling at his eagerness, 'and when you have eaten your dinner you shall ask me as many questions as you please, and see if I speak the truth.'

'I should not doubt that monsieur spoke the truth, but it is wonderful; it is wonderful!'

I noticed that Jean-Marie, as I already called him to myself, devoutly crossed himself on the forehead and on the breast, before and after he took food. I tried to talk French with him, though not always with lucid results, for he had learned French as a second language, and spoke a strange patois, while mine, such as it was, had been acquired in Paris. An acquaintance sprang up rapidly between us, founded on my knowledge of the scenes of his childhood, and the places dearest to him in his manhood. And I grew fond of Jean-Marie, so that my heart sank when I learnt how badly the doctors thought of his case. By degrees he told me the simple story of his life.

Jean-Marie Thégonnec Pipraic was the son of a poor fisherman and his wife who lived near Roscoff, on the coast of Finistère. He and his younger sister, Anne – namesake of *La Bonne Duchesse*, who after four centuries is still spoken of in Brittany as though she had been dead but a generation or so – were the only children, and had been brought up in such poverty and hard work as sounded incredible to my pampered English ears. They never tasted meat. Their food was the coarsest bread, with onions and potatoes, and occasionally on festival days a little fish and milk. They rose at four in the morning to make or mend fishing-nets, or to work on the small plot of ground surrounding the hut in which they lived. The father was out fishing every night, and the mother burnt a taper in the window that in calm weather he could see as a glimmering point of light, when his boat was tossing on the water far from shore. When he came safely home out of the teeth of the western gales that ravage that coast, the pious mother took her children to the church, to thank the Blessed Virgin for her protection. Once when the husband and father had been miraculously preserved in a storm, they made a votive offering of a model of a fishing boat, which was hung suspended, from the roof of the chancel before the altar of their patron saint, in visible token of the mercy of Heaven and the gratitude of man.

But there came a fearful night in autumn when a sudden squall of wind struck the little fleet of fishing boats, and in the dismal dawn, when stormy sea and sky seemed torn together in one grey mist, out of the welter of devouring waves, the drowned bodies of brave fishermen were washed ashore. And among them that of Thégonnec Pipraic, the father of Jean-Marie.

'The sea is cruel on the coast of Finistère, monsieur; it makes many widows and orphans; and on winter nights we hear it howling like a hungry wolf at our door. But in the summer it is often still and blue as the sky above, and the little islands are like clouds floating on its surface. In the summer, monsieur, the sea is like the love of the *Bon Dieu*; in the winter it is like his wrath, and we tremble before it.'

Jean-Marie was to have been a fisherman, like his father before him. But the mother, dreading lest the cruel sea should take from her her son as well as her husband, moved a short distance to St Pol de Léon, where she found work for herself and little Anne in the fields. Jean-Marie, only ten years old, worked his twelve hours daily as a farm labourer for a trifling pittance; but, as he said, 'the *Bon Dieu* saw that I wanted for nothing. I had bread; I had health and strength; and as I grew older I was able to succour my mother and my sister.'

Jean-Marie saw the *Bon Dieu* in everything. I have never met man or woman with the same childlike faith.

When he was twenty years of age his mother died, worn out with toil and scanty living. Work as they would, the three of them, they could not earn more than enough to meet each day's recurring want. They could not lay by a sou against sickness or accident, or afford the weary mother a little rest before she died. Shortly after her death her daughter married a fisherman and went to live on the island of Batzoff, the soil of which is tilled by the women, while the men plough the sea. And there she still lives in many-childed poverty.

'How come you to speak English, Jean-Marie?' I asked him one day when he was free from pain and able to enjoy conversation.

'Monsieur, I learnt it from an excellent compatriot of yours, who lived for many years at Carnac, trying to find out the meaning of the great stones there. Monsieur Smitt was like a father to me. I was his servant, I dug his garden and tended his horse and cow, and he taught me to speak his difficult language. For several years I lived with my master. He was not Catholic, monsieur; Père Croisac would have it that he was not even Christian, but the *Bon Dieu* had given him a good heart, and the poor prayed for him. I tried to convert my master, and I assured him of the miracles that the holy saints still work in Bretagne. But Monsieur Smitt would not be convinced. He had a way like so many Englishmen – pardon me, monsieur, but it is not a good way of jesting at holy things. But in his heart I think my master believed, for he let me go all the way to Helgoet when our cow had cast her calf, and was suffering like a Christian, to intercede with Saint Herbot for the poor beast.'

'I remember Saint Herbot's church perfectly well,' I said. 'He has taken the cattle under his special protection, and I saw tufts of the hair of sick animals laid on his altar by their unfortunate owners, who had come to pray for their recovery.'

'Then monsieur must have seen the very wisp of hair from our poor cow's tail that I laid on the altar of the holy saint myself,' said Jean-Marie with animation. 'It was red, with here and there a white hair mixed; monsieur could not forget it.'

I was obliged to evade the difficulty by saying that when I visited Saint Herbot's church, the altar was so thickly covered with tufts of goats', horses', and cows' hair that Jean-Marie's lock must have been hidden beneath them.

'And did the cow recover?' I asked.

'Monsieur, when I returned from my pilgrimage on the third day the poor beast was dead.'

'What, when you had walked two whole days to lay a tuft of her hair before Saint Herbot? What could the saint be dreaming of?'

'Monsieur, the Holy Saint Herbot has two ways of answering prayer for *les pauvres bestiaux malades*. If he judges it best for them to recover, they will get better; but if not they will die,' and as though unwilling further to discuss the saint with an unbeliever, Jean-Marie passed on to other reminiscences.

'When I was twenty-five years of age my master took me with him to Paris; the first time that I had left my native Bretagne. But, monsieur, what a thing it was, the people there treated me as if I was a savage. They laughed at me in the street, at my long hair, my wide hat, my excellent *bragous bras* – breeches is your English word for them, monsieur, of the pattern that my forefathers had worn since the days of *La Bonne Duchesse*. They jeered at me when I went to mass, and their churches were empty; in Bretagne they are crowded with men. My money was stolen from me, and when I politely asked my way in the street, I was directed to the wrong place. The very children used vile words, and the young girls said things to me that a man in Bretagne would blush to think of.'

One day when we had grown quite intimate, Jean-Marie confided to me the love he had borne to his fellow servant Françoise.

'Monsieur, I have never loved but one woman, my Françoise. For five years we ate at the same table, we worked in the same garden, we went to mass together, we prayed together. We were not married because I desired to save a little money first, that my wife might not have to toil as my poor mother had done. Monsieur, I cannot tell you whether my Françoise was beautiful or not, but the *Bon Dieu* had given her to me, and I never looked in another woman's face. We were to be married: Monsieur Smitt would still keep me as his servant, and we were to live in a little cottage near him, and he would have another woman for his cook, though my Françoise was still to help in the housework. Within a fortnight of our intended marriage our good master fell ill of a fever, and my Françoise nursed him, and took it from him and died. They both died, monsieur, my master and my Françoise, and I tried to take the fever from them that I might die too, but the fever had no more power to kill me than fire has to burn the holy saints. And to think, monsieur, that we might have been man and wife if I had not loved my Françoise so well. Monsieur, this rosary is all that I have that belonged to my Françoise, for she was as poor as the Blessed Virgin herself.'

And Jean-Marie stretched his long, thin arm towards me, and laid on the locker by my bedside a cheap rosary, made of a string of small berries, with a crucifix attached to it.

After the death of his master and Françoise, Jean-Marie returned to the neighbourhood of Roscoff and worked under a well-to-do farmer, who grew great quantities of the onions for which that part of Finistère is renowned. He was an enterprising man, and anxious to find the best market for his produce. Jean-Marie served him faithfully and intelligently, and when he had been with him three years he increased his wages, and as he spoke English he sent him to London, to negotiate for the sale of his onions with English dealers. I was astounded to find how astute my fourteenth-century friend was in business matters. He had made bargains profitable to his employer and to himself, and Monsieur Ploumel was highly satisfied with the honesty and ability of his agent.

And now, on his third journey to England, Jean-Marie was smitten with a mortal illness, and would never return to his native land.

'I have been ill for more than a year, monsieur. I know it by the pain I have suffered. But it does not matter; it is over now. I have finished my work. The day before I came into this hospital, I sent to Monsieur Ploumel every sou I had made for him, and a draft for three hundred francs that I had saved for my poor sister and her children. I have come here to die,' he said, in quiet unemotional tones, as though he were speaking of a stranger.

I listened in silence, for I knew what the doctors thought of his case: that nothing could be done to cure, but only to palliate the disease. Never had there been a more patient sufferer in the hospital. In spite of his mediaeval superstition, Jean-Marie was a most courageous Christian, and put us all to shame. When he was sufficiently free from pain to speak, it was with a gentle courtesy, and no word of complaint or of impatience ever escaped his lips. He was always ready to listen to the egotistic grumbling of his fellow-patients, though he tried, by example and precept, to lift us out of the narrow groove of self-centred suffering.

One day I saw that he was enduring agony. His dark face was livid, and when he could speak he said quietly, 'Monsieur, these pains are pin-pricks compared with those the Blessed Redeemer suffered for us.'

That night Jean-Marie was very ill, and I lay awake, partly from sympathy with him, partly because his restlessness made it difficult for me to sleep, as he muttered and talked to himself without ceasing. The nurse was in constant attendance upon him, and she said to me: 'His sleeping draught has not suited him tonight; he is terribly restless.'

Between two and three o'clock in the morning I thought that she was again leaning over Jean-Marie. On the opposite side of his bed, facing me, a woman stood wearing a white cap, but not such as our nurses wore, and she was bending over Jean-Marie as though she would kiss him. Then she knelt, holding his hand in hers, and the light in the ward was sufficient for me to see that she wore the costume of a Brittany peasant, with the coloured cotton kerchief on the shoulders, tucked into the bib of the black apron in front. I raised myself in bed, and a nurse, who was sitting by the fire, came to me at once.

'Do you want anything?' she asked.

'Yes; who is that woman?' and I pointed to the figure still standing by Jean-Marie.

'What woman?' she said, looking in the direction I indicated.

'That Brittany peasant woman, to be sure, by Jean-Marie's bedside, talking to him and holding his hand.'

'You have been dreaming!' said the nurse; 'there is no-one there. Lie down and try to go to sleep, though I dare say that poor fellow makes it hard for you to rest.'

I had not been dreaming, though Jean-Marie had, for afterwards he awoke with a little sigh as if he were sorry to return to consciousness, and said in his quiet tones, 'Monsieur, the *Bon Dieu* has been very good to me. He has sent my Françoise to me in a dream, and I have seen her and held her hand in mine. I am only to suffer three days more, for on Sunday morning at two o'clock my Françoise is to fetch me!' And he laughed to himself, a little laugh of incomparable happiness, and soon afterwards became again delirious.

All Thursday, Friday, and Saturday, my friend grew steadily worse, though the doctors did not anticipate an immediate end of his sufferings. His mind wandered the whole time, and he talked to himself incessantly in Breton. When occasionally he dropt into French, and I understood what he said, he was imagining he was a child again, playing on the sands, or sitting on the rocks with his little sister, mending their father's fishing-nets. I grew feverish with excitement and anticipation of what would happen to Jean-Marie. I had certainly seen his Françoise, and I dreaded her return. But I did not dare confide in either doctor or nurse. My strange experience could only be regarded by them as a sick man's fancy. But my state of nervous excitement was duly noticed and commented on by one of the house surgeons, a pleasant young man who had shown me much kindness.

'What in the world are you exciting yourself about?' he asked me on the Saturday afternoon. 'You haven't had a pulse like this since before your first operation, and you've nothing of the kind in anticipation to account for it now.'

But I could not tell him the truth, because from me it would appear incredible. I said that I had slept badly for several nights past, and that might account for my not being so well as usual. And I wound up with the apparently inconsequent request, 'Do come and see Jean-Marie at two o'clock in the morning, doctor.'

I spoke so earnestly that the surgeon ceased tapping his palm with the stethoscope he held in his right hand. 'I shall be in the ward at four o'clock under any circumstances, so that unless you have any very good reasons for asking me to see him earlier, your request is absurd. If I could do the poor fellow any good by seeing him, then it would be another thing. And I'm almost run off my legs as it is.'

'But I have a perfectly valid reason for asking you to see Jean-Marie precisely at that hour,' I urged. 'I cannot tell you now what it is, but I will do so afterwards, if you will only come.' And he felt my pulse again, and I knew that he thought I was wandering in my mind.

'Well, well,' he said, good-humouredly, 'if I can wake myself at that hour – two o'clock I think you said – I'll run in and have a look at Jean-Marie.'

About eleven o'clock, when the lights were turned low and all was quiet for the night, Jean-Marie's mind for a short time became clear and tranquil. He was like a man about to set forth on a delightful journey to some place and friends he longed to see; he was full of deep, happy excitement. When the nurse asked him if he wanted anything, his answer was always the same, '*Mon ami*, my wanting days are over, I have everything.' Then he spoke to me. 'I am ready to go when my Françoise fetches me. Monsieur, if I may leave to you my rosary I shall be glad. It may be that the *Bon Dieu* will lead you by it to become Catholic,' and he looked wistfully.

'Jean-Marie, I would become anything that would give me your peace and courage,' I said. But I do not think that he heard my reply, for he was again wandering – talking to himself and singing snatches of old Breton songs, that were not unlike Gregorian tones.

'I wish that French fellow would be quiet and let me go to sleep,' whimpered a fretful voice from my left-hand neighbour.

'It is the last night that he will disturb you; have a little patience,' I said.

Midnight had long past, and in due course I heard the church clocks for a mile round strike one, like irregular file firing. I had not long to wait before I should know whether Jean-Marie's prophetic dream was true or not. In the exalted state of my senses every sound in the ward, every footfall of the nurses, seemed unnaturally loud, as I lay watching in the subdued light the old-world features of Jean-Marie. He was lying on his back with closed eyes, his long, brown fingers telling his beads and his lips moving rapidly. Just then a nurse approached his bedside with a dose of medicine so nauseous that the smell of it as it wafted by made me feel ill.

'Must you disturb him to give him that vile stuff?' I asked, as I looked with compassion on Jean-Marie, tranquil for the first time in many hours. 'Doctor's orders,' she replied briefly, and raised the patient's head to put the glass to his lips. He opened his eyes, and I saw by his expression that his soul revolted at the loathsome draught. Then, with the meekness of a little child, he drained it to the dregs.

It was a few minutes to two o'clock, and I was strung up to an almost intolerable pitch of excitement. When a cinder fell from the grate it sounded like thunder, and I started and trembled. Jean-Marie had fallen into a restless sleep, but he no longer muttered and talked to himself. I could hardly believe my eyes, though I firmly expected what I saw – by the side of Jean-Marie's bed stood the same form I had seen three nights ago, the Brittany peasant woman. Her plain, swarthy face was covered with the sweetest smiles, and she leaned her dark head in its snowy cap over Jean-Marie till her cheek almost touched his. My heart beat to suffocation, and I leaned upon my elbow, determined to watch closely. It was seldom that everyone was asleep in the ward at the same time, and the sister in charge and the nurses were certainly awake. Did no-one but myself see the tall figure by Jean-Marie's bed? It must have been full ten minutes that I saw the woman both standing and leaning over him in her quaint dress, and at length she knelt by his side and I heard him say in a low voice of ecstasy, 'Oh, *ma Françoise! Ma Françoise!*' as he sighed away his last breath.

'Nurse, nurse,' I cried, 'Jean-Marie is dying!' And she hastened to him in a moment, as she did so unconsciously passing through the shadowy form that still hovered over him. Just then the door at the end of the ward opened and the house surgeon entered.

'What is the matter?' he said as he saw me out of bed and the nurse feeling Jean-Marie's pulse.

'Jean-Marie is dead – very suddenly; I only gave him his draught half-an-hour ago,' said the nurse. Then I told the doctor as collectedly as I could what I had seen on Thursday night and how Jean-Marie had told me of his dream, which I had seen fulfilled, and of the ghostly figure of the Breton peasant woman that had but that moment faded from my sight. I dared not tell him the night before, but now that there was confirmation of it he must see for himself that it was true, and I pointed to poor Jean-Marie's corpse. He listened with the greatest attention.

'If it had been any other patient that had told me such a thing,' he said at length, 'I should have known that he was delirious, and have ordered ice to his head, and I don't say but that it mightn't be a good thing for even you. Still, when an educated man like yourself is convinced that he has been brought face to face with the supernatural, he is entitled to a hearing. It is strange, very strange. Jean-Marie was a remarkable man; I have never met a patient like him. There is only one thing that I can be sure of in the whole affair, and that is, that I must have you out of this ward the first thing in the morning, or your nerves will be shattered in addition to your other troubles.'

The body of my poor friend was removed before any of the patients were aware that a death had occurred. In a few hours I found myself in another ward of the hospital, surrounded by fresh faces, and I could hardly be certain whether or not I had dreamed the strange story of Jean-Marie Thégonnec Pipraic.

The Empty Picture Frame

It was a wild day in September. An equinoctial gale had raged since dawn, shaking doors and windows, and battering the walls of Eastwick Court. The orchards were strewed with bruised fruit plucked by the rude hand of the wind. The gardens that yesterday, neat and trim, basked in autumn sunshine, today were littered with branches stript from the trees, and melancholy with uprooted flowers. The paths were cut into channels by torrents of rain, that washed the loose sand on to the grass, where, as the water subsided, it lay in red patches. At sunset there came a sudden lull. The gale fell to a whisper, and the rain ceased. But no flush of light overspread the grey sky. No western glow shone on the sombre walls, or reflected its red light on the rain-washed windows of the old house.

Within doors it was too dark to read or work, and in the enforced idleness of twilight, Miss Swinford laid down her book, and seated herself on a low chair by the fire.

Katherine Swinford was alone in the great drawing-room. As she leaned forward with hands clasped in her lap, watching the bickering flames that played about the logs on the hearth, there was something pathetic as well as dignified in her appearance. The mistress of Eastwick Court was no longer young. Her thick hair was streaked with white, and sundry lines on her brow, and about her clear grey eyes, showed where time's finger had touched her and left its mark. Her features were large but finely formed, her expression firm and self-reliant. Miss Swinford had lived so long alone, mistress of a large property, and a law unto herself in her own domain, that she had acquired the somewhat imperious manner of one who exercises a benevolent tyranny, and has an unquestioned right to be obeyed. She was the only child and heiress of Sir John Swinford who had been dead some twelve years, and she had lost her mother in her infancy.

No-one could have supposed that Miss Swinford, like Queen Elizabeth, was destined to reign alone. She had had as many suitors as the Virgin Queen herself, and they might be classed in three orders. The first, and most numerous, was attracted by the estate to which the lady seemed but the necessary appendage. The second felt the charm of the heiress, and the still greater charm of her wealth, while the third order of suitor was represented by one man only, who loved Katherine for her own sake, and would have sought her for his wife if she had been penniless. No need to tell the story – '*es ist ein altes Liedchen*' – the true love died long ago, and his fever-worn body lay buried in the hot sand of a tropic shore, and Katherine Swinford was still and would always remain Katherine Swinford.

Perhaps as she sat by her lonely hearth in the gathering dusk, she was thinking of what might have been, of the strong arm she might have leaned on, of the children that might have called her mother. She sighed, and rising abruptly, rang for lights. 'This will never do! I shall grow melancholy if I sit by myself in the twilight. It is peopled with ghosts, and with might-have-beens, the worst of all ghosts. I have been too much alone lately. I ought to keep up a succession of visitors. By the way, I wonder why I have not heard from Sir Piers Hammersley. It is ten days since I wrote to him inviting his daughter to come and stay with me.' And an air of bright energy succeeded to her momentary depression, and when the lamps were brought into the room Miss Swinford was looking ten years younger than she had done a short time before.

Sir Piers Hammersley was a cousin of the late Sir John Swinford, and both descended from a common ancestor, Sir Miles Swinford, who lived at Eastwick Court in the time of Charles the First. The Hammersleys were originally Swinfords. But Sir Miles's second son Adam had married an heiress in Cumberland, Anne Hammersley, on the condition that he should bear her name as well as share her fortune. When Adam went to live in the north he took with him his sister Joceline, whose lover Colonel Dacres had been wounded fighting for his king, and died in her father's house, since when she had pined and drooped at Eastwick Court. Joceline was only three-and-twenty years old, and her family thought that absence from home and its tragic associations would restore her to health and cheerfulness. And in this hope she made what was then the long wild journey out of Herefordshire into Cumberland. But no change of air or scene could arrest the decline into which she had fallen. Before the spring came she was laid in the vault of the Hammersleys.

Her sad story and the tradition of her beauty, confirmed by a portrait still preserved at Eastwick Court, had caused her to be remembered both by the Swinfords and Hammersleys, and the name of Joceline had not been allowed to die out in the family. The very reason why Miss Swinford had bestirred herself to write to her father's cousin whom she had not seen since she was a girl, was that his only daughter was named Joceline. Her heart had warmed towards her unknown kinswoman in her loneliness, and she had written asking Sir Piers to allow his daughter to visit her at the house that was the birthplace of the original Joceline. The Hammersleys still lived in Cumberland, and Miss Swinford's letter must have reached its destination the day after it was posted. But she had received no answer to her friendly invitation. She was astonished and almost affronted by chilling silence where she had hoped to meet with a cordial response.

'My cousin Joceline is so much younger than I that perhaps she does not feel very eager about spending a few weeks alone with me,' she argued with herself. 'But at least she should be wishful to see the home of her ancestors, and the portrait of Joceline Swinford, whom she is fortunate if she resembles in personal appearance.'

Here Miss Swinford's soliloquy was cut short by an unexpected interruption. A sound of heavy wheels driving slowly up the avenue by which the house was approached from the high road, and the carriage, waggon, or whatever it was that could be so ponderous, came to a standstill at the front door. 'The storm must have cut the gravel up terribly,' thought Miss Swinford; 'I never heard wheels sound so heavy in the avenue before. Who can be paying an afternoon call so late, just when I am about to dress for dinner!' and the heavy carriage drove slowly away. Immediately afterwards the drawing-room door was thrown open, and Bennet the old butler announced 'Miss Hammersley'. Miss Swinford started with surprise, and advanced to welcome a young and tall lady dressed in black, some fifteen years her junior. She was of a mortal pallor of complexion, with dreamy brown eyes and fair hair, and bearing the most extraordinary resemblance to the portrait of Joceline Swinford.

'My dear cousin! You have dropped upon me from the clouds! I have received no intimation that I should have the pleasure of seeing you today, or I would have driven to the station to meet you myself,' and she kissed her young kinswoman's pale cheek.

'How cold you are, my dear! Come and sit near the fire before you take off your cloak.' And she led Joceline to a low chair, and she sat down by the flickering fire, with her back to the lamp.

'What sort of a journey have you had this stormy day? I'm afraid you had to change trains rather often between Cumberland and our little village station.'

Joceline Hammersley raised her eyes with a strange uncomprehending gaze, as though she were listening to a language she did not understand, and instead of replying to her question merely said, 'I have come a long way, I am very tired.'

'You are not strong, my dear, I am afraid, you look so pale and weary. It is a pity I cannot give you a little of my superfluous strength,' and Miss Swinford smiled kindly on her young cousin. She could not take her eyes from the white oval face with its high marble brow, large dark eyes and heavy eyelids, delicate nose, and small mouth with lips too pale for health. 'It is astounding, perfectly astounding!' at length she said. 'Do you know that you are the living image of our common ancestress Joceline Swinford! You are exactly like the van Dyck portrait in the library! I must show it to you!'

'Oh, not tonight! Not tonight!' pleaded her cousin.

'Very well then, not tonight, but first thing in the morning. By candle-light it might startle you, it would be like looking at the reflection of your face in a mirror. But let me unfasten your cloak for you, my dear.' For her guest was enveloped in a long black silk cloak, with a hood drawn over her fair curls, a quaint garment becoming her so well as to suggest the idea that the pale silent lady was an artist in dress, and studied effects very successfully.

'Do not let me trouble you,' she replied, throwing her hood back upon her shoulders, 'my waiting-woman will give me the help I require.'

'Your waiting-woman! Dear child, what an antiquated phrase! But I suppose odd words and expressions still linger in the wilds of Cumberland. Your maid, yes, I will ring for her, and I will show you to your room, where I am afraid the fire can hardly be lighted yet. It should have been burning all day if you had only done me the honour to announce your arrival beforehand.' And Miss Swinford opened the drawing-room door, when to her amazement her guest with unhesitating step as though she knew her way perfectly, turned towards the old part of the house, that was full of empty rooms.

'Not that way, my dear! You are going to the disused part of the building, that has not been inhabited since my grandfather's time, and belongs nowadays entirely to ghosts and rats. Let me lead you to our comfortable modern rooms, less historically interesting, but better suited to the requirements of a tired traveller like yourself.' And her guest turned to follow her with an expression of disappointment on her pale face.

'May I not see the old rooms?'

'Certainly. I will show you everything, beginning with your own portrait, tomorrow morning. But here is your maid and this is your room; as we dine in half an hour I will leave you now to dress.' And mistress and maid were left together.

Miss Hammersley's maid was no less remarkable-looking than her mistress, with the same extreme pallor, though here the resemblance ended, for the mistress was beautiful and the maid distinctly ugly. Her grey hair was drawn away from her dark bony forehead under a close-fitting white cap. Her eyes were small and black, and her mouth large, with thin compressed lips. Like her mistress, she was dressed in entire disregard of existing fashion, in a dark woollen material, with a deep linen collar and long white apron. At first the sight of a maid wearing a cap that a modern cook would scorn, and an apron suitable in size for a scullion, occasioned rude mirth among Miss Swinford's servants. But their laughter was brief, and succeeded by uneasy fear, for Mistress Galt (as Miss Hammersley called her maid) had queer unaccountable ways, in harmony with her strange and repellent appearance.

The morning after Miss Hammersley's arrival at Eastwick Court, the sun shone brightly on the destruction caused by the storm of the previous day, and the gardeners were busy repairing the damage done by the wind and rain.

When Miss Swinford entered the breakfast-room, her guest was walking on the terrace, dressed in a white close-fitting gown low and open at the front, and her bare neck exposed to the chilly morning air. Miss Swinford hastened to her from the open window, exclaiming, 'My dear child, you will catch your death of cold! Come back and put a shawl over your neck. Is it still the fashion to come down to breakfast in a low dress as my grandmother used to do!' and she led her into the house, and wrapped a soft shawl about her shoulders.

'How cold you are! And the morning air has brought no colour to your face! My dear child, are you always as cold as this?'

'Yes, always,' she replied quietly. Then adding as though speaking to herself, 'yet I am clothed in woollen and sheltered from wind and rain.'

'Drink your coffee, you make me cold to look at you! And after breakfast I will take you upstairs to the library to show you the portrait of your namesake, and you shall tell me if you see the resemblance to yourself which I think so striking. It is an odd coincidence, the dress you are wearing might have been copied from that in the picture. But you shall see for yourself,' and Miss Swinford, pleased to have someone to talk to, continued chatting, and did not notice how silent her cousin remained.

After breakfast she took Joceline's cold hand in hers, and led her upstairs. 'The library was my father's favourite room, and I have made no alteration in it since his time. It was there that I last saw your father, and I remember how greatly he admired Joceline Swinford's portrait. He said he should like to have a copy of it, but he does not need that as long as he has you to look at, my dear.' And Miss Swinford flung the door to the library wide open with a triumphant 'There!'

But she started in astonishment, for over the fireplace, where the portrait of Joceline Swinford had been, hung only the empty frame, its tarnished gilding in sombre harmony with the square of blackened wall that had been covered by the canvas.

Miss Swinford rang the bell impetuously, and ran into the corridor to second its summons with her voice.

'Bennet, Bennet! there is the most extraordinary thing! The old portrait of Miss Joceline Swinford has been taken out of the frame, and carried away bodily! The house has been broken into during the night! Search everywhere, and find out by what door or window it has been entered.'

The servants gathered in a cluster round the library door, looking up at the empty frame with awe-stricken faces, and Miss Swinford sat down and fairly burst into tears. Joceline gently laid her hand on her shoulder, and said in a low voice, 'Do not weep, the picture will be restored to you!' and raising her eyes her cousin beheld the very embodiment of Joceline Swinford's portrait standing beside her. The shawl had slipped from her shoulders, leaving her neck uncovered, and in face, attitude, and costume, she was so amazingly like the figure in the missing picture that Miss Swinford started. And the servants, still peering in at the door, looked from the empty frame to the pale lady, and then at each other with indefinable fear.

No trace of the thieves could be discovered. No lock, bolt, or bar on door or window had been tampered with, and the picture was hung so high that whoever had stolen it, must have accomplished the theft by the help of a ladder. The local superintendent of police came to examine the house, and to take down a description of the missing picture from Miss Swinford's lips, and she advertised a large reward for its discovery or for such information as should lead to the detection of the thief.

'The picture will be restored to you,' repeated Joceline.

'I am afraid not, my dear. The stolen portrait of the beautiful Duchess of Devonshire has never been recovered, and how can I hope to get my picture back again, and to unravel the mystery of its disappearance?' Miss Swinford telegraphed tidings of her loss to her lawyer in London, and followed it up by a long letter of instructions. He was to send a description of the missing portrait to all the picture dealers, and an advertisement was put in the papers warning pawnbrokers to detain the bearer, as well as the picture, if it was offered to them. And having done everything in her power to recover her treasure, Miss Swinford remained inconsolable under her loss.

The excitement in the servants' hall was intense, and the physical difficulty of abstracting from its frame a picture hung at such a height was dilated upon at great length. Finally they all agreed with old Bennet when he gave it as his opinion, 'that it was like as if it had been sperited away!'

Only one person in the house appeared indifferent to the prevailing distress and anxiety, and this was Mistress Galt, who went about chuckling to herself with eldrich laughter.

Several days passed in which Miss Swinford did little but lament her loss, and exhaust conjecture as to how the picture could have been so mysteriously removed. But neither search nor enquiry threw any light on the matter. The portrait had vanished, leaving no more trace than if it had melted into thin air.

Her distraction of mind at first prevented Miss Swinford from noticing her guest, as she otherwise would have done. But as she became less preoccupied, she observed in Joceline Hammersley numberless little peculiarities, that, taken all together, convinced her she was unlike anyone she had ever met before. She had none of the ardour and impetuosity of youth, she was silent and reticent. She was ignorant of everyday matters that a child would know, and yet surprised her by considerable out of the way knowledge, and acquaintance with bygone times, though she knew nothing of contemporary history. Her phraseology was often amusingly antiquated. Sometimes too she would misunderstand the plainest language, and require it to be translated into another form before she appeared to grasp its meaning.

'Does your father never take you to London, my dear?' asked Miss Swinford, thinking it a pity that so lovely a young creature should not see more society than her country home afforded.

'He took me thither once on a time when I was but a child, and I call to mind that while we were at our lodging in Whitehall the Queen was brought to bed of a son, and the rejoicing thereat.'

'My dear Joceline, you positively must not make use of such an old-fashioned, countrified expression as "brought to bed"!' said Miss Swinford, 'it is only fit for an old nurse! Ladies may have spoken in that way a century ago, but it is purely rustic now. If you must date your visit to London by royal domestic events, you should say you were there when the Queen was confined.'

'But that would not be the truth,' replied Joceline, raising her dark eyes and folding her hands in her lap, 'for it was not the Queen's but the King's majesty that was confined in Carisbrook Castle,' and she sighed heavily.

Miss Swinford was confounded. Could it be that her beautiful young kinswoman was mildly deranged? She looked into the dreamy brown eyes fixed upon her, and merely saying, 'I think you have lived too much alone in the country,' lapsed into thoughtful silence.

That night when Miss Swinford was returning to rest and her maid was about to leave the room, she lingered at the door and said, 'There's something I want to speak to you about, miss, but I hardly know how to, for it's about Miss Hammersley.'

'What is it, Dapper? What can you have to say that concerns my cousin?'

'There's something strange about the young lady, miss, and about Mistress Galt too, as she calls her. They walk in their sleep or something as bad. Last night when I was lying awake I heard footsteps, and I got up and opened my door, and crossed the gallery and looked over the bannisters, and there below if there wasn't Miss Hammersley and her maid going into the empty rooms in the old part of the house. I saw them quite plain in the moonlight through the big window. They were in their day dresses, they hadn't undressed for bed though it was past two o'clock, and Miss Hammersley was crying and sobbing. They seemed to know their way about the house in the dark as well as we do by daylight! I felt frightened and went back to bed, and it would be a good half-hour before I heard them creep back to their rooms again. I thought I'd better tell you about it, miss.

'You amaze me, Dapper! It's impossible that they both walk in their sleep. But perhaps my cousin does, and her maid follows her lest she should meet with some accident, or wake suddenly and be alarmed.'

'I hope, miss, that if you hear anything tonight you'll please to get up and see for yourself. I'll put your dressing-gown by the candle and matches, and if you want me I'm a light sleeper, I should wake if you only scratched on the door.' And Dapper retired, leaving her mistress profoundly uneasy.

Many uncomfortable thoughts were suggested to Miss Swinford's mind by what she had heard. She rose and locked the door, that if Joceline walked in her sleep, at all events she would not be startled by her entering the room in the night with wide unseeing eyes. She thought over all her cousin's peculiarities, her strange inanimate expression, her deadly pallor and coldness, her silence and dreamy look, and decided that she was a very likely subject to be a somnambulist. Having settled this painful matter to her satisfaction, Miss Swinford's mind reverted to its favourite theme – the inexplicable loss of the portrait. And she fell asleep to dream that her cousin stood in the tarnished frame over the library mantelshelf, saying, 'I told you that Joceline Swinford's portrait would come back to you!' when she woke suddenly, the clock struck two, and she heard gentle steps in the carpeted gallery.

In a moment she had put on her dressing-gown and opened the door. Dapper had left a lamp burning, and by its light she saw Joceline Hammersley in the gallery on the opposite side of the hall, followed by her maid, walking towards the door leading to the old part of the house.

Miss Swinford hastened along the gallery that ran round the four sides of the hall, till she was close behind the dim figures that had now passed beyond the light of the lamp. Mistress Galt was silent and rigid, but Joceline, pale as death, walked with clasped hands, moaning to herself. They left the door open as they entered the deserted rooms, and Miss Swinford followed unperceived. They passed quickly across stretches of pallid moonlight falling through the dusty windows, alternating with breadths of blackest shadow, opening door after door till they came to a corner room, looking out to the front and end of the house. Then they paused, and Joceline lifted up her face that no moonlight could bleach whiter, and cried, 'It was here that he died! On this spot my love died! Here he lay till they bore him to his last resting place, but far from me!

I lie alone in my narrow bed!' and Miss Swinford, terrified, and convinced that her cousin was either a mad woman or a somnambulist, turned and fled.

She did not pause or look behind her till she had locked herself in her room, when she fell half-fainting upon the bed. 'My poor cousin is insane! She has heard the story of the death of Joceline Swinford's lover in this house, and has brooded over it, till with her peculiar temperament it has turned her brain. And that strange woman Galt is her keeper, I see it all now! How shall I get rid of her? I shall become mad myself if we stay together much longer in this old house. How could she know the room in which Colonel Dacres died? I have not told her, and she has not been at Eastwick Court before. It is hateful, it is uncanny!' and Miss Swinford shuddered.

Presently she heard light footsteps once more, and opening the door saw the dim figures of her cousin and her maid returning to their room. They had made a complete circuit of the house, and regained the gallery by means of a disused staircase, the door leading to which was kept locked. When all was once more silent, Miss Swinford crossed the gallery, candle in hand, to examine for herself if the lock had been tampered with. But the door was fastened as it had been for many years, and the paper pasted round it to prevent draughts was undisturbed. Yet there was no other means of reaching the side of the gallery by which Joceline Hammersley and Mistress Galt had returned to their rooms, except by this staircase.

Miss Swinford slept no more that night, and when she closed her eyes, it was only to open them and assure herself that the pale-faced Joceline was not standing by her side.

At length when morning light filled the room, she drew aside the curtain and looked into the garden. She was startled to see Joceline and Mistress Galt standing together under the window. Neither of them wore hood or kerchief in the keen morning air, and Joceline's bare neck looked white and cold as marble. 'She is as like the old portrait as though she were the original Joceline come back from the dead!' exclaimed Miss Swinford.

Mistress and maid were looking fixedly at a spot in the garden, towards which first one pointed and then another, and in the silence of the early morning Miss Swinford could hear every word.

'And I say, Mistress Joceline, that the bowling green lay yonder!'

'Nay, be not so confident. You were here but for a few months when all was sorrow and confusion, while I dwelt here for three-and-twenty years, and till the cruel wars came had great joy and pleasure in my home. The bowling green was by the sundial, and lay to the north of the maze. But that is gone too. All is changed, the very flowers wear strange faces.'

'Shall you not rest, Mistress, since you have seen that which you prayed to see once more?'

'Yes, I shall rest. I shall sleep till we all wake together.'

'Mad! Stark mad!' ejaculated her cousin as she dropped the curtain and turned from the window.

The day proved wet and stormy, and Miss Swinford had to pass the heavy hours indoors with her uncanny guest. She was now so fully convinced of her cousin's insanity that she felt nervous in her presence, and unable to question her about her mysterious conduct. Joceline was, if possible, quieter and more reserved than ever. She looked fearfully ill, at times scarcely conscious, and as though her dark eyes moved with difficulty from one object to another.

'I am afraid you did not rest well last night, you seem so tired,' Miss Swinford ventured to say.

'I have not slept of late, but soon I shall rest again.' And she seemed almost to fall asleep as she spoke. Only once did she show spontaneous interest in anything, when turning over the leaves of a book, she came upon an engraving of the celebrated portrait of Strafford. Then her pale face seemed to radiate light. 'My Lord Strafford!' she exclaimed, 'and yet how unlike, for no picture can give the dark fire of his eye! O noble soul, that gave thy life for thy king, and yet wast powerless to avert his doom!'

At length the tedious day drew to an end. The two ladies were sitting in silence in the drawing-room, Miss Swinford wondering when her strange cousin would depart. She was resolved that she would write to Sir Piers to say that the change back to the bracing air of the north would be beneficial to his daughter's health, when Joceline rose noiselessly and left the room. 'How shall I get through another night with that unaccountable being wandering about the house, asleep or insane!' she thought, looking after her with a troubled expression. 'I cannot bear the strain of her company! It will be long indeed before I invite a stranger again to pay me a visit!' when the door opened and her cousin stood before her pale as a lily, dressed in her black travelling cloak and hood. Miss Swinford rose in amazement. 'My dear, what is the meaning of this! You came unannounced, you cannot surely be leaving me as abruptly as you arrived!'

'I must go, I am wanted,' she said. And as she spoke the sound of heavy wheels was heard approaching the house. An inexplicable fear fell upon Miss Swinford.

'But how shall you travel? You are too late for any train tonight.'

'I go as I came. I shall soon be at my journey's end. Farewell, cousin Katherine, and be of good cheer, the portrait of Joceline Swinford will be restored to you!' Miss Swinford mechanically followed her downstairs, where Mistress Galt was already waiting, and the servants peering over the bannisters to watch the departure. Miss Swinford stept into the porch with her guest, and there stood waiting a huge coach, drawn by four black horses. By the light of the moon, issuing from beneath a cloud, she saw that the coachman was dressed in as antique a style as his mistress, and that his face like hers was deadly pale.

'Farewell, cousin, farewell!' said Joceline, touching Miss Swinford's cheek with her cold lips, 'the missing picture will be restored to its place.' And followed by Mistress Galt she stepped into the coach, in which six persons could have seated themselves with ease. She leaned out of the window, and bowed to her hostess with solemn formality. Then the horses moving at a heavy trot drew the lumbering vehicle down the avenue towards the high road. Miss Swinford, Bennet, Dapper, and a couple of grooms attracted by the extraordinary sound of the heavy carriage approaching the house, stood awestruck watching it depart. Not one of them could have expressed his fear in words, and the terror each felt was the greater for being unspoken. The huge coach rumbled along the avenue, when it turned into the high road, and still they could hear the heavy waggon-like sound of its wheels.

'They have taken the turning to the left!' cried Miss Swinford, the first to break the silence. 'That great carriage and four horses can never cross the Brook Bridge. They should have turned to the right. See if you can overtake them before the road is too narrow for them to turn!' and the grooms ran down a side path that was used as a short cut to the road. The heavy sound of wheels grew duller and more distant, and suddenly ceased. 'Thank goodness they are stopped in time, they will turn now!' said Miss Swinford. But still no sound was heard. Presently the grooms came back breathless with running, the younger of them looking ready to faint.

'You stopped them in time, Landon, I hope?' asked Miss Swinford of the elder of the two men.

'Oh Lord, Oh Lord, ma'am, there's no coach nor nothing to stop! As I'm a living sinner there's nothing but a three mile stretch o'road clear as day in the moonlight, and not so much as a wheelbarrow on it, and neither man nor beast to be seen! That big coach and four's clean gone, same as if it had sunk into the ground!'

'Come into the house, madam,' said Dapper, supporting her mistress, for she staggered as though she would fall, 'and thank God, however they're gone, those white-faced witches are out of the place at last!' And sick with amazement Miss Swinford suffered herself to be led indoors.

When she had recovered herself, she said with her usual determination, 'Dapper and Bennet, come with me into the library, I want you both!' And they followed their mistress in silence. Miss Swinford paused for an instant on the threshold, then opening wide the door all three entered the room. The lamp stood on the table, a cheerful fire burned on the hearth. Everything was in its accustomed order, and Dapper and Bennet looked vaguely about them wondering why they were wanted. But their mistress pointed to the wall above the mantel-shelf. From its tarnished frame the portrait of Joceline Swinford looked down on them once more, as though it had never been missing from its place. Dapper screamed shrilly, Bennet gazed open-mouthed, Miss Swinford buried her face in her hands and said in a tremulous voice, 'This is dreadful! What does it mean, what can it mean!'

The next morning's post brought Miss Swinford a letter from Sir Piers Hammersley, at Carlsbad, where he and his daughter were staying, apologising for her letter remaining so long unanswered, but it had been carelessly overlooked and only forwarded to him that day. He was exceedingly annoyed to think how uncourteous he must have appeared. Joceline, too, was as sorry as himself. She hoped that her cousin would renew her kind invitation some future time, to give her the pleasure of making her acquaintance, and of visiting the old home of the family.

Then the strange beautiful girl who had come and gone so mysteriously, whose visit had corresponded with the absence of the portrait of Joceline Swinford, was not her cousin after all! Who then was she, or *what* was she? Miss Swinford believed that she knew who her strange guest had been. But she dared not express her conviction in words. Her friends would have thought her mad. She kept her secret locked in her breast. But she was a changed woman from that time forward, and within twelve months the last of the Swinfords was laid to rest in the family burial place. The old servants still tell the story of the pale lady's visit, and her weird ways, and how their mistress fell into pining health from the very night of her mysterious departure.

Sir Nigel Otterburne's Case

It is thirty years since I completed my career at the Eastminster Hospital. I had passed all my examinations successfully, and taken more than my share of medical honours, when one of our most celebrated physicians, Dr Grindrod, asked me to watch an important case for him, the study of which I should find of the deepest professional interest.

Dr Grindrod's patient was suffering from an obscure form of malaria, contracted abroad, which had developed into an extremely rare form of intermittent fever, with really beautiful complications, such as he had never met with before in all his wide practice. But Sir Nigel Otterburne lived a three hours' journey from town in Hampshire, and when the doctor went to see him it practically took a whole day of his valuable time, which was more than he could afford to devote to any one case. Dr Grindrod therefore proposed that he should see the patient himself once a week, and send down one of the most promising of the hospital students to watch the case under him, and to take minute medical notes of its progress.

I was the fortunate man selected for the work, and was to go into the country with Dr Grindrod, taking with us a couple of our most trustworthy nurses. I can never again feel as important as I did on that first day of August when I entered upon my onerous duty. The doctor and I were met at the station, and driven through lovely country to the Hammel, which was the name of Sir Nigel Otterburne's house. It was a fine specimen of Jacobean architecture, and, externally at least, had undergone but little change for a couple of centuries past. It was a three-storeyed building, with tall fluted chimneys, and dormer windows in its high-pitched roof. The front of the house was nine windows wide – narrow sash windows with a great deal of framework in proportion to the glass. The front of the house, with its wings to right and left, made three sides of a quadrangle, the fourth side of which was formed by wrought-iron railings, with great gates in the centre.

Leaving the carriage outside for fear of disturbing the patient by the sound of our arrival, we crossed the wide courtyard on foot. The front door was approached by shallow steps, and sheltered by a richly carved penthouse of black oak. Upon the wall between the second and third storeys was a sundial, and the bright August sunshine threw the sharply defined shadow of the gilded gnomon on the figure denoting the hour of four o'clock in the afternoon.

Above the dial a small turret rose from the centre of the roof surmounted by an elaborate piece of ironwork, with quaintly twisted letters N. S. E. and W., and a glittering arrow for a weather-vane.

I was struck by the appearance of the house, at once stately and homely. But I received from it an impression of melancholy which was not lessened when the door was opened by a grey-headed servant, who led us across the panelled hall into a vast and dreary dining-room. It contained nothing in the way of furniture except a long table with a row of high-backed chairs pushed close against it on either side, and a sideboard of carved oak, on which stood a row of silver flagons. A china bowl on the middle of the table, filled with roses and white lilies, made the atmosphere of the room heavy with their perfume. A few gloomy old portraits looked down from their tarnished frames, some with faces austere and rigid as though they had been painted after death.

Dr Grindrod had acquainted me with the details of Sir Nigel Otterburne's case on our journey, and having nothing further to say till we had seen the patient, he stood with his hands behind his back, looking at the portrait of a lady over the mantelpiece, so lavish of her charms that I assigned her at a glance to Charles the Second's period.

'That is what I call a magnificent woman,' said the doctor, waving his hand sumptuously towards the expanse of bare neck and bosom depicted on the canvas. But I should have rather applied the words to the lady who entered the room while he was speaking, and whom he introduced to me as Miss Otterburne. The doctor had told me that Sir Nigel Otterburne was a widower with an only daughter, but he had said nothing to prepare me for the appearance of so amazingly handsome a creature.

I have never met a woman who so completely fascinated and interested me at first sight. Miss Otterburne was not a girl. She was in the ripe beauty of womanhood, and with a most dignified and haughty carriage. She covered me with a glance of her beautiful dark eyes, and curtsied so low that it was almost a sarcasm to a young man like myself. She was tall and slender, of an ivory pallor of complexion, with fine sensitive features, and a mass of dark hair worn high on her head. She was dressed in some soft, cream-coloured fabric, and her sleeves came only to the elbow, displaying to the utmost advantage her beautifully formed hands and arms.

'I promised you, Miss Otterburne, that I would bring one of our hospital students to watch Sir Nigel's case for me,' said Dr Grindrod. 'You must not mistrust Mr Caxton because he is young. He has had experience in the hospital which many older men might envy. He will post to me daily notes of the patient's condition. I shall be down myself once a week, and you would telegraph for me in any emergency. Indeed, my dear young lady, I can assure you that Sir Nigel is in good hands,' and Dr Grindrod smiled, and attempted a light and easy manner. But Miss Otterburne was entirely irresponsive.

'Heaven grant that you may be right,' she said in chilling tones, and she led us upstairs to the patient's room. As she walked erect before us, there was that in her bearing and appearance which reminded me of some distinguished Frenchwoman at the time of the Revolution, and I thought how many a proud head like hers had fallen from its white shoulders under the guillotine.

Sir Nigel's room was dark and dreary, and he lay in a funereal bed with heavy hangings, and I mentally vowed to have him out of it and in a more cheerful room within four-and-twenty hours. If the house did not contain some light, undraped bedstead, I would send to the hospital for one such as we use for our patients.

Sir Nigel Otterburne was in a half-comatose state when I first saw him, and I judged him to be about sixty-two or -three years of age. He was tall and thin, and looking at his face I saw at a glance whence Miss Otterburne derived her fine features. His hair and moustache were thick and grey, and he looked what he was, a soldier. In his lucid intervals there was a dignity and self-restraint in his manner which again reminded me of his daughter. The local practitioner, Mr Walton, was present in the room, a good-humoured, rustic-looking man, more like a farmer than a doctor, but who, if he was unprofessional in appearance, luckily for me had less than the usual amount of professional jealousy. So far from being annoyed at seeing me installed in the house to watch the case of his distinguished patient for Dr Grindrod, he expressed his approval of an arrangement that relieved him of so much responsibility. But he said nothing before Miss Otterburne, and I saw that she exercised the same repressive influence over him that I felt so strongly myself. But when we were in the dining-room again, and I was receiving my final instructions from

Dr Grindrod, Mr Walton said, as he poured himself out a glass of sherry: 'I don't profess that single-handed I could pull Sir Nigel round. I've not had the opportunity of studying malarious fevers. But if you gentlemen succeed in curing the patient, I share the glory of it, and if he slips through your fingers Miss Otterburne cannot reproach me, for nothing could be expected of me where Dr Grindrod failed.'

'Is Miss Otterburne likely to reproach you, if the case ends fatally?' I asked.

Mr Walton looked round to see if the door was shut, emptied another glass of wine before he spoke, and said in a low voice: 'Miss Otterburne is Miss Otterburne, and it would be unprofessional to gossip about any member of my patient's family. Eyes and ears open, and mouth shut at the Hammel, is my advice.'

After Dr Grindrod's departure I went upstairs to make arrangements for my first night in charge of Sir Nigel. A small room leading out of the patient's had been assigned to my use, and I went to the window to look at the view. My eyes never rested on a more peaceful scene. Immediately in front of the house, bounded on either side by its projecting wings, was the great courtyard, with its wide grass borders bathed in sunshine, and beyond the iron palisades and the high gates stretched an expanse of undulating country thickly wooded with trees in their heaviest summer foliage. On the brow of a gentle ascent, some quarter of a mile distant, stood a grey church with an ivy-grown tower, and the evening sunshine was glittering on the weather-vane.

When I had seen the night nurse enter upon her duties, I went for a stroll in the open air, leaving the house by a door at the back of the hall. I found myself in an old-fashioned garden with grass terraces and clipped yew hedges. I thought that I was alone in the garden, when suddenly I caught sight of Miss Otterburne's light dress, white and ghostly in the gathering gloom, and in a moment we were face to face in the path. I raised my hat and stood aside for her to pass, and I felt the blood mount to my cheeks. She might think that I was intruding on her privacy, and following her on her evening walk. Miss Otterburne did not quicken her pace as she passed me. She regarded me with grave intensity. But her eyes were void of speculation, like those of one who was walking in her sleep. I watched her stately figure recede among the darkening alleys, and heard the door close as she entered the house. I felt chilled and disconcerted, why I could not tell; but I would run no second risk of appearing to intrude upon Miss Otterburne.

At eleven o'clock Miss Otterburne entered her father's room to bid him goodnight. He scarcely knew her, yet I fancied that he smiled faintly as she pressed his hand, or it may have been the flickering of the lamplight on his face that I mistook for a smile.

'I trust Sir Nigel will have a tranquil night,' I said.

'His nights are always tranquil,' she replied in measured tones.

'And yet he has gained no strength the five weeks he has lain here.'

'He never will,' she said in the same passionless voice.

'You speak more positively, Miss Otterburne, than any doctor would dare to do. Such an illness as Sir Nigel's is not necessarily fatal. We do not know . . .'

'But I know,' and her voice sank to a whisper. 'It is useless your staying here. My father will never leave this house alive.'

'It is wrong to speak so,' I said firmly. 'And if Sir Nigel understands what you say, it must cause him the most exquisite pain.'

Not a line in her white handsome face softened or changed.

'My father knows it already,' she said, and swept from the room, leaving me bewildered by her manner.

I slept but little during my first night at the Hammel. My mind was so much occupied with Sir Nigel's case, that I went frequently to see my patient, and to note any change in his condition, however slight. My obstinacy, too, was roused by Miss Otterburne's assertion that her father would die, by the way in which she ignored anything that medical skill could do for him. Her manner was that of a person expressing a profoundly melancholy conclusion forced upon her against her will, and yet that she believed to be irrevocably true.

'If that man's sentence has not gone forth from heaven, he shall live,' I exclaimed, 'and that handsome, obstinate creature shall be taught that she is not infallible!'

My resolution being made, I tried to sleep, but tried in vain. The profound silence of the country after the roar of London had the same effect upon me that noise has upon those who are accustomed to quiet, and kept me wide awake. And from time to time I was startled by the screeching of owls, sounding like the cries of terrified children lost in the dark.

At length the dawn came, and I rose to go into Sir Nigel's room. This time he was conscious, and as I felt his pulse he whispered, 'Are they come?'

'Yes,' I replied, supposing that he alluded to me and the nurses. 'We came yesterday, and we shall try to relieve you as much as we can.'

But he sighed impatiently, closed his eyes, and turned his head from me. It was useless to lie down again, so I dressed myself, and the clock was striking four as I opened the window and leaned out to enjoy the freshness of the morning air. To my great surprise, Miss Otterburne also was looking out of her window in the centre of the right wing of the house. I drew back at once, but she had not heard me throw up the sash, and she was not looking in my direction. Her dark eyes were fixed in a trance-like gaze on the entrance to the courtyard, or on the church crowning the grassy slope. She certainly was not looking at any part of the house. She was ghastly pale, and her eyes wore the same unseeing expression that I had noticed in them on the previous evening.

For more than a quarter of an hour Miss Otterburne remained immovable, and how long she may have been at her casement before I saw her I cannot tell. She was wrapped in a white robe, and her dark hair lay in waves on her shoulders, but her face was not like that of a living woman. It seemed probable that I might have two patients in the house to look after. And I felt a distinct sense of relief when at length she withdrew from the window and I lost sight of her.

That day I carried out my intention with regard to Sir Nigel. We moved him into a small bed and carried him to a bright, cheerful sitting-room on the same floor – a room suggesting pleasant, sunny life as clearly as the gloomy bedroom had suggested death. I felt sure that the patient would appreciate the change, that it would prove beneficial to him. But to my disappointment, he did not appear to notice it, and it produced no effect on his physical condition. I heard him murmuring to himself as he lay, 'It will make no difference; it will make no difference.'

It was singular, too, that Miss Otterburne seemed to take no interest in her father's removal to more cheerful quarters. However, I had Dr Grindrod's approval of what I had done, and I was content.

'How do you get on with Miss Otterburne?' the doctor asked me abruptly on one of his visits, when I had been more than a week in the house.

'You might as well ask me how I get on with that picture on the wall,' I replied. 'But I think she is the handsomest woman I ever saw in my life.'

'You do, do you? Hum! Not my style; I prefer flesh and blood,' and Dr Grindrod shot a glance in the direction of the Charles the Second lady, and fell to talking of purely medical matters.

When I had been in hourly attendance on Sir Nigel for a fortnight, I began to realise not only that my patient was making no progress, but that I was making no progress with my patient. I expected no lively gratitude from him. But it would have been pleasant if there had been any token of recognition, either on his part or his daughter's, that I was doing my utmost for him. I imagine that he regarded me as a servant whose attentions were indispensable to his comfort, but with whom he could not be familiar. It did not annoy me, sometimes it even amused me, for I never count a sick man in the category of sane persons, and should no more think myself insulted by an invalid than by a madman. This excuse, however, did not apply to Miss Otterburne, and I was puzzled more and more by her conduct.

Every morning at earliest dawn, if I looked out, she was leaning on her window-sill, gazing with a tragic melancholy, not I am sure at any tangible object, but on something that presented itself to her mental vision.

Not only did I gain no ground with Sir Nigel and his daughter, but the old housekeeper and butler, though perfectly civil to me, were both exceedingly reserved. Sometimes the housekeeper would have a short confab with me on her master's state, consisting on her part chiefly of sighs and head-shakings, and once the butler went so far as to observe, 'Master Raymond will wish that he'd parted friends with his father when he went to India!' So then Sir Nigel had a son, a fact of which I was not aware, and furthermore it would seem that father and son had had some quarrel or misunderstanding.

Meanwhile there was no disguising the unwelcome fact that my patient was steadily sinking. Dr Grindrod approved of all that I did in carrying out his instructions to the letter, but nothing we could do availed to check the downward course, and we racked our brains for treatment and remedies which should keep the enemy at bay. The disease was not running a normal course. Unexpected complications arose at an unusual period in its progress, and how interesting the battle between the force of disease and the power of science became to me none but an enthusiast in the medical profession can tell. I seldom quitted the patient's room. Only when he was sleeping did I venture to leave him for an hour in charge of a nurse while I went for a stroll in the fresh air.

It was just before sunset one evening, when I had been nearly a month at the Hammel, that I closed the front door gently behind me, and crossing the courtyard, let myself out into the park, and made my way towards the church on the grassy slope. I was exhausted and excited, and I walked bareheaded that the cool breeze might blow about my heated temples. I hated to be baffled. I had been so sure of victory, and now defeat stared me in the face. Miss Otterburne would have a melancholy triumph. She would be right after all, and I should be wrong. I went over every event of the previous weeks in detail. I was satisfied that all that medical science could do for Sir Nigel, at the point to which it had then attained, had been done and was still being done for him. But I reflected with a crushing sense of impotence on the irresistible power of the force with which I was contending. I, a finite being, was measuring my strength against death, the conqueror of man. The contest was hideously unequal. I was sure to be worsted. Even if the patient recovered, it would be at best but a reprieve, and sooner or later he must retrace his anguished steps towards that bourne from whence I was striving with all my strength to turn him back.

I entered the churchyard in the deepest depression of spirit. It was not merely the anticipated loss of my patient that weighed on me; that was but one item in the incalculable total of human misery. In his death I saw the doom of every son of Adam – the death of the whole human race. I was ready to wish that I had died myself before I had embraced a profession which constantly brought me face to face with a terrible elementary fact in nature, with which the utmost skill of man is powerless to cope.

The church door stood hospitably open, and I entered the cool twilight within. Here were tombs of the Otterburnes, from the time when intra-mural burial was a universal custom to the present period, when a memorial tablet or monument is all that is permitted within the church itself. I thought how soon Sir Nigel would be numbered among his ancestors, and be as remote from us who still lived as his own earliest forbears were from him now. Suddenly I heard a deep sigh, and starting, I turned and saw Miss Otterburne close to me, but almost hidden by a great pillar against which she leaned. Her dark eyes were fixed with the wide unseeing gaze which I had noticed in them each early morning as she looked from her window. I spoke to her, and when she heard my voice the pupils of her eyes dilated as though the twilight had deepened round her.

'Miss Otterburne, if there is anything that you wish to say to Sir Nigel, I should advise you to take the opportunity of his next interval of consciousness. It grieves me to be obliged to say this, but I have no choice in the matter. I must tell you the truth.'

'Yes, they will soon come. I know it,' she said with a slight shudder.

I thought that she was wandering in her mind, and, taking no notice of her incoherent reply, I continued.

'I would give my life, Miss Otterburne, if I could prolong the life of one so dear to you.'

But she looked past and through me, as though she were piercing into futurity, and I heard her say: 'When they come you will know that I was right.'

And she glided like a ghost out of the dim church into the amber light of evening. Her manner disquieted me profoundly, and I wished that Miss Otterburne was not so lonely; that her brother in India was at home to take his share of the trouble, and to comfort his sister.

I hastened back to my patient's bedside, and, knowing that it would be impossible to leave him that night, I sat down to copy my notes of the case for my own private use. About eleven o'clock Sir Nigel rallied slightly. I administered a powerful restorative, and sent the nurse to fetch Miss Otterburne at once. As she entered the room, I said: 'If you would like to be alone with your father, I will remain within call outside the door.'

She bowed her head in assent, and I left them together. I remained waiting in my own room, listening to Miss Otterburne's voice distinctly audible in low urgent tones. Then, as Sir Nigel again lapsed into unconsciousness, she spoke a little louder, and I heard her say: 'Father, will you not forgive Raymond?' and then all was silent. I re-entered the room, and Miss Otterburne was kneeling by her father's bedside. She had been weeping, and I saw that beneath the armour of pride and reserve there was a woman's tender heart. But my return was the signal for her to depart, and she left the room hastily, as though displeased that I had witnessed her emotion.

I looked at my dying patient with more regret than I should have thought possible to feel for a man who, in his short intervals of consciousness, had always treated me as a stranger. Certainly I had no affection for Sir Nigel, but I was struck by the pathos of the situation. There he lay, needing, like each one of us, both divine and human forgiveness, but unable to ask it for himself or to grant it to another, even when it was his daughter who knelt weeping by his side, imploring pardon for her brother.

Slowly the night passed, and slowly the patient died. I noted the decreasing temperature, the failing pulse, and I applied restoratives which formerly had power to rally him, though now they had lost their virtue. But the heart still beat, and now and then a sighing breath escaped his lips.

There was nothing more that I could do. But that I might leave no expedient untried, I sent the nurse into my room for an air cushion, which I told her to inflate and bring to me. If I raised the patient's head by means of it, it was possible that he might feel a momentary ease, though he would be unconscious of its cause.

I looked at my watch. It was four o'clock, and the grey light of dawn glimmered through the curtains. I wondered whether Miss Otterburne was at her window, according to her strange custom, when the door opened swiftly and silently, and she entered the room as I had often seen her at that hour, clad in a loose white robe, and her dark hair hanging about her shoulders. There was mortal pallor on her face. She did not cast a glance in the direction of her dying father, but exclaiming in tones that chilled my blood: 'They have come, they have come!' she went to the window, drew back the curtains, let in the cold light of dawn, and stood with clasped hands gazing into the courtyard below. I was by her side in an instant.

'They have come, they have come; I knew they would come!' And I heard the effort she made to speak with a tongue that was dry with terror. In the courtyard beneath, directly opposite to the window, was a strange, silent crowd of men, women, and children, looking up at us in the faint morning light with faces of the dead. And though they pressed and thronged each other on the gravel path, not a sound was heard.

I am not a superstitious man, and in those days my nerves were of iron. But I reeled as I stood, and the blood rushed to my head with a singing sound. I saw the dead of centuries ago, and the dead of yesterday, grey-bearded men who fought in the civil wars, young men and maidens who never were contemporaries in this life, and little children, all gazing at us with upturned faces. Miss Otterburne spoke again as one speaks in nightmare, with deadly effort and oppression.

'I know them. I saw them when they came to fetch my grandfather, and when they fetched my mother. Oh, mother! mother! you are there!' And she leaned forward in an agony, and gazed with set and rigid face at a slim form that drifted through the ghostly throng and lifted its sad eyes to hers. By her side stood a tall man in uniform, whose white face I shall never forget, and he solemnly waved his hand towards us. 'Oh Heaven! my brother Raymond is with them!' shrieked Miss Otterburne, and sank on the floor insensible, at the moment that Sir Nigel gave his last groan. I hastily fetched a cushion and placed it under her head, and then turned once more to the window. But the courtyard was absolutely empty, nor was there a trace of its recent occupation. I could not have been absent from the window a couple of minutes, and the instantaneous disappearance of the ghastly throng shook my nerves fully as much as the sight of it had done. There was not a mark on the untrodden dewy grass. Not a pebble displaced on the broad gravel path that had been so crowded a moment before. On the spot where the tall figure had stood and waved its hand to us a cat was seated, licking her paws, and I heard the fitful chirp of the first awakened birds.

I felt physically ill, and turning from the window I poured out and drank a powerful cordial that restored an artificial calmness to my nerves. Just then the nurse returned. She had not been absent from the room more than five minutes.

'The patient is dead, and Miss Otterburne has fainted,' I said. 'Help me to lay her on the couch.'

I have never in all my experience seen anyone in so deep a swoon. The nurse and I were unspeakably relieved when at length she showed signs of returning consciousness, though I dreaded what she might say when she recovered. I gave her a composing draught which would secure her some hours' rest, and committed her to the care of her maid.

I sent at once for the family doctor, who had seen Sir Nigel on the previous night, to acquaint him with the death of the patient. He was exceedingly inquisitive about every possible detail, and appeared to long for information concerning something he dared not enquire about directly.

'Were there any circumstances of an unusual character attending the death?' he asked anxiously.

'It was the ordinary termination of such an illness as Sir Nigel's,' I replied guardedly.

'And Miss Otterburne, how did she bear the shock?'

'She had a severe fainting-fit, and remained insensible for fully half an hour. She appears to feel her loss acutely.'

Mr Walton agreed with me that I had better remain in the house till the following day, to make the necessary arrangements for the funeral, and to write to Miss Otterburne's relations, with whose names and addresses the butler supplied me, to prevent his mistress from being disturbed. The old man became almost talkative for so taciturn a person.

'The family has died and died till yonder churchyard is full of them,' he said. 'The very soil of it was once Otterburne flesh and blood, and there's no-one left of this branch but Miss Otterburne and the Major in India, that's now Sir Raymond. There's a few cousins up in the north, and a widowed sister of the master's, and they'll like to come for the funeral, if it's only to see where they'll be laid themselves when their time comes, for all the Otterburnes are brought here to be buried.'

'Will one of the ladies of the family stay with Miss Otterburne till her brother returns from India?' I said, and as it was the first question I had asked, the old man cast a suspicious glance at me, resumed his uncommunicative manner, and changed the subject of conversation. By noon I had sent the nurses back to London. Then there remained the long afternoon and evening in which to collect my distracted thoughts and to get my nerves into something like order for a return to the active duties of life. I could not for an instant forget the horror of that early dawn. I saw, as clearly as I now see the pen with which I am writing this narrative, the ghostly throng with upturned, dead faces gazing at us, and Miss Otterburne's words and cry still rang in my ears. Whatever the ghostly vision was, we had both of us seen it. If only one person had seen it, and that one myself, I should not have been convinced of its reality. I should have believed that I was subjected to some terrible hallucination. But we both saw it at the same moment. And Miss Otterburne had seen it twice before, and each time under the same ghastly circumstances. There was no doubt that it had been as visible to us as natural objects are. It was no picture conjured up separately in our brains.

I confess that I was so unnerved I could not look out of that window again, nor could I spend my last night at the Hammel in any room at the front of the house. I asked the housekeeper to give me a bed in one of the back rooms. She cast a peculiar glance at me and said: 'You don't care for a room that looks out into the courtyard, and I don't blame you for it. But you need not mind it now, sir; they won't come again till – till they are sent.'

I made frequent enquiries during the day about Miss Otterburne. But I did not ask to see her, so fearful was I of the effect my presence might have in recalling the horror we had witnessed together. The last thing at night I sent a message to her saying that I should return to town in the morning, and I hoped that she would send for me if I could be of the slightest service to her. But she did not require me, and I retired for the night to a small back room on the second floor.

Sleep was out of the question. I did not undress, but sat smoking pipe after pipe and trying to read, till when the grey dawn came a great terror took possession of me, and I shook like a man in a fit of ague. I scorned myself for my weakness. But the feeling was beyond my own control.

At length, when daylight flooded the room, I threw myself across the bed and fell into a deep sleep which must have lasted for hours, and from which I was awakened by loud knocking at the door. 'Who is there?' I said, starting to my feet, and the knock was again repeated. I ran to the door and opened it. The old butler stood before me pale and trembling.

'Miss Otterburne wishes to see you, sir, in her sitting-room.'

'Tell her I will be with her directly,' and I hastened to make myself fit to enter the presence of a lady, and went downstairs to Miss Otterburne's room, where her maid stood waiting for me with a scared face. She said nothing, but opened the door of her mistress's room. I entered, and she closed it after me.

Miss Otterburne was standing by the table with an open letter in her hand. I should not have known her. Her hair had turned white in the last twenty-four hours, and there was a strange glitter in her eye. She handed me the letter, saying: 'It was Raymond that we saw with them; I knew it.'

I read the letter. It was very short. A few lines written in haste by a friend of the Major's to Sir Nigel, telling him of the death of his son, of cholera at Meerut a month ago, and promising all particulars by the next mail. As my mind took in the meaning of it I grew giddy. The room became suddenly dark to me, and I groped for a chair like a blind man. Miss Otterburne laughed, the cackling laugh of insanity, and it recalled me to myself in an instant through extremity of compassion for her.

'Why do you pretend to be surprised? You knew that Raymond was dead as well as I; we both saw him. Oh, he was merry! They were all a merry company; why should we be sad?' and the poor lady laughed in such an awful fashion I could have shed tears of blood to listen to her.

It was the last time that I saw Miss Otterburne. Twenty long years she continued to live at the Hammel in a state of hopeless insanity, dangerous neither to herself nor to others while she was allowed to remain there. But if any attempt was made to take her elsewhere, her frenzy became ungovernable. 'They would not know where to find me,' she would say. 'They can only fetch me from here, and I want the merry, white-faced folk to come for me;' and her anger would subside into dreadful laughter.

Every day in the early dawn she rose to look out of her window into the courtyard. But one morning she failed to do so, and her attendant was thankful to find Miss Otterburne lying peacefully dead, on the twentieth anniversary of her father's death.

The Ticking of the Clock

Elijah Walrond, or Old 'Lijah as he was commonly called, was a small tenant farmer, who, by dint of hard work, hard living, and saving, had contrived to lay by enough money to make a frugal provision for his old age. 'Lijah's wife died the year before he quitted the farm that had been their home for forty years, and when he lost her it was like losing a part of himself. He was never the same man again. It took the heart out of his work when there was no wife to talk it over with; he could not relish the food prepared by a strange hand, and he lay awake at nights in his loneliness, staring into the darkness with tearless eyes. There was nothing left to make life sweet to him, and his seventy years weighed on him like a hundred. Then he asked his landlord to let him off the short remainder of his lease, and he left the farm to live in the white cottage with the big garden down by the common.

His neighbours said that Old 'Lijah would go silly with loneliness all by himself, for he saw nobody and spoke to no-one but the woman who came to clean and to do his bit of cooking. He seldom left the house, and never went beyond the garden, and he had not entered the church since the day of his wife's funeral. The rector of the parish, who had known Elijah Walrond many years, called to ask him why he never saw him in his accustomed place on a Sunday, but the old man would only reply, 'I canna do it, sir; I canna do it! 'Er'd used to go to church with me, and I canna go alone,' and lapse into silence again. There was no-one at home now to care what he did, or whether he was well or ill, so he ceased to strive against stiffness and rheumatism, and crept along with the help of a stick, with bowed shoulders, as though he carried a heavy burden. Old 'Lijah was in a parlous state, both of body and mind, when one day the very best thing that could happen befell him, though it came about through someone else's sorrow.

'Lijah had an only child – a daughter – who some years previously had married a ne'er-do-well of the name of Grove, and lived with him in the north of England, where, after a short career of idleness and poverty, he died, leaving Jane a widow with one little child. Jane Grove had not a farthing in the world to call her own when she had paid her fare to travel southwards to her father, and her sticks of furniture had been sold to pay for her husband's burial, for her honest pride revolted at a pauper's funeral. She knew that her father had left the farm, but in however poor a place he lived now, he would not shut the door upon his daughter, though he had been displeased with her for marrying as she did. But bygones were bygones, and though the mother, who would have welcomed her child, was dead, Jane could cook and work for her father, and make the meanest place seem like home; and good as her intentions were towards the old man, she could not tell – no-one could have told – the kindness she was about to do him.

Jane Grove reached her father's cottage in the grey of a summer evening, weary and footsore with her long walk from the station, carrying her sleeping child in her arms. She inquired from a man whom she met crossing the common where Elijah Walrond lived, and he pointed out to her the little white cottage with the big garden. Slowly she walked up the long, narrow path, with its straggling border of sweet-smelling pinks, wondering that the place was so untidy and ill-kept, till she stood on the threshold of the half-opened door. She tapped timidly, and no-one replying to her knock, she looked into the kitchen, and there sat her father dozing in his chair by the chimney corner. She was shocked at the change in his appearance. His features were sharp and worn, his hands like birds' claws, and a ragged growth of white beard and moustache covered his once well-shaven face; nor was old 'Lijah as clean as he might have been. His stockings were in holes and his clothes ragged and unmended. It was plain to be seen that he had lost all interest in himself, and that there was no woman to look after him. Jane entered, and quietly seated herself opposite to her father, and her tears fell fast as she took in the meaning of his forlorn and neglected aspect, and whispered to herself, 'Oh, mother, mother!'

When 'Lijah opened his eyes, there sat his daughter on the other side of the hearth, nursing a child on her lap. At first he did not know who it was, and looked vaguely puzzled until he heard her voice.

'It's me, father; it's Jane come to live with you and make you comfortable.'

He did not seem startled, and received the announcement with the most matter-of-fact calm.

'Whatever brings you back i' these parts? It's trouble, I doubt,' and the old man shook a boding head.

'Aye, father, trouble enough it is! My man's dead, and I 'aven't a penny in the world and no home but what you'll give me and this little lad to keep,' and the child, now wide awake, sat up on her lap and looked about him.

'What's that you say about a little lad? You've got a little lad to keep?' and there was a strange stir in the old man's heart as he uttered the words, for he had never had a son of his own, and it had been the great disappointment of his life.

For reply Jane crossed the hearth with her child in her arms, and set him on the old man's shrunken knees – as beautiful a boy of twelve months old as a mother ever doted on.

'Yes, father, that's my little lad as I've got to keep; that's little Peter, your own little grandson; and he's rare good company a'ready for lonely folks. Many's the time he's dried my tears watching 'is pretty ways. 'Old 'im tight, father, for 'e isn't used to old folks, and p'r'haps 'e mayn't take to you.'

No need to tell 'Lijah to hold his little grandson carefully. The touch of the child's firm young flesh, the sight of his golden hair in lamb-like curls, his gentian-blue eyes and moist, innocent breath nourished his old bones, and he felt there was vital warmth in him yet. And when little Peter put up a dimpled hand to grasp his ragged beard, and made pretty baby jabbering, and laughed in his troubled old face, displaying four pearly-white teeth like grains of rice, the frost in the grandfather's heart, that had bound it since his wife died, melted, and he said: 'Jane, if you 'aven't got a penny in the world, your man's left you rich enough wi' a little lad like this! You must bide wi' me – both of you.'

'Aye, father, so we will. But look you how that grey wire beard o' yourn is scratchin' little Peter's face! You'll 'ave to shave it off, and poor mother always thought so much o' your clean chin!'

The ragged beard was duly taken off, and the old man began the trouble of shaving again, and renewed his acquaintance with soap and water, for the little lad's sake; and his daughter washed and mended his clothes, and 'Lijah looked once more himself, but old – very old.

'Lijah's whole heart was garnered up in his little grandson, and as the boy grew older it was a pretty sight to see them in the fields together, the child bringing wild flowers to the old man to name, or a bird's egg or nest; but whatever it was he could tell him everything about it, and nothing short of that would content little Peter. For he had a healthy child's thirst for every kind of knowledge, so long as it was not what schoolmasters teach or what comes out of a book, and he was eager after all country lore and old-world word-of-mouth wisdom. It was wonderful how much the little lad learnt from his grandfather about four-footed creatures, from oxen to stoats and weasels, and he could have passed an examination with honours in the names, songs, and plumage of British birds.

The two were inseparable companions, and Peter would rather play with his grandfather, whom he regarded as an overgrown child with bent back and stiff legs, than with any little boy of his own age.

Jane Grove would stand on the doorstep and smile as she watched her father and his little grandson set out for a walk hand in hand, perfectly happy and content together. 'They're more like a pair o' lovers, them two, than anything else! Father's like wrapped up in that lad, and don't think o' me exceptin' to eat the vittles I cook and set afore 'im; nor little Peter, 'e don't think o' me neither so long as 'e can 'ave 'is grandad! They're both of 'em civil to me, and that's about all they are, they're so took up with each other.'

When little Peter had stuck to his grandfather like his shadow for five years, he began to be aware that his beloved companion could not see very far, and was shaky on his legs, got tired before they were half across the common, had a habit of falling asleep in the midst of the most interesting conversation about rooks and water rats, and was growing deaf, so that he had to speak loud to make him hear. These things grieved little Peter, and as he could not see the necessity for them he asked his grandfather what he did them for.

'Granddad,' he said, as he walked slowly by his side, having hold of his hand, 'grandad, why don't you run as quick as me?'

The old man smiled delightedly at a question that seemed to him to display little Peter's immense intellectual powers.

'It's seventy 'ears too late, my little lad, for grandfather to go running about like a little dog at a fair.'

'But, grandfather, you know a deal more than me; you'd ought to know how to run ever so fast, and climb the bank and gather blackberries same as me.'

'Aye, so I did when I was your age, but blackberries was bigger then than what they are now. They was worth climbing for seventy 'ears ago, I can tell you! But I'm an old man now, Peter,' and 'Lijah looked down on the child's upturned face that was fresh and clear as a flower.

Little Peter walked on a few paces in thoughtful silence. 'But, grandfather, what makes you such an old, old man?' And 'Lijah laughed with delight at the question. Oh, Peter was a rare deep little chap, he'd get to the bottom of everything if he could.

'It's nothing but Anna Dominoes as makes me such a' old, old man, and that's Latin for the 'ear of the Lord. It's Anna Dominoes, that's the matter wi' me, little Peter, and nothin' else,' and the child stored up the mysterious words in his tenacious memory.

Not long afterwards Old 'Lijah, who had grown neighbourly again now that he was happy, went one evening, accompanied by his grandson, to spend an hour with his old friend, Farmer Blewitt. The two old men were seated in armchairs at each side of the table, with a tobacco jar and cider mugs, and a small narrow box before them. Little Peter was lying on the hearth playing with a young spaniel puppy, in whose delightful society he was wholly absorbed, till he heard Farmer Blewitt say: 'Let's have a game o' dominoes, 'Lijah; it's many a day since you and me played together.'

Little Peter sat up.

'I don't mind if I do play a game,' said his grandfather.

Little Peter rose to his feet, pushed the frivolous and seductive puppy aside as being likely to interfere with serious business, and modestly, but firmly, approached the table where the old men were beginning their game. He laid his hand on his grandfather's arm, but he did not feel it at first, so he pressed harder.

'Hallo! little chap, what's up?'

'Don't touch none o' them dominoes, grandfather! Don't touch 'em,' said little Peter urgently.

'Whatever's to do with you, Peter? You're onreasonable!' said 'Lijah, with as near an approach to asperity as was possible towards his little grandson.

But Peter was not to be daunted. 'Grandfather, don't you remember that day when I asked what made you such an old, old man, you said it was Anna Dominoes as did it all? Don't touch 'em, grandfather, don't touch one of 'em!' and Peter's young face was full of anxiety.

Old 'Lijah and Farmer Blewitt laughed till they cried, while 'Lijah told him what he had said to the little chap in the lane about his age; 'for he's that peart, I said Anna Dominoes was the matter wi' me, speaking Latin, and Latin or Greek he'll get to the reason o' things! No, little Peter, these ain't the kind o' dominoes that's made an old, old man o' your grandad; it was the 'ear of the Lord I was speaking on, and when you go to school you'll learn all about un!'

Peter was now an active little slip of seven years of age, never still except when he was sleeping, and not knowing what it was to be tired. He had grown used to his grandfather's increasing infirmities by now, but they irked his restless young body and spirit, and on their walks together, when the old man sat down by the way weary and breathless, little Peter beguiled the time running to and fro as fast as he could, to let off his pent-up energy, after crawling at a snail's pace by old 'Lijah's side.

A few weeks later and little Peter again returned with a child's persistence to the puzzling subject of his grandfather's decaying strength.

'Grandfather, if it isn't the dominoes that does it, do tell me what it is that makes you such an old, old man!'

Old 'Lijah did not laugh at the boy's question now. He felt his life feeble within him, and he did not know what to say in reply that could be intelligible to a child. They were alone in the kitchen, and no sound was heard but the loud ticking of the tall clock, the audible footstep of time. The old man looked into the child's fresh young face as he stood between his knees waiting for an answer, and he smiled feebly, and pressed the firm round cheek with his shaking hand, but he said nothing.

'But what is it, grandfather, that makes you such an old, very old man?'

Then 'Lijah looked up at the tall clock whose loud tick tack penetrated his dull hearing, and it seemed to him as though he had heard it for eighty years, counting out aloud the minutes, hours, days, and years of his whole life.

'It's the ticking of the clock, my little lad, the ticking of the clock, that makes grandfather such an old, old man;' and Peter was satisfied with the reply, and set his young brains to work to find out how he could baffle the evil influences of the clock.

Now the tall case clock was a very big person for a small boy to tackle. He stood six feet without his shoes, with a huge round face behind a pane of glass, and a long front door opening straight into his vitals, and Peter had peeped in on winding-up days, and seen two heavy weights hanging, and the shining brass pendulum swinging to and fro, whose everlasting tick tack had made an old man of his grandfather. Well, never mind, wait till some time when mother was out of the house, and grandfather asleep in the big armchair, as he was nearly all day long now, and little Peter knew what he would do!

Not many days afterwards everything happened as Peter wished, and he looked out of the window to make sure that his mother was at a safe distance at the top of the garden, and there she was, standing with her back to the house, busy pegging clothes on the line, so that no danger need be feared from that quarter. Indoors, too, all was equally favourable to the carrying out of little Peter's deep-laid scheme. Grandfather really was older than ever today. He had not stirred from the big chair since he came down in the morning, and when he was spoken to he said nothing, he only smiled and fell into a doze. He was fast asleep now, and little Peter's heart beat with joy to think what a fine surprise he was preparing for his grandfather. What would the old man think when he felt the stiffness and trembling going out of his legs and back, his eyes growing clear and bright again, and his deafness leaving him? All which would be sure to happen if the clock would only stop ticking.

Grandfather was so fast asleep, with his head leaning forward on his breast, that little Peter was not afraid of waking him. He summoned all his courage to his aid and stepped cautiously up to the great clock, with its menacing tick tack, unlocked its front door, opened it wide, and peeped into the resonant cavern in its inside, with the heavy iron weights hanging and the bright brass pendulum swaying to and fro with its everlasting tick tack, tick tack. Then, without giving himself time to take fright at his own daring, he seized hold of the swinging pendulum and, after a brief struggle, held it in his hand, a silent, motionless thing.

Then little Peter loosed his hold, and glanced over his shoulder at the old man, but he was still quietly sleeping. He cautiously seated himself on a stool at his grandfather's feet, waiting to tell him when he awoke how he had stopped the ticking of the clock that made him such an old, old man.

There his mother found him sitting when she returned from the garden, and neither daughter nor grandson could rouse the old man from the sleep that knows no waking. When the pendulum was set swinging once more, the clock began to tick again as though nothing had happened, and it ticked out the minutes till they grew into years, and little Peter became big Peter, and then he understood what his grandfather had meant.

THE TRAINER'S GHOST
and other stories

The Case of Lady Lukestan

Coeval with the existence of mankind has existed the belief in ghosts. Like other cults, it has had its ups and downs; its periods of exaltation and of persecution.

It has received the sanction of the priesthood and attained the dignity of a special office in the Book of Common Prayer. It has been lashed by the scorn of the materialist, and derided by professors of exact science. Advancing education stripped it to the skeleton as Superstition, and Advanced Thought has reclothed it with the nebulous draperies of Esoteric Philosophy.

The swing of the pendulum and the exertions of the Society for Psychical Research have improved the position of the ghost, but its rights as a citizen have yet to be established. The State recognises it not. Legally, a ghost labours under greater disadvantages than a Catholic before the passing of the Emancipation Bill. It cannot make a will or bring an action at law. It may not, whatever its qualifications during life, celebrate a marriage or give a certificate of death. No judge on the bench would convict on the evidence of a ghost, though, if only subpoenas could be served on the spirit world, many unfortunate souls might be able to escape the gallows and die decently in their beds instead.

Rightly or wrongly, however, the law takes no cognisance of ghosts, and ghosts would seem to be aware of this and occasionally act with the irresponsibility of those who cannot be called to account.

Legally a ghost has no existence. This point was established in the case of 'Lukestan *v.* Lukestan and others'.

The trial, as may be remembered (it was very inadequately reported in the daily papers), involved the succession to the Earldom of Marylebone (1776 G.B.). Mr Baron Collings, before whom the case was tried, ruled there was no evidence of a legal marriage between the late Lord Lukestan and Miss Pamela Ardilaun, that the entry of the said marriage in the parish register was a forgery, and he directed the jury to give their verdict for the defendants, with costs.

I do not pretend to criticise the learned judge's attitude in the matter, though it was apparent from the first that his 'summing-up' was dead against the plaintiff. I merely place before such of the public as may be interested therein the exact facts of one of the most singular cases ever heard in a court of law, and the public, which is always intelligent (is not *vox populi, vox Dei* an all but universally accepted axiom today?), may judge for itself whether Lady Lukestan, otherwise known as Miss Ardilaun, was entitled to the sympathy due to a deeply injured woman, or the contumely which is justly heaped on the head of an unsuccessful adventuress.

Morally, Miss Ardilaun was not entirely innocent. She undoubtedly played with the feelings of a nervous and hyper-sensitive man. Other women have done the same without any very serious result. The mistake in Miss Ardilaun's case was that she did not take the trouble to study the mechanism of her plaything. The truth is, that years of over-work, enforced solitude, and rigorous self-repression had reduced the Rev. Cyprian Martyn to a condition of mind closely bordering on insanity, and in this condition he construed an ordinary flirtation into a cardinal sin.

He believed that in falling in love with Miss Ardilaun and acquainting her with the fact, he had broken his faith with God and man, and incurred the curse pronounced on those who, 'having put their hand to the plough, turn back'.

In a moment of delirium he told the girl that his choice lay between the Creator and the creature – between Good and evil – and that he had deliberately, and with his eyes open, chosen the latter; that he was prepared to risk all penalties here and pains hereafter for the gratification of his passion; and as he had proved himself unworthy of the high office of the priesthood, he would resign his cure, marry her, and claim the privileges he had purchased at the price of his very soul.

It is at all times dangerous to disclose the inmost workings of the heart to a woman, who rarely comprehends, and can never realise, the length, breadth, and depth of a man's passion, and this mad avowal was the seal of Cyprian Martyn's fate.

Miss Ardilaun probably resented the position assigned her by the terms of her lover's choice. She certainly thought him insane, and the event proved her to be absolutely correct. She very curtly stated that at no period of their very informal acquaintance had she reckoned on him as a factor in her future life. She had tolerated his attentions solely because she was bored to distraction in the rural solitude periodically insisted on by her aristocratic and tyrannical invalid aunt; and as to her marriage, the only part he could possibly take in the ceremony would be that of marrying her to another man, for she should never dream for a moment of marrying him. With this rather cruel speech, Miss Ardilaun would have parted from her clerical admirer, but before she could realise his intention, Martyn had caught her in his arms and kissed her passionately full on the mouth. 'You have ruined me body and soul,' he said, when at last he released her; 'but remember, I *shall* marry you, if not to myself, then to another man. Living or dying I will have my revenge.'

This was his farewell. A week later he was found dead in his study, with an empty bottle, which had contained morphia, lying on the table at his side.

That the unhappy man had deliberately taken his own life was beyond a doubt. All his affairs had been set in order, his liabilities paid, and his correspondence and diaries destroyed. He had written to his brother and only near surviving relative, requesting him to receive such goods as he might die possessed of, and begging him to carry out certain directions as to the disposal of his body.

The letter, which was produced at the inquest, also referred to some unpardonable sin committed by the writer, which rendered him unfit for prolonged existence. As the dead man had borne the most exemplary character, and was universally respected, this allusion was generally regarded as a symptom of mental derangement.

The local practitioner stated in evidence that the deceased had consulted him professionally before starting on his annual holiday. He was then in a very low, nervous state, and complained of depression and insomnia. He (the medical man) attributed his condition to overwork and insufficient nourishment. Mr Martyn was a strict Anglican, and held extreme views on matters of self-discipline. Hallucination as to the commission of some unpardonable sin was a common and painful feature in cases of religious mania, from which, in his (Dr Garrod's) opinion, the deceased was undoubtedly suffering at the time of his death.

The jury brought in a verdict of 'Suicide whilst of unsound mind', and the unfortunate man was buried in the shadow of the village church which for ten dreary years had been the scene of his ministrations.

All this happened in the autumn of 1886. During the following winter I made the acquaintance of Miss Ardilaun at a crowded 'At Home' given by the wife of a legal luminary of the first magnitude.

She was kind enough to give me a dance, and inquired if I knew many people. I confessed I was practically a stranger, brought by my cousin and particular chum, Charley Roskill, who as a dancing man and a rising 'junior' was a *persona gratissama* with his hostess.

I think it was then Miss Ardilaun owned to being tired and suggested that, as the rooms were hot and overcrowded (which was certainly true), we should find a seat outside, and she selected one immediately opposite the stairs.

Our conversation turned chiefly on Roskill, in whom my companion appeared to take more than a little interest. She said Sir Charles had spoken of him as an Attorney-General of the future, and she asked what struck me as rather a singular question.

'Is he,' she said, 'the sort of man to whom you would advise a woman to go if she were in urgent need of assistance and advice?'

I replied, I was convinced that Roskill, like myself, would at any time be ready to place his entire professional resources at Miss Ardilaun's service, and that he was undoubtedly clever.

She laughed a little. 'I wasn't sure,' she said; 'but you ought to know.'

Then she went away on the arm of a young man, who had arrived to claim his partner.

It was Lord Lukestan. I saw them several times in the course of the evening, always sitting out in sheltered corners, and engaged in earnest conversation. Lukestan was a good-looking boy, a year or two Miss Ardilaun's junior, and it struck me that she accepted his manifest admiration in a serious manner, which indicated that she meant business.

I mentioned this to Roskill as we walked home together, and he laughed the suggestion to scorn. Lukestan's people would never permit such a match. It was well known that old Lord Marylebone destined his nephew for his cousin, Lady Adeliza Skelton. It was quite possible that the boy himself might prefer Miss Ardilaun as a bride-elect, but he could not afford to run counter to his uncle's wishes. He was dependent on his prospects as Lord Marylebone's heir, and more than half the property was unentailed.

'Besides,' he concluded, 'the girl hasn't a penny. She is virtually the companion and white slave of her aunt, old Lady Catermaran. Take my word, it's only a common or garden flirtation, and it won't last long at that.'

Roskill speaks with authority on social matters, and I let the subject drop, but somehow I wasn't convinced.

People talked a good deal about Miss Ardilaun that winter, but with the new season interest in her seemed to die down. She was seldom seen, and I heard, through Roskill, that she was devoting herself entirely to her aunt, who had become a confirmed invalid, and went nowhere. It seemed a dreary life for a young and beautiful woman, and I wondered whether Lord Lukestan's engagement to his cousin, which had been formally announced in all the Society papers, had anything to do with the girl's sudden retirement from the world.

In June Lord Marylebone died. For the past six months he had been hovering on the brink of the grave, and no-one had expected him to last so long. He was, from all accounts, a very disagreeable old gentleman, and I should doubt if any of his relatives, even including his only daughter, much regretted his removal to another sphere.

Lukestan attended the funeral as chief mourner, and was present at the subsequent reading of the will. There were a few legacies to servants and dependents, and a suitable provision for Lady Adeliza. The bulk of the property went with the title.

Lukestan was now Lord Marylebone, and a free agent, but the dead man's shoes, for which he had waited, were destined to be fitted on a dead man. He left Marylebone Castle for town on the evening of the funeral, an evening made memorable by the occurrence of the worst railway disaster of recent years. The night mail from the North collided with a goods train a little beyond Settringham Junction, and while the confusion and dismay, incidental to such a misfortune, were at their height, the Lowton and Wolds express dashed into the rear of the wrecked passenger train, and completed a scene of horror rarely equalled in the annals of modern travel.

The daily papers chronicled in full the ghastly details of the catastrophe. The boiler of the express engine burst within a few minutes of the second collision, and steam and fire alike wreaked their fury on the unhappy passengers imprisoned in the overturned carriages. First on the long list of victims published by the evening press, was the name of Lord Lukestan.

The compartment which had been reserved for his use was reduced to matchwood, and it was only after immense exertions on the part of the officials that the bodies of the young man and his valet could be removed from the mass of smoking *débris*.

'Poor fellow!' said Roskill, as he put down the paper. 'His luck has come too late. I wonder' – he paused to light his cigarette over the lamp – 'how Miss Ardilaun will take it?'

We had dined early, preparatory to looking in at the Frivolity, but somehow the smash on the Great Northern had taken the edge off our interest in the new burlesque. Roskill's acquaintance with Lukestan had been of the slightest; to me he was hardly more than a name, but the tragic circumstances attending his death evoked a sympathy that was almost personal.

'I wonder,' Charley repeated, meditatively, 'how Miss Ardilaun will take it?'

The words were barely past his lips when the servant appeared with a message.

'Lady to see you, sir. She wouldn't give her name, but I was to say her business was most urgent.'

She must have followed close on Stevens's heels, for before he had finished speaking she was in the room. A tall, slender woman, wrapped from head to foot in a long cloak of softly rustling silk. She wore a thick veil, but even under this disguise I was struck by something familiar in her gait and carriage.

The moment the door had closed upon the retreating man, she lifted the thick folds of black gauze. It was Miss Ardilaun. Her eyes were red with weeping, and her face as white as a sheet.

'I hope you will forgive me for disturbing you at this hour,' she said, going straight to Charley, 'but I knew you lived in chambers, and I wanted to find you at home. I am in great trouble, Mr Roskill, dreadful trouble, and I must have advice without delay. I thought – I felt sure you would help me.'

If Roskill was surprised (and I think he was) he did not show it. He said simply, 'I shall be very glad to give you any assistance in my power, Miss Ardilaun,' and looked at me.

She followed the direction of his eyes, and became aware, for the first time, of the presence of a third person. I intimated my readiness to withdraw, but she cut me short.

'Please don't go, Mr Bryant. I am not sure that I don't require a solicitor's rather than counsel's opinion – at present. In any case you may as well hear my story – if you do not mind.'

I was only too glad of the opportunity, for I own my curiosity was a good deal excited. We sat down and waited.

Miss Ardilaun's manner was that of a woman who has nerved herself to go through anything. She was unnaturally, almost horribly, calm. She began without any hesitation, speaking in a dry, metallic tone, which was devoid of the least trace of emotion.

'You have seen in the papers that Lord Lukestan was killed last night in the railway accident? I had better tell you at once that he was my husband. We were married last January. There were strong reasons for keeping the marriage secret. Lord Lukestan was entirely dependent on his uncle, who had other views for him, and he dare not risk the consequences of openly disregarding those wishes. At that time Lord Marylebone was not expected to live more than a few weeks, and *he* (Arthur) felt sure that a private marriage would be the easiest way of extricating ourselves from the many family difficulties which surrounded us. We never anticipated the necessity for secrecy lasting so long. Of course Lord Marylebone's partial recovery placed us in a most painful position, but we knew it could only be temporary, and we resolved to chance it and wait. That was why Lord Lukestan's engagement to his cousin was formally announced. What would have happened if the old earl had insisted on their immediate marriage I don't know; fortunately, or unfortunately, he did not make a point of that, and when circumstances rendered it necessary that our marriage should be acknowledged, Lord Marylebone died. I cannot tell you how rejoiced I was to receive the news, and only last night I went down on my knees and thanked God for this.'

She drew a telegram from her pocket and laid it on the table before us. The message had been handed in at Marfleet, the post town for Marylebone Castle, and ran –

THANK HEAVEN, ALL RIGHT AT LAST, AM LEAVING BY NIGHT MAIL. SHALL BE WITH YOU ELEVEN TOMORROW. WILL SEE CRAIKE ON WAY.
ARTHUR

'I thought my prayers had been answered,' she went on, in the same low, even voice, 'that my troubles were over; but you see I was premature in my thanksgivings. Today I am in the most horrible position in which any woman could be placed – a widow who has never been acknowledged as a wife. I have neither father nor mother. My aunt has never desired my confidence; she has always regarded me in the light of an unpaid servant, and even if I wished to do so, I could not consult her now, for the doctors inform me that in her present state of health any sudden shock might prove fatal. I have no other relations, no-one to whom I can turn for help. I *must* make my marriage public. What am I to do?'

The first step was manifestly to procure the necessary proofs of the marriage. We said so and inquired whether she was provided with a copy of the certificate.

She replied she was quite certain that no such document had been given or demanded.

'I know nothing about the preliminary arrangements,' she said, 'I left them entirely to Lord Lukestan. I cannot even tell you the name of the village where we were married, though I should be able to find my way there. It is a tiny place, quite out of the world, about ten miles from Garstang Junction. Parker, Lord Lukestan's confidential servant, met us there with a cart and we drove straight to the church. It stands above the village on the top of a hill. We were married by the vicar. I know his name – it is Martyn.'

I referred to Crockford, and presently found 'Martyn, Lucian John, Vicar of Slumber-le-Wold, Yorkshire.'

'That is the man, I suppose. Was he a personal friend of your husband's?'

'He was a stranger to both of us,' she replied, emphatically.

I undertook to obtain a copy of the certificate and wrote the same night to the Rev. Lucian Martyn. To my utter dismay I received in reply a courteous note regretting his inability to comply with my request, as the marriage to which I referred had never been solemnised.

Mr Martyn's letter reached me by the first post. Two hours later I presented myself at No. 20, Berkeley Square, asked for Miss Ardilaun and was shown into the library. In a few minutes she joined me, and I broke the news as gently as I could.

She seemed utterly overcome. 'It is impossible,' she repeated; 'he cannot deny it. Beside, there are our signatures in the register. Surely he can be made to produce that.'

'You are certain that Martyn is the right man?' I asked. 'You could swear to his signing the register in that name?'

'No,' she replied. 'I never saw his signature. I wrote my own name and I saw Arthur write his. Then Parker witnessed our signatures. Mr Martyn followed, but I did not see what he had written.'

'You must excuse my asking questions, Lady Lukestan, where they are necessary. You mentioned that the clergyman who married you was a stranger to both you and your husband. How do you know that he was Mr Martyn?'

She hesitated. 'I knew him from his likeness to his brother.'

'You are acquainted with his brother, then?'

'I was. The subject is very painful to me. Mr Cyprian Martyn is dead. I believe he committed suicide, but our – our friendship had entirely ceased before that took place. I never corresponded with him, and our people were not aware of our acquaintance. It was merely an affair of a few weeks, and terminated very abruptly.'

'And the likeness between the brothers was so striking that you recognised Mr Lucian Martyn immediately.'

'The likeness was more than striking, it was – horrible' – she shivered – 'if they were both living I should not have known them apart. I was aware that Cyprian Martyn had a brother, who was vicar of a remote parish in Yorkshire, but until the last moment I did not know that he was to marry us. If I had heard the name sooner, I should have used every means in my power to prevent it.'

'You are prepared to affirm on oath that your marriage was solemnised by Mr Martyn in due form, and recorded in the parish register?'

She looked surprised at my question. 'Certainly I am. You surely do not doubt my word?'

'Not at all, but this is a very serious matter. Will you now tell me every detail connected with the ceremony?'

'As I said, I know nothing of the preliminary arrangements. During the third week in January, Lord Lukestan and I were both staying at Chilworth Priory. My aunt was also to have been of the party, but a severe cold detained her in town. Lady Chilworth has great influence with Aunt Maria, and persuaded her to let me go to Yorkshire without her; I was to take part in some theatricals, and my place could not be supplied at the last moment. It was the opportunity for which we had been waiting, and we decided not to let it slip. Lord Lukestan's plans were complete. He showed me a special licence, and he said Parker knew a village where we could be married, and that all the necessary steps had been taken. We left Chilworth on the morning of the 23rd of January. I had previously wired home that the heavy snow would delay my return twenty-four hours. Lady Chilworth was going abroad almost immediately, and as I write all my aunt's letters I was not afraid of the deception being discovered. We left the train at Garstang, where Parker was waiting with a hired trap, and we drove to this church. There was no-one about. The clergyman was waiting for us at the chancel step. He began the service at once. Parker gave me away, and we afterwards signed our names in the vestry. We drove back to the station and caught the next train to Doncaster. I returned to town the following day.'

'Was there any conversation between Mr Martyn and yourselves?'

'None; he did not speak to either of us. Lord Lukestan put the fee on the vestry table. It was a ten-pound note, and he remarked afterwards, that the vicar might have wished us luck. There was no luck for us, I suppose,' she concluded bitterly.

I was a good deal puzzled by this sudden check. However, I said what I could to comfort her, and suggested that the clerk could be produced as a witness.

'There was no clerk,' she replied, 'there was no-one in church, but the clergyman, Parker, and ourselves.'

From Berkeley Square I hurried to the Temple, found Roskill, and decided with him that I should go up to Slumber-le-Wold, see Martyn, and examine the register.

I found the vicar at home, and acquainted him with my errand. He received me civilly, and in reply to my questions informed me that I was quite at liberty to inspect the register, but it was not possible that I could find any entry of the marriage.

'Since I received your letter,' he said, 'I have referred to my diary, and I will gladly give you all the information in my power. I find that on the 20th of January I received intimation of an intended wedding. The note, which was brought by a man who looked like a superior servant, had neither address nor date, and was signed Arthur Evelyn Lukestan. I am quite ignorant of the various titles of our aristocracy, and was not aware of the existence of such a person as Lord Lukestan. I was informed the marriage would be by licence, and that, owing to certain circumstances, which could be explained to me, if needful, before the ceremony, it was to be of a strictly private character. I ascertained that the contracting parties were of age, and fixed the time for one o'clock on the 23rd. Early that morning I was called to the sickbed of a distant parishioner. As I had been advised that the wedding was to be as private as possible, I did not inform the clerk that his services would be required. I intended to do so on my return from Bretwell. Unfortunately I met with an accident. My horse set its foot on a stone, stumbled, and threw me heavily. I lay for some time unconscious, and when I came to myself I found my ankle so severely sprained that I was unable to move. The road is a lonely one, and it was at least two hours before I could obtain assistance. I reached home at three o'clock, and immediately sent to the church. There was no-one there. I afterwards ascertained that a lady and two men, strangers, had passed through the village in the direction of the church, and had returned after the lapse of half an hour. I waited in daily expectation of hearing of or from them, but no news came, and as I did not know Lord, or as I thought, Mr Lukestan's, address, I was unable to communicate with him. I ought to mention that an open envelope containing a ten-pound note was found on the vestry table. I kept it for three months, anticipating some explanation from the donor, then, as none came, I concluded the money was intended for an offering, and devoted it to the relief of the poor.'

I inquired if it were possible that in his absence any other clergyman could have been pressed into the service.

'Quite impossible,' he replied. 'If any priest could be found willing to commit such a breach of etiquette, he would certainly have informed me of it afterwards; and, in any case, the clerk would have been called.'

I said I should like to see the register, and Mr Martyn led the way to the church.

It stood, as Miss Ardilaun had said, on an eminence at some distance from the village, and was separated from the vicarage by the entire length of the garden and churchyard.

'Is this door always open?' I inquired, as we entered the south porch.

'Between matins and evensong the church is open for private prayer, though,' with a sigh, 'my parishioners do not often avail themselves of the privilege.'

We went up to the vestry. It was furnished with a table, two chairs, a hanging cupboard, and a massive, iron-bound chest of black oak.

The vicar took a bunch of keys from his pocket, selected one of peculiar shape, unlocked the chest, and produced the register.

'We have not many marriages here,' he said. 'I have only solemnised two in the last six months. The last was in April.'

He turned to the place. There were two entries at the top of the page. The final date on the preceding leaf was for the 30th of December.

I made a minute examination of the pages. Then I glanced keenly at my companion.

'Mr Martyn,' I said, 'these two leaves are stuck together.'

'Impossible!' he answered.

'Feel them,' I rejoined. 'This page is thicker than the rest, and the edges are not quite even at the bottom.'

He scrutinised the book, testing the substance of the paper between his thumb and forefinger.

'You are quite right,' he said, quietly; 'though I should never have noticed it. Have you a knife?'

I opened my penknife and very carefully inserted the thinnest blade.

How the leaves had been secured, it was impossible to say. There was not the slightest trace of mucillage on the edges of the paper, and the incision once made, they parted easily.

At the top of the left-hand page was the entry of a marriage between Arthur Evelyn Lukestan, bachelor, and Pamela Mary Ardilaun, spinster. The witness was William John Parker.

'My God!'

The exclamation came from the vicar. His eyes were fixed on the register and his face was white to the very lips.

'What is it?' I asked, in surprise.

He pointed speechlessly to the fourth signature. It was written in a firm, very uncommon hand, 'Cyprian George Martyn'.

'That is not your name, Mr Martyn?'

He faced me suddenly. 'It is not,' he answered. 'It is that of my brother Cyprian, who died last October.'

I confess I felt horribly taken aback. Miss Ardilaun's admission that she had been acquainted with the younger Martyn, taken in connection with the other peculiar circumstances attending her marriage, gave rise in my mind to a most uncomfortable suspicion.

I regarded my client with the sincerest admiration and sympathy. I was anxious to prove the validity of her claims and the truth of her statements, but I could not blind myself to the fact of her position being desperate, and I knew that a desperate woman is frequently unscrupulous.

For a few seconds we remained silent, each, I believe, suspecting the other's complicity in what was evidently a deep-laid plot. Then I pulled myself together. 'You say that is your brother's name, Mr Martyn – is it also his handwriting?'

'It is like it, very like it, but it can only be a forgery, since, as I told you, my brother is dead.'

I examined the entry carefully.

'The particulars are filled in by the same hand, and it would not, I imagine, be an easy one to imitate. Had you seen this signature during your brother's lifetime, should you have had any doubts as to its being genuine?'

'If he were living, none.'

'I should like to compare it with an authenticated specimen of his writing, if you have one by you. I need not apologise for the trouble I am giving you, since you will understand that this is, to my client, a matter of life and death, or rather of what is more important than either, to a woman of honour.'

'I understand that, and you will have any assistance I can render, but –'

He broke off abruptly, and proceeded to re-lock the chest.

'We will carry the register up to the house. I have some of my brother's letters there, which will serve your purpose.'

'Is the register usually kept here?'

'Always.'

'And the key, have you more than one? I see it is of a very uncommon pattern.'

'So far as I know, there has never been a duplicate.'

'And it has not, to your knowledge, left your possession?'

'I am sure it has not. I carry it constantly about my person.'

'Had you those keys with you on the 23rd of January?'

'Yes, I am certain of it.'

'How, then, was it possible for anyone to get at the register?'

'I cannot tell. It would appear impossible, were it not for that extraordinary entry.'

'It would be impossible to tamper with that lock,' I said, pointing to the coffer.

'I should have thought so.'

We retraced our steps, the vicar carrying the register, which he placed on the table in his study. He then produced a bundle of letters, selected two or three, which he glanced through and handed to me. We compared the signatures with that in the register. They were identical. If a forgery, it was the work of an expert. No amateur could have counterfeited so perfectly those singular characters.

'Your brother's handwriting bears very little resemblance to yours,' I remarked. 'Were you much alike in person?'

'There was a family likeness, not, I think, very strong; but you can judge for yourself. This is my brother's photograph.'

He pointed to a massive silver frame which occupied the centre of the mantelpiece. I went over and studied the portrait. It was a large, three-quarter, platina-type of a tall, handsome man, apparently several years younger than the vicar of Slumber-le-Wold. There was, as he had said, a family likeness between the two faces, but it was not remarkable, and no-one could for a moment have mistaken one for the other.

I returned to town, sorely perplexed, drove straight to the Temple, where I had wired, requesting Roskill and, if possible, Miss Ardilaun, to wait for me, and told my story.

Charley was furious. He made some very intemperate and highly absurd charges against the clergy in general, and Mr Martyn in particular, and declared himself as firmly convinced of Lady Lukestan's good faith as he was of his own.

I ventured to suggest that in this case his convictions were of less moment than those of the judge and jury, and I doubted if any judge would share the opinion he had so confidently expressed. For my part, I could see only three possible solutions of the mystery.

(1) That Martyn, who was the only person having access to the register, had, for some private motive, tried to suppress the fact of the marriage, in which case the history of his accident and absence on the 23rd of January was an invention, and could easily be disproved. (2) That Lord Lukestan, finding the vicar absent, had obtained the services either of another clergyman or someone personating the same, and had gone through the marriage ceremony, by way of satisfying Miss Ardilaun's scruples. (3) That the story of the marriage was an entire fabrication, the last resource of a despairing woman, in which case it was impossible to account for the entry in the register.

At this juncture Lady Lukestan was announced. She was dressed in deep, but not widow's, mourning, which became her admirably. She was certainly a very beautiful woman, and, looking into her clear blue eyes, it seemed impossible to doubt her integrity.

I questioned her closely as to her previous statements, but she never swerved a hair's breadth from her original story.

I had brought with me a photograph of Mr Lucian Martyn, and one of his brother. She looked at the former, and failed to recognise it, though she thought there was something familiar in the expression. I then handed her the portrait of Cyprian Martyn. She gave an involuntary shudder.

'That is the man who married us,' she said, and laid the photograph, face downwards, on the table.

'Are you quite sure,' I urged, 'that you are not making a mistake? The first portrait is that of the present vicar of Slumber-le-Wold, the other that of his brother, who, as you know, is dead.'

I shall never forget her expression at that moment, the mingled horror, fear, and repulsion written on her colourless face.

'Then it *was* he!' she cried. 'I knew it. My God! how horrible!'

She made an uncertain step forward, stretching out both hands towards Roskill, with the sudden uncontrollable impulse of blind terror, and slid helplessly to the ground in a dead faint.

I felt certain then of what I had suspected from the beginning, viz., that Miss Ardilaun knew more of the mystery than she had chosen to confess, and I considered she was treating us unfairly, for a lawyer cannot, any more than a physician, advise on an incomplete diagnosis. She had voluntarily placed herself in our hands, and she ought to have taken us unreservedly into her confidence.

I found an opportunity of expressing these sentiments to Roskill before he escorted her home, and advised him to try to get at the truth. She might speak freely to him. I was sure she had not done so to me.

The more I thought over the bearings of the case, the more I questioned the expediency of taking it into court. The whole weight of evidence told against the plaintiff. She could not produce a single witness to corroborate her story.

That Lukestan intended to marry her there was no reasonable doubt; but the sole proof of the ceremony having taken place was an entry in the parish register, which was manifestly a forgery.

The only witness whose evidence would have carried any weight, the valet Parker, was dead. It was the bare word of a woman, and a woman in desperate straits, against the reason and common sense of the whole world.

In my opinion, Miss Ardilaun's wisest course would be to keep quiet. Lady Catermaran was now lying in a state of semi-consciousness, and her decease could only be a question of days. Presumably she would have made some provision for her niece, and at her demise Miss Ardilaun would be her own mistress. She might retire somewhere abroad, and her unhappy story need never be given to the world.

But to drag the case into court seemed to be absolutely courting publicity and shame. She might consider herself Lukestan's wife, but, in the eyes of the law and of society, she was simply his mistress, and her child would be declared illegitimate.

And then there remained the question, *had* she really believed herself legally married, or was her story only a last desperate expedient to avert the consequences of a fatal error?

The doubts in Miss Ardilaun's sincerity, which her presence invariably tended to dispel, had an awkward way of returning very forcibly when the magnetism of her personal influence was removed.

Late in the afternoon Roskill returned. I saw at once that he had something to tell me. He threw his hat and gloves on the table, and began to pace restlessly up and down the room.

'It is the most extraordinary case that ever has or will be heard,' he said.

'She has told you everything?'

'Yes.'

'Did the marriage ever take place, then?'

He looked at me murderously.

'You heard her say so, that ought to be proof enough for you.'

It wasn't, but I did not attempt to argue the point. I inquired who had performed the ceremony.

'The man whose name you saw in the register, Cyprian Martyn.'

'But he's been dead for the last nine months,' I objected. 'How could he reappear in the flesh to solemnise a marriage?'

'I don't know,' he answered, 'how the devil works, or by what laws he is bound. There are some things which cannot be explained. That brute – well, the man is dead, and I won't abuse him, though, living and dead, he's behaved like a brute – got acquainted with Pam – Miss Ardilaum, fell in love with her, and wanted to marry her. She refused him, whereupon he conducted himself in a manner for which his only excuse could be that he was insane at the time. He told her that she had ruined him body and soul, that he meant to have his revenge, and if ever she married, he should marry her, if not himself, then to another man. Then he went back to his parish, somewhere in Dorsetshire, and committed suicide.'

'Well,' I said, 'what has that to do with the Lukestan marriage?'

'Everything – the man kept his word. He did marry her to Lukestan. The poor girl had a secret terror all the time that he had done so, but the thing seemed so incredible that she fought it down and hoped against hope, until it was impossible to doubt any longer.'

I sat and stared at him blankly. He was absolutely serious.

'Do you really expect me to believe,' I said at last, 'that a man who has been dead for nine months could rise from his grave, assume bodily form and material clothing, go through a form of prayer, extract a register from a locked chest, make that entry and disappear again into the limbo of the unknown?'

'I don't expect anything. I tell you facts.'

'Good Heavens, Charley, you must be mad! You can't believe such a monstrous story!'

'I believe it entirely. It is the only rational explanation of that entry.'

'*Rational!*' I echoed, contemptuously.

'Yes, rational; for what do we know of the powers and limitations of what we are pleased to call spirits? Nothing. On the other hand, is it reasonable to suppose that three people could obtain access, without a key and without damaging the lock, to a secured chest, abstract the register, the whereabouts of which they were entirely ignorant, and make an entry in the name and handwriting of a dead man – a piece of penmanship, moreover, unrivalled in the annals of forgery? Surely the latter theory is as great a strain on your credulity as the former.'

'Take it into court and see what they say to it there.'

'I intend to do so,' he answered, quietly.

'No solicitor will undertake the case.'

'If you mean that you won't, I shall find someone who will, though I would much rather receive instructions from you than from a stranger.'

Then I gave tongue. For two hours I used every argument in my power. I stormed, I persuaded; I believe I threatened, but he remained quite unmoved.

'It isn't the least use, Jack,' he said, when at last I stopped, exhausted. 'Legally and morally Pamela is Lukestan's widow, and I mean to fight to the last gasp for her rights. If we succeed, so much the better for her and her child. If we fail, well, we shall have done our best to vindicate truth and justice. In either case, I may as well tell you I intend to make her my wife. Her aunt is not expected to live through the night. She will be alone in the world then, and I shall marry her as soon as I decently can. I believe she has cared for me from the first,' he added, softly, with the sublime and overweening credulity of a man who loves.

I doubted it, but what was the use of saying so. Roskill's will has all through our joint lives dominated that of his weaker brother; and when a few days later I heard from Miss Ardilaun's lips the particulars of her extraordinary story, I succumbed to that personal influence which would subdue any man save an incorruptible and unprejudiced judge.

The long and the short of it was that Roskill had his way, and in process of time the case of 'Lukestan *v.* Lukestan and others' came on for hearing. Miss Ardilaun's appearance created a profound sensation in court. She told her story simply and directly, and the most severe cross-examination failed to shake her in the smallest detail.

The fact of Lukestan's having taken out a special licence, together with his letters (produced), proved he had desired to be, and believed he was, legally married. The evidence of the stationmaster at Garstang, of the innkeeper from whom the trap was hired, of the villagers who saw the party pass through Slumber-le-Wold, all confirmed their progress to the very door of the church, but there stretched a gulf which no human witness could bridge.

The personality of the officiating priest, the authorship of the entry in the register, alike remained an inexplicable mystery.

It was admitted on all hands that Roskill's speech was a model of forensic rhetoric. He surpassed the utmost expectations of those who had prophesied for him a brilliant future, and placed himself at once in the front rank of the Junior Bar. But no argument, however powerful, could have convinced a dozen hard-headed practical Englishmen of the possible existence of ghosts. They were called upon to decide whether Cyprian Martyn, being dead, had resumed his fleshly habit to solemnise a marriage which consigned the woman who had rejected him to shame and obloquy, or whether, on the other hand, Pamela Ardilaun had, with the late Lord Lukestan and Parker, the valet, fraudulently obtained access to the parish register and therein forged the entry of a fictitious marriage – and the twelve good men and true unhesitatingly decided against the ghost.

Judgement was given for the defendant, with costs, and Pamela Ardilaun left the court a ruined woman. The slender fortune left her by her aunt was more than swallowed up by the expenses of the trial. Her fair fame was blasted, she was branded before the world as an impostor and an adventuress. Verily, if her story were true, Cyprian Martyn had taken a complete revenge.

Yet the woman was not left utterly desolate. Through all stress of weather Roskill's love stood firm. He absolutely refused to be dismissed. He assumed the management of her affairs, provided her with a home, and procured the first medical advice when, broken down with anxiety and despair, her life hung trembling in the balance. He followed to the grave the hapless infant, who lived just long enough to receive its father's baptismal names of Arthur Evelyn, and, finally, in spite of her repeated refusals to burden him with her wrecked life, made her his wife.

A year after Lukestan's tragic death the two were married before the Registrar. Nothing would have induced either to risk a repetition of the horrors of that other wedding, and as the law takes no cognisance of ghosts, Cyprian Martyn's uneasy spirit was unable to interfere in the civil ceremony which made Miss Ardilaun Charley Roskill's wife.

The Trainer's Ghost

The Cat and Compass was shut in for the night. The front of the house was dark and silent, for it was long past closing time, but from one of the rear ground-floor windows a thin shaft of yellow light gleamed through the falling rain, and indicated that behind the shutters of the snug bar-parlour, in a cheerful atmosphere of tobacco smoke and the odorous steam of hot 'Scotch' Mr Samuel Vicary, licensed victualler, and two other congenial spirits, were 'making a night of it'.

'It's too late for Downey now,' the landlord remarked, with a glance at the clock, as he leaned forward to knock out his pipe on the hob. 'Twenty past twelve, and raining like blazes. Damn the weather; if it holds on like this, The Ghoul will have his work cut out to get round the old course on Thursday with 8 stone 9.'

'Not with that lot behind him,' rejoined a seedy individual who sat on the farther side of the table. 'I've watched them pretty carefully. The race lies between us and the favourite, and with Downey up, she's safe enough. It's real jam this time – eh, Mr Davis?'

The gentleman indicated drained his glass with an unctuous smile. His exterior suggested the prosperous undertaker. As a matter of fact he was a bookmaker in a big way of business, and suspected, moreover, of having considerable interest in a stable notorious for the in and out running of its horses.

'That's about the size of it,' he answered, drawing in his thick lips with a gentle, sucking sound, expressive of inward satisfaction.

'Prime whisky this, Vicary! I'll take another tot. Yes, it is a big thing, and, after this, Davis, Smiles, and Co. must lie quiet for a bit. There'll be plenty of fools to cry over burnt fingers by Monday, and what with stewards meddling where they've no cause to interfere, and the press writing up a lot of rot about "rings" and such like, and the Jockey Club holding inquiries, a man must mind his P's and Q's in these days. Racing is going to the dogs, and soon there'll be no making a decent living on the turf. How it does rain to be sure! I shouldn't care to find myself abroad tonight.'

'Here's some poor devil as has got to face it,' said the tout, as the sound of horse-hoofs echoed down the quiet road. 'Ain't he coming a lick, too! He's not afraid of busting his cattle.'

'Small blame to him either in weather like this,' grunted the landlord, removing his pipe to listen. 'Why, that's Downey's hack. I'd swear to her gallop among a thousand. To think, now, of his turning up at this time of night!'

The clatter of hoofs ceased, and the men sprang to their feet. In the silence that followed they heard the muffled slam of a closing gate, and the clink of shoes on the stones of the yard outside. Vicary snatched up the lamp and hurried to the door, while the visitors looked at each other.

' 'Tis Downey sure enough,' said the bookmaker, spitting energetically into the fire. 'Now, what brings him here so late? He hasn't pelted over from Hawkhurst in the teeth of this storm for the pleasure of our company, I'll go bail.'

The newcomer had swung himself off his horse before the landlord could unfasten the door.

'Yes, it's me – Downey,' was his answer to that worthy's cautious challenge. 'Look sharp with that chain and let me get under cover. I'm stiff with the cold, I can tell you, and the mare is about beat.'

The chain fell with a clank, and Vicary flung back the door.

'Come in, come in,' he cried, holding the lamp above his head to get a better view of his visitor.

'Lord! how it do rain! Get out of that coat and put a tot of whisky inside you, while I see to the mare. 'Tis all right,' he added, as the other jerked his head interrogatively in the direction of the bar-parlour, 'there's only me and Slimmy and Davis. Go right in and help yourself.'

Thus assured, the fresh arrival went forward, the water dripping from his soaked hat and covert coat, and trickling in little black streams over the well-stoned passage; while Vicary, flinging a rug across his shoulders, led the tired horse round to the stables.

When he returned to the parlour Downey was drying himself before the fire, a smoking tumbler in his hand, and a good cigar between his lips.

'Well?' inquired the landlord, setting down the lamp with a keen glance at the disturbed countenances of the three men. 'I take it, you did not come through this rain for nothing. Is aught the matter?'

'Matter enough,' ejaculated Slimmy. 'Here's Coulson got a rod in pickle that is going to upset our pot.'

Vicary laughed. 'Go on with you,' he said derisively, 'they've nothing at Malton as can collar The Ghoul.'

'Don't you be so precious sharp,' the tout retorted. 'Wait till you hear what Downey's got to say.'

The jockey shifted his cigar to the other side of his mouth. 'It is this way,' he began. 'One of Coulson's lads was at our place this afternoon, and he let on to me in confidence that they have a colt over there they think a real good thing for the Ebor. It is entered in Berkeley's name – the Captain, him as sold the Malton place to Coulson.'

'The Captain's been stony broke this three year,' put in Vicary. 'How did he come by the colt?'

'Picked him up in the dales, from what I gather (he'd always a rare eye for a horse had the Captain), and fancied him so that he got young Alick to take half-share, and lend the purchase-money into the bargain, I reckon. The Coulsons always thought a lot of the old family. It wouldn't be the first time one of them had helped a Berkeley out of a tight place.'

'That's true,' assented the landlord. 'Markham told me old Alick held enough of the squire's paper to cover a room. There wasn't anything he'd have stuck at to keep him on his legs. I remember him saying once in that very bar there, "I'd come from hell," he says, "to stand by one of the old stock." Fifteen years ago this very day it was, just before the Ebor, and the last time I ever saw the old chap alive, for Blue Ruin kicked the life out of him in his box at Malton on the morning of the race. Nothing would serve the squire but the horse must be shot the same night. Lord, what a shindy there was! And if it weren't like one of old Berkeley's fool's-tricks to "blue" twelve hundred pounds that way, and him not knowing where to turn for the ready! But about this colt: if he's such a clipper, how is it nobody's heard of him before this?'

'Coulson has kept him dark. He's been trained at Beverley, and they only brought him to Malton three weeks back. The lad tells me he has been doing very good work, and he is to be tried in the morning with Cream Cheese – that is schoolmaster to the Leger crack. Now look here, if the colt can beat Cream Cheese at a stone, he's a moral for the Ebor. On a heavy course he'll walk right away from The Ghoul, and put us in the cart.'

The landlord whistled. 'You are sure the lad's square?'

'I'd peel the flesh off his bones if I thought he was putting the double on me; but he daren't try it. Coulson as good as swore the boys over to hold their tongues, but Tom says the stable is that sweet on his chance, they'll put their shirts on the colt at starting-price.'

'Who's to ride him?'

'Alick's head lad. The brute has a temper, and won't stand much "footling" about; but Jevons and he understand each other, and his orders are to get him off well, and sit still.'

'I suppose now,' suggested the bookmaker, 'this Jevons ain't a reasonable sort of chap?'

Downey grinned. 'As well try to square Coulson himself. He is one of your Sunday-school-and-ten-commandments sort, is Jevons. Besides, his father was the old squire's second horseman, and the lad was brought up in the stables. He swears by the Berkeleys, and would never lend a hand to put a spoke in the Captain's wheel.'

'Do you know what time the trial is to come off?'

'About six. I reckoned on Slimmy's being within call, for there is precious little time to lose. It is light by four.'

'I'm game,' said the tout, 'if Mr Vicary will lend me something to take me over.'

The landlord consulted his watch. 'Half-past one,' he said. 'Let's see; it's close on fifteen mile to Coulson's. I'll drop you at the Pig and Whistle. You can get over the fields from Gunny's corner in twenty minutes.'

'You know your way?' queried Davis, uneasily.

'Every yard of it, guv'nor. Coulson and me is old friends so long as we don't happen to meet. There is a nice bit of cover at the end of the ground where I can lie snug. Will you wait for me, Mr Vicary?'

'Aye, I'll be on the road by Gunny's at seven. What for you, Downey; can we give you a shakedown here?'

'No thank you; I'm off,' answered the jockey, laughing; 'you're altogether too warm in this corner for a nice young man like me. I'm putting up at the Great Northern, and shall see you and Davis for the first time on the course, and not more than I can help of you then.'

The rain had cleared off, and the first pale rifts in the eastern sky were broadening into grey dawn before Mr Slimmy, from the convenient elevation of a friendly elder bush, caught sight of a line of dark specks moving across the wold, and gradually resolving themselves into a string of horses.

'Here they come,' he murmured, pocketing the flat bottle from which he had been refreshing his inner man, and working himself cautiously forward on the stout bough, while he parted the leaves with his left hand to command a better view. 'And here's young Alick and the Captain. I thought as much,' he added, triumphantly, for the trainer and Berkeley had cantered up and reined in their hacks within ten paces of his hiding-place.

In a very few minutes the horses were stripped and got into line.

'They will start themselves,' said Coulson, 'and take it easy for the first half mile. Then you'll see, Captain, that there is very little fear but what the colt will give a good account of himself tomorrow. There they go, and a good start too.'

The horses jumped off together, a big chestnut, which even in the half light Slimmy had recognised as Cream Cheese, coming to the front, with a clear lead. The soft drum of the hoofs on the moist ground died away, and the two men stood up in their stirrups, following with keen eyes the dim outline of the horses as they rounded the curve and swept into the straight, the chestnut still showing the way, with his stable companion and a powerful-looking bay in close attendance. 'There he goes!' was the tout's mental ejaculation, for, at the bend for home, a dark horse crept up on the inside, and, taking up the running at half distance, came on and finished easily with a couple of lengths to spare.

Coulson turned to his companion with a smile.

'He'll do, Captain. The money is as good as banked. You can put on his cloths, Jevons, and take him home. He's a clipper, and no mistake. He came up the straight like a – '

'Rocket,' suggested Berkeley. 'How's that for a name? By Gunpowder out of Falling Star – not bad, I think.'

'Couldn't be better,' was the hearty answer.

'A few more of his sort, and we'll soon have you back at the Hall, Master Charles. I shall live to lead in a Derby winner for you yet. Lord! I think it would almost bring the old man out of his grave to know the Berkeley's had their own again.'

The words were hardly past his lips when a crack, like the report of a pistol, close behind them, made both men jump as if they had been shot.

Mr Slimmy, who, having heard and seen all he wanted, and was in the act of beating a masterly retreat, had unfortunately set his foot on a rotten branch, which instantly snapped beneath his weight. Taken by surprise, the tout lost his foothold and his balance at the same time, made an ineffectual grab at the swinging boughs, pitched forward, and, despite his wild endeavours to recover himself, descended precipitately in a shower of leaves and dry twigs on the wrong side of the hedge.

'Where the deuce did the fellow come from?' ejaculated Berkeley, as he gazed blankly at the heap on the ground. Coulson's only answer was to swing himself off his horse and fling the bridle to his companion. The quick-witted trainer had reckoned up the situation in a moment, and before the luckless Slimmy could gather himself together Coulson's hand was on his collar, and Coulson's 'crop' was cracking and curling about his person, picking out the tenderest parts with a scientific precision that made him writhe and twist in frantic efforts to free himself from that iron grip. But the trainer stood six feet in his socks, and was well built. He held his victim like a rat, while his strong right arm brought the lash whistling down again and again with a force that cut through the tout's seedy clothing like a knife.

'For God's sake, Coulson,' cried Captain Berkeley, 'hold hard, or you will kill the man.'

'And a good thing, too,' said the trainer, relinquishing his hold on Slimmy with a suddenness that sent him sprawling into the muddy ditch. 'I know him, and I'll have no touting on my place. If he shows his face here again, he'll find himself in the horsepond. Stop that row,' he went on, turning to where Slimmy lay in the ditch, crying and cursing alternately; 'and get off my ground before I chuck you over the fence.'

White with rage and pain, the tout picked himself up and scrambled through the gap in the hedge as fast as his aching limbs could carry him. But when he had put a safe distance between himself and Coulson, he turned and shook his fist at the trainer's retreating figure.

'Curse you,' he said, with a horrible imprecation. 'I'll pay you out for this. I'll be even with you, if I swing for it, swelp me if I ain't.'

Owner and trainer rode home in silence.

Coulson was a good deal upset by the discovery that his horse was being watched. He had recognised Slimmy, and Slimmy was known to be in the employ of a party popularly supposed to stick at nothing, and quite capable of trying to get at a horse that threatened to upset their game. Then, again, the arrangements and time of the trial had been kept so quiet that it seemed impossible the tout could get wind of it, except from someone directly connected with the stables. Altogether Coulson felt uneasy, and, after some consideration, he mentioned his suspicions to his head lad, in whom he had the most implicit confidence. Jevons thought things over for a bit. Then he suggested the colt's box should be changed, and that he should sit up with him.

'Put him in the end box next the saddle-room, sir; it is so seldom used that an outsider would not think of trying it, and there isn't many of the lads as would like to rux about in there tonight, leastways not one as has a bad conscience.'

Coulson knew what he meant. In the box next the saddle-room his father, old Alick Coulson, had come by his end, kicked to death by the Ebor favourite on the very eve of the race. A training-stable is not exactly a hotbed of superstition, but, without doubt, a feeling did exist in connection with that particular box, and, as Jevons had said, it was very rarely used.

'Shall you like to sit up there yourself?' the trainer asked bluntly.

Jevons did not mind at all. He said he did not hold with ghosts and such like, and he was sure a sportsman like the old master would know better than to come upsetting the colt and spoiling his, Jevons's, nerve just before the race. Still, as there was gas in the saddle-room and a fire, if Mr Coulson had no objection, he might as well sit there, and look in every now and again to see his charge next door was getting on all right.

The trainer readily agreed. He had a high opinion of the lad's coolness and common sense, but he also felt that to pass the night alone and without a light in a place which, however undeservedly, had the reputation of being haunted, and that, too, on the very anniversary of the tragedy from which the superstition took its rise, was a performance calculated to try the strongest nerves, and he preferred that Jevons should not face the ordeal.

Indeed, it struck him as he left the lad for the night that he would scarcely have cared to undertake the watch himself. It might be fancy, but there was a queer feel about the place.

'Fifteen years ago tonight,' thought Coulson, 'since an Ebor crack stood in that box. It was a dark horse, too, and owned by the squire. It is a coincidence, anyway. No, I shouldn't care to take on Jevons's job.'

Nor was he alone in his conclusions. Several other people expressed a similar conviction, notably Jevons's subordinate, who had heard of the arrangement in the morning.

'I wouldn't be in Bill's shoes tonight – no, not for fifty down,' he said, and slipped off unobserved to the nearest box to post a letter.

The communication he despatched was addressed to 'S. Downey, Esq., Great Northern Hotel, York', and was marked 'immediate'. The lad was going over to the races in the afternoon, and felt tolerably certain of getting speech with the jockey; but he was a careful young man, and wisely left nothing to chance.

It wanted fifteen minutes to midnight. Outside, the night was as black as your hat: not a vestige of a moon, not a single star to break the uniform darkness of the sky. With sunset a noisy blustering wind had sprung up, rattling about the chimneys, clashing the wet branches, and deadening the sound of cautious footfalls creeping across the paddock in the direction of the stables. Jevons was sitting over the saddle-room fire, with his pipe and the *Sporting Life* for company, and the remains of his supper-beer on the table beside him. From time to time he took a lantern and went to look at his charge. The colt had been quiet enough all the earlier part of the evening, but for the last half-hour Jevons fancied he could hear him fidgeting about on the other side of the wall.

'What ails the brute?' he said to himself, laying down his pipe to listen.

The wind dropped suddenly, making the silence all the more intense by contrast with the previous roar; and through the stillness Jevons heard the clink of a bucket and the sound of someone moving about in the loose-box.

He sprang to his feet and snatched up the lantern. His sole idea was that someone was trying to get at the horse, and his hand was on the revolver in his breast-pocket when he opened the door. So strong was the impression that he was positively surprised to find no sign of an intruder. The colt was lying in the farthest corner and perfectly quiet. Jevons looked all round. There was certainly nothing to see, but it struck him that the air felt very cold, and he shut the door. The instant it closed behind him, a dark shadow fell across the square of light issuing from the entrance to the saddle-room.

'Now's your time, Slimmy,' whispered Mr Vicary. 'Nip in and doctor his liquor. This is getting precious slow.'

The beer stood on a table barely two paces from the door. Stretching out his arm, the tout emptied the contents of a small bottle into the jug, and crept noiselessly back to his hiding-place.

'There's a deuce of a draught in here,' said Jevons to himself, 'and where it comes from fairly beats me.'

He held up his hand at different heights, trying to test the direction of the chill current of air. But it seemed to come from every quarter at once, and shifted continually.

The lad struck a lucifer, and held it level with his shoulder. To his utter astonishment the flame burned clear and steady, though he could feel the cold draught blowing on his face, and even stirring the hair on his closely cropped head.

'That's a rum go,' he said, staring at the match as it died out. He backed a few steps towards the wall, the draught was fainter; when he came level with the horse it ceased altogether.

'You are wise, my lad, to stick to this corner,' Jevons remarked as he looked at the colt; 'it's enough to blow your head off on the other side. Well, it must have been the wind I heard, for there ain't nothing here.'

He locked the door and went back to the saddle-room. The hands of the American clock on the narrow mantelpiece pointed to twelve. Jevons loaded his pipe, poured out the rest of the beer, and took a long pull. Then he kicked the fire together, and looked about for a match.

'Now, where did I put that box,' he said, staring stupidly around. 'Where did I put that – what is it I'm looking for? What's got my head? It's all of a swim.'

He felt for a chair and sat down, holding his hand to his heavy eyes. The lids felt as if they were weighted with lead. The gas danced in a golden mist that blinded him, and the whole room was spinning round and round. Then the pipe dropped from his nerveless fingers, and his head fell forward on the table.

'He's safe,' muttered Vicary, as he softly pushed the door ajar and surveyed the unconscious lad. 'That's prime stuff to keep the baby quiet. Here's the key, Slimmy; I'll bring the light. When we've damped the powder in that there rocket, Coulson will wish he hadn't been so handy with his crop this morning.'

Slimmy turned the key in the lock and looked into the box; then he gave a slight start, and drew quickly back.

'What's up?' inquired the landlord. 'Go on, it's all right.'

'Sh!' whispered the tout, 'he might hear you.'

'Hear us? Not he, nor the last day neither, if it comes now.'

He was thinking of Jevons, but Slimmy pulled to the door and held it.

'There's someone in there,' he muttered, 'an old chap. He's sitting on a bucket right in front of the horse.'

'Did he see you?'

'I don't know, his back was turned and he looked asleep like.'

He leaned forward, listening intently, but not a sound came from behind the closed door.

'Coulson didn't mean to be caught napping,' said Vicary, under his breath. 'Is it a stable hand?'

'A cut above that,' returned the other, in the same tone. ' 'Tis queer he should keep so quiet.'

They waited a few minutes, but everything was still.

'See here,' whispered Slimmy, untwisting the muffler he wore round his neck, 'there ain't no manner of use standing here all night. Give me the stick. If I can get past him quiet, I will; but if he moves, you be ready to slip the handkerchief over his head. He can't make much of a fight agen the two of us, and we ain't got this far to be stalled off by an old crock like him; keep well behind him. Never mind the lantern. He's got a light inside.'

There was a light inside, but where it came from would have been difficult to say. It fell clear as a limelight over half the box, and beyond the shadow lay black and impenetrable, a wall of darkness.

As he crossed the threshold Slimmy felt a blast of cold air sweep towards him, striking a strange chill into his very bones.

Straight opposite stood a horse, and before him an old man was sitting on a reversed bucket, his elbow resting on his knee, his head on his hand. To all appearances he was asleep. But even in that intense stillness the tout could catch no sound of breathing. His own heart was thumping against his ribs with the force of a sledge-hammer. He felt his flesh creeping with a sensation of fear that was almost sickening. Fear? Yes, that was the word; he was horribly afraid. And of what? Of a weak old man, for whom he would have been more than a match single-handed, and they were two to one. What a fool he was, to be sure! With a desperate effort he pulled himself together and went forward, his eye warily fixed on the silent figure. Neither man nor horse moved. Slimmy thrust his hand into his pocket and felt for the bottle which was to settle the Rocket's chances for the Ebor! His fingers were on the cork, when the silence was broken by a sound that brought a cold sweat out on his forehead and lifted the hair on his head. It was a low chuckling laugh. The man on the bucket was looking at him. The gleaming eyes fixed him with a sort of mesmeric power, and the bottle fell from his trembling fingers.

'Quick with the rag, Sam,' he gasped, 'he's seen me.' But Vicary stood like one turned to stone. His gaze fastened on the seated figure, taking in every item of the quaint dress, the high gill collar and ample bird's-eye stock, the drab coat and antiquated breeches and gaiters. His mouth was open, but for the life of him he could not speak. He was waiting in the helpless fascination of horror to see the face of a man who had been dead and buried for fifteen years.

Slowly, like an automaton, that strange watcher turned his head. The square, resolute mouth was open as if to speak; the shrunken skin was a greenish yellow colour, like the skin of a corpse; along the temple ran a dull blue mark in the shape of a horse's hoof; but the eyes burned like two living coals, as they fixed themselves on the face of the terrified publican.

With a single yell of 'Lord ha' mercy on us! 'Tis old Alick himself!' Vicary turned and fled.

Slimmy heard the crash of the lantern on the stones and the sound of his flying feet, and an awful terror came upon him, a great fear, which made his teeth chatter in his head and curdled the blood in his veins.

The place seemed full of an unnatural light – the blue flames that dance at night over deserted graveyards. The air was foul with the horrible odours of decay. Above all, he felt the fearful presence of that which was neither living nor dead – the semblance of a man whose human body had for fifteen years been rotting in the grave. It was not living, but it moved. Its cold, shining eyes were looking into his, were coming nearer. Now they were close to him. With the energy of despair, Slimmy grasped his stick by the thin end and struck with his full force at the horror before him. The loaded knob whistled through empty air, and, over-balanced by the force of his own blow, the wretched tout pitched forward, and with one piercing shriek fell prone on the straw.

'Did you hear that?'

'What the deuce was it?'

The two men, who were sitting over the fire in the comfortable smoking-room, sprang to their feet. Coulson put down his pipe and went into the hall. Someone was moving about in the kitchen.

'Is that you, Martin?' he called. 'What was that row?'

The man came out at once.

'Did you hear it too, sir? It made me jump, it came so sudden. Sounded like someone hollering out in the stables.'

'Get a lantern. I must go across and see what it was. Are you coming, too, Captain? Then bring that shillelagh in your hand. It might be useful.'

Martin unbolted the side door, which opened on the garden, and the three men crossed the gravel path and went through the yard. Here they saw the gleam of another lantern. Someone was running towards them. It was one of the lads, half dressed, and evidently just out of bed.

'Is that you, Mr Coulson?' he said breathlessly. 'Did you hear that scream? It woke us all up. Bryant can see the saddle-room from his window, and he says the door is wide open.'

'Come on,' was Coulson's answer, as they hurried across to the stables. The square of light from the saddle-room showed clearly through the darkness.

'Here's Jevons,' said the trainer, who was the first to enter. 'He is only asleep,' he added, as he lifted the lad's head and listened to the regular breathing. He shook him roughly, trying to arouse him, but Jevons was beyond being awakened by any ordinary method; he made an inarticulate grunt, and dropped back into his former attitude.

'Drunk?' ejaculated Martin, blankly.

'Drugged, by gad!' Captain Berkeley had taken the empty jug from the table and smelt it. The sickly odour of the powerful opiate clung about the pitcher and told its own tale.

'Then,' cried the trainer, 'as I'm a living man, they've got at the colt.' His face was white and set as he seized the lantern and ran to the loose-box. The door was open; the key was in the lock. The men crowded up. There was scarcely a doubt in their minds but that the mischief was already done. Coulson held up the lantern and looked round. The colt was standing up in the corner, snorting and sniffing the air. He, too, had been startled by that terrible cry.

On the ground, straight in front of the door, a man lay prone on his face. There was no mistaking the look of that helpless body, the limp flaccidity of those outstretched arms.

'He's dead, sir,' said Martin, as he turned up the white face; 'hold the light down; his coat's all wet with – something.'

It was not blood, only a sticky, dark-coloured fluid, the contents of a broken bottle lying underneath the body. Just beyond the reach of the clenched right hand was a heavy loaded-stick, and near the door they found a thick woollen handkerchief. Berkeley bent down and looked at the drawn features.

'Surely,' he said, in a low voice, 'it is the same man you thrashed this morning?'

Coulson nodded. 'He meant squaring accounts with me, and he has had to settle his own instead. It is strange that there should be no marks of violence about him, and yet he looks as if he had died hard.'

And truly, the dead man's face was terrible in its fixed expression of mortal fear. The eyes were staring and wide open, the teeth clenched, a little froth hung about the blue lips. It was a horrid sight.

They satisfied themselves that life was absolutely extinct. Then Coulson gave orders for the colt to be taken back to his old box, locked the door on the corpse until the police could arrive, and spent the remainder of the night in the saddle-room, waiting till Jevons should have slept off the effects of the opiate.

But when the lad awoke he could throw very little light on the matter. He swore positively there was no-one in the box when he paid his last visit at five minutes to twelve, and he could remember nothing after returning to the saddle-room. How the tout had effected an entrance, by what means his purpose had been frustrated and his life destroyed, remained for ever a mystery. The only living man who knew the truth held his tongue, and the dead can tell no tales. But Mr Vicary, as he watched Captain Berkeley's colt walk away from his field next day, and, cleverly avoiding a collision with the favourite on the rails, pass the post a winner by three lengths, was struck by the fact that the Rocket had grown smaller during the night, and he could have sworn the horse he saw in the loose-box had some white about him somewhere.

'He's one o'raight sort,' exclaimed a stalwart Yorkshireman who stood at Vicary's elbow. 'When aa seed him i' t'paddock, aa said aa'l hev a pound on th' squoire's 'oss for t'saake of ould toimes, for he's strange and loike Blue Ruin, as won th' Ebor in seventy-foive. 'Twas fust race as iver aa'd clapped eyes on, and aa'd backed him for ivery peeny aa'd got.'

The publican turned involuntarily to the speaker. 'Did you say yon colt was like Blue Ruin?' he asked hoarsely.

'The very moral of him, barring he ain't quite so thick, and ain't got no white stocking. I reckon you'll remember Blue Ruin,' added the farmer, referring to a friend on the other side, 'him as killed ould Coulson?'

Vicary was a strong man, but at the mention of that name a strange, sickly sensation crept over him. The colour forsook his face, and when, a few minutes later he called for a brandy 'straight', the hand he stretched out for the glass was shaking visibly.

Once, and once only, did the landlord allude to the events of that fatal night. It was when Mr Davis, loudly deploring his losses, expressed an opinion that Slimmy was 'a clumsy fool, and matters would have come out very differently if he had been there.'

'You may thank your stars,' was Vicary's energetic rejoinder, 'that you never set foot in the cursed place. The poor chap is dead, and there ain't no call for me to get myself mixed up in the business.

Least said, soonest mended, say I; but you mind the story I told you the night Downey brought the news of that blooming colt, about ould Coulson swearing he'd come back from the dead, if need be, to do a Berkeley a good turn.'

'I remember right enough. What's that go to do with it?'

The landlord glanced nervously over his shoulder. 'Only this,' he answered, sinking his voice to a whisper, '*he kept his word*!'

The Ghost in the Chair

This story requires explanation. The explanation will never be given, because no one of the theories of cerebral pressure, spectral illusion, or hypnotic influence, by which people try to explain away the inexplicable, can get rid of the single fact that, shortly after three o'clock on a certain Friday afternoon, one hundred and fifty sane and sober men saw, or thought they saw, Curtis Yorke take the chair at a general meeting of the San Sacrada Mining Company, Limited, at which time, according to subsequent medical evidence, he must have been dead for several hours.

For some time his friends had known that Yorke was going a little bit too fast. While hardly more than a boy, one brilliant hit had gained him a reputation in the City far beyond his years, and at an age when most men are expending their superfluous energy on the tennis-court or river, he was finding brains for the working out of several big undertakings.

Six years of unbroken success taught him to believe his luck infallible. When that changed, as sooner or later it was bound to do, he began to lose confidence in himself. Like many men who keep a level head in prosperity, he could not play a losing game, and for months past anxiety and overwork had been telling steadily on his nerves.

Moreover, he was superstitious, and though he made no profession of religion, he retained an odd belief in the Puritanical dogmas of hell-fire and a personal devil. This in some measure accounts for what he said to Fielden four days before his tragic end.

The directorate of the San Sacrada Mining Company had been holding an extraordinary meeting. A crisis was impending, and things looked black for the company, which was no 'bubble speculation', but a sound and solid concern, suffering from the effects of a persistent run of bad luck.

Now, luck has more to do with the making or marring of mines and men than the moralists would have us believe, and the luck of the San Sacrada Mining Company had all along been execrable.

Unexpected hitches had occurred in securing the title of the property. The contractors had seen fit to export the machinery reversely to the order in which it was required. Delays had been caused by scarcity of water, and when at last the returns promised to justify the small fortune sunk in the shaft, the Yankee manager, whose appointment had been backed by flaming testimonials, demonstrated his native 'cuteness by 'skipping out' with twenty-five thousand dollars of the company's money. His place was filled by an Englishman in every way qualified for the post; but before the good effects of this change of administration could become apparent the mine was flooded, and all operations for the time being perforce suspended. Nor was this all.

Unpleasant rumours began to circulate as to the stability of the concern. It was said that money had been borrowed at a ruinous rate of interest; that the company was insolvent; that the very plant had already been seized by their creditors.

One of the financial journals got hold of the story, and treated it after its own inimitable fashion. The company brought an action against the paper, and won their case, thereby incurring heavy law expenses and advertising the scandal, for the public to a man read the offending article, while only a very small section took the trouble to acquaint themselves with the proofs of its inaccuracy.

The shareholders grew restive, and it became known that the forthcoming general meeting was likely to be stormy. It was then that the Board held their extraordinary council. There was much discussion, and many futile suggestions, but no resolution was passed, because, if the situation were to be saved, it would be the work of one man, and he hadn't had time to think out a plan of action. This was the chairman, Curtis Yorke, who, having nothing to say, had said it exceedingly well, and was now aimlessly scribbling on the back of some papers lying before him on the table.

The board-room was almost deserted. Four of the five directors had gone home; the fifth remained at the special request of the chairman, who had then relapsed into silence and hieroglyphs.

A casual observer might have judged his occupation mere idling, and interrupted him without hesitation. Fielden knew better.

He not unfrequently annoyed his own clients during important interviews by adorning his blotting-pad with minutely detailed presentments of cutters and yawls, and he understood that miscellaneous sketching may be on occasion the outcome of deep thought.

Therefore he waited, leisurely drawing on his gloves, until at the end of twenty minutes Yorke, without lifting his head from the paper, began to speak.

He said in a low, even voice that the company was going to the devil; that there was only one man who might be induced to see them through, and he was on the Continent, and his exact address uncertain.

That the most important thing now was to gain time, and for that purpose they must find a smart junior, a man who could talk and wasn't too well known; give him five shares and a cheque for fifty guineas, and put him on at the general meeting to impress the shareholders with the necessity for keeping quiet.

He went on to say that the San Sacrada Mine was the third venture that had gone wrong within six months, and that he, Yorke, regarded it as an omen. That if it came to grief he should never do another stroke of business; that he would be down and done for.

But that it should *not* come to grief, because he intended to pull it through at the price of his own soul. That he was prepared to sell his soul for that end, and he believed the sale would shortly be concluded.

At that moment the fire crackled, and Yorke jumped as if he had been shot. Then he laughed rather awkwardly, and explained that he had not slept for a fortnight, and his nerves were all to pieces.

'I believe,' he said apologetically, 'that I've been talking damn rot. To tell the truth, I don't know all the time what I'm saying. It's this beastly insomnia. But you understand what I want for Friday. I made that clear. We must have someone to tackle this Simpson brute, or he'll carry the whole meeting with him. Nothing the Board can say will weigh with the shareholders; but a split among themselves may gain time, and time is money to us just now.

Fielden thought he knew a man who would do, and he asked who Simpson was.

'A dirty little outside broker. The miserable beast hasn't more than a hundred shares in all; but he's quite capable of upsetting our cart as things are at present.'

'It is always the small holders who give the most trouble,' said Fielden, preparing to go. 'I'll see my man tonight, and send you a wire in the morning. If I were you, Yorke, I'd look in at my doctor's on the way home, and get him to give me some bromide or something. You're running under too big a strain. It isn't nice to hear a sensible man talking nonsense about his soul. If you came out with that sort of thing at a meeting the reporters would say you were drunk. Besides, there's no demand for the article nowadays. They are altogether too cheap. Goodnight.'

Yorke went with him to the door.

It was raining hard, and the evening air felt raw and chilly. He shivered as he returned to the empty board-room. His head felt heavy, and there were two pink spots on the green cloth which worried him.

He sat down again at the table and began to play with his pen, writing odd words on the blank sheet of paper.

He certainly had been a fool to let himself go in that way before Fielden. He must have been a bit off his head. And yet it was true. He would sell his soul if that would ensure his coming safely through this business.

His soul! Fielden had said souls were cheap. If City men had souls, what mean, shabby things some of them would be. Yorke tried to imagine what one would look like and laughed. His laugh was not good to hear.

And yet it was a big price to offer, for it was the last possession of the human being – the only thing he has to carry out of this world into the blank Beyond. And it could burn!

He remembered a picture he had seen as a child in an old Bible, of souls burning in hell. Souls with human faces horribly distorted by pain. Yes, that was the end of lost souls – hot fire.

The rain swirled against the long windows, and Yorke's teeth chattered. He was cold now, and the company was going to smash. He had said all along, if this venture went down he should go with it. It had come to mean everything or nothing to him, and to know for certain that he was going to pull it through he *would* sell his soul.

He began writing again, the words forming themselves automatically beneath his fingers –

> I, the undersigned, hereby covenant and agree to guarantee the loan of such moneys as shall cover the working expenses of the San Sacrada Gold Mine for the space of six calendar months, and further to ensure the complete success of the company, in consideration of the surrender of the soul of Curtis Yorke, chairman, at such time and for such purpose as I may hereafter determine.
>
> (Signed) X his mark

It was the merest vagary of a disordered brain, but Yorke's heart gave a great bound as he read and re-read the words.

Then his jaw fell, and his face grew set and rigid with terror, the terror that wipes out all manly strength and courage, and leaves room for nothing but an abject, shaking cowardice. The perspiration stood out in great drops on his forehead, and his eyes were bolting out of his head as he gazed at the paper before him.

On the blank space left for the signature five letters had come out in characters that shimmered and glowed as if they were traced in flame.

Every drop of blood in Yorke's body went to his heart. For one awful moment he remained paralysed and immovable. The next, with a desperate effort, he had seized the sheet of foolscap, and, staggering across the room, flung it into the fire.

The thick paper shrivelled, curled, and broke into a blaze. Yorke snatched up the poker and stirred the coals to a fiercer heat, crushing the charred fragments into the glowing embers.

Then the poker fell from his hand with a crash, and he sank into the nearest chair, shaking and sweating like a scared pony.

The clock on the mantelpiece struck six, and the sound recalled him to a sense of mundane things. He stood up and passed his hand across his damp forehead.

'Good God!' he muttered, 'my head must be going. It wasn't real. It couldn't be real. Fielden's right. I'm running under too big a strain. I'll see Jones at once, and get something to pull me together.'

He put on his overcoat and went downstairs.

A clerk was coming up the passage with a telegram in his hand.

Yorke stopped under the gas-burner to open the yellow envelope, and his face turned a shade paler as he read the contents.

It was the message for which he had been waiting all day. The address of the one man who could save the company.

This happened on Monday. By Wednesday afternoon Yorke had reached Paris, seen Van Hooten, and brought their conference to a successful issue.

His conduct of the transaction was throughout masterly, and aroused the great financier to an almost paternal expression of admiration.

'You are von ver' clever young man,' he said to Yorke at the close of the interview. 'I haf watched you for three, four, five years, and I say to myself, "He does go far, zat boy; but he will arrive." What! you made von leetle mistake last Spring about those "Guatemalas", zat is nothing. I myself haf also made mistakes. You are young; you buy your experience. So! But, in ze end, you will succeed, for you haf a head. *Mein Gott!* What a head for a man so young. You see, I haf belief in you. I lend you my influence. I trust you with my money, because I look for you one day to do great things. There is no fear. You will succeed.'

'I shall succeed this time,' said Yorke.

He took leave of the big man gratefully, for Van Hooten had been a good friend to him.

When he got back to his hotel he locked himself into his room and drew a paper out of his pocket-book. It was an exact duplicate of the weird bond he had burned in the boardroom on the Monday evening. Impelled by an insane desire to see if the horrible delusion would repeat itself, he had three times rewritten the document, watching with a painful admixture of interest and dismay the ghastly signature come out on the white paper. Then, in an access of terror, he would destroy the evidence of his unholy compact, only to reproduce it on the first occasion he found himself alone.

Meanwhile, the treatment prescribed by his doctor exercised a slightly beneficial effect. He did not sleep, but his brain, on the single point in which he was vitally interested, became phenomenally clear, and his powers of endurance appeared to be practically unlimited.

In the three days intervening between the board and general meetings Yorke did the work of ten men. On the Thursday night he devoted himself to the preparation of his speech. He told his servant, who left him in his own room at eleven o'clock, to put a glass of milk and a syphon of soda beside the bed, and on no account to disturb him in the morning until he rang for his shaving-water.

He was then writing. The man went to bed. Yorke must have worked late into the night, for he had made a fair copy of the rough draft of his speech and added several sheets of notes.

When the speech was delivered, it was noticed that, contrary to custom, the chairman used no notes at all. He brought with him no papers whatever, and he arrived very late.

The room was packed, and the general temper of the meeting so manifestly turbulent that Fielden's neighbour had given it as his opinion that if Yorke did not turn up soon, neither he nor anyone else would be able to obtain a hearing.

The words were scarcely past his lips before the tall figure of the chairman became visible amidst the crowd surging about the door. He wore a heavily-furred overcoat, which he did not attempt to remove, though the atmosphere was oppressively close.

As he made his way up the room and took his place at the table, a peculiar stillness became apparent. It originated with those in the immediate neighbourhood of the chair, and passed like a magnetic wave over the entire audience. Gradually the indeterminate hum of voices dropped, wavered, and died away. When Curtis Yorke rose to address the meeting, he was received in absolute silence.

The speech which followed was the most remarkable piece of oratory ever delivered at a company's meeting. It comprised the entire history of the San Sacrada Gold Mine, with details and statistics, several of which, unknown at the time even to the directors, were subsequently verified by telegram and proved to be absolutely exact.

Yorke's manner created a profound impression. He spoke for an hour without a single hesitation, and he held his hearers spellbound. Not an argument was wasted, not a point lost, not a possible objection left unanswered. The man was transfigured by his intense earnestness. His face was inspired, his whole person dilated. He predicted the future success of the company with the authority of one who *knew*. Every word he uttered carried conviction; and when at last a vote of confidence in the Board was put to the meeting, it was carried without a single dissentient.

Then an odd thing happened.

Without a word, the chairman rose and left the room. The crowd fell back, making a way for him to the door. His disappearance was succeeded by a second of dead silence. Then Fielden, acting on an impulse, for which he could never afterwards account, sprang up and followed.

He wasn't more than a minute in gaining the stairs; but when he reached the passage Yorke was nowhere to be seen.

He hurried out on to the pavement.

A brougham had just pulled up at the kerb, and someone called him by name.

It was the doctor whom Yorke was in the habit of consulting.

He said something, the drift of which Fielden did not catch, for he was looking up and down the street, and answered by the question uppermost in his mind –

'Have you seen Yorke?'

The reply was startling. 'Yes, poor fellow; but there was nothing to be done. He must have been dead for hours. His servant begged me to come to you. He says there are some important papers which you – '

'What the deuce are you talking about?' Fielden interrupted impatiently. 'Yorke's no more dead than I am. He has been at the meeting since three o'clock. He has only just this minute left. I followed him downstairs.'

Then, catching the peculiar expression of the medical man's face, he added warmly – 'I'm neither mad nor drunk, Dr Jones. If you don't believe me, go upstairs. The whole meeting's there, reporters and all. Ask them who took the chair this afternoon. Dead men don't make such speeches as Yorke has just given us.'

There was no doubting the sincerity of his tones.

Dr Jones considered a moment; then he asked a rather singular question –

'Did you,' he said, 'speak to Mr Yorke yourself?'

'No; he left the room suddenly, without addressing anyone individually. I thought the strain had been too much for him – he had spoken really magnificently – and I followed, but – '

'Ah!' interjected the other softly; 'I think, Mr Fielden, I must ask you to come back with me. There are papers about of which you, as an intimate personal friend of Yorke's and a representative of the company, had better take charge. Besides, you may be able to elucidate – '

'Do you,' said Fielden, 'seriously expect me to believe in the death of a man whom I have seen within the last five minutes?'

'I expect nothing. I merely tell you that Mr Yorke was found dead in his room at half-past two this afternoon. He had given orders overnight that he was not to be disturbed until he rang; but his servant, knowing he was to attend an important meeting at three o'clock, became uneasy, and, after repeated attempts to obtain admission, broke open the door and found his master as I have said. The man at once sent for me, also for Dr Lewis, of Harley Street; but, of course, there was nothing to be done. Mr Yorke must have been dead for at least five hours. The body was quite cold. The cause of death was cerebral apoplexy, brought on by nervous pressure and prolonged mental strain. I have known for some days that he was in a serious condition of health.'

The brougham rolled noiselessly on its way. Fielden was staggered. His mind refused to take in the full meaning of the doctor's words. Neither man spoke again till the carriage drew up at the chambers which Yorke occupied. His servant was waiting for them in the hall, and led the way upstairs. The bedroom was in disorder; the candles had burned down in their sockets; papers were scattered over the writing-table and floor.

On the bed, which had not been occupied during the night, lay the dead body of Curtis Yorke.

'He was found here,' said the doctor, indicating the writing-table. 'Evidently he was working up to – the end.'

Fielden had been standing by the bed, reverently looking down at the still face on the pillow. The door of a wardrobe opposite had swung back. As he raised his head, his eyes fell upon Yorke's furlined overcoat, and the events of the afternoon came back upon him in all their weird improbability. He crossed the room and laid a shaking hand on the doctor's arm.

'What does it mean?' he asked hoarsely. 'What does it mean? I saw him, I tell you, not half an hour ago. I heard him speak, and yet – he is dead. For God's sake, what *does* it mean?'

'I don't know,' the other answered, simply. 'There are some things that won't bear explanation. The affairs of the company were very much on his mind;' and, turning over the papers lying on the table, he added: 'He was preparing his speech when the end came. Look here; is this anything like what you heard?'

Fielden looked, and a smothered exclamation escaped his lips as he glanced down the closely-written pages. He was reading, word for word, the speech to which he had listened barely an hour before.

The eyes of the two men met, and Fielden nodded. There was a pause, broken only by the rattle of a passing cab. A corner of the hearthrug was turned up, and the doctor stooped mechanically to straighten it. Under the fold lay a piece of paper. It had dropped from the dead man's hand and remained there unnoticed since the removal of the body.

Fielden heard his companion draw in his breath with a soft, sibilant sound, and looked up.

'What is it?' he asked.

'Convincing proof, if any were needed, of that poor fellow's mental condition. Good God! what a strain he must have been running under before things got to this pass. Read it for yourself. What do you make of it?'

Fielden read, and there came back to his mind the words Yorke had spoken in the board-room four days before –

'I am prepared to sell my soul for that end, and I believe the sale will shortly be concluded.'

It was the last copy of that extraordinary document by which the unhappy man believed he had saved the San Sacrada Mining Company and lost his own soul.

On the back of the paper Yorke had written:

My friend Fielden has said that there is no demand for souls nowadays – that they are altogether too cheap – but he is wrong.

The devil is never weary of bringing men to destruction, as I am proving, at what cost is known only to myself. Though I am now past hope in this world or the next, I solemnly swear that I did not seriously intend to register this shameful bargain with the powers of darkness.

In a moment of abstraction, hardly knowing what I did, I wrote out the original of this agreement. Three minutes later *it was signed*, and I knew that I was lost.

I saw the vile name come out in letters of fire – the fire of hell, in which my soul, that I have bartered away, must burn hereafter.

Six times I have destroyed the outward evidence of this cursed bond, only to be compelled, by a power stronger than myself, to reproduce it, and watch the awful signature again affixed. *His* share of the compact will soon be completed. My part is yet to come. The surrender of my soul 'at such time and for such purpose'. The purpose I know only too well. The time is yet uncertain, but I feel that it will not be long. I am now tormented by one terrible fear: that the call may come before I have seen the success of the company assured; that after all I may be cheated out of my dearly-bought triumph. But that I am resolved not to suffer. Surely my body will have strength to resist; my will-power suffice to claim that last privilege. Come what may, I *will not* yield up my immortal self before Friday's meeting. After that I care little how soon the summons comes. This hourly suspense is torture, worse than any actual suffering. My brain is burning already. My mind is already in hell. But –

Here the writing ceased, with a faint downward stroke of the pen, as it had slipped through the nerveless fingers.

It was Curtis Yorke's last word.

The summons had come.

Fielden's eyes were wet as he finished reading.

'Poor fellow,' he said under his breath. 'Poor Yorke. My God! What he must have gone through!'

He turned the paper over, and looked at the strangely worded agreement.

The space left for the signature was blank.

This is the truth of a story to which no-one will give credence, least of all the hundred and fifty odd men who heard Yorke's speech at the general meeting of the San Sacrada Mining Company. They will prefer to believe that two competent medical authorities made a mistake of five hours in assigning the time of his death. For there is nothing to which human nature objects so strongly as contact with the supernatural, and no credulity equal to the credulity of the incredulous.

In the Séance Room

Dr Valentine Burke sat alone by the fire. He had finished his rounds, and no patient had disturbed his post-prandial reflections. The house was very quiet, for the servants had gone to bed, and only the occasional rattle of a passing cab and the light patter of the rain on the window-panes broke the silence of the night. The cheerful glow of the fire and the soft light from the yellow-shaded lamp contrasted pleasantly with the dreary fog which filled the street outside. There were spirit-decanters on the table, flanked by a siphon and a box of choice cigars. Valentine Burke liked his creature comforts. The world and the flesh held full measure of attraction for him, but he did not care about working for his *menus plaisirs*.

The ordinary routine of his profession bored him. That he might eventually succeed as a ladies' doctor was tolerably certain. For a young man with little influence and less money, he was doing remarkably well; but Burke was ambitious, and he had a line of his own. He dabbled in psychics, and had written an article on the future of hypnotism which had attracted considerable attention. He was a strong magnetiser, and offered no objection to semi-private exhibitions of his powers. In many drawing-rooms he was already regarded as the apostle of the coming revolution which is to substitute disintegration of matter and cerebral precipitation for the present system of the parcels mail and telegraphic communication. In that section of society which interests itself in occultism Burke saw his way to making a big success.

Meanwhile, as man cannot live on adulation alone, the doctor had a living to get, and he had no intention whatever of getting it by the labour of his hands. He was an astute young man, who knew how to invest his capital to the best advantage. His good looks were his capital, and he was about to invest them in a wealthy marriage. The fates had certainly been propitious when they brought Miss Elma Lang into the charmed circle of the Society for the Revival of Eastern Mysticism. Miss Lang was an orphan. She had full control of her fortune of thirty thousand pounds. She was young, sufficiently pretty, and extremely susceptible. Burke saw his chance, and went for it, to such good purpose that before a month had passed his engagement to the heiress was announced, and the wedding-day within measurable distance. There were several other candidates for Miss Lang's hand, but it soon became evident that the doctor was first favourite. The gentlemen who devoted themselves to occultism for the most part despised physical attractions; their garments were fearfully and wonderfully made. They were careless as to the arrangement of their hair. Beside them, Valentine Burke, handsome, well set up, and admirably turned out, showed to the very greatest advantage. Elma Lang adored him. She was never tired of admiring him. She was lavish of pretty tokens of her regard. Her photographs, in costly frames, were scattered about his room, and on his hand glittered the single-stone diamond ring which had been her betrothal gift.

He smiled pleasantly as he watched the firelight glinting from the many-coloured facets. 'I have been lucky,' he said aloud; 'I pulled that through very neatly. Just in time, too, for my credit would not stand another year. I ought to be all right now if – ' He broke off abruptly, and the smile died away. 'If it were not for that other unfortunate affair! What a fool – what a damned fool I was not to let the girl alone, and what a fool she was to trust me! Why could she not have taken better care of herself? Why could not the old man have looked after her? He made row enough over shutting the stable-door when the horse was gone. It was cleverly managed though. I think even *ce cher papa* exonerates me from any participation in her disappearance; and fate seems to be playing into my hand too. That body turning up just now is a stroke of luck. I wonder who the poor devil really is?'

He felt for his pocket-book, and took out a newspaper cutting. It was headed in large type, 'MYSTERIOUS DISAPPEARANCE OF A YOUNG LADY' –

> The body found yesterday by the police in Muddlesham Harbour is believed to be that of Miss Katharine Greaves, whose mysterious disappearance in January last created so great a sensation. It will be remembered that Miss Greaves, who was a daughter of a well-known physician at Templeford, Worcestershire, had gone to Muddlesham on a visit to her married sister, from whose house she suddenly disappeared. Despite the most strenuous efforts on the part of her distracted family, backed by the assistance of able

detectives, her fate has up to the present remained enshrouded in mystery. On the recovery of the body yesterday the Muddlesham police at once communicated with the relations of Miss Greaves, by whom the clothing was identified. It is now supposed that the unhappy girl threw herself into the harbour during a fit of temporary insanity, resulting, it is believed, from an unfortunate love affair.'

Valentine Burke read the paragraph through carefully, and replaced it in the pocket-book with a cynical smile.

'How exquisitely credulous are the police, and the relatives, and the noble British public. Poor Kitty is practically dead – to the world. What a pity – ' He hesitated, and stared into the blazing coals. 'It would save so much trouble,' he went on after a pause, 'and I hate trouble.'

His fingers were playing absently with a letter from which he had taken the slip of printed paper – an untidy letter, blotted and smeared, and hastily written on poor, thin paper. He looked at it once or twice and tossed it into the fire. The note-sheet shrivelled and curled over, dropping on to the hearth, where it lay smouldering. A hot cinder had fallen out of the grate, and the doctor, stretching out his foot, kicked the letter closer to the live coal. Little red sparks crept like glow-worms along the scorched edges flickered and died out. The paper would not ignite; it was damp – damp with a woman's tears. 'I was a fool,' he murmured, with conviction. 'It was not good enough, and it might have ruined me.' He turned to the spirit-stand and replenished his glass, measuring the brandy carefully. 'I don't know that I am out of the wood yet,' he went on, as he filled up the tumbler with soda-water. 'The money is running short, and women are so damned inconsiderate. If Kitty were to take it into her head to turn up here it would be the – ' The sentence remained unfinished, cut short by a sound from below. Someone had rung the night-bell.

Burke set down the glass and bent forward, listening intently. The ring, timid, almost deprecating, was utterly unlike the usual imperative summons for medical aid. Following immediately on his outspoken thoughts, it created an uncomfortable impression of coming danger. He felt certain that it was not a patient; and if it were not a patient, who was it? There was a balcony to the window. He stepped quietly out and leaned over the railing. By the irregular flicker of the street-lamp he could make out the dark figure of a woman on the steps beneath, and through the patter of the falling rain he fancied he caught the sound of a suppressed sob. With a quick glance, to assure himself that no-one was in sight, the doctor ran downstairs and opened the door. A swirl of rain blew into the lighted hall. The woman was leaning against one of the pillars, apparently unconscious. Burke touched her shoulder. 'What are you doing here?' he asked sharply. At the sound of his voice she uttered a little cry and made a sudden step forward, stumbling over the threshold, and falling heavily against him.

'Val, Val,' she cried, despairingly. 'I thought I should never find you. Take me home, take me home. I am so tired – and, oh, so frightened!'

The last word died away in a wailing sob, then her hands relaxed their clinging hold and dropped nervelessly at her side.

In an emergency Dr Burke acted promptly. He shut the outer door, and gathering up the fainting girl in his arms, carried her into the consulting-room, and laid her on the sofa. There was no touch of tenderness in his handling of the unconscious form. He had never cared much about her, when at her best, dainty in figure and fair of face; he had made love to her, *pour passer le temps*, in the dullness of a small country town. She had met him more than half-way, and almost before his caprice was gratified he was weary of her. Her very devotion nauseated him. He looked at her now with a shudder of repulsion. The gaslight flared coldly on the white face, drawn by pain and misery. All its pretty youthfulness had vanished. The short hair, uncurled by the damp night air, straggled over the thin forehead. There were lines about the closed eyes and the drooping corners of the mouth. The skin was strained tightly over the cheekbones and looked yellow, like discoloured wax. His eyes noted every defect of face and figure, as he stood wondering what he should do with her.

He knew, no-one better, how quickly the breath of scandal can injure a professional man. Once let the real story of his relations with Katharine Greaves get wind and his career would be practically ruined. He began to realise the gravity of the situation. Two futures lay before him. The one, bright with the sunshine of love and prosperity; the other darkened by poverty and disgrace. He pictured himself the husband of Elma Lang, with all the advantages accruing to the possessor of a charming wife and a large fortune, and he cursed fate which had sent this wreck of womanhood to stand between him and happiness. By this time she had partially recovered, and her eyes opened with the painful upward roll common to nervous patients when regaining consciousness. With her dishevelled hair and rain-soaked garments, she had all the appearance of a dead body. The sight, horrible as it was, fascinated Burke. He turned up the gas, twisting the chandelier so as to throw a full light on the girl's face.

'She looks as though she were drowned,' he thought. 'When she is really dead she will look like that.' The idea took possession of his mind. 'If she were dead, if only she were really dead!'

Who can trust the discretion of a wronged and forsaken woman, but – the dead tell no tales. If only she were dead! The words repeated themselves again and again, beating into his brain like the heavy strokes of a hammer. Why should she not die? Her life was over, a spoiled, ruined thing. There was nothing before her but shame and misery. She would be better dead. Why (he laughed suddenly a hard, mirthless laugh), she *was* dead already. Her body had been found by the police, identified by her own relations. She was supposed to be drowned, so why not make the supposition a reality? A curious light flashed into the doctor's handsome face. A woman seeing him at that moment would have hesitated before trusting her life in his hands. He looked at his unwelcome visitor with an evil smile.

She had come round now and was crouched in the corner of the sofa sobbing and shivering.

'Don't be angry with me, Val, please don't be angry. I waited till I had only just enough money for my ticket, and I dare not stay there any longer. It is so lonely, and you never come to see me now. It is ten weeks since you were down, and you won't answer my letters. I was so frightened all alone. I began to think you were getting tired of me. Of course I know it is all nonsense. You love me as much as you ever did. It is only that you are so busy and hate writing letters.' She paused, waiting for some reassuring words, but he did not answer, only watched her with cold, steady eyes.

'Did you see the papers,' she went on, with chattering teeth. 'They think I am dead. Ever since I read it I have had such dreadful thoughts. I keep seeing myself drowned; I believe I am going to die, Val – and I don't want to die. I am so – so frightened. I thought you would take me in your arms and comfort me like you used to do, and I should feel safe. Oh, why don't you speak to me? Why do you look at me like that? Val, dear, don't do it, *don't* do it, I cannot bear it.'

Her great terrified eyes were fixed on his, fascinated by his steady, unflinching gaze. She was trembling violently. Her words came with difficulty, in short gasps.

'You have never said you were glad to see me. It is true, then, that you don't love me any more? You are tired of me, and you will not marry me now. What shall I do? What shall I do? No-one cares for me, no-one wants me, and there is nothing left for me but to die.'

Still no answer. There was a long silence while their eyes met in that fixed stare – his cold, steady, dominating, hers flinching and striving vainly to withstand the power of the stronger will. In a few moments the unequal struggle had ended. The girl sat stiff and erect, her hand grasping the arm of the sofa. The light of consciousness had died out of the blue eyes, leaving them fixed and glassy. Burke crossed the floor and stood in front of her.

'Where is your luggage?' he asked, authoritatively.

She answered in a dull, mechanical way, 'At the station.'

'Have you kept anything marked with your own name – any of my letters?'

'No, nothing – there.'

'You *have* kept some of my letters. Where are they?'

'Here.' Her hand sought vaguely for her pocket.

'Give them to me – all of them.'

Mechanically she obeyed him, holding out three envelopes, after separating them carefully from her purse and handkerchief.

'Give me the other things.' He opened the purse. Besides a few shillings, it contained only a visiting-card, on which an address had been written in pencil. The doctor tore the card across and tossed it into the fireplace. Then his eyes fastened on those of the girl before him. Very slowly he bent forward and whispered a few words in her ear, repeating them again and again. The abject terror visible in her face would have touched any heart but that of the man in whose path she stood. No living soul, save the 'sensitive' on whom he was experimenting, heard those words, but they were registered by a higher power than that of the criminal court, damning evidence to be produced one day against the man who had prostituted his spiritual gift to mean and selfish ends.

In the grey light of the chilly November morning a park-keeper, near the Regent's Canal, was startled by a sudden, piercing shriek. Hurrying in the direction of the sound, he saw, through the leafless branches, a figure struggling in the black water. The park-keeper was a plucky fellow, whose courage had gained more than one recognition from the Humane Society, and he began to run towards the spot where that dark form had been, but before he had covered ten yards of ground rapid footsteps gained on his and a man shot past him. 'Someone in the canal,' he shouted as he ran. 'I think it is a woman. You had better get help.'

'He was a good plucky one,' the park-keeper averred, when a few days later he retailed the story to a select circle of friends at the bar of the Regent's Arms, where the inquest had been held. 'Not that I'd have been behindhand, but my wind ain't what it was, and he might have been shot out of a catapult. He was off with his coat and into the water before you could say Jack Robinson. Twice I thought he had her safe enough, and twice she pulled him under; the third time, blest if I thought they were coming up any more at all. Then the doctor chap, he comes to the surface dead-beat, but the girl in his arms.

' "I'm afraid she's gone," he says, when I took her from him, "but we won't lose time," and he set to and carried out all the instructions for recovering the apparently drowned while I went for some brandy. It wasn't a bit of use. The young woman were as dead as a doornail. "If she'd only have kept quiet, I might have saved her," he says, quite sorrowful-like, "but she struggled so", and sure enough his hands were regularly torn and bruised where she'd gripped him.'

Dr Burke and the park-keeper were the chief witnesses at the inquest. There were no means of identifying the dead woman. The jury returned a verdict of *felo-de-se*, and the coroner complimented the doctor on his courageous attempt to rescue the poor outcast.

The newspapers, too, gave him a nice little paragraph, headed, 'Determined Suicide in Regent's Park. Gallant conduct of a well-known physician'; and Elma Lang's dark eyes filled with fond and happy tears as she read her lover's praises.

'You are so brave, Val, so good,' she cried, 'and I am so proud of you; but you ran a horrible risk.'

'Yes,' he answered, gravely, 'I thought once it was all up with me. That poor girl nearly succeeded in drowning the pair of us. Still, there wasn't much in it, you know; any other fellow would have done the same.'

'No, they would not. It is no use trying to pretend you are not a hero, Val, because you are. How awful it must have been when she clung to you so desperately. It might have cost you your life.'

'It cost me my ring,' he replied, ruefully. 'It is lying at the bottom of the canal at this moment, unless some adventurous fish has swallowed it – your first gift.'

'What does it matter,' she answered, impulsively, 'I can give you another tomorrow. What does anything matter since you are safe?'

Burke took her in his arms, and kissed the pretty upturned face. She was his now, bought with the price of another woman's life. Bah! he wanted to forget the clutch of those stiffening fingers and the glazed awful stare of the dead eyes through the water.

'Let us drop the subject,' he said, gently. 'It is not a pleasant one, and, as you say, nothing matters since I am safe' – he added under his breath, 'quite safe *now*'.

The carriage stood at the door. In the drawing-room Mrs Burke was waiting for her husband. She had often waited for the doctor during the four years which had elapsed since their marriage. Those four years had seen to a great extent the fulfilment of Burke's ambition. He had money. He was popular, sought-after, an acknowledged leader of the new school of Philosophy, an authority on psychic phenomena, and the idol of the 'smart' women who played with the fashionable theories and talked glibly on subjects the very A B C of which was far beyond their feeble comprehension. Socially, Dr Burke was an immense success. If, as a husband, he fell short of Elma's expectations, she never admitted the fact. She made an admirable wife, interesting herself in his studies, and assisting him materially in his literary work. Outwardly, they were a devoted couple. The world knew nothing of the indefinable barrier which held husband and wife apart; of a certain vague distrust which had crept into the woman's heart, bred of an instinctive feeling that her husband was not what he seemed to be. Something, she knew not what, lay between them. Her quick perceptions told her that he was always acting a part. She held in her hand a little sheaf of papers, notes that she had prepared for him on the series of *séances*, which for a month past had been the talk of the town. A medium of extraordinary power had flashed like a meteor into the firmament of London society. Phenomena of the most startling kind had baffled alike the explanations of both scientist and occultist. Spiritualism was triumphant. A test committee had been formed, of which Dr Burke was unanimously elected president, but so far the attempts to expose the alleged frauds had not been attended with any success.

It was to Mme Delphine's house that the Burkes were going tonight. The *séance* commenced at ten, and the hands of the clock already pointed to a quarter to that hour, when the doctor hurried into the room.

'Ready?' he said. 'Come along then. Where are the notes?'

He glanced hastily through them as he went downstairs.

'Falconer and I have been there all the afternoon,' he explained as they drove off. 'I had only just time to get something to eat at the club before I dressed. We have taken the most elaborate precautions. If something cannot be proved tonight – ' he paused.

'Well?' she said, anxiously.

'We shall be the laughing-stock of London,' he concluded, emphatically.

'What do you really think of it?'

'Humbug, of course; but the difficulty is to prove it.'

'Mrs Thirlwall declares that the fifth appearance last night was undoubtedly her husband. I saw her today; she was quite overcome.'

'Mrs Thirlwall is a hysterical fool.'

'But your theory admitted the possibility of materialising the intense mental – '

Burke leaned back in the carriage, laughing softly.

'My dear child, I had to say something.'

'Valentine,' she cried, sorrowfully, 'is there no truth in anything you say or write? Do you believe in nothing?'

'Certainly. I believe in matter and myself, also that the many fools exist for the benefit of a minority with brains. When I see any reason to alter my belief, I shall not hesitate to do so. If, for instance, I am convinced that I see with my material eyes a person whom I know to be dead, I will become a convert to spiritualism. But I shall never see it.'

The drawing-room was filled when they arrived at Mme Delphine's. Seats had been kept for the doctor and his wife. There was a short whispered consultation between Burke and his colleagues, the usual warning from the medium that the audience must conform to the rules of the *séance*, and the business of the evening began in the customary style. Musical instruments sounded in different parts of the room, light fingers touched the faces of the sitters. Questions written on slips of paper and placed in a sealed cabinet received answers from the spirit world, which the inquirers admitted to be correct. The medium's assistant handed one of these blank slips to Burke, requesting him to fill it up.

It struck the doctor that if he were to ask some question the answer to which he did not himself know, but could afterwards verify, he would guard against the possibility of playing into the hands of an adroit thought-reader. He accordingly wrote on the paper, 'What was I doing this time four years ago? Give the initials of my companions, if any.'

He had not the vaguest idea as to where exactly he had been on the date in question, but a reference to the rough diary he always kept would verify or disprove the answer.

The folded slip was sealed and placed in the cabinet. In due time the medium declared the replies were ready. The cabinet was opened, and the slips, numbered in the order in which they had been given in, were returned to their owners. Burke noticed that there were no fresh folds in his paper, and the seal was of course unbroken. He opened it, and as his eye fell on the writing he gave a slight start, and glanced sharply at the medium. Beneath his query was written in ink that was scarcely yet dry:

> On Wednesday, November, 17, 1885, you were at No. 63, Abbey Road. Only I was with you. You hypnotised me. – K.G.

The handwriting was that of Katharine Greaves.

The doctor was staggered. In the multiplied interests and distractions of his daily life he had completely forgotten the date of that tragic visit. He tried to recall the exact day of the month and week. He remembered now that it was on a Wednesday, and this was Monday. Calculating the odd days for the leap year, 1888, that would bring it to Monday – Monday the 17th. Four years ago tonight Kitty had been alive. She was dead now, and yet here before him was a paper written in her hand. He sat staring at the characters, lost in thought. The familiar writing brought back with irresistible force the memory of that painful interview. It suggested another and very serious danger. Burke did not believe for a moment that the answer to his question had been dictated by the disembodied spirit of his victim. He was racking his brains to discover how his secret might possibly have leaked out, who this woman could be who knew, and traded on her knowledge, of that dark passage in his life which he had believed to be hidden from all the world. Was it merely a bow drawn at a venture, which had chanced to strike the one weak place in his armour, or was it deliberately planned with a view to extorting money?

So deeply was he wrapped in his reflections, that the manifestations went on around him unheeded. The dark curtain which screened off a portion of the room divided, and a white-robed child stepped out. It was instantly recognised by one of the sitters – a nervous, highly-strung woman, whose passionate entreaties that her dead darling would return to earth fairly harrowed the feelings of the listeners. Other manifestations followed. The audience were becoming greatly excited. Burke sat indifferent to it all, his eyes fixed on the writing before him, till his wife touched him gently.

'What is the matter, Val?' she whispered, trying to read the paper over his shoulder. 'Is your answer correct?'

He turned on her sharply, crushing the message in his hand. 'No,' he said audibly. 'It is a gross imposture. There was no such person.'

'Hush.' She laid a restraining hand on his arm. 'Do not speak so loudly. That is a point in our favour, anyway. Mr Falconer has proposed a fresh test. He has asked if a material object, something that had been lost at any time, you know, can be restored by the spirits. Madame returned a favourable answer. Mr Falconer could not think of anything at the moment, but I had a brilliant inspiration. I told him to ask for your diamond ring – the ring you lost when you tried to save that poor girl's life.'

Burke rose to his feet, then recollecting himself, sat down again and tried to pull himself together. There was nothing in it. If this Madame Delphine was really acquainted with the facts of his relations with Katharine Greaves she could not know its ghastly termination. He tried to reassure himself, but vainly. His nerve was deserting him, and his eyes roved vacantly round the semi-darkened room, as if in search of something. A sudden silence had fallen on the audience. A cold chill, like a draft of icy air, swept through the *séance* chamber. Mrs Burke shivered from head to foot, and drew closer to her husband. Suddenly the stillness was broken by a shriek of horror. It issued from the lips of the medium, who, like a second Witch of Endor, saw more than she expected, and crouched terror-stricken in the chair to which she was secured by cords adjusted by the test committee. The presence which had appeared before the black curtain was no white-clad denizen of 'summer-land', but a woman in dark, clinging garments – garments, to all appearance, dripping with water – a woman with wide-opened, glassy eyes, fixed in an unalterable stony stare. It was a ghastly sight. All the concentrated agony of a violent death was stamped on that awful face.

Of the twenty people who looked upon it, not one had power to move or speak.

Slowly the terrible thing glided forward, hardly touching the ground, one hand outstretched, and on the open palm a small, glittering object – a diamond ring!

It moved very slowly, and the second or so during which it traversed the space between the curtain and the seats of the audience seemed hours to the man who knew for whom it came.

Valentine Burke sat rigid. He was oblivious of the presence of spectators, hardly conscious of his own existence. Everything was swallowed up in a suspense too agonising for words, the fearful expectancy of what was about to happen. Nearer and nearer 'it' came. Now it was close to him. He could feel the deathly dampness of its breath; those awful eyes were looking into his. The distorted lips parted – formed a single word. Was it the voice of a guilty conscience, or did that word really ring through and through the room – 'Murderer!'

For a full minute the agony lasted, then something fell with a sharp click on the carpet-less floor. The sound recalled the petrified audience to a consciousness of mundane things. They became aware that 'it' was gone.

They moved furtively, glanced at each other – at last someone spoke. It was Mrs Burke. She had vainly tried to attract her husband's attention, and now turned to Falconer, who sat next to her.

'Help me to get him away,' she said.

The doctor alone had not stirred; his eyes were fixed as though he were still confronted by that unearthly presence.

Someone had turned up the gas. Two of the committee were releasing the medium, who was half-dead with fright. Falconer unfastened the door, and sent a servant whom he met in the hall for a hansom.

When he returned to the *séance* room the doctor was still in the same position. It was some moments before he could be roused, but when once they succeeded in their efforts Burke's senses seemed to return. He rose directly, and prepared to accompany his wife. As they quitted their seats, Falconer's eyes fell on the diamond ring which lay unnoticed on the ground. He was going to pick it up, but someone caught his hand and stopped him.

'Leave it alone,' said Mrs Burke, in a horrified whisper. 'For God's sake, don't touch it!'

Husband and wife drove home in silence. Silently the doctor dismissed the cab and opened the hall-door. The gas was burning brightly in the study. The servant had left on the side-table a tray with sandwiches, wine, and spirits. Burke poured out some brandy and tossed it off neat. His face was still rather white, otherwise he had quite recovered his usual composure.

Mrs Burke loosened her cloak and dropped wearily into a chair by the fire. A hopeless despondency was visible in every line of her attitude. Once or twice the doctor looked at her, and opened his lips to speak. Then he thought better of it, and kept silent. Half an hour passed in this way. At last Burke lighted a candle and left the room. When he returned he carried in his hand a small bottle. He had completely regained his self-possession as he came over to his wife and scrutinised her troubled face.

'Have some wine,' he said, 'and then you had better go to bed. You look thoroughly done up.'

'What is that?' She pointed to the bottle in his hand.

'A sleeping-draught. Merely a little morphia and bromide. I should advise you to take one, too. Frankly, tonight's performance was enough to try the strongest nerves. Mine require steadying by a good night's rest, and I do not intend risking an attack of insomnia.'

She rose suddenly from her chair and clasped her hands on his arm.

'Val,' she cried, piteously, 'don't try to deceive me. Dear, I can bear anything if you will only trust me and tell me the truth. What is this thing which stands between us? What was the meaning of that awful sight?'

For a moment he hesitated; then he pulled himself together and answered lightly – 'My dear girl, you are unnerved, and I do not wonder at it. Let us forget it.'

'I cannot, I cannot,' she interrupted wildly. 'I must know what it meant. I have always felt there was something. Valentine, I beseech you, by everything you hold sacred, tell me the truth now before it is too late. I could forgive you almost – almost anything, if you will tell me bravely; but do not leave me to find it out for myself.'

'There is nothing to tell.'

'You will not trust me?'

'I tell you there is nothing.'

'That is your final answer?'

'Yes.'

Without a word she left the room and went upstairs. Burke soon followed her. His nerves had been sufficiently shaken to make solitude undesirable. He smoked a cigar in his dressing-room, and took the sleeping-draught before going to bed. The effects of the opiate lasted for several hours. It was broad daylight when the doctor awoke. He felt weak and used up, and his head was splitting. He lay for a short time in that drowsy condition which is the borderland between sleeping and waking. Then he became conscious that his wife was not in the room. He looked at his watch, and saw that it was half-past nine. He waited a few minutes, expecting her to return, but she did not come. Presently he got up and drew back the window-curtains.

As the full light streamed in, he was struck by a certain change in the appearance of the room. At first he was uncertain in what the change consisted, but gradually he realised that it lay in the absence of the usual feminine impedimenta. The dressing-table was shorn of its silver toilet accessories. One or two drawers were open and emptied of their contents. The writing-table was cleared, and his wife's dressing-case had disappeared from its usual place. Burke's first impulse was to ring for a servant and make inquiries, but as he stretched out his hand to the bell his eyes fell on a letter, conspicuously placed on the centre of a small table. It was addressed in Elma's handwriting. From that moment Burke knew that something had happened, and he was prepared for the worst. The letter was not long. It was written firmly, though pale-blue stains here and there indicated where the wet ink had been splashed by falling tears.

> When you read this [she wrote] I shall have left you for ever. The only reparation in your power is to refrain from any attempt to follow me; indeed, you will hardly desire to do so, when I tell you that I know all. I said last night I could not endure the torture of uncertainty. My fears were so terrible that I felt I must know the truth or die. I implored you to trust me. You put me off with a lie. Was I to blame if I used against you a power which you yourself had taught me? In the last four hours I have heard from your own lips the whole story of Katharine Greaves. Every detail of that horrible tragedy you confessed unconsciously in your sleep, and I who loved you – Heaven knows how dearly! – have to endure the agony of knowing my husband to be a murderer, and that my wretched fortune supplied the motive for the crime. Thank God that I have no child to bear the curse of your sin, to inherit its father's nature! I hardly know what I am writing. The very ground seems to be cut away from under my feet. On every side I can see nothing but densest darkness, and the only thing that is left to us is death.
>
> Your wretched wife,
>
> ELMA

From the moment he opened the letter, Burke's decision was made. He possessed the exact admixture of physical courage and moral cowardice which induces a man worsted in the battle of life to end the conflict by removing himself from the arena. He had taken the best of the world's gifts, and there was nothing left worth having. His belief in a future life was too vague to cause him any uneasiness, and physically, fear was a word he did not understand. He quietly lighted his wife's letter with a match, and threw it into the fireless grate. He smoked a cigarette while he watched it burn, and carefully hid the charred ashes among the cinders. Then he fetched from his dressing-room a small polished box, unlocked it, and took out the revolver. It was loaded in all six chambers.

Burke leisurely finished his cigarette, and tossed the end away. He never hesitated a moment. He had no regret for the life he was leaving. As Elma had said, there was only one thing left for him to do, and – he did it.

[illegible]

[illegible] the [illegible] generally [illegible] the language [illegible]

[illegible]

[illegible] one [illegible]

[illegible]

[illegible] must be equal [illegible] is lost.

The Missing Model

'A plague on all marrying and giving in marriage, say I.'

Gordon Mayne flung aside the sheaf of brushes he had been washing and began to stride impatiently up and down the studio.

'Why the deuce does the woman want to get married?' he demanded. 'What business has a model to marry at all? She is the property of the artistic public, and no single man should be permitted to monopolise her – least of all a Philistine of a shop-walker who refuses to allow his wife to sit, even to her oldest friend. It is all very well for you to lie grinning there, Faucit; but let me tell you it is no laughing matter. Here am I with an idea, a masterpiece evolving itself in my mind – a picture that should make my name and lift me among the gods on high Olympus; a sublime conception, which I should, of course, have treated sublimely. And now, at the eleventh hour, my only model, the one woman who is the living embodiment of my dream, coolly sends me word that she has married a shop-walker – a *shop-walker*, if you please – and can undertake no more engagements. It is absurd! It is brutal! To what end has Nature endowed her with that faultless form and divine length of limb, with that superb carriage, if the one is to be hidden by the stylish abominations of Westbourne Grove clothiers, and the other ruined by wheeling the eternal perambulator down Bayswater slums? Any healthy female of four foot nothing would have answered the purpose equally well. It is a sacrilege that – '

'That divine form should be clasped in the arms of a low-born peasant,' quoted Faucit from the divan, where he lay luxuriously among the cushions, puffing little clouds of smoke rings into the warm air, and laughing softly at his friend's vehemence. 'So it is, old chap. I sympathise. Have a cigarette?'

'I don't care a blue cent who clasps the divine form, so long as I can paint it,' retorted the other crossly, ignoring the proffered case; 'but it *is* sacrilege that such a model should be wasted on mere matrimony. I shall never meet her equal! My picture is lost.'

'Rot!' responded Faucit, with conviction. 'London is stiff with models. There is always as good fish in the sea as ever came out. See here, De Croissac is off to Rome next week. He has a capital girl, "brunette, statuesque – the reverse of grotesque". I'll ask him to send her address. You might arrange with her while he is away. He won't be back till October.'

The studio was full of the soft gloom of a late afternoon in January. Outside the dying sunset threw a crimson glow on the gathering mists which were turning the prosaic villas of the St John's Wood Road into enchanted palaces of mystery. Within a wood fire burned between the dogs on the great open hearth and flickered over the unfinished sketches alternating with plaster casts on the walls, over the two or three big easels, and the odds and ends of draperies and Eastern embroideries scattered about. Gordon Mayne had but recently taken possession of the studio. It had been standing empty for some time, and he had secured it at a comparatively low rental.

'It is an odd thing,' remarked Faucit, meditatively, 'that the very last time I was here Deverill was tearing his hair over the disappearance of a model. You remember his "Vanity", don't you? No? Ah, then it was exhibited in '87, when you were in Paris. Well, it was one of the pictures of the year, and the girl who sat for it was lovely, perfectly exquisite. Deverill found her, and she sat to no-one but to him and Flint, who is his great chum, you know. One day she did not turn up as usual. It was the first time she had ever failed him, and Deverill fancied something unforeseen had kept her at home, swore a little, and thought no more about it, till late in the evening the girl's father came to inquire at what time his daughter had left the studio. Then it turned out that she had not gone home the previous night, and she never did go home. They searched for her high and low, had the canal dragged, put on detectives, and advertised for weeks, but it wasn't the least use. She had vanished off the face of the earth, and not a word has been heard of her from that day to this.'

'Bolted with someone, I suppose,' said Mayne conclusively.

'No, that was the odd part of it. Her name had never been mixed up with a man's. She wasn't that sort of young woman at all. When they searched her room they found no letters, nothing that gave the smallest clue to any affair of the kind. Besides, she took no clothes with her; absolutely nothing. Deverill was in despair. She was sitting for "Oenone Forsaken", the picture he painted for McCandlish, the colonial millionaire, and he had not quite finished it. I can't tell you how much he spent over trying to find her. After that, he threw up the classic, and went in for Scriptural subjects. Queer fellow, Deverill,' concluded Faucit, lighting a fresh cigarette. 'Would any other man exile himself for three years in some stinking Arab village, for the sake of painting his virgins and disciples on the spot?'

'Lucky for me he went,' said Mayne, 'or I should have lost the chance of a rattling good studio. Well, if we really mean to dine with Mrs Lockhart at seven, I must dress. There is some sherry and a bottle of Angostura bitters in that cupboard, and here is a glass. Help yourself while you are waiting. I shall not be long.'

Mrs Lockhart was noted for her little dinners. Covers were invariably laid for eight, and both guests and *menu* were selected with infinite care. Under the congenial influences of good wine and good company, Mayne forgot his grievances, and it was not till the two men were parting for the night, that he again recurred to the subject of the model. Faucit was going to the club, the artist to St John's Wood.

'Don't forget to ask for that girl's address,' he said, as he stepped into his hansom, and the other nodded assent. In the artistic world Gordon Mayne was generally spoken of as a rising man. He had been rising for several years, without having attained to any considerable height. Not that his work wasn't good, for it was, and the dealers seldom left anything on his hands, but since his first exhibit on the walls of Burlington House he had produced nothing very striking, and the critics, who had prophesied great things of the creator of 'Pelagia', felt they had been taken in and let him know it.

By portraits and potboilers a man may gain lucre, but not fame; and Gordon had begun to realise that it was high time he should be represented in the summer exhibitions by something more important than young ladies in evening gowns and the pretty green and grey landscapes, with which city gentlemen of artistic predilections like to adorn their suburban dining-rooms. He had waited a long time for an inspiration, and at last the inspiration had come. On the afternoon following Mrs Lockhart's dinner, Mayne was busily engaged in roughing out his idea with a bit of charcoal, a single female figure – three-quarter-length and life-size – against a curtained doorway. The left hand drew aside the heavy draperies. The right raised the veil from the face.

The picture was to be called 'Avenged', and the expression of the woman was to convey its own story to the spectator. If only he could find an adequate model Mayne felt the composition must prove a success. He was sensible of an enthusiasm for the subject which had latterly been wanting in his work, and he was deeply engrossed in the sketch when someone knocked at the outer door – it was a low, almost timid knock, which had to be twice repeated before the artist's attention was fairly arrested. Rather reluctantly he rose to answer the summons. It was almost dark outside, and his eyes, dazzled by the bright light of the studio, took in with difficulty the lineaments of the woman standing on the threshold. She did not speak, only stood looking wistfully into the lighted room.

'You want to see me?' Mayne inquired courteously. 'Will you come in?'

He threw back the door. As she stepped forward, he saw that his visitor was a young woman, considerably above the average height, and that she moved superbly, with the natural grace of a perfectly-formed and healthy girl.

A second glance assured him that she was undeniably pretty. She was well, but not fashionably, dressed in some black clinging material which hung in straight, almost classical folds. As she reached the centre of the room she turned and threw back the veil she wore with a gesture that brought an involuntary exclamation to the painter's lips. It was the precise action he had attributed to the figure in his sketch. His eyes devoured the faultless features, the exquisite colouring of the face before him, the rich tint of the chestnut hair visible beneath her hat, the expression of the wonderful eyes. For a few moments he stood silently gazing, lost in admiration of her singular beauty. Then, finding she made no effort to explain her errand, he became conscious of the absurdity of the situation.

'You wish to see me?' he said. 'What can I do for you?'

Her eyes rested on the unfinished sketch, as she answered in a low voice – 'You require a model?'

It flashed across Mayne that this must be the girl Faucit had mentioned, and he inwardly endorsed his friend's encomiums on De Croissac's *protégée*. He began at once to explain his requirements, hours, &c. She listened quietly, answering his direct questions, but never volunteering a remark. When the arrangements were completed, she declined his offer of refreshment and went to the door. As he showed her out, the young man reminded her that he knew neither her name nor address. The girl raised her beautiful eyes slowly to his face.

'I shall be here at ten,' she answered, and slipped past him into the darkness.

Later in the evening a telegram was delivered at the studio. It was from Faucit, stating that he was on the point of starting for Athens, in consequence of a despatch apprising him of the sudden death at the British Embassy of his eldest brother.

Mayne threw himself heart and soul into his new work. The model proved an admirable sitter. She caught the spirit not only of the pose, but of the facial expression, and her powers of endurance were remarkable. She could stand for almost any length of time without evincing the slightest fatigue. As the work grew under his hand, Mayne became more and more fascinated. His artistic sensibilities were roused to a species of exultation. The picture was never absent from his thoughts by day, and all night long he dreamed of it. The singular beauty of his model exercised over him an almost magnetic influence. The hours he spent with her in the studio were like an introduction into a new and unknown world. Without analysing the cause, he was conscious in her presence of a keen delight to which he had hitherto been a stranger. He was jealous of any eye but his resting on that exquisite face, and denied himself to all visitors during the sittings. He worked for the most part in silence. The girl never spoke unless directly addressed. She was surrounded by an atmosphere of mystery. She showed the strongest aversion to meeting with strangers, and on two occasions on which in the early days of her engagement Mayne had received friends, she disappeared and did not return until he was again alone.

It was not until after she had been sitting to him for several weeks that the artist learned her name and address, and then only on condition that he should make no use of his knowledge except under urgent necessity. He gave the promise readily, as he would have agreed to anything she required, for she had obtained a remarkable influence over the young man. Without a word having passed between them, he was deeply in love with his model, and he believed that she understood his unexpressed sentiment towards her.

At the end of April Faucit returned to town. Family affairs had detained him abroad far into February, after which he had accompanied a relative on a protracted yachting trip. One of his first visits was paid to the studio in St John's Wood. He found Mayne at home, and disengaged. The two men had not corresponded, and Faucit inquired with interest after the progress of his friend's work.

'How did you manage about your model?' he asked, when he had settled himself on the divan and lighted the usual cigarette. 'I thought once of writing to De Croissac about that girl, but I didn't know his address in Rome, and the news of poor Bob's death drove everything else out of my head before I left England.'

Mayne stared at him blankly.

'But you did send her,' he said. 'She came the very next day.'

'She – who?'

'The model, of course; and I can never thank you sufficiently for what you did for me. She is an inspiration. I can honestly say that picture is the best thing I have ever done. It is splendidly hung, on line at the end of the second room. See here,' he pointed to the black-and-white study which hung on the opposite wall; 'that gives you a faint idea of it.'

Faucit pulled himself up, and went over to the sketch. As his eyes rested on it his face changed.

'Good God!' he exclaimed, 'who sat for that?'

'De Croissac's model, the girl you sent, and the most perfect woman in the whole world.'

'Are you off your head?' cried Faucit; 'that is no more De Croissac's model than I am, and I never sent anyone. That is – Great Heavens! Mayne, don't play the fool. Where did you find her? How did she get here? Answer me,' as the artist stood in silent amazement at this unprecedented outburst of excitement on the part of his impassive friend, 'where in the name of all that is wonderful did you come across Violet Lucas?'

'You know her name?'

'Know her name,' repeated the other impatiently. 'Wasn't her name advertised in every paper, at every police station in London? I tell you the original of that picture is none other than Deverill's lost model, the girl who disappeared three years ago.'

The private view of the Royal Academy was, if anything, more largely attended than usual. All sorts and conditions of notabilities thronged the principal rooms. Lady journalists taking hasty notes of the costume worn by a charming young duchess who was making a tour of inspection under the President's guidance. A leading scientist was arm in arm with a well-known writer of burlesque; R.A.'s and A.R.A.'s by the dozen, stars of the artistic and dramatic firmament, authors, critics, a mammoth picture-dealer, a host of people merely smart, and a smaller sprinkling of those who could not boast even that most modern of all claims to notoriety.

'Very fine picture. Long way the strongest thing we have seen of yours since "Pelagia".' The great dealer nodded approvingly at Mayne, who stood chatting with Faucit at a short distance from his work. 'I said just now to McCandlish (he's the man for you), "if you want to see the picture of the year," I said, "there it is. Mayne is a coming man. If you don't take it I shall." Don't you let him have it a penny under six hundred. I'll give five hundred myself for it any day; it's a very fine work.'

'Yes,' put in the critic of a leading journal, who was also an old friend of the artist, 'it takes a lot of punishment to make you try, old man, but when you are screwed up to the point, you are capable of cutting down your field. I've had my knife into you consistently for about four years now, and at last I have succeeded in driving you to produce a picture worth criticising.'

'Here is McCandlish,' said Bignold. 'You don't know him, I think?'

He turned to the newcomer with a few words of explanation, and presented Mayne. The millionaire was a big man, verging on fifty, with immense shoulders and a fresh-coloured, rather sensual face.

He acknowledged the introduction in a somewhat offhand manner, and glanced at the picture. The eyes of three of the little group turned in the same direction; but Faucit, who happened to be looking at the Australian, saw him give an irrepressible start.

'When was this picture painted, Mr Mayne?' he asked, in a tone that was a trifle too casual.

'I finished it three weeks ago.'

'Did you work from a – a model?'

'Certainly, and it is a very faithful portrait.'

McCandlish could not take his eyes off the canvas. It had evidently made a great impression on him. With an attempt at carelessness which was not lost on one at least of his auditors, he continued –

'The picture bears a striking resemblance to one already in my possession, but the lady who sat for that is dead, I am told.'

'Perhaps' – to his dying day Faucit will never know what prompted the remark – 'Miss Lucas is not dead. Perhaps before long she may be – '

'Avenged,' said a clear voice at his elbow, 'No. 112.'

The lady who had spoken passed on, but Faucit, turning, saw that every vestige of colour had died out of the Australian's face. His jaw dropped, his eyes were staring straight before him, where, close by the barrier, stood a tall, graceful woman, dressed in black. With her right hand she raised the veil she wore, and disclosed the exquisite features of Mayne's mysterious model – the original of the picture behind her – the missing Violet Lucas!

For a brace of seconds Faucit held his breath. Then he caught sight of Mayne's face, beaming with delight, and knew that he was not dreaming. With a stifled cry of 'My God!' McCandlish staggered back and clung to Bignold's arm for support.

The exclamation distracted Faucit's attention; when he looked again for the girl she was gone. Mayne had also vanished among the crowd, and Bignold, with consternation written on his broad, red face, was inquiring of the colonial what the deuce was the matter with him? McCandlish looked ghastly.

'It is nothing,' he stammered; 'a sort of attack I have sometimes – over directly. Help me to get out of this. The heat is stifling.'

The good-natured dealer shouldered a passage through the crowd. Faucit turned to the critic.

'Did you see that girl?' he asked.

'The one in green? Hardly a girl – forty if she is a day, but a handsome woman still.'

'No, no,' impatiently; 'the girl in black who was standing in front of Mayne's picture.'

The other stared.

'Is it a riddle?' he inquired. 'I'm not good at riddles. Ask me another.'

'You must have seen her,' Faucit urged, 'It was Mayne's model. What is the joke?' he added, shortly, as his companion broke into a broad smile.

'My dear chap, if it were anyone but you I should ask where you had been lunching.'

'I don't know what the devil you mean,' was the retort. 'The girl *was* there. McCandlish saw her, so did Mayne, so must you unless you are blind. She was standing *there*,' indicating the spot.

The other man instantly became grave.

'You have been overdoing it a little,' he said. 'I know the sort of thing: get it myself sometimes. Go and see your doctor and take it easy for a bit.'

'Do you think I am mad or drunk?' said Faucit, indignantly.

'Neither; but a little overworked. On my honour, old man, there was no-one there.'

Without another word Faucit left him. Elbowing his way to the door, he met Bignold.

'Where is McCandlish?' he asked.

'I've put him into a cab and sent him home. He seemed all right when I got him outside. Queer sort of attack, wasn't it?'

'Very,' Faucit assented, dryly. 'The sight of that girl startled him, I suppose.'

'What girl?'

The situation was becoming critical. The young man pulled himself together.

'Did you not see,' he inquired, trying hard to keep his temper, 'a woman in black, standing before Mayne's picture?'

'What the deuce are you driving at? I was straight opposite the picture, and there wasn't any woman that I saw.'

There was no mistaking the sincerity of his tone. Faucit muttered something about a mistake, and went in search of Mayne. He found the artist returning breathless from the hall.

'I cannot find her anywhere,' he began. 'I have been through all the rooms and out into the street. I asked the constable downstairs, but no-one seems to have seen her. It is very odd.'

'Very odd, indeed,' was Faucit's answer. 'Come outside, where we can talk quietly. There is more in this than meets the eye.'

'Look here,' was his next remark, when he had related what had passed during Mayne's absence. 'There is a screw loose somewhere. I do not believe in spiritualism and that sort of thing, but I mean to get to the bottom of this business. You say Miss Lucas gave you her address; you must communicate with her.'

'But,' objected Mayne, 'she said I could not see her for three weeks, and I promised not to use the address except under urgent necessity.'

'The necessity is urgent. I met Flint last night, and he told me (I was making inquiries about her) that Miss Lucas's people know nothing of her whereabouts. They believe her to be dead. Now she was a good girl, and devoted to her father and sister; if she were living in town, a free agent, would she keep them in ignorance of her fate?'

'Then you think – ?'

'Never mind what I think. What is her address?'

'Alma Cottage, St Cyr Road, Hampstead. Shall I write?'

'No,' said Faucit, 'we will go. You shall see her while I wait in the cab. If she is not home you can write tonight.'

They hailed a hansom, and gave the address. Faucit sat back in the cab, smoking and thinking; Mayne leaned forward, with his arms on the doors, his face flushed with excitement and expectation.

'Suppose she is not in?' he said once. 'Of course she won't be in. She will not have had time to get home.'

'Then we will wait till she is in,' was the quiet reply.

After an interminable drive they reached St Cyr Road. It was a dreary, out-of-the-way sort of place, bordered on either side by small detached villas, each surrounded by a wall the top of which was encrusted with broken glass. All were dismal, several were unoccupied. Before one of the latter the hansom stopped, and the driver lifted the trap.

'This is Alma Cottage, sir,' he said, 'but there don't seem to be anyone living there.'

Mayne sprang out.

The name was clearly painted on each of the dingy stuccoed gate-posts. The gate was padlocked, the garden neglected. The shutters were closed, and the blinds drawn down.

There was a bell at the gate, and the artist pulled it vigorously. It was very stiff, and beyond the creaking of the wire elicited no response.

'Perhaps there is another house of the same name,' Faucit suggested to the man; 'drive up the road and back, slowly.'

The cabby obeyed. He walked his horse along by the kerb, scanning the names on every gate. There was no other Alma Cottage.

Mayne was still struggling with the bell. An old man, carrying an armful of gardener's tools, had stopped to look at him.

'There ain't no manner of use your ringing there, sir,' he said presently; 'the place has been empty this three year.'

'Who does it belong to?' asked Faucit, who had come up in time to hear the last sentence.

'I've heard tell as the last party who had it was called Johnson, but I never seed anyone but the servant there. The gen'elman only came down irreg'lar like – of a night,' and he grinned significantly.

'Is the place to let?'

'There's never been no board up; but Mr Standing, the agent, used to have the letting of it.'

'Where is he to be found?'

The man told him. Faucit gave him a shilling and got into the cab.

'We will see the agent,' he said.

The agent proved to be an affable gentleman who wore a checked suit, a crimson tie, and several rings.

Yes, he had the management of the St Cyr Road property; knew Alma Cottage perfectly, but it was not to let. The present owner was abroad. Yes, he had been abroad for some time; but he had no intention of letting the house; had refused several offers for it already.

'I have rather a fancy for the place,' Faucit suggested mendaciously; 'I should be quite willing to meet your client on his own terms.'

'Not the least use, sir; Mr Johnson won't let at any price. He may return to England some day soon, and he would require the house again.'

'It must get very damp,' said Mayne, thoughtfully; 'but I suppose there is a caretaker who looks after it.'

The agent did not know.

There was nothing for it but to return to town. When Faucit had left his friend at the club he took a fresh cab, drove to a large house in Park Lane, and inquired for Mr McCandlish. The servant informed him that his master had left for the Continent two hours before, and did not know when he would be back. The journey was quite unexpected. Mr McCandlish had left no address; he would wire in the morning where his letters were to be sent.

Faucit gave the man his card.

'I wished particularly to see Mr McCandlish,' he said; 'but I suppose I must wait now. Let me have his address as soon as you know it.'

He slipped half a sovereign into the servant's hand, and went back to the club.

On the way he stopped at a telegraph office, and despatched a message.

ALMA COTTAGE, ST CYR ROAD, HAMPSTEAD. FIND OUT ALL POSSIBLE ABOUT OWNER AND CARETAKER, IF PRACTICABLE TO GET INTO HOUSE. URGENT. FAUCIT.

The telegram was sent to Hayward, 112 Denbigh Street, Pimlico.

'One thing is certain,' he said later on to Mayne, 'and that is that McCandlish knows something about the girl. He saw the likeness, and he recognised the original. He was awfully upset, and he bolts forthwith. If she is alive, he is afraid of meeting her, and – '

'*If* she is alive,' interrupted the artist, 'why, we saw her this afternoon.'

'Three of us saw her' – Faucit struck a match very deliberately – 'or *thought* we did.'

'I did see her,' said Mayne, doggedly.

'But Bignold and Vernon did not. Why did she give you that address?'

'I don't know' – very unwillingly.

'I do. It was because that house was the last address she had to give, and I believe that it is there we shall find her.'

'You think it possible that she can be concealed about the premises?'

'Yes,' said Faucit, coolly.

Four days later Mayne received an urgent summons to his friend's chambers. He found him closeted with a short, commonplace man, whom he introduced as Mr Hayward. The artist recognised the name as that of a detective whom Faucit had come across professionally, and of whose judgement and tact he held a very high opinion.

'Another link in the chain,' he remarked, without wasting time in preliminaries. 'Now, Hayward, tell your own story.'

'Not much of a story yet, sir; but Mr Johnson, the owner of Alma Cottage, is really McCandlish the millionaire. He took the house on lease from February '86, and put in a housekeeper. He was never there in the daytime; used to go down late at night with a friend, not always the same, and leave in a few hours or early next morning. In April '87 he bought the place, and has never occupied it since. A caretaker goes in and opens the windows now and again. Crusty old party, of the name of Short. Not to be bought; says her orders are to admit no-one, and she ain't going to lose a good job along of strangers.'

'What is there at the back?'

'Garden of house in Randolph Street unoccupied. Windows of adjoining houses don't overlook the premises, leastways only the garden.'

Mayne rose suddenly.

'I am going over that house tonight,' he said, in a hard, strained voice.

'Yes,' agreed Faucit, quietly. 'Will you bring some tools, Hayward?'

'It is a criminal offence, Mr Faucit.'

'I have already told you that I take the entire responsibility. You shall lose nothing by the business. What time?'

'About eleven,' answered the detective, shrugging his shoulders. 'Better meet me at the end of the Hampstead Road. Can't go up in hansoms, you know, sir.'

At half an hour to midnight the three men reached the gate of the empty house. They had taken the precaution of separating *en route*, Faucit and Mayne keeping together, the detective following on the opposite side of the street.

The road was absolutely deserted. The inhabitants were apparently early people, and all the houses were dark. By the light of the last lamp Hayward consulted his watch. 'Half-past,' he said. 'Constable won't pass till 11.50, we have twenty minutes to do it.' He took off his coat, folded it, and threw it over the broken glass on the wall.

'I'll give you a leg up, Mr Faucit. Drop carefully, there are bushes on the other side.'

Faucit clambered over and the others followed.

Guided by the detective, they made their way round to the back. Once down the area, Hayward showed a light. Slipping a knife up the shutter of the kitchen window, he worked open the bolt, broke a pane of glass, turned the fastener, and raised the sash. They made a careful inspection of the house. Dust lay thick on the covered furniture and carpetless floors. From room to room their footsteps echoed noisily in the dead stillness of the night. They began at the garrets and worked their way back to the basement, without finding the smallest trace of any human being, living or dead.

When they reached the door of the kitchen, Mayne's face was very pale. There were black circles round his eyes. His expression was one of utter despondency.

'We'd better go, gentlemen,' said Hayward; 'there is nothing more to be seen, I think.'

He held up the lantern and looked round.

'Wait a bit,' he added. 'There is a cellar.'

A stout oak door opened from the darkest corner of the passage. It was secured by a couple of heavy bolts, and across the lock was drawn a tape fastened by two seals.

'Wine-cellar,' suggested Faucit.

He slid the bolts, which were rusty and moved with difficulty.

Hayward took a small bag from his pocket, and proceeded scientifically to pick the lock. In five minutes they were standing inside. It was a wine-cellar, fitted with bins, most of which were empty. There were a few bottles of champagne and half a dozen or so of spirits.

'Not enough stuff to justify all that precaution,' remarked Faucit.

The detective stooped, holding the lantern close to the ground.

'Bricks loose here,' he said. 'This floor has been taken up and never properly relaid.'

He knelt down, sifting the dust and little bits of loose mortar in his fingers. Presently he drew out what looked like a dustweb, and held it carefully to the light, gently disengaging the clinging particles and smoothing it between his thumb and forefinger. It was a long, silky hair.

'Look here, sir,' he said, 'here's a clue at last. There's a light poker in the kitchen that will serve our turn. Just you wait a minute till I fetch it.'

Faucit laid his hand on Mayne's arm, and felt in the darkness that he was shaking from head to foot.

Hayward was back in a second. He slipped the thin end of the poker between the bricks, using it as a lever. Very little effort dislodged them. When he had removed a dozen, he thrust his arm into the hole, scraping up handfuls of rubbish and loose earth. Each handful he examined by the light of the lantern. The upper layer was chiefly brickdust and earth. Lower down the dust was largely mixed with a white substance.

'Quicklime,' ejaculated the detective. 'I should not wonder, Mr Faucit, if you weren't right after all.'

He lengthened the aperture, working with a will, till the bricks were removed for a space of nearly six feet. Then he and Faucit scraped up the earth.

Two feet below the surface they came upon a complete bed of lime.

'Gently,' said Hayward; 'we've come to what we are looking for.'

Taking out his handkerchief, he carefully swept away the white dust.

The two men bent forward, with a sickening instinct of what lay beneath that thin covering. Suddenly the detective looked up.

'Mr Faucit,' he remarked, quietly, 'just see to your friend. He'll be off in a second.'

The warning was not a minute too soon. Before the words were fairly past his lips, Mayne had reeled and pitched heavily into Faucit's arms, in a dead faint.

As he caught the unconscious man, the barrister looked down into the cavity and saw lying at his very feet – *the perfect skeleton of a woman.*

It was all that remained of the most beautiful model in London – the girl whose fate had for three years been wrapped in mystery – the original of Deverill's 'Oenone', Violet Lucas.

A Ghost's Revenge

It was a dismal evening. Heavy clouds covered the sky. The air was full of a raw dampness, which hung like a veil over the flat marshy district through which the London train was winding its way, like some huge fiery serpent, now pausing in its sinuous course, now darting forward with a writhe and a shriek, to vanish under a lurid cloud of steam.

'Mallowby,' shouted the hoarse voice of the porter, 'Mallowby.' The door of a first-class smoking carriage was reluctantly opened, and a solitary passenger alighted.

'What a beast of a night!' he muttered, hastily buttoning up his fur-lined overcoat, 'and what a beast of a place!' peering discontentedly across the low white railing at the monotonous stretch of snow-powdered fallow and pasture. 'What on earth has induced Forster to bury himself in such a desolate hole?'

'Any luggage, sir? Two portmanteaus and a gun-case – very good, sir. Where for – the Rectory? The cart is just outside, through the gate on the left.'

With another malediction on the rawness of the atmosphere, the passenger from town picked his way across the sloppy platform and climbed into the dogcart which was in waiting for him. He was cold, hungry, and, if the truth must be told, considerably out of temper; and, as he splashed down the mile of a muddy road which lay between the station and the village, Gerald Harrison was half inclined to repent his promise of spending a couple of days with his old college chum on his way to Scotland.

A hearty welcome, a sherry and bitters, a roaring fire, and a hot bath went a long way towards dispelling his ill-humour. The Reverend Richard Forster, now acting as *locum tenens* for the absent rector of Mallowby, thoroughly understood the art of making his guests comfortable.

'You will not have too much time, old fellow,' he said, when he had conducted Harrison to his room. 'I am sorry to hurry you, but dinner is at half-past seven, and I cannot well put it back because I have asked another man. His name is Granville. He has lately come to the old Hall, and we are going to shoot over one of his farms tomorrow.'

Twenty minutes later, when Gerald (with temperature and temper alike restored to their normal condition) descended to the library, he found his host in earnest confabulation with the visitor – a slight dark man, with an anxious, rather worried expression, and a trick of glancing nervously over his shoulder.

'I give you my word, Forster,' he was saying, 'that it is going on worse than ever. I can't get a servant to sleep in the front of the house, and if I were not ashamed of acknowledging myself a fool, I would cut the place tomorrow and go back to town.'

The opening of the door put an end to the discussion. Forster changed the subject by introducing his guests, and as dinner was almost immediately announced, the conversation fell into general channels – such as the Irish question, pheasant-rearing, and the chances of an open season. It struck Harrison that Mr Granville had all the appearance of a man who has received some severe mental shock. Though he talked intelligently and even well, it was evident that his attention was never wholly given to the subject in hand. He seemed to be constantly listening for some expected sound, and once, when footsteps were audible on the gravel without, he started violently and turned as white as a sheet.

'It is only Kenwell bringing back the keys of the church,' remarked Forster. 'He has been taking the choir practice for me this evening. There is the bell.'

A servant answered the door, and the footsteps died away again, accompanied by the distant clash of the iron gate. Granville sank back in his chair with a long breath of relief. He had let his cigar out, and now looked round for a light. Harrison offered him a match, and, as the elder man took it, he could feel that his hand was cold and shaking.

The evening passed in pleasant desultory chat. At eleven o'clock Granville rose. 'Will you order my cart?' he said. Then, in answer to his host's demur, he answered nervously, 'Don't tempt me to stay, Forster; it only makes matters worse. Yes, I know it is quite early and all that; but they will take ten minutes to put the horse in, and,' with a ghastly attempt at a smile, 'I am like Cinderella, I must be indoors before midnight. You will come up early tmorrow, and of course you both lunch with me. I would ask you to dine as well, only – only I am not good company in my own house now.'

Forster's hand was on the bell. He paused, and looked keenly into his friend's face.

'Don't go back, Granville,' he said, earnestly. 'Let me tell your man that you will stay the night here. I can easily put you up.'

'No, thanks; no,' with the nervous haste of one who fears that his resolution may fail him, 'I cannot do that. After all I have said, I dare not show the white feather to the servants. They would think me a fool; but, my God! they don't hear it as I do. Tell them to bring the cart round, Forster. For pity's sake, man, don't waste time! It is ten minutes past eleven already.'

The order was given. As the minutes wore on, Granville became increasingly uneasy. He could not restrain his restless anxiety to be off, and it was a relief to everyone when the grating of wheels outside announced that the trap was in readiness. Forster accompanied him to the door, whither Harrison presently followed.

'It is not much of a night,' he commented, peering out into the chill darkness. 'Your friend will have a coolish drive.'

Forster was standing on the step.

'Hush!' he said, holding up his hand. 'Listen! He is galloping.'

From the old grey tower on their left chimed the half-hour, and, as the notes died away, they could hear the receding rattle of a cart being driven at a furious pace along the road below.

'He must be cracked to drive at that rate in the dark,' cried Gerald, as the clatter of hoofs grew fainter and finally died away. 'It will be more by luck than management if he doesn't upset at the first corner. What is the matter with him, Dick – does he drink, or is he off his head?'

'Neither at present. He thinks his house is haunted, and it is getting on his nerves.'

'Oh, he must be cracked, then,' with easy decision. 'No-one but a lunatic believes in ghosts in these days. Accept the possibilities of terrestrial elementaries and left-hand magic if you like; but the common or garden ghost, never.'

'There is something queer about the old Hall, though,' persisted Forster. 'I do not believe that any consideration you could offer would induce a Mallowby man to sleep there alone. The place has a bad name. It stood empty for years before Granville bought it. He spent no end of money in repairs and furniture too, which makes it additionally hard on him to be driven out by – '

'A ghost,' concluded Harrison, with a shout of laughter. 'My dear Dick, it is too absurd. Let us exorcise the place. I will back my six-shooter at thirty feet against any combination of goblins and blue fire. We will arrange a match tomorrow. Fifty pounds a side, to be paid in material currency only. Come, admit now that the thing is a huge joke.'

'It is a good deal more like death to Granville,' returned Forster, seriously. 'His nerves are regularly gone to pieces. He is not like the same fellow who came down in the autumn.'

'Have the ghosts been trying to evict him ever since?'

'Sounds weak, I dare say,' Dick answered, 'but I am inclined to believe, Gerald, that there is more in it than meets the eye. Last October Granville was every bit as sceptical as you are. If he heard anything he treated it with contempt. When the servants complained of mysterious noises, he laughed them to scorn. You saw for yourself that he does not laugh at it now. He told me this evening that these – these manifestations are of nightly occurrence. I am afraid it is taking serious effect upon his health. I wish I had kept him here tonight.'

'Oh, he will be all right,' said Harrison, lightly. 'Funk is a deuced unpleasant complaint, but it don't often kill. Twelve o'clock; I think I'll be turning in. This time tomorrow, I suppose, we shall be wishing each other a happy new year.'

But the glad new year was destined to be ushered in by no hearty shaking of hands, no joyous congratulations at Mallowby Rectory. In the grey dawn of the December morning Harrison was awakened by the flashing of a candle before his eyes. Forster was standing beside the bed, with a pale and horror-stricken face.

'Gerald,' he said hurriedly, 'will you get up at once? I want you to come with me to the Hall. Something terrible has happened. Poor Granville is dead.'

'Dead!' repeated the other blankly, 'dead! Why, he only left here at eleven.'

'I know that. Seven hours ago he was here, only seven hours ago, and now they are carrying his body up from the pond where it was found. Why did I not keep him here?' he cried, pacing the room in deep agitation. 'Why did I let him go back to that accursed house? I knew his mind was unhinged by what he had heard there. Poor fellow! Poor Granville! And now it is too late.'

Harrison was already out of bed.

'I will be downstairs in five minutes,' he said. 'Of course, I know no particulars, but has anyone thought of sending for a doctor?'

Forster caught eagerly at the implied hope.

'Someone shall go for Mr Tilling at once, he said, hurrying out of the room.

It was a relief to be able to do something, but long before the surgeon arrived they knew that his services would be useless. Death had sealed the master of Ravenshill for his own. The cold and rigid limbs refused to respond to the revivifying influences of hot blankets and artificial respiration.

Harrison was of the opinion, as he assisted in his friend's frantic endeavours to restore some semblance of life, that poor Granville had been dead for several hours.

It was a painful task. In vain Forster tried to close the dull, lack-lustre eyes, fixed in a wide stare of indescribable horror. The tense features would not relax. Never had a human being passed away from life leaving behind him so terrible an impression of fear. At seven o'clock the surgeon for whom Forster had sent appeared on the scene. One glance at the body was sufficient for him.

'He's dead,' said the plain-spoken country practitioner. 'Dead as a door-nail. How did it happen?'

Ah! how indeed? That was a mystery. A secret known only to the dead man and to those unspeakable powers who work behind the veil.

In the early morning of the last day of the year the household at the Hall had been startled from their slumbers by a wild, agonised cry, followed by shriek upon shriek of demoniacal laughter. The horrible sounds lasted only for a minute. Before the terrified servants were fairly aroused and crowding together into the corridor, to learn the meaning of this strange alarm, the house was wrapped in its customary silence. For a few moments they had been too scared to do more than wonder at their master remaining undisturbed; then someone, bolder than the rest, suggested that it would be as well to waken him. They knocked at his door and received no answer. They called, but no voice replied. At last the butler ventured into the room. It was empty. The night lamp, which Granville had lately used, was burning brightly, the fire was nearly out. The bed had not been occupied. Thoroughly alarmed now, a search party was formed, and, armed with lights and a brace of revolvers, the men descended to the ground floor. In the library the lamp was also burning. The odour of tobacco still hung in the air; a few embers glowed in the grate; the spirit decanters and an empty soda-water bottle lay on the table beside an open book. There was no trace of any disturbance, and there was no sign of Granville.

The servants looked at each other in silence. No-one dared to put into words the fear that lay chill at his heart. Suddenly the butler uttered an exclamation. His eyes had fallen on one of the windows. The long curtains were swaying gently backward and forward in the current of cold air from without.

The shutters were thrown back, and the casement stood wide open. They crowded round. 'Steady, keep back a bit,' protested one man, more astute than his fellows, 'there is snow enough to hold footmarks. It's a pity to tread it about till we've got a lantern and struck the trail.'

In a few minutes a covered light had been procured, and the threshold of the window was examined. There could be no doubt as to the way in which Granville had quitted the room. Straight from the sill the footprints were distinctly traced in the light snow. Along the path they tracked the marks, round the corner of the house, across the lawn to the edge of the pond. And there, beneath the willows, half-hidden by the drooping frost-browned ferns, they found the body of their master, still in evening dress, with clenched fingers, and features transfixed in an expression of ghastly dread.

The quiet little village was shaken to its core. All day long the people gathered in knots to discuss the awful tragedy which had been enacted in their midst. Horror was in the air. Old superstition reasserted its sway with renewed strength. Old stories were repeated with bated breath; for once again the curse of the Deverels had fallen, and the truth of the half-forgotten legend was triumphantly vindicated.

By nightfall every human being quitted the precincts of the fateful Hall. The scared domestics absolutely refused to remain on the premises, and the big house was deserted, save for the silent form lying so still beneath the white sheet on one of the sofas in the library, in which room the body of Philip Granville had been laid to await the coroner's inquest.

To Forster this desertion of the helpless corpse seemed terrible. He would have spent the night in watching beside the poor fellow who had so lately been his guest, and was only dissuaded from his purpose by the earnest solicitations of his churchwarden, a stalwart farmer, on whose grey head seventy odd years sat lighter than most men's fifty.

'Parson,' said the old man, solemnly, 'theer's noa good a-flyin' in the faace o' Providence. Noa body thinks as you're a coward, but what sort o' use be theer in flingin' good loives a'ter bad uns? Yon poor lad tried it, and see how they've served him. Thirty year back Lord Broadborough's agent died in same way. My feyther used to tell how, when he were a little lad, one of the Dawbenys caam doon hissen' and boasted as how he'd better the Deverels. It was i' the summer toime, and all went well enow. But as soon as winter caame on, "they" were at work ag'in, and t'ould squoire, he began to grow graave and stern-like. He would na gi'in, till, on New Year's Eve, the house were fetched up by a fearful cry, and next mornin' they found his body in the pond theer, with a look on t'faace as, God forbid, should iver be sean on yours or moine. Mony an' mony a good mon has met that death, sin' the noight that Katharine Deverel stood in yon winder and cursed the mon who had robbed her of her husband's naame, an' theer lad of his lawful inheritance. "You hev ta'an it by fraud," she croid; "but the Lord will avenge me. Noa good shall it bring thee. You shall neyther live in it yoursen, nor shall another receive it at your hands. Though I lose my immortal soul," she says, "I'll hev revenge. You may tak' my choild's birthright, you may slur ma fair naame, but noa mon – be he young or auld, good or evil, so that he does na' bear th' naame o'Deverel – shall live to see a new year sawn wi'in these walls. I'll die on Deverel land," says she; "and he who braves ma curse shall die even as I hev died." Then she called on the God of the feytherless to hear her words and turned awa', and next mornin' they found her body stiff an' stark in yonder pond, with the dead baby still clasped in her arms. You'll bear in moind, sir, what the Lord did to the mon who built up the walls o' Jericho. It's His will, an' you bein' a parson, should knaw better than to goa agin' Him. What harm can taake yon poor bit o' clay now? But you hev a wark to do i' the warld, and you ain't got no reet to chuck your loife a'ter his'n.'

'Mr Dawson is right, Dick,' urged Harrison; 'you can't do the poor fellow any good. Your nerves are shaken, and I am free to confess, ghost or no ghost, to spend the night in that dismal house with a dead man is more than I should care about.'

Very unwillingly Forster at last agreed to yield.

Three days later the local jury brought in a verdict of 'Died by the visitation of God', and once again the spirit of Katharine Deveril had triumphed and the home of her ancestors stood empty.

Five years had come and gone, bringing with them many changes. Dick Forster, now Bishop of Honduras, was doing good work for God and man in his far-off colonial diocese. His place in Harrison's daily life had been filled by another friend of his schoolboy days, who was also shortly to become his brother-in-law. Jack Chamberlayne was a handsome, genial young fellow, blessed with a fine constitution, a sweet temper, and a very considerable fortune, and the match between his favourite sister and his special chum was a source of unmixed satisfaction to Gerald. The two men were constantly together until a matter of business obliged Harrison to visit the South of Europe. The transaction occupied him for some months, and it was not till the end of December that he found himself once more on English soil. He reached Dover at noon on the last day of the year, and went straight to the Lord Warden. A packet of letters was awaiting him. They had been forwarded from San Carrémo after his departure, and among them was an envelope addressed in Chamberlayne's characteristic handwriting.

> Dear Old Boy [ran the letter] what do you mean by spending Christmas in a dirty Italian village, instead of returning to the bosom of your family like a respectable Englishman? I don't believe a word about the vineyards. Tell your agent to go to the devil, and come to us for the new year, or neither Elaine nor I will have anything more to do with you. The Hunt Ball is on the 5th, the Cardwell's on the following evening. On the 7th Mrs Verelst is giving some theatricals in which we are going to distinguish ourselves, and there are three or four other minor events which you ought not to miss. Also I want your valuable advice as to the wisdom of buying a place in Creamshire. I only heard of it last week, and have already made up my mind to purchase, so your counsel must tend in that direction if you wish me to profit by it. It is a jolly old house, with capital stabling, and nice gardens. There is a ripping tennis-lawn (room for two courts, if I fill up a pond at the end), and a lot of old oak indoors. I forgot to say the house is furnished. It is in the best part of the Broadborough country, and within reach of the outside meets of Lord Cremorne's and the Turton. Plenty of shooting, and the whole thing going for a mere song. I believe there is even a family ghost thrown in. I am running down on Friday for a week to see how I like it; but of course you will put up at my place as you come through town whether I am there or not –

Harrison waited to hear no more. In a moment the letter was crushed into his pocket, and he was out in the street, and, hurrying to the nearest telegraph-office, without a second's delay he wrote the message and handed it in to the clerk –

CHAMBERLAYNE, 112 PICCADILLY. ON NO ACCOUNT GO TO RAVENSHILL HALL TILL YOU HAVE SEEN ME. SHALL BE IN TOWN THIS AFTERNOON AND WILL EXPLAIN. – GERALD

Then he hastened back to the hotel and ordered some luncheon. While he was eating he looked out the trains for town. The next was due in twenty minutes. His portmanteaus had not been unstrapped. Harrison sent for a cab, paid his bill, and in less than an hour was well on his way to London. From the moment of reading Chamberlayne's description of his projected purchase, he had decided on the course he must pursue. Though the name of the place was not mentioned he knew, by a sudden swift intuition, that it was Ravenshill Hall. Back to his mind, with the freshness of yesterday, swept the memory of that terrible night five years ago, and he shuddered as he recalled the old farmer quoting the words of Katharine Deverel.

'"No man – be he young or old, good or evil, so that he does not bear the name of Deverel – shall live to see the new year break within these walls. I will die on Deverel land, and he who braves my curse shall die even as I have died."

'Many and many a good man has met that death since,' the farmer had declared. Was another victim destined to be added to the long roll-call of that terrible vengeance, and that victim his old playmate, his friend, his almost brother? No, thank God; there was yet time to avert the stroke of fate. Jack must have received his wire by now. He would be waiting for the promised explanation. The slow hours wore on; the train rattled and ground its way through the wintry landscape. The sky was leaden and dull. On the horizon lay dense masses of clouds, black and heavy with snow. By the time they ran into Charing Cross, large flakes were floating lazily down to join their crushed and mud-stained comrades on the dirty pavement. Evidently there had been a considerable fall earlier in the day, for the roofs down the Strand were gleaming white, and great heaps of snow had been scraped up from the roadway and piled behind the pillars of the station gates. Harrison got his luggage on to a hansom and drove straight to his friend's chambers. As he glanced up at the windows, it struck him as odd that no lights were to be seen.

The housekeeper answered his ring.

'Oh, is it you, Mr Harrison? Very glad to see you back, sir. There is a letter for you upstairs and three telegrams. The first came on Wednesday, sir. The note Mr Chamberlayne left for you; he expected you would be here on Wednesday.'

'Left for me,' repeated Gerald, anxiously. 'He has not gone, surely? Did he not get my wire?'

'I sent it on with the other letters this morning, sir. Mr Chamberlayne has been gone a week – him and Mr Curtis. He is staying at Creamshire, at Ravenshill Hall, Mallowby.'

Harrison's brain reeled. He saw it all now. That letter had been a week in travelling to Italy and back again to England. He had cried, 'Peace, peace', when there was no peace; when all the time he was too late, and Jack had gone to that accursed house, and – this was New Year's Eve.

'Fetch the letters, Mrs Williams; or, stay, I will get them myself.'

He tore upstairs, two steps at a time, snatched the envelopes from the mantelpiece and was back to the cab before the astounded housekeeper could utter a syllable.

'King's Cross!' he shouted to the driver; 'and a double fare if I catch the 7.05 for the north. It is a matter of life and death.'

'I'll do my best, sir,' said the man, dubiously; 'but it's darned bad going.'

Never had the way seemed so long; never did time go faster and horse more slowly. To Harrison's overwrought fancy they crept along, and again and again he raised the trap and implored the man to whip up. The agony and anxiety in his white drawn face moved the cabby's heart to pity, and he generously refrained from swearing at his impetuous fare.

'A cove is that onreasonable when 'e's in trouble,' he growled to himself aloft. 'Does 'e want me to let the mare down and make sure of losing 'is blooming train?'

At last they turned into the Euston Road. The snow was coming down in good earnest now, and Gerald could hardly see the hands of the clock for the blinding flakes. It wanted eight minutes to seven.

'Thank God!' he murmured, as the hansom turned into the yard of the Great Northern. Before the man had time to pull up, he was out on the ground.

'Mallowby,' he called to the porter, 'can I do it?'

'Four minutes,' was the response.

Gerald flung half a sovereign to the driver, and rushed into the booking-office. The bell was ringing when he got on to the platform. The porter had put his portmanteaus into a carriage and was holding open the door. He threw himself into a seat with a sense of gratitude that he was to have the compartment to himself.

To maintain an appearance of indifferent calm at this moment would, he felt, have been impossible. He was enduring a martyrdom of suspense. If his friend's life had not already paid the forfeit for another's sin, every second that ticked its course was bringing him nearer to its end. He conjured up with horrible distinctness the dark library, the deep recesses on either side of the fireplace lined with books, the massive oak furniture. He could hear the weird murmur of voices, without, the ghostly steps on the drive; then the heavy velvet curtains trembled, parted, and a woman's figure stood framed in the long window – a woman with dripping garments and a white set face, lighted by strange, lurid eyes – eyes which were dead, and yet alive in their fierce hatred and unquenchable thirst for revenge. How they glittered! They were close to him now, looking in through the carriage window, and Harrison, who had once laughed contemptuously at the mere notion of supernatural manifestations, was perilously near raising a ghost for himself from the intensity of his nervous excitement. Fortunately, at this juncture he remembered that Jack's letter and the telegrams were still unopened in his pocket, and the break in the sequence of thought gave him time to pull himself together.

With a half-laugh at his own weakness, he drew the curtains across the windows, and, lighting a cigar, tore open the yellow envelopes.

All three messages had been handed in at Mallowby Station. The first was dated December 29, and said:

COME DOWN AS SOON AS POSSIBLE. DULL AND SEEDY. WANT CHEERING UP. – CHAMBERLAYNE

'He is getting nervous,' Gerald said to himself, 'and did not like to acknowledge it.'

The second telegram was more urgent, and enclosed a reply form.

MUST SEE YOU TODAY. IMPORTANT. WIRE WHAT TRAIN. DON'T FAIL ME. – JACK

The third was signed by Chamberlayne's valet.

SOMETHING SERIOUSLY WRONG HERE. PLEASE COME AT ONCE, VERY ANXIOUS ABOUT MASTER.

Harrison's face grew very grave. Something must indeed have been wrong before the punctilious Curtis would take upon himself to send a wire like that. His fears returned with renewed force. It was torture to think of Jack sending message after message only to meet with blank silence. There was a piteous reproach in the last appeal, 'Don't fail me'.

'As if I were likely to do that so long as I am above ground,' thought Gerald. 'Poor old Jack, he might have known I should have answered if I'd ever got the things.'

At Peterborough he went to the refreshment-room and swallowed a sandwich and a few mouthfuls of soup while his flask was replenished with brandy. Very few passengers joined the train, and no-one came into Harrison's carriage. As the hours dragged out their weary length he grew more and more restless and nervous. He paced the six feet of floor like a caged animal. He let down the window. A cloud of fine snow blew in through the opening. All around hedges, fields, and trees were wrapped in a dense white mantle. It was bitterly cold. Despite his fur-lined coat, hot tin, and a couple of rugs, his teeth were chattering and his hands were like ice.

He looked at his watch. It was half-past nine. In thirty minutes the train was due at Mallowby, and they had not passed Grantham yet. Surely, too, they were slackening speed. Half doubting the evidence of his senses, he again opened the window. The train was unmistakably at a standstill, but there was not the slightest sign of a station. The wind had risen, and whistled through the telegraph-wires overhead. Between the gusts he could hear the murmur of voices. Presently a man passed along the footboard. It was the guard. Harrison inquired the cause of the delay.

'Line blocked, I'm afraid, sir,' was the reply, 'but I will let you know as I come back.'

With an exclamation which was almost a groan, Gerald flung himself back in his seat. Were the fates in league against him, that now, when every moment might seal Jack Chamberlayne's death-warrant, he must perforce sit idle, bound hand and foot by the victory of the forces of nature over the inventions of man? Five minutes passed, ten, twenty, thirty. Then the guard put his head in at the door.

'All right, sir, line is clear; we shall go on directly.'

At one minute past eleven the London train, more than an hour behind its time, set down a single passenger at Mallowby. Harrison at once addressed himself to the stationmaster, and inquired how he could get to the old Hall. The man had been on the coroner's jury five years before, and remembered his face.

'Going to the Hall tonight, sir? Why, were not you here when poor Mr Granville was drowned? You don't want to see it a second time, surely!'

'God forbid!' answered Gerald, quickly, 'but I want to prevent it. A dear friend of mine is at that devilish house tonight. He does not know his danger, and I mean to save him.'

'You can't do it,' returned the man, bluntly. 'Best keep clear of the black work that will be going forward up there. There is no baulking the Deverel curse. It will have its victim. God help him I say, and all those who sleep under that roof on New Year's Eve. You can do nothing for them.'

'I mean to try,' answered Harrison, with set teeth. 'I have no time to waste. Where can I get a trap?'

'Nowhere nearer than the village. It will take you as long as walking the whole way. The roads are awful.'

'Then I must walk. Can you find me a lantern? For Heaven's sake be quick. Every minute may mean his life now. What do I care about the danger? Man, I tell you he is my friend. He is to marry my sister in a fortnight, and I will either save him or die with him.'

The stationmaster hesitated a moment.

'Look here, sir,' he said, hurriedly, 'you're a brave man, and I'll do what I can to help you. That was my last train till 1.30. I'll come with you as far as the gates. It will save you losing the way, and perhaps a bit of time getting through the drifts beside.'

Gerald thanked him heartily, and side by side they turned their backs to the lights of the little station, and struck into the lonely road which lay between the railway and the haunted house. It had ceased snowing now. A few stars gleamed out between the rifts in the cloudy sky. From time to time a pale moon showed her face, now flooding the white landscape with a cold grey light, now hiding herself in a veil of fleecy vapour, as though she feared to see those things which should be done on the earth. By the help of the stationmaster's lantern the two men managed to keep to the narrow cart tract. The road was desperately bad. In places the snow was fully two feet deep. With the rising moon a keen wind had got up, which came sweeping over the level fields right in their faces, and cut like a knife. At the turning into the village where the land sloped a little, the drifts were almost impassable. At every step they sank above the knee. Harrison could hear his companion's breath coming thick and short. He was evidently getting done. For himself he was impervious to all outward discomfort. Cold, fatigue, hunger; he was vaguely conscious that he should know them all, if he were not past feeling now. His whole mind, will, nerve, aye, his very being, were centred in the one intense determination to save his friend. At length they gained the main street of the village. Here the snow was trodden down, and the going comparatively easy. Hardly a light was to be seen in any of the cottages. Involuntarily Gerald's eyes turned towards the rectory. It was wrapped in shadow and silence; but from the old grey tower, looming up behind, gleamed a small point of yellow light. Slowly it crept from window to window, steadily rising, rising. A cold shudder ran through the man who watched it. He knew what it meant; that the last sands were falling from the hour-glass of time; that the life of the old year must now be measured by minutes. The ringers were going up to the belfry.

'Oh, God!' he groaned inwardly, 'give me strength, give me time.'

'Have you got a drop of brandy about you, sir?' suggested the practical Miles. 'It would help to keep the spirit in us a bit.'

Without slackening his pace, Gerald held out his flask.

'A'ter you, sir, a'ter you.'

'I don't want any, thanks.' His ears were strained for the first stroke of that ominous bell.

'Oh, come now, sir, fair do's. You will need your strength more than me, and I say a'ter you.'

To save discussion, Harrison put the flask to his lips. The spirit sent a warm glow through his sluggish veins. At the same moment the stillness of the night was broken by the solemn tolling of the passing bell. With a cry of horror he thrust the brandy into his companion's hands, and began to run as if for his life. Immediately before him the road curved sharply to the left, and far ahead through the skeleton branches of the leafless elms gleamed half a dozen irregular patches of light. They shone from the windows of the Hall.

Slowly, mournfully pealed the muffled notes from the belfry. The knell of the old year, dying hard in the chill winter night; the knell of a human soul, who might even now be passing from life and love to the horror of unknown darkness, through the gate of a fearful death. The thought was torture. How he lived through those moments of suspense Harrison never knew. He could not have told how he covered the ground, or when he passed the gates which led up to the house. His brain burned like molten iron, on which the slow, monotonous clang of the bell fell like the strokes of a heavy hammer. He forgot the stationmaster, plodding along in the rear – forgot everything but that his goal was reached, if only he had not come too late.

The lower windows were closed, but from the chinks in the shutters stole the warm glow of fire and lamp, and as he reached the corner of the house he could catch the sound of approaching voices.

Voices, yes! – but what sort of voices? Nearer they came, now swelling louder, now sinking to a whisper, but ever drawing nearer, till he could hear the words repeated in every shade of tone, from malignant exultation to concentrated passion of resolve.

'We shall have him tonight!' they said, with ghastly reiteration. 'We shall have him tonight!'

Like a wave of ice-cold air, the horrible sounds passed by him, receded, and died away with an echo of fiendish laughter.

Despite an inexpressible thrill of fear, that sent a shudder through his whole frame and nearly raised the hair on his head, Harrison was conscious of a faint hope that all was not over yet. Slowly and more slowly came the tolling of the bell. It was on the verge of midnight.

Suddenly from within the closed windows of the library issued a wild awful cry. The shutters were flung back, as if by magic the casement was thrown open, and the dark shadow of a man crossed the sill.

The moon emerging suddenly from behind a bank of clouds poured down a flood of silvery light on the stone wall, the snow-covered path, and on the figure of Jack Chamberlayne, who, with hands clenched as if in mortal pain, his eyes fixed with an expression of nameless horror on some object, invisible to all but him, was slowly following the ghostly vision along the drive, across the lawn, to –

With a supreme effort Harrison threw off the paralysing numbness which was creeping over him. Instinctively he dashed across the grass and stood between Chamberlayne and the fatal pond. Twelve paces from him his friend was advancing, slowly, unswervingly, like one who walks in his sleep.

'Jack,' he shouted, 'Jack, it is I, Gerald. Don't you know me?'

There was not a quiver of the tense eyeballs, not a sign that his voice had reached those ears, deaf now to all earthly sounds, but from the open window of the library a man rushed towards them, crying wildly, 'Stop him, for God's sake, stop him before it is too late.'

Gathering all his strength, Gerald flung himself upon the approaching figure. A frantic struggle ensued, for Chamberlayne was the taller by a head, and was at this moment, moreover, endowed with abnormal strength. It was then that his knowledge of wrestling, acquired during a 'long' spent in the Cumberland dales, stood Harrison in right good stead. He closed with his antagonist, and by a sudden dexterous manoeuvre threw him heavily to the ground, while overhead across the snowy fields the bells rang out their joyous welcome to the glad new year.

'Is he – dead?'

The valet on his knees beside his master's prostrate form had torn open Chamberlayne's vest and shirt, and was feeling for the faint pulsation which tells that the spirit has not yet quitted its earthly tenement.

'Fainted, I think; I can feel his heartbeat.'

'Thank God, sir, you came when you did. I should have been too late. Can you help me to carry him, Mr Harrison? No, not to that damned place!' as Gerald glanced involuntarily towards the lighted windows. 'They are all up at the gardener's cottage. I wanted Mr Chamberlayne to sleep there tonight; but you know what he is – told me to go myself if I was frightened. I had not been out of the room five minutes when I heard that awful cry, and – Holy Virgin! What is that?'

Harrison turned instinctively towards the library window. From the open sash a long tongue of yellow flame leaped out, curling round the edge of the curtain and licking up the thick silk cording as though it were a mere thread. Then another, and another. Fanned by the fresh breeze from without, the yellow glare broadened and deepened till the whole room was filled with a fierce lurid glow, succeeded by dense clouds of smoke and an ominous crackling sound.

'The place is on fire!' cried Gerald. 'There is not a moment to lose. We must get your master into shelter and give the alarm!'

'Holy Saint Patrick, defend us!' murmured Curtis, hastily crossing himself, as he stooped to raise the helpless form of poor Chamberlayne. Then, as best they could, the two men carried their burden across the lawn, along the drive, and up the side path leading to the fruit-gardens.

'Who is in the house?' gasped Harrison, as staggering and breathless, they reached the door of the cottage. 'Are any servants there?'

'Not a soul. Mrs Bamfield here came in the day. She left directly dinner was served. There is no-one in the place to burn but the devil's spawn as lighted it.'

The valet's resonant knocks soon brought the gardener to the door, and while his wife was helping Curtis to restore his master to consciousness, Bamfield hurried Gerald off to the village to obtain assistance.

Just outside the gates they encountered the stationmaster, who was hanging about in great distress of mind, too anxious on Harrison's account to return to Mallowby, yet not daring to adventure himself within the fatal precincts of the Hall. His relief and joy at finding

Gerald still alive knew no bounds, and he readily undertook to see a messenger despatched for the nearest doctor on his way back to the station. Meanwhile an alarm had been raised, and the sleeping village was raised by the hoarse cries of 'Fire!' The ringers had been the first to see the red glare through the tress; but before long some forty men had turned out to join the little crowd already assembled before the burning house. Under Harrison's direction a body of labourers, headed by the gardener and bailiff, made an attempt to check the progress of the flames. But their efforts were scarcely perceptible. With a sharp wind blowing, and no better appliances at command than a line of buckets and a couple of garden-hose, it was evident from the first that the Hall was practically doomed. The old oak, of which the interior was chiefly built, burned like tinder. Within twenty minutes of the first outbreak the flames had spread to the upper storey. Window after window lent its aid to the weird illumination. The great carved bedsteads, the massive presses and cabinets, glowed and crackled in the fierce heat. Deverel after Deverel, clothed in dainty satin or shining armour, shrivelled and cracked away from their frames, to go down calm and unflinching as became true knights and brave gentlewomen into that burning fiery furnace. Still the fire-fiend raged on, vast clouds of black smoke mingling with the glare, while from time to time could be heard the heavy crash of falling beams and flooring. As the clock of the old church chimed the first hour of the new year, with a sound like the roll of distant artillery, swelling gradually into a deafening roar, the roof fell in and there shot up to heaven one mighty sheet of flame, which turned the sky into a crimson pall, and lighted up the snow-clad country for miles around. Was it a trick of over-heated imagination, a play of superstitious fancy, or did those who stood by at that moment really hear that hideous peal of shrill triumphant laughter, which made the stoutest heart among them quail, and forced each man to edge involuntarily nearer his neighbour? It lasted but for an instant, then nothing was audible but the continuous roar of the flames. Before the pale dawn had warmed into the red flush of sunrise, Ravenshill Hall was a heap of smouldering ashes enclosed in four grim, smoke-blackened walls. From attic to cellar not a corner had been spared. The fire had done its work thoroughly, and of the original structure nothing remained save the bare tottering shell.

'It wer' th' Lord's will,' said old Dawson, who had come down to inspect the scene of the late catastrophe, 'that Katharine Deverel should hev her reets; and now as He's proved as mon caan't go agin' Him, He's maade awa' wi' th' dommed ould plaace, an' a good riddance too. The Lord avenges the widder and the feytherless, though He keeps 'un waitin' a bit first soomtoimes, and it seams to me,' concluded the farmer, thoughtfully, 'as soom o' they poor bodies in Oireland should be hevin' theer turn afore long.'

'It will be a bad look-out for the Moonlighters when they do,' answered Harrison, with a quiet smile.

He was a little oppressed by the situation in which he found himself; for the events of that New Year's Eve were the talk of the countryside, and Gerald the hero of the hour. A man who, single-handed, had braved the Deverel ghosts and baulked them of their prey ranked, by the Mallowby standard, above Gordon, and only a little lower than Nelson. The worthy Miles was never tired of recounting the incidents of that midnight walk, and drew upon his imagination for certain effective touches to that part of the adventure to which he had not been an eyewitness.

The rustic mind is slow to receive a new impression; but when it does get a sensation, it makes the most of it. The people would listen to the story twenty times a day. They repeated it to each other; they turned it inside and out and discussed it threadbare, beginning it over again for the benefit of every fresh comer. To Gerald, who was heartily sick of the place and the subject, this lionising was inexpressibly irritating, and he was thankful when the doctor at last gave permission for Chamberlayne to be removed.

Thanks to his splendid constitution, backed up by the devoted nursing of Curtis and his friend, Jack escaped brain fever; but he had received a terrible shock, and his nerves were sorely shaken. It was not till the snow-wreaths had melted on the Creamshire Wolds, and crocuses were showing their gold and purple heads above the dark earth in suburban gardens, that Harrison was called upon to officiate as best man at a very pretty wedding in a certain fashionable London church, after which ceremony Mr and Mrs Jack Chamberlayne went off to the Riviera, where it was hoped that southern sunshine and a little judicious excitement at Monte Carlo would efface from the bridegroom's memory the experiences of that terrible New Year's Eve.

Of what he had actually seen and heard in the awful interval between his servant's departure and his subsequent return to consciousness Chamberlayne never speaks.

'I used to wonder,' he once said to Gerald, 'why Lazarus and those other fellows who were raised from the dead never told what they did and how they felt. I think I understand now. It was too terrible. They could not put it into words, and that is how I feel about that night – as if I had been brought back from the dead.'

The Blue Room

It happened twice in my time. It will never happen again, they say, since Miss Erristoun (Mrs Arthur, that is now) and Mr Calder-Maxwell between them found out the secret of the haunted room, and laid the ghost; for ghost it was, though at the time Mr Maxwell gave it another name, Latin, I fancy, but all I can remember about it now is that it somehow reminded me of poultry-rearing. I am the housekeeper at Mertoun Towers, as my aunt was before me, and her aunt before her, and first of all my great-grandmother, who was a distant cousin of the Laird, and had married the chaplain, but being penniless at her husband's death, was thankful to accept the post which has ever since been occupied by one of her descendants. It gives us a sort of standing with the servants, being, as it were, related to the family; and Sir Archibald and my Lady have always acknowledged the connection, and treated us with more freedom than would be accorded to ordinary dependants.

Mertoun has been my home from the time I was eighteen. Something occurred then of which, since it has nothing to do with this story, I need only say that it wiped out for ever any idea of marriage on my part, and I came to the Towers to be trained under my aunt's vigilant eye for the duties in which I was one day to succeed her.

Of course I knew there was a story about the blue tapestry room. Everyone knew that, though the old Laird had given strict orders that the subject should not be discussed among the servants, and always discouraged any allusion to it on the part of his family and guests. But there is a strange fascination about everything connected with the supernatural, and orders or no orders, people, whether gentle or simple, will try to gratify their curiosity; so a good deal of surreptitious talk went on both in the drawing-room and the servants' hall, and hardly a guest came to the house but would pay a visit to the Blue Room and ask all manner of questions about the ghost. The odd part of the business was that no-one knew what the ghost was supposed to be, or even if there were any ghost at all. I tried hard to get my aunt to tell me some details of the legend, but she always reminded me of Sir Archibald's orders, and added that the tale most likely started with the superstitious fancy of people who lived long ago and were very ignorant, because a certain Lady Barbara Mertoun had died in that room.

I reminded her that people must have died, at some time or other, in pretty nearly every room in the house, and no-one had thought of calling them haunted, or hinting that it was unsafe to sleep there.

She answered that Sir Archibald himself had used the Blue Room, and one or two other gentlemen, who had passed the night there for a wager, and they had neither seen nor heard anything unusual. For her part, she added, she did not hold with people wasting their time thinking of such folly, when they had much better be giving their minds to their proper business.

Somehow her professions of incredulity did not ring true, and I wasn't satisfied, though I gave up asking questions. But if I said nothing, I thought the more, and often when my duties took me to the Blue Room I would wonder why, if nothing had happened there, and there was no real mystery, the room was never used; it had not even a mattress on the fine carved bedstead, which was only covered by a sheet to keep it from the dust. And then I would steal into the portrait gallery to look at the great picture of the Lady Barbara, who had died in the full bloom of her youth, no-one knew why, for she was just found one morning stiff and cold, stretched across that fine bed under the blue tapestried canopy.

She must have been a beautiful woman, with her great black eyes and splendid auburn hair, though I doubt her beauty was all on the outside, for she had belonged to the gayest set of the Court, which was none too respectable in those days, if half the tales one hears of it are true; and indeed a modest lady would hardly have been painted in such a dress, all slipping off her shoulders, and so thin that one can see right through the stuff. There must have been something queer about her too, for they do say her father-in-law, who was known as the wicked Lord Mertoun, would not have her buried with the rest of the family; but that might have been his spite, because he was angry that she had no child, and her husband, who was but a sickly sort of man, dying of consumption but a month later, there was no direct heir; so that with the old Lord the title became extinct, and the estates passed to the Protestant branch of the family, of which the present Sir Archibald Mertoun is the head. Be that as it may, Lady Barbara lies by herself in the churchyard, near the lychgate, under a grand marble tomb indeed, but all alone, while her husband's coffin has its place beside those of his brothers who died before him, among their ancestors and descendants in the great vault under the chancel.

I often used to think about her, and wonder why she died, and how; and then It happened and the mystery grew deeper than ever.

There was a family-gathering that Christmas, I remember, the first Christmas for many years that had been kept at Mertoun, and we had been very busy arranging the rooms for the different guests, for on New Year's Eve there was a ball in the neighbourhood, to which Lady Mertoun was taking a large party, and for that night, at least, the house was as full as it would hold.

I was in the linen-room, helping to sort the sheets and pillow-covers for the different beds, when my Lady came in with an open letter in her hand.

She began to talk to my aunt in a low voice, explaining something which seemed to have put her out, for when I returned from carrying a pile of linen to the head-housemaid, I heard her say: 'It is too annoying to upset all one's arrangements at the last moment. Why couldn't she have left the girl at home and brought another maid, who could be squeezed in somewhere without any trouble?'

I gathered that one of the visitors, Lady Grayburn, had written that she was bringing her companion, and as she had left her maid, who was ill, at home, she wanted the young lady to have a bedroom adjoining hers, so that she might be at hand to give any help that was required. The request seemed a trifling matter enough in itself, but it just so happened that there really was no room at liberty. Every bedroom on the first corridor was occupied, with the exception of the Blue Room, which, as ill-luck would have it, chanced to be next to that arranged for Lady Grayburn.

My aunt made several suggestions, but none of them seemed quite practicable, and at last my Lady broke out: 'Well, it cannot be helped; you must put Miss Wood in the Blue Room. It is only for one night, and she won't know anything about that silly story.'

'Oh, my Lady!' my aunt cried, and I knew by her tone that she had not spoken the truth when she professed to think so lightly of the ghost.

'I can't help it,' her Ladyship answered: 'besides I don't believe there is anything really wrong with the room. Sir Archibald has slept there, and he found no cause for complaint.'

'But a woman, a young woman,' my aunt urged; 'indeed I wouldn't run such a risk, my Lady; let me put one of the gentlemen in there, and Miss Wood can have the first room in the west corridor.'

'And what use would she be to Lady Grayburn out there?' said her Ladyship. 'Don't be foolish, my good Marris. Unlock the door between the two rooms; Miss Wood can leave it open if she feels nervous; but I shall not say a word about that foolish superstition, and I shall be very much annoyed if anyone else does so.'

She spoke as if that settled the question, but my aunt wasn't easy. 'The Laird,' she murmured; 'what will he say to a lady being put to sleep there?'

'Sir Archibald does not interfere in household arrangements. Have the Blue Room made ready for Miss Wood at once. *I* will take the responsibility – if there is any.'

On that her Ladyship went away, and there was nothing for it but to carry out her orders. The Blue Room was prepared, a great fire lighted, and when I went round last thing to see all was in order for the visitor's arrival, I couldn't but think how handsome and comfortable it looked. There were candles burning brightly on the toilet-table and chimney-piece, and a fine blaze of logs on the wide hearth. I saw nothing had been overlooked, and was closing the door when my eyes fell on the bed. It was crumpled just as if someone had thrown themselves across it, and I was vexed that the housemaids should have been so careless, especially with the smart new quilt. I went round, and patted up the feathers, and smoothed the counterpane, just as the carriages drove under the window.

By-and-by Lady Grayburn and Miss Wood came upstairs, and knowing they had brought no maid, I went to assist in the unpacking. I was a long time in her Ladyship's room, and when I'd settled her I tapped at the next door and offered to help Miss Wood. Lady Grayburn followed me almost immediately to inquire the whereabouts of some keys. She spoke very sharply, I thought, to her companion, who seemed a timid, delicate slip of a girl, with nothing noticeable about her except her hair, which was lovely, pale golden, and heaped in thick coils all round her small head.

'You will certainly be late,' Lady Grayburn said. 'What an age you have been, and you have not half finished unpacking yet.' The young lady murmured something about there being so little time. 'You have had time to sprawl on the bed instead of getting ready,' was the retort, and as Miss Wood meekly denied the imputation, I looked over my shoulder at the bed, and saw there the same strange indentation I had noticed before. It made my heart beat faster, for without any reason at all I felt certain that crease must have something to do with Lady Barbara.

Miss Wood didn't go to the ball. She had supper in the schoolroom with the young ladies' governess, and as I heard from one of the maids that she was to sit up for Lady Grayburn, I took her some wine and sandwiches about twelve o'clock. She stayed in the schoolroom, with a book, till the first party came home soon after two. I'd been round the rooms with the housemaid to see the fires were kept up, and I wasn't surprised to find that queer crease back on the bed again; indeed, I sort of expected it. I said nothing to the maid, who didn't seem to have noticed anything out of the way, but I told my aunt, and though she answered sharply that I was talking nonsense, she turned quite pale, and I heard her mutter something under her breath that sounded like 'God help her!'

I slept badly that night, for, do what I would, the thought of that poor young lady alone in the Blue Room kept me awake and restless. I was nervous, I suppose, and once, just as I was dropping off, I started up, fancying I'd heard a scream. I opened my door and listened, but there wasn't a sound, and after waiting a bit I crept back to bed, and lay there shivering till I fell asleep.

The household wasn't astir as early as usual. Everyone was tired after the late night, and tea wasn't to be sent to the ladies till half-past nine. My aunt said nothing about the ghost, but I noticed she was fidgety, and asked almost first thing if anyone had been to Miss Wood's room. I was telling her that Martha, one of the housemaids, had just taken up the tray, when the girl came running in with a scared, white face. 'For pity's sake, Mrs Marris,' she cried, 'come to the Blue Room; something awful has happened!'

My aunt stopped to ask no questions. She ran straight upstairs, and as I followed I heard her muttering to herself, 'I knew it, I knew it. Oh Lord! what will my Lady feel like now?'

If I live to be a hundred I shall never forget that poor girl's face. It was just as if she'd been frozen with terror. Her eyes were wide open and fixed, and her little hands clenched in the coverlet on each side of her as she lay across the bed in the very place where that crease had been.

Of course the whole house was aroused. Sir Archibald sent one of the grooms post-haste for the doctor but he could do nothing when he came; Miss Wood had been dead for at least five hours.

It was a sad business. All the visitors went away as soon as possible, except Lady Grayburn, who was obliged to stay for the inquest.

In his evidence, the doctor stated death was due to failure of heart-action, occasioned possibly by some sudden shock; and though the jury did not say so in their verdict, it was an open secret that they blamed her Ladyship for permitting Miss Wood to sleep in the haunted room. No-one could have reproached her more bitterly than she did herself, poor lady; and if she had done wrong she certainly suffered for it, for she never recovered from the shock of that dreadful morning, and became more or less of an invalid till her death five years later.

All this happened in 184—. It was fifty years before another woman slept in the Blue Room, and fifty years had brought with them many changes. The old Laird was gathered to his fathers, and his son, the present Sir Archibald, reigned in his stead; his sons were grown men, and Mr Charles, the eldest, married, with a fine little boy of his own. My aunt had been dead many a year, and I was an old woman, though active and able as ever to keep the maids up to their work. They take more looking after now, I think, than in the old days before there was so much talk of education, and when young women who took service thought less of dress and more of dusting. Not but what education is a fine thing in its proper place, that is, for gentle-folk. If Miss Erristoun, now, hadn't been the clever, strong-minded young lady she is, she'd never have cleared the Blue Room of its terrible secret, and lived to make Mr Arthur the happiest man alive.

He'd taken a great deal of notice of her when she first came in the summer to visit Mrs Charles, and I wasn't surprised to find she was one of the guests for the opening of the shooting-season. It wasn't a regular house-party (for Sir Archibald and Lady Mertoun were away), but just half-a-dozen young ladies, friends of Mrs Charles, who was but a girl herself, and as many gentlemen that Mr Charles and Mr Arthur had invited. And very gay they were, what with lunches at the covert-side, and tennis-parties, and little dances got up at a few hours' notice, and sometimes of an evening they'd play hide-and-seek all over the house just as if they'd been so many children.

It surprised me at first to see Miss Erristoun, who was said to be so learned, and had held her own with all the gentlemen at Cambridge, playing with the rest like any ordinary young lady; but she seemed to enjoy the fun as much as anyone, and was always first in any amusement that was planned. I didn't wonder at Mr Arthur's fancying her, for she was a handsome girl, tall and finely made, and carried herself like a princess. She had a wonderful head of hair, too, so long, her maid told me, it touched the ground as she sat on a chair to have it brushed. Everybody seemed to take to her, but I soon noticed it was Mr Arthur or Mr Calder-Maxwell she liked best to be with.

Mr Maxwell is a Professor now, and a great man at Oxford; but then he was just an undergraduate the same as Mr Arthur, though more studious, for he'd spend hours in the library poring over those old books full of queer black characters, that they say the wicked Lord Mertoun collected in the time of King Charles the Second. Now and then Miss Erristoun would stay indoors to help him, and it was something they found out in their studies that gave them the clue to the secret of the Blue Room.

For a long time after Miss Wood's death all mention of the ghost was strictly forbidden. Neither the Laird nor her Ladyship could bear the slightest allusion to the subject, and the Blue Room was kept locked, except when it had to be cleaned and aired. But as the years went by the edge of the tragedy wore off, and by degrees it grew to be just a story that people talked about in much the same way as they had done when I first came to the Towers; and if many believed in the mystery and speculated as to what the ghost could be, there were others who didn't hesitate to declare Miss Wood's dying in that room was a mere coincidence and had nothing to do with supernatural agency. Miss Erristoun was one of those who held most strongly to this theory. She didn't believe a bit in ghosts, and said straight out that there wasn't any of the tales told of haunted houses which could not be traced to natural causes, if people had courage and science enough to investigate them thoroughly.

It had been very wet all that day, and the gentlemen had stayed indoors, and nothing would serve Mrs Charles but they should all have an old-fashioned tea in my room and 'talk ghosts', as she called it. They made me tell them all I knew about the Blue Room, and it was then, when everyone was discussing the story and speculating as to what the ghost could be, that Miss Erristoun spoke up. 'The poor girl had heart-complaint,' she finished by saying, 'and she would have died the same way in any other room.'

'But what about the other people who have slept there?' someone objected.

'They did not die. Old Sir Archibald came to no harm, neither did Mr Hawksworth, nor the other man. They were healthy, and had plenty of pluck, so they saw nothing.'

'They were not women,' put in Mrs Charles, 'you see the ghost only appears to the weaker sex.'

'That proves the story to be a mere legend,' Miss Erristoun said with decision. 'First it was reported that everyone who slept in the room died. Then one or two men did sleep there, and remained alive; so the tale had to be modified, and since one woman could be proved to have died suddenly there, the fatality was represented as attaching to women only. If a girl with a sound constitution and good nerve were once to spend the night in that room, your charming family-spectre would be discredited for ever.'

There was a perfect chorus of dissent. None of the ladies could agree, and most of the gentlemen doubted whether any woman's nerve would stand the ordeal. The more they argued the more Miss Erristoun persisted in her view, till at last Mrs Charles got vexed, and cried: 'Well, it is one thing to talk about it, and another to do it. Confess now, Edith, you daren't sleep in that room yourself.'

'I dare and I will,' she answered directly. 'I don't believe in ghosts, and I am ready to stand the test. I will sleep in the Blue Room tonight, if you like, and tomorrow morning you will have to confess that whatever there may be against the haunted chamber, it is not a ghost.'

I think Mrs Charles was sorry she'd spoken then, for they all took Miss Erristoun up, and the gentlemen were for laying wagers as to whether she'd see anything or not. When it was too late she tried to laugh aside her challenge as absurd, but Miss Erristoun wouldn't be put off. She said she meant to see the thing through, and if she wasn't allowed to have a bed made up, she'd carry in her blankets and pillows, and camp out on the floor.

The others were all laughing and disputing together, but I saw Mr Maxwell look at her very curiously. Then he drew Mr Arthur aside, and began to talk in an undertone. I couldn't hear what he said, but Mr Arthur answered quite short: 'It's the maddest thing I ever heard of, and I won't allow it for a moment.'

'She will not ask your permission perhaps,' Mr Maxwell retorted. Then he turned to Mrs Charles, and inquired how long it was since the Blue Room had been used, and if it was kept aired. I could speak to that, and when he'd heard that there was no bedding there, but that fires were kept up regularly, he said he meant to have the first refusal of the ghost, and if he saw nothing it would be time enough for Miss Erristoun to take her turn.

Mr Maxwell had a kind of knack of settling things, and somehow with his quiet manner always seemed to get his own way. Just before dinner he came to me with Mrs Charles, and said it was all right, I was to get the room made ready quietly, not for all the servants to know, and he was going to sleep there.

I heard next morning that he came down to breakfast as usual. He'd had an excellent night, he said, and never slept better.

It was wet again that morning, raining 'cats and dogs', but Mr Arthur went out in it all. He'd almost quarrelled with Miss Erristoun, and was furious with Mr Maxwell for encouraging her in her idea of testing the ghost-theory, as they called it. Those two were together in the library most of the day, and Mrs Charles was chaffing Miss Erristoun as they went upstairs to dress, and asking her if she found the demons interesting. Yes, she said, but there was a page missing in the most exciting part of the book. They could not make head or tail of the context for some time, and then Mr Maxwell discovered that a leaf had been cut out. They talked of nothing else all through dinner, the butler told me, and Miss Erristoun seemed so taken up with her studies, I hoped she'd forgotten about the haunted room. But she wasn't one of the sort to forget. Later in the evening I came across her standing with Mr Arthur in the corridor. He was talking very earnestly, and I saw her shrug her shoulders and just look up at him and smile, in a sort of way that meant she wasn't going to give in. I was slipping quietly by, for I didn't want to disturb them, when Mr Maxwell came out of the billiard-room. 'It's our game,' he said; 'won't you come and play the tie?'

'I'm quite ready,' Miss Erristoun answered, and was turning away, when Mr Arthur laid his hand on her arm. 'Promise me first,' he urged, 'promise me that much, at least.'

'How tiresome you are!' she said quite pettishly. 'Very well then, I promise; and now please, don't worry me any more.'

Mr Arthur watched her go back to the billiard-room with his friend, and he gave a sort of groan. Then he caught sight of me and came along the passage. 'She won't give it up,' he said, and his face was quite white. 'I've done all I can; I'd have telegraphed to my father, but I don't know where they'll stay in Paris, and anyway there'd be no time to get an answer. Mrs Marris, she's going to sleep in that damned room, and if anything happens to her, I – ' he broke off short, and threw himself on to the window-seat, hiding his face on his folded arms.

I could have cried for sympathy with his trouble. Mr Arthur has always been a favourite of mine, and I felt downright angry with Miss Erristoun for making him so miserable just out of a bit of bravado.

'I think they are all mad,' he went on presently. 'Charley ought to have stopped the whole thing at once, but Kate and the others have talked him round. He professes to believe there's no danger, and Maxwell has got his head full of some rubbish he has found in those beastly books on Demonology, and he's backing her up. She won't listen to a word I say. She told me point-blank she'd never speak to me again if I interfered. She doesn't care a hang for me; I know that now, but I can't help it; I – I'd give my life for her.'

I did my best to comfort him, saying Miss Erristoun wouldn't come to any harm; but it wasn't a bit of use, for I didn't believe in my own assurances. I felt nothing but ill could come of such tempting of Providence, and I seemed to see that other poor girl's terrible face as it had looked when we found her dead in that wicked room. However, it is a true saying that 'a wilful woman will have her way', and we could do nothing to prevent Miss Erristoun's risking her life; but I made up my mind to one thing, whatever other people might do, *I* wasn't going to bed that night.

I'd been getting the winter-hangings into order, and the upholstress had used the little boudoir at the end of the long corridor for her work. I made up the fire, brought in a fresh lamp, and when the house was quiet, I crept down and settled myself there to watch. It wasn't ten yards from the door of the Blue Room, and over the thick carpet I could pass without making a sound, and listen at the keyhole. Miss Erristoun had promised Mr Arthur she would not lock her door; it was the one concession he'd been able to obtain from her. The ladies went to their rooms about eleven, but Miss Erristoun stayed talking to Mrs Charles for nearly an hour while her maid was brushing her hair. I saw her go to the Blue Room, and by-and-by Louise left her, and all was quiet.

It must have been half-past one before I thought I heard something moving outside. I opened the door and looked out, and there was Mr Arthur standing in the passage. He gave a start when he saw me. 'You are sitting up,' he said, coming into the room; 'then you do believe there is evil work on hand tonight? The others have gone to bed, but I can't rest; it's no use my trying to sleep. I meant to stay in the smoking-room, but it is so far away; I couldn't hear there even if she called for help. I've listened at the door; there isn't a sound. Can't you go in and see if it's all right? Oh, Marris, if she should – '

I knew what he meant, but I wasn't going to admit *that* possible – yet. 'I can't go into a lady's room without any reason,' I said; 'but I've been to the door every few minutes for the last hour and more.

It wasn't till half-past twelve that Miss Erristoun stopped moving about, and I don't believe, Mr Arthur, that God will let harm come to her, without giving those that care for her some warning. I mean to keep on listening, and if there's the least hint of anything wrong, why I'll go to her at once, and you are at hand here to help.'

I talked to him a bit more till he seemed more reasonable, and then we sat there waiting, hardly speaking a word except when, from time to time, I went outside to listen. The house was deathly quiet; there was something terrible, I thought, in the stillness; not a sign of life anywhere save just in the little boudoir, where Mr Arthur paced up and down, or sat with a strained look on his face, watching the door.

As three o'clock struck, I went out again. There is a window in the corridor, angle for angle with the boudoir-door. As I passed, someone stepped from behind the curtains and a voice whispered: 'Don't be frightened Mrs Marris; it is only me, Calder-Maxwell. Mr Arthur is there, isn't he?' He pushed open the boudoir door. 'May I come in?' he said softly. 'I guessed you'd be about, Mertoun. I'm not at all afraid myself, but if there *is* anything in that little legend, it is as well for some of us to be on hand. It was a good idea of yours to get Mrs Marris to keep watch with you.'

Mr Arthur looked at him as black as thunder. 'If you didn't *know* there was something in it,' he said, 'you wouldn't be here now; and knowing that, you're nothing less than a blackguard for egging that girl on to risk her life, for the sake of trying to prove your insane theories. You are no friend of mine after this, and I'll never willingly see you or speak to you again.'

I was fairly frightened at his words, and for how Mr Maxwell might take them; but he just smiled, and lighted a cigarette, quite cool and quiet.

'I'm not going to quarrel with you, old chap,' he said. 'You're a bit on the strain tonight, and when a man has nerves he mustn't be held responsible for all his words.' Then he turned to me. 'You're a sensible woman, Mrs Marris, and a brave one too, I fancy. If I stay here with Mr Arthur, will you keep close outside Miss Erristoun's door? She may talk in her sleep quietly; that's of no consequence; but if she should cry out, go in at once, *at once*, you understand; we shall hear you, and follow immediately.'

At that Mr Arthur was on his feet. 'You know more than you pretend,' he cried. 'You slept in that room last night. By Heaven, if you've played any trick on her I'll – '

Mr Maxwell held the door open. 'Will you go, please, Mrs Marris?' he said in his quiet way. 'Mertoun, don't be a damn fool.'

I went as he told me, and I give you my word I was all ears, for I felt certain Mr Maxwell knew more than we did, and that he expected something to happen.

It seemed like hours, though I know now it could not have been more than a quarter of that time, before I could be positive someone was moving behind that closed door.

At first I thought it was only my own heart, which was beating against my ribs like a hammer; but soon I could distinguish footsteps, and a sort of murmur like someone speaking continuously, but very low. Then a voice (it was Miss Erristoun's this time) said, 'No, it is impossible; I am dreaming, I must be dreaming.' There was a kind of rustling as though she were moving quickly across the floor. I had my fingers on the handle, but I seemed as if I'd lost power to stir; I could only wait for what might come next.

Suddenly she began to say something out loud. I could not make out the words, which didn't sound like English, but almost directly she stopped short. 'I can't remember any more,' she cried in a troubled tone. 'What shall I do? I can't – ' There was a pause. Then – 'No, *no*!' she shrieked. 'Oh, Arthur, Arthur!'

At that my strength came back to me, and I flung open the door.

There was a night-lamp burning on the table, and the room was quite light. Miss Erristoun was standing by the bed; she seemed to have backed up against it; her hands were down at her sides, her fingers clutching at the quilt. Her face was white as a sheet, and her eyes staring wide with terror, as well they might – I know I never had such a shock in my life, for if it was my last word, I swear there was a man standing close in front of her. He turned and looked at me as I opened the door, and I saw his face as plain as I did hers. He was young and very handsome, and his eyes shone like an animal's when you see them in the dark.

'Arthur!' Miss Erristoun gasped again, and I saw she was fainting. I sprang forward, and caught her by the shoulders just as she was falling back on to the bed.

It was all over in a second. Mr Arthur had her in his arms, and when I looked up there were only us four in the room, for Mr Maxwell had followed on Mr Arthur's heels, and was kneeling beside me with his fingers on Miss Erristoun's pulse. 'It's only a faint,' he said, 'she'll come round directly. Better take her out of this at once; here's a dressing-gown.' He threw the wrapper round her, and would have helped to raise her, but Mr Arthur needed no assistance. He lifted Miss Erristoun as if she'd been a baby, and carried her straight to the boudoir. He laid her on the couch and knelt beside her, chafing her hands. 'Get the brandy out of the smoking-room, Maxwell,' he said. 'Mrs Marris, have you any salts handy?'

I always carry a bottle in my pocket, so I gave it to him, before I ran after Mr Maxwell, who had lighted a candle, and was going for the brandy. 'Shall I wake Mr Charles and the servants?' I cried. 'He'll be hiding somewhere, but he hasn't had time to get out of the house yet.'

He looked as if he thought I was crazed. 'He – who?' he asked.

'The man,' I said; 'there was a man in Miss Erristoun's room. I'll call up Soames and Robert.'

'You'll do nothing of the sort,' he said sharply. 'There was no man in that room.'

'There was,' I retorted, 'for I saw him; and a great powerful man too. Someone ought to go for the police before he has time to get off.'

Mr Maxwell was always an odd sort of gentleman, but I didn't know what to make of the way he behaved then. He just leaned against the wall, and laughed till the tears came into his eyes.

'It is no laughing matter that I can see,' I told him quite short, for I was angry at his treating the matter so lightly; 'and I consider it no more than my duty to let Mr Charles know that there's a burglar on the premises.'

He grew grave at once then. 'I beg your pardon, Mrs Marris,' he said seriously; 'but I couldn't help smiling at the idea of the police. The vicar would be more to the point, all things considered. You really must not think of rousing the household; it might do Miss Erristoun a great injury, and could in no case be of the slightest use. Don't you understand? It was not a man at all you saw, it was an – well, it was what haunts the Blue Room.'

Then he ran downstairs leaving me fairly dazed, for I'd made so sure what I'd seen was a real man, that I'd clean forgotten all about the ghost.

Miss Erristoun wasn't long regaining consciousness. She swallowed the brandy we gave her like a lamb, and sat up bravely, though she started at every sound, and kept her hand in Mr Arthur's like a frightened child. It was strange, seeing how independent and stand-off she'd been with him before, but she seemed all the sweeter for the change. It was as if they'd come to an understanding without any words; and, indeed, he must have known she had cared for him all along, when she called out his name in her terror.

As soon as she'd recovered herself a little, Mr Maxwell began asking questions. Mr Arthur would have stopped him, but he insisted that it was of the greatest importance to hear everything while the impression was fresh; and when she had got over the first effort, Miss Erristoun seemed to find relief in telling her experience. She sat there with one hand in Mr Arthur's while she spoke, and Mr Maxwell wrote down what she said in his pocket-book.

She told us she went to bed quite easy, for she wasn't the least nervous, and being tired she soon dropped off to sleep. Then she had a sort of dream, I suppose, for she thought she was in the same room, only differently furnished, all but the bed. She described exactly how everything was arranged. She had the strangest feeling too, that she was not herself but someone else, and that she was going to do something – something that must be done, though she was frightened to death all the time, and kept stopping to listen at the inner door, expecting someone would hear her moving about and call out for her to go to them. That in itself was queer, for there was nobody sleeping in the adjoining room. In her dream, she went on to say, she saw a curious little silver brazier, one that stands in a cabinet in the picture-gallery (a fine example of *cinque cento* work, I think I've heard my Lady call it), and this she remembered holding in her hands a long time, before she set it on a little table beside the bed. Now the bed in the Blue Room is very handsome, richly carved on the cornice and frame, and especially on the posts, which are a foot square at the base and covered with relief-work in a design of fruit and flowers. Miss Erristoun said she went to the left-hand post at the foot, and after passing her hand over the carving, she seemed to touch a spring in one of the centre flowers, and the panel fell outwards like a lid, disclosing a secret cupboard out of which she took some papers and a box. She seemed to know what to do with the papers, though she couldn't tell us what was written on them; and she had a distinct recollection of taking a pastille from the box, and lighting it in the silver brazier. The smoke curled up and seemed to fill the whole room with a heavy perfume, and the next thing she remembered was that she awoke to find herself standing in the middle of the floor, and – what I had seen when I opened the door was there.

She turned quite white when she came to that part of the story, and shuddered. 'I couldn't believe it,' she said; 'I tried to think I was still dreaming, but I wasn't, I wasn't. It was real, and it was there, and – oh, it was horrible!'

She hid her face against Mr Arthur's shoulder. Mr Maxwell sat, pencil in hand, staring at her. 'I was right then,' he said. 'I felt sure I was; but it seemed incredible.'

'It is incredible,' said Miss Erristoun; 'but it is true, frightfully true. When I realised that I was awake, that it was actually real, I tried to remember the charge, you know, out of the office of exorcism, but I couldn't get through it. The words went out of my head; I felt my will-power failing; I was paralysed, as though I could make no effort to help myself and then – then I – ' she looked at Mr Arthur and blushed all over her face and neck. 'I thought of you, and I called – I had a feeling that you would save me.'

Mr Arthur made no more ado about us than if we'd been a couple of dummies. He just put his arms round her and kissed her, while Mr Maxwell and I looked the other way.

After a bit, Mr Maxwell said: 'One more question, please; what was it like?'

She answered after thinking for a minute. 'It was like a man, tall and very handsome. I have an impression that its eyes were blue and very bright.' Mr Maxwell looked at me inquiringly, and I nodded. 'And dressed?' he asked. She began to laugh almost hysterically. 'It sounds too insane for words, but I think – I am almost positive it wore ordinary evening dress.'

'It is impossible,' Mr Arthur cried. 'You were dreaming the whole time, that proves it.'

'It doesn't,' Mr Maxwell contradicted. 'They usually appeared in the costume of the day. You'll find that stated particularly both by Scott and Glanvil; Sprenger gives an instance too. Besides, Mrs Marris thought it was a burglar, which argues that the – the manifestation was objective, and presented no striking peculiarity in the way of clothing.'

'What?' Miss Erristoun exclaimed. 'You saw it too?'

I told her exactly what I had seen. My description tallied with hers in everything, but for the white shirt and tie, which from my position at the door I naturally should not be able to see.

Mr Maxwell snapped the elastic round his note-book. For a long time he sat silently staring at the fire. 'It is almost past belief,' he said at last, speaking half to himself, 'that such a thing could happen at the end of the nineteenth century, in these scientific rationalistic times that we think such a lot about, we, who look down from our superior intellectual height on the benighted superstitions of the Middle Ages.' He gave an odd little laugh. 'I'd like to get to the bottom of this business. I have a theory, and in the interest of psychical research and common humanity, I'd like to work it out. Miss Erristoun, you ought, I know, to have rest and quiet, and it is almost morning; but will you grant me one request. Before you are overwhelmed with questions, before you are made to relate your experience till the impression of tonight's adventure loses edge and clearness, will you go with Mertoun and myself to the Blue Room, and try to find the secret panel?'

'She shall never set foot inside that door again,' Mr Arthur began hotly, but Miss Erristoun laid a restraining hand on his arm.

'Wait a moment, dear,' she said gently; 'let us hear Mr Maxwell's reasons. Do you think,' she went on, 'that my dream had a foundation in fact; that something connected with that dreadful thing is really concealed about the room?'

'I think,' he answered, 'that you hold the clue to the mystery, and I believe, could you repeat the action of your dream, and open the secret panel, you might remove for ever the legacy of one woman's reckless folly. Only if it is to be done at all, it must be soon, before the impression has had time to fade.'

'It shall be done now,' she answered; 'I am quite myself again. Feel my pulse; my nerves are perfectly steady.'

Mr Arthur broke out into angry protestations. She had gone through more than enough for one night, he said, and he wouldn't have her health sacrificed to Maxwell's whims.

I have always thought Miss Erristoun handsome, but never, not even on her wedding-day, did she look so beautiful as then when she stood up in her heavy white wrapper, with all her splendid hair loose on her shoulders.

'Listen,' she said; 'if God gives us a plain work to do, we must do it at any cost. Last night I didn't believe in anything I could not understand. I was so full of pride in my own courage and common-sense, that I wasn't afraid to sleep in that room and prove the ghost was all superstitious nonsense. I have learned there are forces of which I know nothing, and against which my strength was utter weakness. God took care of me, and sent help in time; and if He has opened a way by which I may save other women from the danger I escaped, I should be worse than ungrateful were I to shirk the task. Bring the lamp, Mr Maxwell, and let us do what we can.' Then she put both hands on Mr Arthur's shoulders. 'Why are you troubled?' she said sweetly. 'You will be with me, and how can I be afraid?'

It never strikes me as strange now that burglaries and things can go on in a big house at night, and not a soul one whit the wiser. There were five people sleeping in the rooms on that corridor while we tramped up and down without disturbing one of them. Not but what we went as quietly as we could, for Mr Maxwell made it clear that the less was known about the actual facts, the better. He went first, carrying the lamp, and we followed. Miss Erristoun shivered as her eyes fell on the bed, across which that dreadful crease showed plain, and I knew she was thinking of what might have been, had help not been at hand.

Just for a minute she faltered, then she went bravely on, and began feeling over the carved woodwork for the spring of the secret panel. Mr Maxwell held the lamp close, but there was nothing to show any difference between that bit of carving and the other three posts. For a full ten minutes she tried, and so did the gentlemen, and it seemed as though the dream would turn out a delusion after all, when all at once Miss Erristoun cried 'I have found it', and with a little jerk, the square of wood fell forward, and there was the cupboard just as she had described it to us.

It was Mr Maxwell who took out the things, for Mr Arthur wouldn't let Miss Erristoun touch them. There were a roll of papers and a little silver box. At the sight of the box she gave a sort of cry; 'That is it,' she said, and covered her face with her hands.

Mr Maxwell lifted the lid, and emptied out two or three pastilles. Then he unfolded the papers, and before he had fairly glanced at the sheet of parchment covered with queer black characters, he cried, 'I knew it, I knew it! It *is* the missing leaf.' He seemed quite wild with excitement. 'Come along,' he said. 'Bring the light, Mertoun; I always said it was no ghost, and now the whole thing is as clear as daylight. You see,' he went on, as we gathered round the table in the boudoir, 'so much depended on there being an heir. That was the chief cause of the endless quarrels between old Lord Mertoun and Barbara. He had never approved of the marriage, and was for ever reproaching the poor woman with having failed in the first duty of an only son's wife. His will shows that he did not leave her a farthing in event of her husband dying without issue. Then the feud with the Protestant branch of the family was very bitter, and the Sir Archibald of that day had three boys, he having married (about the same time as his cousin) Lady Mary Sarum, who had been Barbara's rival at Court and whom Barbara very naturally hated. So when the doctors pronounced Dennis Mertoun to be dying of consumption, his wife got desperate, and had recourse to black magic. It is well known that the old man's collection of works on Demonology was the most complete in Europe. Lady Barbara must have had access to the books, and it was she who cut out this leaf. Probably Lord Mertoun discovered the theft and drew his own conclusions. That would account for his refusal to admit her body to the family vault. The Mertouns were staunch Romanists, and it is one of the deadly sins, you know, meddling with sorcery. Well, Barbara contrived to procure the pastilles, and she worked out the spell according to the directions given here, and then – Good God! Mertoun, what have you done?'

For before anyone could interfere to check him, Mr Arthur had swept papers, box, pastilles, and all off the table and flung them into the fire. The thick parchment curled and shrivelled on the hot coals, and a queer, faint smell like incense spread heavily through the room. Mr Arthur stepped to the window and threw the casement wide open. Day was breaking, and a sweet fresh wind swept in from the east which was all rosy with the glow of the rising sun.

'It is a nasty story,' he said; 'and if there be any truth in it, for the credit of the family and the name of a dead woman, let it rest for ever. We will keep our own counsel about tonight's work. It is enough for others to know that the spell of the Blue Room is broken, since a brave, pure-minded girl has dared to face its unknown mystery and has laid the ghost.'

Mr Calder-Maxwell considered a moment. 'I believe you are right,' he said, presently, with an air of resignation. 'I agree to your proposition, and I surrender my chance of world-wide celebrity among the votaries of Psychical Research; but I *do* wish, Mertoun, you would call things by their proper names. It was *not* a ghost. It was an – '

But as I said, all I can remember now of the word he used is, that it somehow put me in mind of poultry-rearing.

* * *

Note – the reader will observe that the worthy Mrs Marris, though no student of Sprenger, unconsciously discerned the root-affinity of the *incubator* of the hen-yard and the *incubus* of the *Malleus Maleficarum*.